*In the shimmering tradition of*

## THE SWORD OF SHANNARA
## *and* THE LORD OF THE RINGS

Behind him was the secluded castle of his queen mother. Ahead was the Round Table —and glory. But the Round Table ruffians scoffed at his innocence and dubbed him "Parsifool."

Yet Parsival was destined to triumph again and again in mighty deeds of the sword and the soul. And only Parsival of all King Arthur's knights would come to know the glory beyond joust victorious and rescued damsel.

Only he would be worthy to find the Holy Grail.

Begin, for there is magic here. . . .

**"Epic scope . . . abounds in the trappings of Arthurian romance"**

—*Los Angeles Times*

# RICHARD MONACO

# PARSIVAL
## OR A
# KNIGHT'S
# TALE

Illustrated by
David McCall Johnston

PUBLISHED BY POCKET BOOKS NEW YORK

POCKET BOOKS, a Simon & Schuster division of
GULF & WESTERN CORPORATION
1230 Avenue of the Americas, New York, N.Y. 10020

Published by arrangement with MacMillan Publishing Co., Inc.
Library of Congress Catalog Card Number: 77-22150

ISBN: 0-671-82225-X

First Pocket Books printing December, 1978

10 9 8 7 6 5 4 3 2 1

Trademarks registered in the United States and other countries.

Printed in the U.S.A.

*For my mother and father.*
*For Judy.*
*Thanks to Peter Lampack.*
*Love to Chen, Tui and Tip.*

With grateful acknowledgements to
Michael Denneny
Tony Gardner

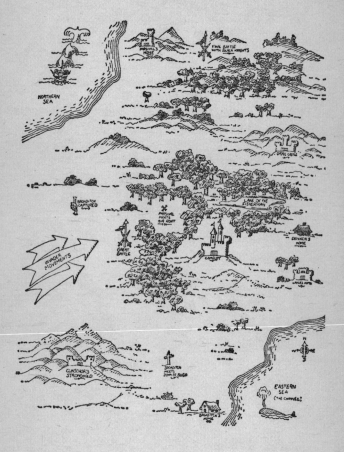

# illustrations

# PARSIVAL

## OR A

# KNIGHT'S
# TALE

# i

The field was like a lawn. Late morning. The grass was dry under his bare feet. Sunlight and treeshadows flickered over him as he moved quietly across the glade, glanced once around at the brilliant green, the intense stainless blue sky, then paused, set his feet on the soft earth, sunheat steady on his bare back, tilted the short spear until his knotted fist gripped the shaft close by his ear, held a deep breath of spring air his body seemed to breathe in through the flesh itself and waited, completely still. His mind was light and easy as the drifts of breeze and he watched with absolute intentness the liquid light-dappled brownish stillness fifty steps away: the gleaming horntips enmeshed and almost lost in the shadowed netting of branches, bush and treetrunks just where the deep woods ended. And then the graceful neck dipped, seeming to delicately balance the outsized, spiked crown, as the deer bent to drink from a splash of pool, then straightened suddenly, flipping an ear up. Its eye saw him and his heart went off, the blood banged in his head, and he was working to breathe steadily, in and slow out, in and slow out, eyes wide and blue; long, golden-tinted hair stirring slightly, strong young body now coiled within, as if around his racing heart, like a spring. He was giddy, afraid, motionless . . .

Then the buck broke loose from the background and he perceived (only later remembered) the spray of water as it thundered through the pool, the percussion of its hooves shockingly loud, drumlike, and he was already running, arm cocked, as it bounded in a short, violent half circle whose arc would close among the trees; his legs seemed filled with unlimited power, seeming to run without his will, in one continuous fluid motion (his mind merely

1

watching from a calm distance) whipped the shaft away
and felt, as if his nerves were somehow strung to it, its
shallow arcing and keen impact as the beast staggered
(felt a knot and tearing in his own belly), stumbled,
reared, then plunged to its knees, trembling terribly, head
madly erect, antlers vibrating, bloody pinkish foam gathering at the lips below the lost, startled eyes . . .

And he dropped to *his* knees in the soft earth staring at
the great buck leaning against the spear's tilt. The blood
spurted into the bluegreen shadowed background; its
breath shuddered, rasped, exploded like a burst bellows.
He couldn't look away, a cool interest, floating somehow
apart from his shocked reactions, followed each unfolding
detail of the struggle to death: the meaningless prance of
the forelegs, tosses of head, ripples of flesh, mad sucking
of the mouth like, he thought, a fish . . .

## ii

The midday was hazy and hot. The heavy trees hung still. The Red Knight sat his charger just within the deep bluish shadow of the woods. His red helmet was open for whatever drifts of breeze might cool his sweaty face. A bright butterfly suddenly rose and flickered across the motionless wheatgrass and bright field of goldenrod where the sun glittered on countlessly dipping and fumbling bees. Across the field was a low, square castle and narrow moat. Beyond, hazy fields of crops and the squat huts of serfs.

Two men were leaning at ease on the wall above the gate which was creaking and grinding open. The drawbridge swung down. A party of knights and men-at-arms came riding and marching over the booming boards, raising a fine dust as they reached the narrow roadway. A lady in a bright yellow silk gown mounted sidesaddle on a pony emerged next, followed by more spearmen on foot. She waved and kept looking back. A man and two more women in everyday dress now stood in the shadow of the gate and returned her farewells.

The Red Knight shook his head to toss the sweat from his eyes and closed his helmet. He held his lance and shield firmly, the shaft straight up. He waited, invisible in the shadows, as they crossed the drowsy, glowing field toward him. Then he kicked his mount forward lightly and moved out on the dusty trail in full sight of them all.

He constantly turned his head to scan the area through the narrow eyeslits in his helmet. He watched the five knights rein up as everyone suddenly saw him. The men on the wall came to attention, the lord and ladies in the gateyard stepped forward shielding their eyes against the noonglare and a rank of spearmen formed protectively

3

around the mounted woman. He noticed she was very graceful, even as he was starting to build up the dark, concentrated rage he was going to need in a moment.

The five knights lowered their lances, horses pawing restlessly, churning the yellowish dust, silvery armor shining; the unarmed lord took a few steps onto the drawbridge. Helmet visor raised, one of the five called over to the slowly advancing red warrior.

"You, hold!" No response. He tried again, "You, coming there, what is your—" and broke off speech as the Red Knight lowered his long lance and began an easy, watchful charge straight across the golden field seeing through the slits the men-at-arms in their leather jerkins and steel caps, digging spear-butts into the earth and crouching behind them as the mounted men now began moving forward, spreading out from the road into the wash of flowers that swayed and splashed around the horselegs. The lord on the bridge was shouting something and calling more men from the castle. The two lookouts on the wall were frantically pointing and shouting too because the golden flowers were suddenly full of men with spears and axes standing up and charging the trapped party as three knights in blue and green armor, brandishing mace and sword, broke from the tree shadows at full gallop in support of the Red Knight who was already among the five, shield going up to fend off a vicious lance jab that scraped past, ducking to avoid a second, the glittering tip ripping just past his neck and then he twisted around in the saddle and stabbed the passing horse in the rump, the keen tip slicing into the genitals, and watched briefly as the animal screamed and bucked the massive rider into the dust with a dull clang. Then he tossed away his lance (at close quarters) and, already past the knights who were now faced with the blue and green newcomers, he cut his cursing, yelling way into the thick of the spearmen, red sword chopping flesh and bone as the futile spears swung against him and his powerful mount.

"Die, you common filth!" he kept grunting in cold, professional rage, voice hollow in his helmet.

He veered violently out of their broken line in front of the pale woman, seeing a flash of her outraged frightened face through his eyeslits. Now the howling men came pouring from the field into the combat, hacking and spearing, holding up wood and leather shields.

The Red Knight saw the party was completely cut off

from the little castle now. He looked back as one of the five horsemen, lance shattered, helmet battered, tried to escape across the clearing and was knocked from his saddle and his life by a tossed mace. Two others and a horse lay dead in the road. That left one riding still, he noted, and one down and the spearmen had him: he was on his knees, several of them around him and when he tried to stand they'd tangle his feet with the shafts as he flailed his sword in desperate defense, blood spilling bright from his gleaming armor joints. The Red Knight was furious at this, reined his horse toward them, feeling himself in the fallen warrior's place, hating the foot soldiers, thinking only a knight may slay a knight . . . and then a spear point poked into the fellow's visor and he tilted over, screaming, into the golden flowers as if falling underwater as the last rider, with three at his back, came on swinging mace and chain and the Red Knight caught just the shadow of his motion at the eyeslit corner and turned in time to catch the chain on his swordblade. It spun and locked, chipping the edge, and as the confident opponent pulled at him savagely, he freed his ax with his left hand (letting the shield dangle from the neck thong) and sent it spinning over the other's too-slow shield to split the man's face, folding the helmet in with a terrible mushy explosion. He jerked his blade free and turned back toward the castle: the men-at-arms were killing wounded in the roadway and the three knights were charging the gate where a few men had rallied around the unarmored lord who had a shield and sword now.

He just sat and watched, raising his faceplate, sweating and puffing in the hot, dusty air, the horse nearly up to his flanks in golden, crushed and bloodspattered flowers. Around the body of the nearest man the bees were already stirring and fumbling to work again. He watched, heard the pleas and shouts, curses and clashing steel . . .

Well, he'd done his work, his share. It was up to them to kill the lord and his family. That was Arthur's politics and was nothing to him. He'd kept his bargain and only needed to be paid . . .

A thinner cry . . . he looked around. The lady. She was running across the dazzling clearing, gown fluttering like a butterfly. The spearmen were scrambling to cut her off. He watched her fall and get up again. Smoke was now billowing up inside the castle. The fight had passed through the open gate. *Well*, he reflected, *no unarmored men on foot*

*could stand up to a concentrated charge of even one knight
if the mount were well protected.* He began to consider
some of the technical problems involved as he idly watched
the last thrashings of the conflict . . .

# iii

She watched him coming across the glade, crossing bars of
sunlight, flicking in and out, dark, then bright, moving with
that grace which always checked her breath for a moment,
watching him (in one easy lope) take the low stone fence
at the end of this outer garden, whose inner side was the
stone of the castle itself, his bare skin the color of pale
honey, muscle shadows playing over him like the stirrings
of a pond.

She felt his hurt before she saw his eyes or saw the
spatters of blood that marked him like, she thought, a pox.

*Oh, my son,* she was thinking, *can I keep you?*

Seeing him casually stride over the fence brought home
to her that all future time was borrowed, that she'd kept
him enclosed so long now she'd forgotten she never really
believed it possible. He had the legs to step out of this
harmonious world of serfs, servants and women and pass
through the gates she'd shut before he was born, sealing
herself and the rest off in this high country in the north of
what was later to be called Wales. At this time it was one
of many small kingdoms, each complete and a law unto
itself. The last noblemen had come over fifteen years before, her husband's squire and two knights, cantering
across those fields: she'd seen them from a high window
and thinking, hoping, it was Gahmuret returning she'd
rushed down the steps out into the rosecolored twilight,
reaching the grass as the three men were dismounting, sun
at their backs pushing long shadows before them. She'd
known, instantly, completely. The whole world darkened
and lost substance. She hadn't heard their words at first but
understood anyway. And the only bright thing now was
memory and she held it like a precious candle flame that a

7

stranger in an unknown house dares not let blow out. The little squire unwrapped a stiff and stained piece of silk and held out a blood-darkened spearpoint to her with both hands as if presenting a precious jewel and she'd thought: *What is this boy giving me?* Then picking up, from far away, his meagre, sing-song voice: ". . . so my master, struck through the helm by this . . ." *So big,* she'd thought, *for his poor head.* It was larger than her whole hand. ". . . and sent these to you, my queen, who fought nobly and died without sin." And then she'd admitted no more words to her mind.

*Oh, my son,* she was thinking as he stopped near her. At his feet were bright, white flowers. She remembered those terrible nights, the dreams and torments as the child the father would never see kept growing within her, remembered the dream of the dragon in her womb, how it clawed out, the hooked paws reaching around as it gave birth to itself in blood and agony, climbing from her, pulling the burning, scaly form from between her helpless thighs, then turning and biting, sucking her nipples, lapping the milk dry with rough, greedy tongue; then the gusts and slapping of huge wings unfolded, the terror of that movement all around her as it rose and crashed like lightning from the chamber, darkened the bright window and sky as it burst outside . . .

*Oh, my son, my son.* She saw the blood spots on his body.

"Mother," he said.

"Yes, Parsival?"

"I don't know why I did it. It made me sick to do it."

She showed nothing.

"You killed something," she stated, quietly.

*Oh, my son . . .*

Later she was inside the cool cavern of a hall. Whitish daylight was intense at the embrasures. In the silence she knelt at a little niche where two faint candles burned, unshaking, on an altar. Her gown was ghostly white. Her lips moved as she prayed.

At some point she half turned and saw her mother-in-law was standing behind her, tall, narrow, dressed in black silk. Neither spoke. Nothing stirred in the vast hall. Faintly, from outside came the windwrung cry of a crow in the distance. A breath or two and it cawed again, fainter . . .

"Well, Queen," the old woman wanted to know, "are you weary of it yet?"

"Don't chide me."

"For living in dreams?"

The queen sighed.

"For anything," she said.

The narrow ax of a face tilted down at her.

"For what you've done to the boy?"

Queen Herzelroyd bowed her head slightly.

"He's not to die," she whispered, "like his father."

The old but somehow unworn voice said:

"His father's defense was weakened by treachery."

The queen drooped there, a strange, pale flower in the twilight of the hall.

"No," she whispered, "his own."

That too was part of the story, how a jealous groom (or some other, convenient, baseborn figure) rubbed hot hegoat's blood on the helmet that gave way and she'd thought: *No, it was his own goat's blood that betrayed him,* because she knew about the black bride in the Holy Land and the other son whose flesh was (they said) marked in mockery: her imagination tried many images, glossy and pale. One had him divided down the middle like a jester's suit, half night, half day . . . another showed a boy who first seemed light and then as you looked a dark glow like distant smoke dimmed his form . . . the image that persisted had him specked like a leopard: Parsival himself only spotted black (she thought), stained . . .

"What would he have said," the old voice wondered, "if he could have seen what's been done to the boy? Raised by women. Never seeing a noble man with blood in his veins in his life . . ." The edged voice sighed. "Locked away here . . . getting too thick with every common swine and Jack. No chivalrous training at all! None at all . . . God's wounds, what would my son have said to this disgrace?"

The old woman's hands clenched into bony fists and trembled. The queen said nothing.

"Disgrace," the old woman muttered, furious, "disgrace and stain."

The queen shut her eyes. Clasped her praying hands.

The following weeks of spring opened and closed around her. She was waiting now. She neither counted nor didn't count the days. It was as if it had already happened somewhere far away and she was simply expecting the inevitable but needless word that he was lost to her, that her son was lost to her too . . .

She bent her graceful neck, looked at the pale, hushed tones of the flowerbeds, the grayish shadows peaked to pure, softened colors. She sighed. A light, drizzling rain began flicking the grass and petals: slight twinkles, sudden, here and there . . .

A mile away in the forest Parsival squatted on the damp ground. He was poking the head up with a twisted stick: the eyes stirred with swarming life, an edge of jawbone was bare white; a cloud of scintillant flies rose like a cloth and grated, dropped back in sudden, bright flickers to the feast. Part of one haunch was chewed away. The belly was immensely fat, legs standing out stiffly. In the pittering rain low ground fog smoked around the body, drifted over gleaming grass and brush.

He let the head flop back, arousing the flies again. Threw away the stick. Remained hunkered down there, watching like a serious student at his lessons . . .

# iv

The Red Knight's armor was a dull emberglow in the violet twilight shadows on the rutted trail. The other three were abreast and behind him as they went on into the woods. The common fighting men marched further back. Though the castle was out of sight a mile or more there was a faint stinging of smoke on the wind. Steel clinked and pinged, leather creaked as they moved along and the men in the rear were singing something about a girl, a juggler and five stout lads . . .

With helmet open the breeze was cool on his ruddy face.

"How far will you ride with us?" asked Galahad, leader of the raiding party.

"How far?" the Red Knight wondered in return, twisting in the saddle to look at the other man's blank faceplate bobbing beside him.

"Are you not weary of this road?" Galahad suggested.

"Weary? I'm weary of waiting for the rest of Arthur's gold." He turned his head to cover his rear for a moment. The two other warriors were riding silently behind. "Why don't you pry open your purse now?" he asked. "There's no good reason to wait."

"You want to be paid, then?" Galahad confirmed, needlessly enough.

The Red Knight became very alert. *Keep it themselves and say he was killed? Possibly . . . More likely Arthur himself, since Galahad was supposed to be rich . . . Why? Why create a debt and make an enemy? It made little sense. He ought to pay and be glad of the price for a sword like his.* Which weapon his hand was resting lightly on. The twilight deepened rapidly. *How far back were those men?* He could still hear them singing.

11

"Will you pay?" he demanded, letting his horse drift to
the side a little so as to be able to see everybody's outline
at once. Automatic on his part.

"Didn't we agree to it?" Galahad wanted to know.

And now he was sure. Was waiting now. It would
happen soon, he was certain. Three first-rate fighters. But
it wouldn't be easy and they knew that too.

"Is it worth it?" he asked Galahad, his voice cold and
hard.

Galahad understood. They were rounding a bend. It was
almost night here. Wisps of glowing sky showed through
the dense branches overhead.

"The king desires your silence," he finally said.

*What were they waiting for then?* He carefully scanned
around and behind himself. No one had moved perceptibly
closer.

"It's treachery," he told him.

"Not to my king," was the answer.

His heart was pounding now. He carefully controlled his
breathing. Then he saw the dim shapes on the twisting
trail, the blotted outline of spears and men. They'd somehow gone ahead and cut him off. Held his breath and
whipped the massive broadsword out and cut in one terrific
move backhand at Galahad who had been waiting for this
and caught the ringing blow on his shield, jarred by the
impact as the Red Knight spurred forward crying:

"You bastards!"

and went into the wall of men before him, their shadowy
shapes striking at him, a spear painfully grinding against
his chest mail but not ripping through and his downstroke
caught a piece of the man anyway, he noted as the next
fellow struck his shield and then another had his horse by
the bit and Galahad was yelling:

"Hold him! Hold him!"

And he swung beside the animal's head and felt an arm
part sickeningly, heard a howl and twisted the kicking,
frenzied charger around in a tight circle, met the two other
knights, steel gleaming and flashing dimly, sparks spurting
and hissing as he snapped out blows in a frenzy, furious,
bellowing hoarsely, grinding his teeth, landing two blows
to their one on either side of himself as Galahad tried to
work in behind, and then one knight's sword shattered and
another blow toppled him, cursing, from his saddle. The
Red Knight took a blow on the helmet which jarred stars

in his head and then, snarling berserkly, gave back one that split the upraised shield, broke away and charged back down the trail toward the marching foot soldiers, raging over his shoulder at Galahad:

"I'll be behind you, you bastards!"

Hanging his shield behind his back as he rode, lifting his ax with his left hand and poising his sword in his right he veered suddenly to cut around the spears that were braced in the earth of the trail and came in on the flank of the soldiers close to the trees and wooden shields split and heads shattered and splashed.

"Don't let him scatter our foot!" he heard Galahad shouting, coming closer. But the ones who weren't screaming in the dirt were dodging away into the woods and he rode on down the trail, smiling grimly, aware he'd scored an unexpected (and, to a degree, unmerited) tactical victory. Now the hunt could begin. He'd give them a day or two and they wouldn't know where to look or when . . . *Those bastards,* he thought, *he'd collect his damned pay from those damned bastards* . . . Cantering on at an easy pace now, the wind humming in his helmet, the dim trees flowing past . . . *he'd collect, by God's pain he'd collect in full* . . .

# V

The sun was hot and golden, dripping in the still forest,
lying on the hilly fields, the rich syrup of August. All
greens were darkly ripe, flowers gushed full and heavy
from the dense earth seeming to shoulder one another aside
as if choked for space to swell and burst in.

Arms one way, heads another, foot of one crossed over
the shin of the other, deep in the surf of dandelions that
broke against the shore of grassy weeds, floating, utterly
still in the long, slow swells of afternoon, two men lay
like sacks. A fat and a thin sack. Bees droned. Breezes
coiled and uncoiled. The sun was steady and above the
drowsy stir of the day rasped a wavering pair of inter-
woven snores . . .

Out across the field two horsemen came on steadily,
seeming to float over the waves of deep grasses. The thin
sleeper opened his eyes suddenly, flapped his bones as he
struggled to surface from sodden sleep. He shook his companion, violently. Armor was clanking not far away. The
heavy man lay unmoving, a mound of greasy hides.

"Broaditch," the thin one was hissing, "Broaditch, stir
yourself!"

"What?" Broaditch sighed, then cursed without any real
force. "Damn you, loose me. Am I a girl?" He pushed
himself free easily without even having to sit up. He'd
gone to fat but stayed strong.

"You been asleep," chided the other. The clinking of
armor was further off now. He craned his skinny neck and
long face around. They were already out of sight over the
crest of the hill.

"You're a creature of vast wit, Waleis," Broaditch returned, massively unmoved.

14

"Horsemen just passed," the wit said.

The other tilted his hide cap to shadow his eyes. Nodded with private satisfaction.

"You'll make your name yet, Waleis," he prophesied. "You know a horse from a snore."

"Broaditch," he cried, "they were *knights!*"

Broaditch was scratching himself under his rough tent of shirt. His thick yellowed nails caught and vengefully pinched a louse. He sighed with pleasure.

"Knights," he muttered, "are fit for dreams." He belched softly, thoughtful eyes belying his remarks.

"But they were knights," Waleis repeated, staring. "We're supposed to keep all such away from these lands and . . ."

Broaditch looked at him.

"Why did you fail your duty then?"

The other was exasperated.

"Finally," he said, "the fat has reached your brain! *It was too late!*"

Broaditch shook his head.

"You couldn't have stopped them anyway," he observed. "Your common knight has no time for anything but gullet-slitting. And they'd have slit ours, Waleis, my friend." He locked his hands behind his head and stretched. "I haven't held an ax in many, many soft years now . . . Did I ever tell you how I stood in the battle of—" he started as the other cut nervously in.

"We were supposed to say we've plague here."

"True," Broaditch nodded. "But your common knights, what can they hear behind those visors? They're pretty well sealed off, that's been my experience."

"What are we to do?"

Broaditch pointed down the valley.

"You can chase *him* back," he suggested.

Waleis turned to see a single horseman moving rapidly through the beaten wake of grass the first two had ploughed. His armor flashed in the sunlight, his yellow surcoat flapped like a banner.

Waleis stood up, hesitant.

"He comes," Broaditch dryly observed.

They watched the man thunder up the hill without a glance in their direction, looming suddenly immense on his black charger, a rain of earth spraying from the mashing hooves, in a welter of bellowing horsebreaths, grunts, ring-ings, a storm of steel and massive flesh crashing up and over the crest.

"He goes," Broaditch concluded.

# vi

The Red Knight was armorsore and covered with dust. The country was hilly but open now. All he could do was follow steadily and hope they decided to stand and fight. His fury was constant, slowburning and necessary because he was not rich and couldn't afford against his reputation to be cheated even by a great king. So he followed them through the lush, green countryside, as inexorable as the earth turning. He'd almost had them a week ago: not Galahad but one of the others had fallen behind to wash himself in a stream, armor on, just dipping his face and arms. He was remounting as the Red Knight emerged from the pines on the far bank. The thrown ax missed the startled man by inches and took down an arm-thick tree beside him. By the time his horse had forded the surprisingly deep stream the quarry was too far away again for a sprint chase . . .

## vii

Parsival knelt on the low bank of a narrow, unrippled
stream where a formation of trout hung motionless as if
embedded in glass. Overhanging trees greenly shadowed
the water. The dark tails flickered slightly. When the
javelin hissed among them the gray shapes exploded away
in a scattering of silver glitter as their sides caught the
light. One stayed, pinned to the mud: it curled against the
shaft, flipped its tail a few times, shuddered.

He leaned close to the water, watching. It didn't shock
him this time. He'd watched those fish for years never
really connecting them with the plump bodies that turned
up on skewers, split and broiled at meals. Now he understood this too and felt no pleasure or disgust. It was just
another thing to know . . .

He was so intent that the two horsemen were very close
before he reacted and stood up, holding the spear with the
impaled fish, taking a step or two onto the narrow trail
that bent with the stream across the marshy fields.

He looked up just as they broke from the shade of a
line of trees, moving with clank, dust and glitter into the
intense sunlight. The sound surprised him but the dazzling,
reflecting armor stunned him. He squinted his shocked
eyes, heart banging; remembered:

night in his bedchamber, tapers gleaming, he sat in his
nightclothes on the silken edge of his bed. A dog and two
servants were sleeping in one corner of the room where
they'd gathered a mound of the rushes that covered the
floor. He had just been praying and the queen still knelt
beside him.

He'd just asked her what God was like and she'd tilted
her graceful neck and long, smooth face so that the vague

18

light glowed on her flesh as if a pale flame burned beneath the skin.

"Son," she'd said, "He is brighter than day, like . . . like a mirror without stain. And yet, he took on the form of a man . . ."

He'd listened without a word.

"Against Him," she'd gone on, "there is the darkness." She'd pointed, her hand pale and vague in the shadowy air. "We are like those flames there, a little speck against such vast night!" She'd paused and sighed. Then had continued: "But if we hold fast to Him, our flames will grow and grow until the dark is everywhere pressed back!" She'd gripped both his knees with soft, fierce, long fingers as she'd spoken. "Our flesh," she'd fiercely whispered at him, "is like the melting wax! It must feed that pure light!" She'd stopped and seemed breathless. He'd been frightened and sad. And though he didn't know why, he remembered he'd wept . . .

The sunlight lanced and shattered, sprayed from the polished silvery chain mail that seemed faceted like his mother's jewels. He dropped to his knees, crying out:

"Help, O God!"

He let fall the spear, the fish reflexively kicking again, and clasped his hands in prayer. He blocked the narrow lane and the riders were forced to rear back their mounts, shouting through closed visors, voices muffled and ringing, then, in the same motion, as if on cue, both flipped their helmets open the better to rage at and abuse the worshipful boy. Then in silence they stared at him.

"He's mad," one said, as his thickbodied charger struggled, stifflegged, against the wrenched reins in a rocking quarter circle, panting and blowing.

The other sat perfectly still on a suddenly motionless horse. He gave an impression of being about to move, violently, without warning. The first one kept glancing behind. Parsival stayed on his knees looking reverently up at them.

They stared, baffled, curious and struck by his beauty.

"Here comes Galahad," the first said as the third rider came thundering up behind them, mount snorting fiercely.

"Who blocks our path?" he called out, slamming to a halt. His armor was silverbright inwrought with gold tracings and much brighter, in that August intensity of sun, than that of the first two. Parsival was stunned by this new flash and glitter; he thought a man made of mirrors was before him.

"O Lord," he suddenly called out, "show me thy mercy and help!" Addressed to the knight.

Galahad lifted his faceplate and frowned down at Parsival who was trembling with fear and excitement, his powerful, graceful hands clenched with such force that a tiny drop of blood oozed over one whitened nail.

"I am not God," Galahad said, only his eyes showing in the shadow of his helm. "Are you mad, boy?"

"Did you see him?" the first man asked.

"No," Galahad said.

"Perhaps he's lost heart for it."

"Stay here and see," Galahad said, coldly.

"Have you never seen knights, boy?" the second, quiet man on the unmoving horse asked.

"I have seen nights and days too," returned Parsival, "for that is God's work. And my mother told me he took the form of a man as bright as the sun."

The second man laughed; the first was too busy looking behind; Galahad tapped his own chestplate.

"These are but suits that come off," he informed him, "though knights hope to be bright in their glory, boy."

The first man had no shield and his headpiece was severely dented and slashed. Galahad's armor was barely marred or stained. Parsival stood up, still in awe.

"What power makes you . . . *knights?*" he wanted to know.

"The king, boy. King Arthur. A great king."

The first man frowned.

"Why do we talk here like fools?" he demanded, nervously. "Go to King Arthur," he snarled at Parsival, "perhaps he'll make you a knight yourself and you'll know all these things then." To Galahad: "What keeps us?"

Parsival, meanwhile, had moved closer and was touching the armor. He saw his face reflected there: his long, bright hair, intent, distant eyes like windows flashing a clear sky.

"What's this suit good for then?" he wanted to know, picking at it. "I don't see how you can get out of it."

The second man and Galahad laughed this time. The leader drew his sword and turned the fine blade to catch the light and little chips of sun flickered over Parsival.

"When a man strikes me with one of these," he said, "the metal dulls the blows."

Parsival nodded.

"If that fish," he said, pointing to the one stuck on the end of his spear, "had scales like these he'd be swimming still."

The second man laughed again and Galahad smiled. The first was already walking his horse past them along the trail.

"Wait here and dull some blows, why don't you?" he snapped back over his shoulder.

"We must go and do the king's work," Galahad said, urging his mount ahead as Parsival moved aside.

"God keep and shield you, boy," the second said, not untenderly. "Pity he made you not less lovely and given you deeper wits instead." He shut his visor with a click. And then the three horses exploded down the trail, following the bends of stream as if yoked together by invisible wire. A fine dust hung and slowly sank over the path. Then even the sound was gone. A bird trilled, paused, then trilled again in the still, golden afternoon.

# viii

A little later the Red Knight paused there and pondered
the ground. There were deep prints and a punctured fish
in the dust. Did they stop to catch it and then throw it
away? It seemed senseless. And whose were the naked feet
among the horses' hooves? He poked the trout with his
own lance and lifted it up, then idly tossed it into the
water where it turned bright belly up and slowly floated
downstream.

No matter. They went on. And he was a little closer, he
thought, all the time. He kicked his spurs and his mount
pounded off again . . .

# ix

*There's no being prepared*, the queen was thinking. *When you see someone start to fall from a height it is no less a shock when he finally strikes the earth. There's no being prepared for it.*

She received her son in the main hall, seated on the smaller of two raised thrones. The narrow windows streaked the dim air with light. One beam lit her. As he walked down the length of the chamber the rays seemed to wink on and off him.

She was thinking how the black queen and herself both had a son and an empty seat to sit beside. She tried to picture the woman but only saw a strange, barbaric robe, clusters of boars' tusks and circlets of gold with the face itself a deep, dark blur, a lightless hole in her mental vision . . . *perhaps,* she thought, *they had the whole of his memory between them . . .*

Parsival had stopped and was standing in the cool dimness between two lightshafts. Neither spoke.

*It's like a wound*, she was thinking, *mortal . . . we're born wounded . . .*

When she suddenly spoke her eyes were unfocused and he was invisible.

She was nothing but light and shadow, blurred, deep, without walls or source.

"Let me instruct you," she said, "before you leave."

# X

As the lush fields drifted slowly past he kept remembering that last talk with his mother. The bony horse rocked unevenly. For a while he watched a huge, solitary tree float toward him across the hot, motionless afternoon. Hills and forests were faintly suggested on the horizon where the haze seemed to gather. The horselegs swooshed softly through the long grass.

He'd kissed her at last though she hadn't invited it. She'd never seemed to look at him and her unresponsive lips were hot and dry. He'd been startled by the heat of her flesh. Had drawn back. She'd spoken as if he were still standing at a distance, as if unaware of what he was doing, as if he were vague as a mist.

"I will give you a horse," she'd said, "for your journey."

# xi

Two young peasant girls were peering around the entrance arch, looking down the long, high, empty hall. At the far end they could see her sitting in the indirect, grayish light. Nothing was distinct. One pulled back suddenly, then inched her face around the bend again.

"I thought she moved," she whispered.

"No," said the other.

"Is she watching us?"

"No."

The second girl was pale, dark and thin. Sad. The first was nervous and very short.

"Why is she staying there?" she wondered in an unnecessary whisper. "They say she won't answer anybody. . . . She didn't eat today . . . Is it because the young lord went away? . . . I spoke to him once, he's so handsome and tall. . . . What's going to happen?"

The other was weeping, silently, she wasn't sure why.

"I don't know," she said.

# xii

The horse sagged in the middle and strayed to the left steadily because of a defect in his joints. Parsival was unconcerned; he barely noticed. He moved without urgency: "Arthur's court," the groom had told him, gesturing vaguely, "why, young master, that's somewheres east to be sure. Somewheres east. You'll meet with strange folk in those places but if you find some sensible fellow you speak right up, you ask him and he'll point the way, he will." The old man, gray, bent, sweatreeking, strong, nodded with a single quick jerk of his head.

"How will I know he's sensible?" Parsival wondered.

The man tilted his head to the side and squinted at the boy as if they shared a sly secret between them. He'd winked, saying:

"Why, if he looks much like meself, young master." Winked again. "But if he looks like Mill Jack, or Waleis the Fisher, pass him by, pass him by!" Chuckled. "Always trust a gray old man to be wise, young master." Chuckled.

Parsival nodded, taking this in. They were standing in the stable yard within the walls. A sweetish, rich tang of dung and mud cloyed in the damp air. A brief storm had just passed and the sun flashed on and off as the clouds stretched and fluffed apart. Ducks splashed in the standing pools; horses moved restlessly.

As Parsival had turned to go he saw the massive mudsplattered form of Broaditch and the jaunty bones of Waleis splashing across the yard.

"Lord," piped Waleis, holding up what seemed a mass of rags and hide. "Wait, my lord."

They stood together in the middle of the yard as the sun went bright and dark almost rhythmically. The two of

26

them were rainsoaked, dark hair greasy and flattened on
their heads. Waleis held out the damp bundle to Parsival.

"From your mother, the queen, young lord," he announced.

Parsival frowned.

"These?" he asked.

Broaditch nodded, seriously.

"Aye," he said. "This scarecrow speaks the truth, lord."

"Scarecrow?" Parsival was puzzled.

Broaditch gestured at Waleis.

"Him," he said, noting the strange literalness of the boy.

"She says for you to wear these clothes," Waleis said in
his high, toneless voice. "My lady says they will keep you
from harm and that she weeps—"

"No," broke in Broaditch, "the queen says, my lord, that
she *will* weep if you ever fail to wear them."

Parsival shook out the damp garments: sackcloth and
raw hides, breeches and shirt of one piece that would leave
the calves bare; shapeless calfskin bags for boots.

"Why these are—" muttered Waleis. Broaditch nudged
him.

Parsival seemed to come to a decision. Nodded.

"Very good," he said. "I thank you both."

The day went dark again though the pulses of light were
now longer and longer as the clouds were shredded by
brisk winds. He studied them both for a moment as if there
were something in their manner he should read. He sensed
something, narrowed his eyes, then seemed to put it from
his mind. A moment later he was striding across the
muddy, suddenly sunbright yard, the clothes under his arm.
The air was cool and clear. He breathed it in feeling his
heart and blood, a sense of excitement, impatience, joy . . .

He remembered for a while as the canted horse rocked
on. He had no specific course, no sense of urgency now
that he was on his way. The way seemed sufficient, the
steady unrolling of days and nights ahead and behind. . . .
For a while he tried to catch the sun actually moving . . .

# xiii

He had known from the tracks for hours now that one of their mounts had thrown a shoe. The print was unmistakable. There were rocky, twisting hills thick with highland flowers and berrybushes here. Morning mists drifted in long, smoky coils. The sun was just clearing the steep peaks. *Nine or ten o'clock,* he thought. He knew he was close and freed his lance and held it upright. That hoof was down to the quick by now.

His instinct stopped him in the middle of a little glade where the mist lay like a wall before him. A moment later he was almost certain he heard a horse snort. He kept his visor open and watched the slow mist unwind and shift before him.

"Throw your ax," he called into the fog. "For when it lifts I have you." He smiled faintly. To either side of him there was no cover so his quarry had to be in front, looking out from the fog. He knew he was already visible. Biting his lip, very tense, he eased his charger a little closer. "Easy there," he murmured, soothingly. "Easy . . ." Closer, closer. He had to chance it now, this was the hidden man's best hope. The Red Knight was sweating chill sweat. He had to relax, couldn't strain to see, had to sit easy and unfocused and wait and wait agonizingly to react when the attack came. . . . Closer. . . . He thought he could see a dim outline in the mists suddenly as his lance just reached into the shifting white wall and then the cold, bright steel appeared spinning out of the blankness a few feet away coming so fast his mind didn't register it until after the edge of his shield part-blocked the ax which merely glanced off the side of his helmet with a stunning bang and he thought *Ah, a good toss!* even as he went straight in at the

28

vague outline which became a desperate knight, the quiet, second man of the three, on a crippled steed having to stand still and take the charge on his shield. There was nothing else to do. He braced and was knocked flying over the rocks. He rolled and scrambled to his feet. His helmet had been twisted to one side, blinding him. As he stood there in the mist, sword drawn, desperately trying to free his visor, staring at blackness, his mind kept rapidly replaying the last few moments: the thinning mist, the dim rubyred figure drifting slowly closer, knowing there was no escape, aware this was life and death, recalling the sinking in his stomach when the horseshoe flew loose and he knew it was over and he was alone, totally alone and he didn't even bother to tell them to go on ahead because the first knight wouldn't wait and Galahad had to reach Arthur if he could. As he struggled there, dizzy, blind and in pain, he never felt the blow that spun his head off or heard the clinking bounces of his gushing helmet . . .

# xiv

He sat at ease, moving on across hills and fields, one leg
crossed on the saddle. The sun was tilting down through
the afternoon. He was reading a parchment his mother had
given him. He read it again and again. It was yellowed at
the edges and waterstained. The characters were very
graceful, the hand virile and sure. It read:

> On strange paths beware of dark places.
> Cross not strange rivers at dark fords,
> But pass where the shallows run clear.
> Greet every man politely.
>
> If you win the ring and greeting of a noble lady,
> Take them both and free your heart from care.
> Kiss and embrace her for if she be chaste
> Your strength will grow and you will lose nothing.

As the horse, Spavint, rocked and veered along, he folded
the parchment and put it away. The words raised some
questions in his mind but as there was no one to ask he
decided it was better to have good advice you didn't entirely understand than poor precepts that were perfectly
clear.

The sun was low in the sky and fiercely red, directly in
his face. Partly for this reason he kept closing his eyes
but riding steadily all day through the lush heat had
drained him so now he dozed and half dreamt, moving
back and forth between sleep and waking with the sharper
jerks of the horse. Shadows deepened, then grew long from
scattered trees and gathered in rills behind stone dolmens,
massive roughhewn monuments where druids still gathered

on sacred nights. . . . The western forests were dark; the air cool and fragrant; grasses grayed to pale silver . . .

As he tried to imagine King Arthur and the land of the knights the dreams would begin and blend gradually into his images: walls and towers multiplied and rose like mountains of jewel and mirror and in rainbow explosions of light men, like individual suns, walked and rode blindingly in a world of blazing, vibrating crystal . . .

Eventually he woke among dark trees. The horse had entered a spur of woods. Directly overhead where the branches thinned, there was a grayish ghost of twilight . . .

He dismounted, tethered and rubbed down Spavint; sat with his back to an immense tree and ate from his foodsack, slowly chewing the dried fruit and salt meat. . . . After a time there was no light at all above the treetops. At some point he passed into sleep . . .

# XV

Sunbeams stabbed down from the high embrasures into the dim throneroom where a cluster of attendants (motley as such went since the queen had barred highborn men and ladies for fear of their influence on Parsival) had gathered at the foot of the steps leading up to the motionless Herzelroyd, who sat silent and brooding like a sibyl. Her mother-in-law stood apart from the others and aimed the long edge of her face upward.

"Queen," she said, "come away from here!"

Herzelroyd didn't stir. One of the attendant ladies whispered to a groom:

"She's sat like that for three days now."

No one mentioned the smell. It hung in the air, vague and disquieting, a tone higher than the ordinary musty, acrid, sweet and bitter background of human and animal odors and the faint decaying of floor rushes and flowers.

"Queen!" cried the mother. "Queen!"

# xvi

A little after dawn Parsival was already being walked deeper into the forest by his strangely canted mount that seemed to lean on the air to its left as it wandered steadily and imperceptibly away from any straight course that happened to present itself. The groom had well understood his mother's instructions to prepare a horse that would win no envy anywhere nor speed any rider with dangerous swiftness. *So,* the man had thought, *this Spavint, if the young master were to meet with no obstacles and the world be wide enough as they say, will eventually circle him home again . . .*

A deep white mist flowed all around so that the morning light glowed directionless and the trees seemed to float rootless and dark above the earth where they lifted into thinner fog. The grasses gleamed dark and wet. A bird suddenly piped, unseen.

He rode, relaxed, spear across his lap. He was wiping the wood dry with a cloth as Spavint was about to step across a narrow brook that barely creased the earth. Thick reeds and flowers clustered along the banks. He looked down at the dark shadowed water and reined back the wandering horse.

"Hold," he said, thinking: *Cross not strange rivers at dark fords.* "What use is advice," he asked Spavint, rubbing his serrated back, "if a man ignores it at first test?"

So Parsival aimed the beast to the right and headed downstream and Spavint's left-turning tendencies kept his head to the brook following all the wendings and doublings that coiled under the dark, cool treeshadows and as the mists lifted little splinters of sunlight broke through the foliage and flickered here and there.

At one point a rabbit casually hopped over the thread of water from one bank to the other. Seeing this, Parsival smiled with the first stirring of irony:

"Poor creature," he told Spavint, pointing out the rabbit, "he has had no good advice from his mother."

# xvii

Broaditch, Waleis and another man were advancing up the long stone hall (deserted, lit near the throne by three feeble candles) to where the pale figure on the high seat was barely visible in the guttering of deep shadows. They each had wrapped cloths over mouth and nose and resembled bandits or the surgeons of later ages. Their voices were blurred.

"Where went the dead king's mother?" Waleis wanted to know.

They walked slowly, the sickly sticky smell in the warm, damp air seeming to cling to flesh and clothes.

"Went to her cousin, they say," responded the third man. "They say she wants men to hunt for the young prince, Parsival." His voice rasped with age.

Broaditch shuddered with sudden nausea.

"God's mercy," he muttered, "there's no end of wisdom to be come upon."

"What's that?" asked Waleis, breathing short and shallow.

"That's there's no such a thing as royal shit, lad." He swallowed hard, sweating coldly.

He stopped and they all stopped.

"It's the season," the old man rasped. "Damp heat. A sweet cheese won't keep a day unsalted."

"Aye," rumbled Broaditch, "sweet spoils fast enough." His tone was tender.

They went on again and near the foot of the steps Waleis crossed himself with sudden violence and clunked to his knees, staring up at the obscure figure on the exalted seat, the head, traced by the uncertain candle flashes, bent forward as if in deep reflection. The old man bowed reverently.

"Forgive us, Your Majesty," he said harshly, nervously.

Broaditch stood frowning, looking still as a man carved of stone on his massive legs, somehow indestructible, hewn for the ages. He had noticed one of her arms stuck straight out from under the vague robes, the fingers hooked half-closed as if frozen while desperately gripping at some unseen, incorporeal form. The light and shadow trembled over the curve of flesh. The stiff, awkward arm, *too stiff, too awkward,* he thought, reaching out of the shadows.

"God keep you, my lady," he said. His voice stayed tender though he shuddered with another wave of nausea. The other two stayed on their knees.

"We were sent, Your Majesty," Waleis was saying, his nervous high tone penetrating, looking with habitual sheepish awe at the queen though he accepted her as hopelessly mad. "We were sent to—"

"Waleis," cut in Broaditch, sad and somehow angry in an unfocused way he didn't quite understand, "try squeaking louder and if that fails go where she is yourself to tell her." He sighed and shut his eyes. "God's sweet mercy," he murmured.

# xviii

It was soon after sunrise when Parsival reached a plain where the forest opened out and the stream vanished underground among a tumble of mossy rocks. He urged Spavint across where the trickle would have been flowing into a misty meadow. The sun was still below the wooded hills, and as he rode on, the moist dewsmoke thickened and nothing could be seen but a few feet of damp parklike vale in every direction. Spavint had imperceptibly begun (as the stream no longer checked him) his steady straying left again.

Suddenly, in front of him, a huge, unfamiliar shape loomed up revealed by a shift in the drifting clouds. He stopped the horse, heart beating faster. It was wide, dark, tall, tapering toward the top: he thought of a man, more than twenty feet high, wearing a full cape. Just before it was cut off by another swelling of fog he thought it moved. Couldn't be certain.

Gripping his spear firmly he walked Spavint forward. A moment later hooves were plopping into marshy mud, then knee deep in pond water, lilypads tangling and ripping rubberlike around the bony legs. The mists filled and steamed up here like smoke.

Since the shadowy thing was obviously on the other side, he backed out and headed Spavint around the outskirts of the ooze and then again, startlingly, the shape was rising over him and an instant later he felt a cold, wet touch like a thin snake across his chest and neck that seemed to be trying to coil around and drag him from the saddle. As he was pushed back he gripped it with silent fury and fear, holding the horse still in the ironlock of his

legs, and snapped what at the same moment he recognized
was a rope. A tentrope.

He smiled and shook his head and dismounted. Secured
Spavint to a stake and went around the big tent, padding
under the net of guycords. Parted the entrance flaps and
stepped inside.

It was dim and close. He blinked, stooped and poked
the carpet: rich and thick. Heard a faint sigh and spun
around: at the far end of the spacious, round interior someone lay stretched out. Thinking whoever it was might be
ill or injured he went over to see.

He knelt beside a sleeping woman: she'd struggled out
of her fine sable covers (because of the humid heat) and
most of her lay pale and naked on the twisted pelts. His
heart was loud in his ears; his stomach clenched up.

Breathless, he took in her long, bare limbs, the fluff of
dark hair at her legs' joining; the rich, full aureoles . . .

He gently cupped the breast, curious but not-quite-con-
sciously, and wondered at the sheer skin and soft, full
weight, like something infinitely ripened. . . . Let his hand
rove freely along her bends and sleeknesses. Giddy, not
understanding but enjoying it, he smelled her, sniffed a
strange fragrance, bending closer to her loins, inhaling it,
stunned and delighted as she opened her eyes and stared
at him bending over her like a thirsty man at a pool.

"Who dishonors me?" she cried, then scrambled backwards trying to free herself but he pressed closer, caressing
and inhaling. "Lord Jesus," she moaned, pushing feebly at
him, "help me . . . help me . . ."

He barely felt her hands. She seemed to herself to be
struggling in a nightmare: the beautiful young man in
coarse hides that chafed her soft flesh, holding her with
effortless, astounding strength, stroking, exploring her with
an intensity and delight, she was starting to realize, that
was strangely innocent.

"In God's name," she said, "how can this be?"

He sat back suddenly and caught her wrist, stared at a
wide gold ring she wore.

"What do you want with me?" she asked, more calmly,
seeing that he was apparently satisfied with very little as
such things might be expected to go. She was shocked
when he suddenly tugged the ring from her finger and
kissed her dryly on the lips.

"Are you a thief?" she whispered as he abruptly let her

go and sat up on his knees over her, smiling with obvious satisfaction. She lay there for a time silently looking up at him. Then, belatedly, she tugged the cover up not quite over her breasts, staring totally confused.

"That was wonderful," he finally said.

She frowned. She couldn't decide if he was actually mad, witless or sly. His soft, bluegreen eyes and curled golden lashes troubled her appraisal. His innocence, she concluded, was impossible.

"Which part of it, pray?" she finally asked.

"Why all of it, my lady." He looked at her as at a wonder of the world. "My mother had this written down." He nodded, pleased. "I remembered. I have known nothing like it. I am learning so many new things my head swims."

"Ah," said the lady, "your mother loosed you upon the world, did she?"

He frowned slightly, beautifully, she thought. Like a troubled god.

"Not all willingly," he said. "She felt I was not yet ready to leave."

"What an idea!" insisted the lady with, she realized, useless sarcasm.

"I convinced her," he said. "But is it not a marvelous thing to be touched and kissed? It's true, as it was written, it took away my cares!" He beamed at her.

She sighed.

"It's but the beginning of cares, boy," she murmured with, she thought, wasted wisdom. She just lay back watching him and realized (as from far off) that she should be acting, crying out for help, or at least getting him out somehow but there was still a vague dreaminess to all of this and she lingered (she was later to think) like a foolish deer in the eye of the hunter. Except this hunter seemed oblivious to the aiming of arrows . . .

"There is so much to learn about," he said, and turning he noticed a cold partridge, garnished, laid out on a low table. He seated himself on a pillow and began to feast. "This is good," he said, mouth full.

"Poor creature," she said, gently, "eat if you must, but return my ring. Did your mother teach you not to steal, boy?"

"Steal?" he frowned. "I but took your favor. As it is written."

"My favor? Ah. Look you, a lady *bestows* such things

and then only to knights, not to poor, foolish, mad boys."
She covered her breasts and sat up. "However comely,"
she added, as if to reprimand herself.

"I shall soon be a knight," he declared, wiping a dribble
of sweet grease from his chin with the back of his hand.

He stood up.

"Strange is the knight," she said, "who feasts without
his hostess' bidding, Sir Boy." She smiled more securely
now, certain he was demented. "Return my ring and I'll
give you a greater favor."

He squinted at her, then laughed.

"I know better than that," he told her. "I have your
favor and must keep it and win honor."

He went to the entrance.

"How will you know honor," she asked him, "to win
it?"

He considered this, parting the flap. A stream of morning sunlight enhaloed him and brightened the tent. She
blinked against it.

"God will make it clear to me," he replied, at length.

She sighed and nodded, tenderly.

"May He shield you," she said quietly as he went out
and the flap shut behind him.

As he mounted his horse he noticed two smaller tents
nearby. The fog was gone except for a few threads drifting
in the hollows of the ground. A young woman was just
coming out of a tent holding a large, silver bowl. She
stopped and silently stared at him.

"God shield you, lady," he called and waved to her as
he rode away.

# xix

In a vast, dim, cool pine forest, rich-scented, Galahad and the shieldless knight were walking their mounts over the thick, muffling floor of dried needles. Thin strands of moonlight gleamed here and there through the dense canopy.

"We go straight on," Galahad was saying.

"Into that red-suited swine-kisser's own damned country?" the other protested, half-whispering. "That's a sound plan, Galahad. Worthy of your wisdom. Hear me, I say we double south and swing back later."

"South of here," Galahad said, "there are worse things than Sir Roht, the Red."

The other man cradled his helmet in his arms and kept jerking his head around nervously.

"Do you really believe the invader has come?" he wanted to know, staring out into the dim stillness pressing all around. "I think Arthur starts at shadows. I think—"

"Think what you please, Gunkar."

"I say we go south."

"Say what you will."

"Damn Arthur! Why couldn't he pay the bastard and have done with it? 'When you hire the wolf,' they say, 'to guard your sheep you—' "

"Be still. If you've no trust in my—"

"Trust? In you? And see where we are, O Galahad," he said with broad sarcasm.

Galahad strode on, tugging the reins behind him as the horse quietly followed. Steel rang and pinged faintly. Gunkar remounted.

"Alright," he said, turning his horse aside. "We part."

41

Galahad went on, said nothing more. "I'll risk jousting shadows while Roht makes sausage of you!" Gunkar called after him. No reply came as he drifted down a slope now into the breathless darkness . . .

# XX

The two mules drank as if chewing the water, their long necks stretched out side by side. Waleis paced nervously. Broaditch lay flat on his thick back, hands clasped under his head, looking up through the interstices of the sunlaced trees at splinters of bright sky. The breeze was sweet. The air was rich with earth and water.

"Broaditch," his companion complained, "why do I ever heed you?"

"Because I am wiser," was the peaceful reply.

Waleis spat; then turned and stepped to the stream, unlacing his codpiece. He urinated, watching the hissing bubbles with a certain satisfaction.

"Wiser," he said, scornfully. "Mark well the wisdom of it: leave a good home to chase after a mad prince, God alone knows to where. . . . This is wisdom indeed!"

He turned, scooping his organ out of sight after thoughtfully flicking it a few times with his middle finger.

"He's a king now," Broaditch pointed out.

"Aye. So much the worse for him. Better only a mad pup than a mad hound."

"Better a mad king than a mad serf," Broaditch reflected. "It's heavily more profitable and small boys don't pelt you with mud and stones. Still," he admitted, "your cursed relatives try to do for you. But they will whether your wits be whole or in parts."

"So you finally agree he's an empty jug."

"No. Parsival is young and odd in his way, but he's sound. But you must know, with the queen reigning from under the earth, how do you think our particular lot would fall out back there so long as we walk above ground?"

43

Waleis frowned, contracted his whole face to focus around his red and bony nose. This shot told.

"That family," Broaditch went on, "aunts, uncles, cousins, the whole sack of them, they'll have that kingdom peeled and sliced soon enough."

"Well. We might still live in peace there." Waleis was truculent.

"Aye? But we were advantaged and raised up by the old queen and we'd soon be raised in the other direction by the new." He sat up, stretching. Tugged a flask of wine from a bundle and tilted it up to his lips. Sighed and belched softly. "Young Parsival, with or without his wits, stands between us and an unkind life." Broaditch was so (as ever) matter-of-fact that Waleis gave it up. His voice was wistful as he complained:

"What's the price, then, of a quiet life?"

Broaditch stood up. His shrewd, somehow dreamy eyes (incongruous in the wide, impassive face that some woman had tenderly compared to a sack of ripe apples) weren't looking at Waleis. Women, he had discovered, rarely missed those eyes, men always did.

"You've not the purse for it," he said. He pointed at the now grazing mules. "Collect your brothers," he said, "the hunt goes on."

# xxi

She was in midstream, holding up her skirts, feeling her way across the wide, shallow, pebbly river in the sparkling noon sunlight when she turned and saw them coming down the green hill she'd just passed herself: two men on muleback, one tall and all angles like, she decided, clothes hung on a pole to dry; the other massive, weighing his mount down like, she thought, a load of stones. When they reached the far bank they held up and sat looking at her. Rogues don't ride mules by and large, she reasoned with herself.

"The tracks all lead to here," she heard the tall one say.

"Woman," called the bulky man in a deep, rather mellow voice.

She watched him urge his heavyladen beast into the inches-deep water. The stream flowed cool and pleasant over her bare feet and ankles. She heard pebbles moistly crunch under the hooves of the mule. When he drew close she studied his face and felt reassured. His mouth looked ready to smile though it didn't.

"Woman," he repeated, "have you seen a rider pass?"

She looked coolly and skeptically at them: the bony fellow, all nose and ears, was entering the stream too.

"If you go on," she said, "I soon may."

She saw he was amused.

"I'm called Broaditch," he said.

"By those who call you, I think," she replied, smiling slightly. "Anyway, you seem broad enough for the name."

She turned and stepped on through the stony shallows toward the far side.

"Curse him!" the bony one cried out and she turned to

see him suddenly plip-plopping past her as his mule rushed
forward. The fellow's clothes and limbs flapped together,
she decided, like a broken ship's mast in a storm. He sped
by, raging and kicking the beast's flanks and beating at its
head, to which the animal remained utterly indifferent.

"Curse you by God's blood! See, Broaditch, again it
does—" and was cut off as the mule charged out on the
far shore and instantly stopped, spraddlelegged as if it had
run into an invisible wall and, she thought, the mast broke
off and came crashing down sails fluttering wildly. She
laughed; glanced at big Broaditch: he simply shook his
head and sighed.

She watched the man scramble to his feet and, shouting,
grab up a fistful of stones from the shallow water.

"Foul lump of dung!" he cried and fired the missiles
with terrific fury at point-blank range.

"It's far safest to be his target," remarked Broaditch as
the stones splashed everywhere and the mule turned a
placid eye on his attacker.

"He has a way with beasts," she suggested.

Broaditch opened his thick hands.

"Strange roads," he declared, "unite strange travelers."

They were across now and she sat on the grassy bank to
let her feet dry in the sun. She didn't quite watch him as
he dismounted and squatted near her, unlacing a flask of
wine. The other came and stood restlessly nearby, touching
his nose from which ran a trickle of blood. She decided
he'd need to wear a tent just to keep that remarkable organ
out of the rain. *Whoever kissed him,* she thought, *would
run the risk of impalement.*

"His name's Waleis," said Broaditch fraternally, looking
closely at her.

Later they shared a supper of hare and greens. As they
dipped their fingers in the cooling pot, she kept staring
down the length of river to where it blended into the
twilight summer haze. The nightbug whirred and skreecked
all around now. A pair of fireflies winked against the dark
tree shapes. She kept remembering the millpond on summer
evenings at home: the rough huts just shapes, mysterious
in the dusk, and on the shadowed, glimmering, still water,
concentrating all the elusive, hinting illumination, swans
sailed, pure white, silent. . . . *Ah,* she thought, *on windless
nights you couldn't smell the serfs . . .*

Broaditch had just said something.

"What?" she asked.

"Where were you bound, woman?"

He wiped his greasy hands on his trousers.

"Home," she said.

"Home," he repeated as if that word explained some deeper thing.

She suddenly wanted to talk. *He has a gentle look for such a rough man,* she thought.

"It's been years," she said. "I remember a pond there I . . ." She broke off. There was no way to express it, the memory too real for talking, the image a concentration of form, color, youth, the sheer richness of life, of growing up, a joy and sadness—she felt it in her chest as the whole of her past became one inexpressible feeling . . .

"Your people are castle folk," he said.

"Aye," she replied. "My father was swordsmith to the lord."

Waleis poked into the conversation, impressed.

"Ah," he said, "I spoke many times to a Master Denis of Alquerry. He was a swordsmith too. That's a fine position in life. Ah," he reflected, "if I but had such a skill I wouldn't be here following my lord fool . . . Master Denis had *gold,*" he went on, "I know this for a fact . . . why he showed me a *fur,* a nobleman's fur! He was given it for a duke's blade . . ."

He rubbed his sore nose and dourly considered his fate.

"So you're going home, then?" Broaditch said.

She glanced at him, cocking an eyebrow.

"Better than trackin' about the countryside," put in Waleis, voice rising to a complaining pitch, "in all manner of danger and distress of rogues and cutthroat bandits, better to be goin' home!" He threw himself back on the earth in disgust. There was a silence. Then she spoke, thoughtfully:

"You were in gentle service?"

"Our fathers wore the collar," Broaditch said, matter-of-factly.

"And you do not?" She widened her eyes. "Are you runaways? Outlaw men?"

"No," he said, "We were improved by our mistress. And I was taught by monks." He chuckled. "And I learned some things they never meant for me to know," he murmured, suggestively.

"Are you on pilgrimage, then?"

"Heh," muttered Waleis from the background; he was taking long pulls at the wineflask now. "Pilgrimage to the Devil."

She quickly, mechanically, crossed herself.

"Why are you here," Broaditch asked, "and alone?"

She sighed. Looked downstream again: now the shadows had closed in and the water merely traced an elusive glimmering.

"My lord's good temper," she said.

Broaditch nodded. His powerful, square hands gripped his knees. He studied her face in the vague light: in her thirties, sharp featured, the look he always liked. He smiled, recalling a few incidents from the past with lean, fiery ladies. Redhaired, like this one. An astrologer had looked up from a chart he'd cast: "You have moon with Mars in your seventh house," he'd said, amused. "In fire. You find yourself unsteady in love with sharp-faced, sometimes redheaded women with sharp tempers." Broaditch had sighed and admitted this. "Sometimes," the dreamy-eyed old man went on, "they have a scar on their cheeks or somewhere on the face or a great dark or inflamed-looking mark, due to the afflictions I see." "Well," said Broaditch, "someone has to love them." He explained well enough, Broaditch reflected, but failed to provide the cure. Still, there's nothing new in that. It's more than plain lust but, call it what you will, nothing's lasting, it comes to a great heat and a great cooling in the end . . .

He sighed. Took out his pipe and clicked it between his teeth. Sighed again. He glanced at Waleis who seemed asleep already. Then he stared closely at her trying to see if she had a mark on her face. It was too dark now and he hadn't noticed before. He smiled slightly. She wasn't quite looking at him.

"You served many years, then?" he asked her, quietly.

"Aye. And this day I was left behind. Or left myself behind too, if you turn it another way. And glad of it."

"Oh?" He lit his pipe with the glowing end of a stick. Each puff brought his face out, redly glowing, seeming to float in the air, a massive bronze, twinkle-eyed, rough carving.

"Glad of it," she confirmed, stretching her feet out, wriggling her toes near the dull embers. "Ah, but my poor feet are full sore . . ."

He picked one up in his gentle, thick hands.

"I'll rub them," he said.

She glanced over at where Waleis lay. Said nothing. Sighed with a hint of resignation, perhaps . . .

"I've good hands for it," he said.

# xxii

Gunkar had gone south. He was watching the stars as he moved through the wide, shadowy plains that curved around the mountains. This route would save him days over Galahad's plodding climb and struggle against the grain of the country. He was slightly nervous, naturally, but confident and satisfied with his progress. He would have been less satisfied had he known that two or three miles behind him Sir Roht the Red Knight was following the same strategy. But a few moments later he was to be totally unsatisfied: he'd just noticed a red glow on the horizon which at first he took for the sun until he realized he was looking west; *it must be flames*, he decided, *a forest fire* . . . then, much closer, something seemed to move between him and the distant light. What he needed, he thought, was to get to Camelot and rest. A few days' rest and he'd have his confidence back. Here he was, shaken, sore, half starved and battered. A few days of sleep and good food . . . he pictured a lady he knew very well resting in a soft bed with him, could almost taste the wine . . . *just a few days*, he thought like a prayer . . .

Even with the night close around him he felt naked, exposed here. He kept swiveling in his saddle. Screwed his helmet back in place. Toyed with the hilt of his broadsword. Something moved he was certain now. *Just ahead like a blot of darker shadow. . . . A bear? A deer? Too large. . . .* He was suddenly sweating. Drew the blade out carefully. Moistened his lips. . . . He felt something close behind too, and out on his flanks as if he were enclosed in the center of a hunting circle. *Were these the invaders, the wizards?* He shivered in the warm air with exhaustion and fear. How bright the image of the bed and the woman was and he remembered running from the woods one evening as a child, feeling the deadly shadow creatures reaching for his prickling back, racing for the castle yard, shouting for his mother. . . . With fear then and desperate rage he kicked his horse into a full gallop, bared his teeth, raised his blade and let the scream in his throat burst into a great warcry . . .

Which the Red Knight heard, faintly, on the wind. And he reined up, leaned forward, listening . . .

# xxiii

Later the moon was above the treetops, the world all deep shadows and soft gleaming. Their voices were quiet. She lay near him, weary, peaceful, watching the moon rise and telling the story.

"So you heard shouting?" Broaditch primed her in a pause.

"Aye," she said. "One of my lady's maids, a face like sweet cream though it were curdled now, all in tears pushes into my tent where I was, as I said, taking a few extra minutes of ease, as was well my due, I think, when you consider—"

"No doubt, no doubt," he put in, impatient for the meat of the tale.

"So as sweet cream was all shouts and no sense I went out and, I must tell you, it didn't take long for me to see my master had come back from one of his forays . . ." She sighed. "God's mercy, they strut on horseback like small boys, ride down the serfs, and strike hard blows at one another. Why marry them, will you find them home before you come gray?" She sighed again. "Still, they're some fine figures of men, and life keeps on the move . . ."

"He was back, then?"

"Duke Orilus. A gentle man. Proud enough to die of it. Why once in battle he was struck through the cheek with an arrow and was shortly knocked to earth and as he lay stunned a friend stooped to pull loose the arrow shaft and braced his foot on my lord's chin whereupon my lord rose up all in a rage and struck at the man, shouting out: 'Rather let me bleed than suffer a man's foot in my face!' and so on in like wise . . ."

"Very lordly," commented Broaditch.

"Aye," she said. "So the duchess was on her knees and his sword was flashing over her head—it takes strength to heft such a weapon—and I thought, Holy Mother, this is murder before my eyes, except he rushed forward shouting some proud thing, I'm sure, I was running but still too far off to hear closely . . ."

"He slew his wife like that?"

"No," she said. "He went past her, the great lord did, and his lady followed on her knees, walking on her knees like a monk on St. Alman's Day, full of tears, and then Adela—"

"The lady?"

"Ah, no, the *slightly* noble girl who served her, whose father had not enough grass to keep one horse under him and yet *she* was gentle blood . . ."

Broaditch took this in.

"Well, well," he said, "it's a lumpy world, woman."

She wasn't listening.

"My father has four horses," she said, in the tone of one who feels goaded to finally speak out, "and how many cows and goats I don't know and land enough, aye, land enough . . ."

"To be sure, to be sure. What was she shouting?"

"Who?"

"Adela."

"Oh. Well, it made no sense which leaves me not stunned. 'It was a fool,' she said, 'just a fool!' I thought maybe she'd seen her reflection. I said: 'That's the duke there, you silly girl,' and she said: 'The boy, the boy!' But I had no time for her: the duke was now striking at the *tent!* What a mad thing!"

"It was empty," Broaditch remarked shrewdly, "the tent? None came out of it?"

"No. He struck it to the earth and trampled on it as though it were flesh and blood! What a mad thing . . . I must tell you, that tent held out not long against his rage! Ah, but his face was red as beet blood, his great sword whirred in the air and everywhere feathers fell like snow . . ."

"Feathers? He slew a bird there?"

"From my lady's pillows." She was all afire with her tale now. "Ah, but he'd grunt and smite and the fluff would fly up and there was so much—she had brought I know not how many comforts with her for they were going to his sister's and there's little comfort there I—"

"Surely, surely, there was so much?"

"What? . . . Oh, aye, aye, the feathers fell as though he struggled in a winter's storm, all around him, settling on his hair and mail, and these seemed to rouse him all the more and double for he struck out at them too and I learned when swords fly it's well to be a feather."

Broaditch chuckled approvingly at this morsel of wisdom.

"By the time he tired of this lordly sport, my lady had come on her knees right to him and the down was catching in her hair too and I was waving my hands to keep some out of my eyes as I ran nearer because he had the blade up over her head. Then he fetched me a fair blow on my shoulder with his great hand which, I must tell you, kept me from staying a long time close to him and my feet no longer had the trouble of standing on the ground . . ."

"Ah," breathed Broaditch, "but you did all you could."

"And his big red face shouted: 'So he pleased you, did he?' and I could see from where I lay, his big fist bang between her eyes and blood spurt from her nose and she fell down . . . Adela was on *her* knees, shouting whatever she shouted or pleaded, and my lady, God knows how, managed to sit up and said through her blood which kept choking her: 'God forbid,' she said, 'he was but a poor fool, a mad boy.' But Orilus seemed more anxious to speak than listen: 'That one whose feet trod here . . . and here,' he pointed his sword at where the earth was marked by footprints but for all I could tell they were his own . . ."

"Well," mused he, "these things are bound to happen. It's in the nature of things, of men and ladies."

"So?" she said, sharply, "if we women had great fists as big as yours there might be a juster spurting of noseblood, Broad One."

He laughed.

"Aye," he allowed.

" 'That one whose feet trod here,' he shouted, 'think of his life as something brief!' and the weeping lady swore her innocence . . ." She paused, thoughtfully. "As I would myself . . . women are weak, that's what men love to say . . ." Her voice was softer now as she came out of the story a little and turned toward the bulk of Broaditch sitting across from her. "So I've been told a time or two."

"And when was this?" he asked, feeling his blood draw somehow thicker, looking at the moonsoft form of her lying back on the rich silvered grass.

She laughed lightly and stretched her arms back and turned her body on the warm ground.

"Ah, when?" she asked the air, or perhaps the moon. "Alienor, you were *so* weak . . ."

"Alienor," he repeated, softly.

"Well," she said, "my husband who's dead, he never tore down *my* tent."

"Had you a tent?"

"A small point," she insisted, laughing. "What pleasures can a poor matron have in these times?"

"You have known others, then?"

"Oaf," she told him. "What questions!"

"I meant other *times*, woman Alienor."

She snorted. Then they paused and his mind came back to the story.

"So he didn't slay her," he murmured, "because he would have done that right away in his heat. . . . Well, the lady protested, but what did the lord?"

"What indeed? Why he smashed her fine saddle, tore her fine garments to tatters, even the ones she wore . . ." She sighed. "Such samite cloth as you rarely see—she had it on to flaunt before his sister, well, you must know, the way he left her dressed was not in the fashion. . . . He set her shoeless on her palfrey. 'We will ride together, you thus,' he told her, 'for I long to meet your friend,' he said, 'my heart beats,' he said, 'like a maid's with my longing.' But he looked little enough like a wooer to me, good Broad One . . ." she took thought for a moment, then concluded: "Adela and I he drove off, cursed us as midwives to this birth of shame, I think he said, for I listened ill at this point, feeling some little anger myself. I gave him a few words to consider from a safe distance . . ."

"Ah, did you?" he remarked, mildly.

"Adela followed after them, making a muddy trail with her tears . . . well, why not? Could she return to her one-horse baron father? She had high cause to weep, that one . . ."

They sat in silence for a while to let the tale set. She reveled like a kitten on the warm earth, stretching and twisting. There was a purr in her saying:

"So, Broadman, you see what a poor woman can come to . . ."

It was not until hours later (the moon down, stars clustered thick and rich like crushed diamonds) with her sleeping sound and close under his arm that it struck him:
*A boy,* he thought, *she said it was a fool, a mad boy . . .*

# xxiv

The rain pittered high in the trees that massed so thickly over the steeply sloping hill path that only a stray drop now and then struck him as he walked Spavint down over the rocks and ruts. The afternoon was dark gray as twilight.

They worked their way down the twisting incline, slipping now and then on the strange crumbly rocks, moving deeper into the grim valley. He had never seen country like this, so steep and dense with pine trees that hushed the damp air. For days now he'd seen no person of any degree or sign of habitation.

He kept remembering pieces of his past life. He had never had so much time for reflection. There was one morning when he escaped his mother's close watch and hid himself in a stable on festival day to watch the sport: in a wicker enclosure four husky serfs were blindfolded, given cudgels and, while the rough crowd went mad, a blowing, terrified porker was released. . . . He remembered the sour smell of the hay where he hid looking out through broken planks; the view of the castle nearly a mile away up the hillside; the rows of huts and muddy streets; the young serf boys, already wearing collars on their thin necks, his own age (nine or ten at that time) running naked in the noisy crowd. . . . 'Beating the blindfolded pig,' they called it . . .

The fat animal snorted and squealed and its speed as it tore around the enclosure surprised him: the mud flew, the crowd shouted, the four men staggered and spun, flailing at sounds and movement, the pig now bowling one over, now shaking the wicker pen, the meaty thwack as

57

clubs struck man and beast alike, the pig stunned on its
back, legs vibrating, a man hit in the chest, crawling
breathless as the others tripped and skidded and swung
and the mob went into ecstatic hilarity, laughing, screaming, surging, now a man pounding at the downed animal,
now a club thwocking *his* head, the sound clear and solid
over all the outcry, men falling and getting up, dripping
black stinking mud, dying squeals, cries of pain . . .

"We are all," a voice said behind him, he turned, recognized Broaditch, "in that pen in some capacity, young
lord."

Parsival sat up in the damp hay and looked at the man
standing with that quality of utter repose as if he might
never move or breathe, his eyes somehow about to smile
from the ruddy browned face, standing just inside the
stable door, needles of light scattered around him, stab-
bing through the bent and uneven boards. Then he reached
out his thick hand and Parsival took it, feeling the warmth
and strength of it. Whenever he recalled the man he recalled what he called to himself "the chestnut smell" because somehow that was nearest the odor of Broaditch. At
least that day.

They'd walked together up the long, grassy slope through
the open, warm fields.

"I wanted to see," he told Broaditch, who led the way.

"Well," was his reply, "didn't you, young lord?"

"But I wanted to stay."

"Ah. So you did." Broaditch didn't turn when he spoke.

"I could run back right now."

"So you could."

They went on, steadily, unhurried. He moved closer to
the big man. Smelled the chestnuts.

"Your mother," Broaditch said, "is not your common
run of queen. She talks to monks. And she *reads*."

"I can read."

"You know not yet the full stretch of your uncommon-
ness."

Parsival tilted his head.

"Are you uncommon, Broaditch?" he asked.

Broaditch chuckled, deep in his chest.

"Enough to displease some gentle ladies," he replied.
"Some who think your mother a mad lover of serfs." He
nodded, still looking straight ahead up the hill. "Some who
think Adam and Eve had servants."

"Did they, Broaditch?"

He enjoyed talking with him. There was something sure and solid that he liked. Something else that he sensed he'd have to grow up to understand.

"It seems," Broaditch told him, "to have been overlooked in holy writ."

Then Parsival noticed his grandmother was standing before the archway in the rough stone and log wall that circled the towering, windowless keep. She was watching them, her narrow head tilted at a thoughtful angle. Broaditch automatically tugged off his cap and bowed.

"God has made us all," his mother had told him when he'd asked. "Our differences are according to our vices and advantages. We all serve him equally from our various places in life, my son. We must ever be kind and wise and fair to those whose vices have brought them less profit, as the good friar says. For when you are truly good, my son, you forget yourself and feel only for others. You feel their sorrow and joy as a mother for her babe . . . How many say these things, how few *know* their truth!" and she sighed, her long, nervous hands trembling with her intensity . . .

Remembering his talks with the queen again, he came to a steep, twisting turn where the loose, damp soil and black pebbles slipped away under each hoof and footstep and he and Spavint half skidded and half ran around the bend, struggling to stop suddenly when he saw the girl seated on a rock off the trail, crouched over a man in armor, his head in her lap. The massive, dark pines tilted against the slope, dense around them there. He noticed the armor was dull gray in the drizzling dull light. He angled himself back against the horses chest and forelegs and strained all his terrific strength to check their steady half slide past as if the lady and knight were on a madly tilted shoreline and he and the horse floating down on a slow, inexorable current. Though the soil kept breaking away he was able to keep their loss of ground down to mere inches for the moment as he called out to her:

"Who are you? Is that knight dead? What happened here?"

She looked up at him, wan, tired, dark hair loose and wet. She stared without replying, astonished by this apparition that she later talked about with a girl friend at a feast where they sat together at noon watching the acrobats form a trembling human pyramid in the castle yard, the master cook hacking hunks from a roast boar that serving men placed on chunks of bread for plates and passed among the reclining nobility: ". . . and what did I see," she said, delicately cracking and drawing the marrow from a braised thrush wing, "but a handsome boy in rags of hide, leaning against a knock-kneed nag as they both slipped and slid down the hill—" "Where?" asked her companion, a sturdy, flaxen girl, sucking at a piece of crisped boar's fat; "—at Valmit, the hills above the great field where *he* fell . . ." She paused for a moment, remembering. Sighed. "For all my grief," she said, "I scarce kept from laughing at the sight of that boy . . ." "Were you ever kind to him?" her friend wondered, meaning the knight. The other stopped chewing and stared, not seeing the acrobats, the bustle and excitement of the feast. She sighed. "I meant to be," she said, "but then he was killed . . ." "Look," her friend said, pointing, eyes excited, "they're about to fall!" As the human tower suddenly sagged in the middle and crumpled, men and the young boys on top all came smashing down onto the sunbaked clay, some rolling safely, some hitting flat and hard as an involuntary sigh went up as one from the crowd . . .

"Can you hear?" cried Parsival.

"I hear you, boy," she replied.

The slippery, crumbly trail stayed at the same pitch right up to the edge of the flat, black rock she was seated on so it didn't help him any to try and work Spavint nearer since his tacking course would take him below the spot before he ever reached it.

Panting with strain, Parsival said:

"How was he killed, lady?"

She brushed a hand at her tears, too curious to weep now. She couldn't get over the incongruity of form and dress. Later at the feast she and her friend were to look into this question: "He was dressed like a fool?" her friend wondered. "Yes. In skins." They both washed their fingers in a bowl held for that purpose by a serving man. "You know," her friend said, "you should have fucked him." "The boy?" she wondered, frowning. "No, no. The knight." "But he was old. More than thirty years." "Well," was the response, as the fingers were rubbed rapidly together in the sunshine to dry, "that's not *so* old, when you love . . ." The man, whose presence they'd noticed no more than a fly's, passed on. "I'll wait till I marry to fuck with strange knights," she said, smiling, "like all great ladies." Her friend laughed, then pointed again. "Look," she said, "the singers are ready."

"He fought a hard joust today," she told Parsival. "He was slain by a lance though he lived to ride this far with me. He wanted to die alone with me, he said." And she looked down into his face, tenderly for a moment, then back up as Parsival slipped to one knee and lost several feet of ground before he could brace himself back to his feet.

"You're going to fall," she observed.

"My name is Parsival," he told her, for no particular reason.

Later, at the feast, after the singing, she and her friend were walking with two squires in the nearby meadowlands. The boy with her kept reaching for her hand which she kept skillfully disengaging.

"He said he was son of Gahmuret the King," she said to her friend. "Who?" the boy with her asked. "Some beautiful fool," she told him. "Ah," said the boy, "if he offended you I'll fight him." "You can't. He was a peasant and without his wits." "Well, I'll beat him then!" The other boy laughed overloud at this retort, then turned from the flaxenhaired girl for a moment to ask: "Is she truly sixteen?" The first, dark girl tossed back her loose hair, giggling. "She's a liar," she said, "we're the same age." "Both fifteen, liar," said the boy, triumphantly . . .

Her leg was going to sleep so she shifted the dead man's bearded head with the trickle of blood creasing one corner of the bruised mouth to another spot on her lap. She was getting tired of sitting and wanted to go home.

"So you're the king's son?" she asked Parsival who had to twist his head around to look up at her now. Better to even talk to him than sit alone any longer. She was getting very hungry all of a sudden.

"Yes," he called back. "But why do you sit there like that?"

"It was this knight's wish, O king."

"I cannot keep my footing here," he called back, "though I wish I could stay . . ."

And he went, faster and faster around the bend and suddenly out of her view.

He had wanted to see the man's death wound. He

couldn't imagine how armor could be pierced, even by his own spear. *There must be a way,* he decided, and he wished he could try it himself. Curiosity burned in him the way lust for flesh or power burned in other men . . .

He was skidding and slipping, unable to hold the horse at all now as he reached an angle where all semblance of roadway ceased and he was suddenly running full tilt down the crumbling hillside deeper and deeper into the dark, foggy woods. He gripped Spavint's reins and raced the final distance to the bottom, finally able to stop and look back up at what from there was virtually a cliff face, massive, curving around him, equally steep, as far as he could see, in both directions. He was like an ant walled in the bottom of a basin except that straight before him was a level break in the thick forest. Since there was no choice and it made no real difference, he shrugged, remounted and rode on through the silent pine darkness . . .

# XXV

Sir Roht, the Red Knight, waited until daylight to move up to investigate the cry he'd heard just before dawn. With the pine mountains on his left and the sweeping, green plains on his right he went about a mile or so. The day was cloudless and sparkling except on the horizon, beyond the scattered clumps of trees, a vast mass of dark, oily looking smoke hung stagnant and slowly spread. Toward the coast, he observed and wondered if a whole town might not have burned there. . . . And then he saw the man he'd been hunting: the helmeted head and the head of his horse (the bodies were nowhere in evidence, which was remarkable in itself) both sat tilted up on poles. The blood had run the length of the wood and dried dark and crusty. The face was shadowed by the visor, which looked strangely like an open mouth. Coming closer he heard the snarling buzz of flies and saw them bunched and flickering. The heads were facing the mountains as if outposts at the end of the plains. It seemed to have some significance and looked like, he thought, barbarian work. The horse's jaw had fallen as if in speaking. *Well, it told its tale well enough,* he reflected, looking around, scanning the dense and rocky pine forest above him before urging his mount up among the trees, thoughtfully. His instinct told him that Galahad had kept on straight and his common sense said it was better to struggle through the hills than ride this smooth track to hell.

# XXVI

Since he distrusted the mule anyway it hadn't been hard to reason Waleis into the advantages of walking and complaining over riding and grumbling. So he went out in front of Broaditch and Alienor, his bony legs wading through the fine dust they raised on the hot, windless road that twisted and doubled back on itself like (he had pointed out several times) a sick snake. Under the steady pressure of the sun they went up and down short, steep, green hills. *As level as the sea,* mused Broaditch.

They stopped on a slope where the road divided and writhed away in two directions. Alienor pulled back her hood, wearily. Broaditch wiped the sweat from his eyes. Waleis paced and gesticulated nervously with random fierceness.

"See, see," he said, "now where are we? . . . We lost his trail if it ever *was* his. . . . Now where are we?"

"Sometimes, I think," Alienor said, "that it's just the breeze blowing through your mouth that makes the sound spill from you."

Waleis looked bitterly at her.

"See how I'm used by this woman," he said. "I walk, she rides, and what benefit do I get of her? Tell me that!"

"The benefit of my gentle counsel," she told him.

Waleis paid her no mind.

"I have to shit," he announced.

She shook her head.

"You ask our help?" she wondered. "Want us to squeeze your belly?"

"When are we going to eat?" he wanted to know suddenly sitting down, crosslegged, in the roadway, like a bony, brooding troll, she thought.

Broaditch leaned slightly forward, shading his eyes with his hand.

"I thought I saw riders on the leftwards road," he said, "there, some hills on . . ." He pointed.

"I see nothing," she said. "I think that is the way to the damp country. I passed near there once. . . . Arthur's sister, the witch, has her lands there."

Broaditch looked at her, eyes soft and serious. She returned the look in kind.

"Your home lies neither way," he said.

She shrugged.

"It has waited years enough for me," she said. "Arthur's court is west." She pointed down the righthand road.

Broaditch thought it through.

"I've no doubt the boy will find his way there," he said.

"Which road leads to the land of food and drink?" Waleis wanted to know.

# xxvii

Parsival halted Spavint in a now steady, heavy rain that spattered and gushed from the trees and gathered in dark pools on the sodden earth. His long hair was pressed wet and flat along his cheeks and neck.

He dismounted and walked through the mud to the door of the dark, windowless hut that sagged under the trees. Dark smoke seeped out through the spaces in the walls and roof. The gray rain beat at the soggy thatch and streamed down in random rivulets into the bubbling yard. Blinking the water from his eyes he reached to try the latch but before he touched it the door swung inward and a stinging reek billowed out.

Parsival stood there in the roaring rainfall, drops shattering on his head, facing a short, damply pale serf with eyes washed out to whitish gray, seeming pupilless. The tip of the man's nose had been sliced off, somehow, and the scar was red and raw. He ran a twisted finger around the inside of his serf's collar, staring without apparent focus. Behind him, in the cave-like gloom, Parsival saw a naked child poking at some small, dead, furry thing with a short stick.

"God keep you," the young king said. "I am hungry."

The bent man stood there, working his teeth together as if pondering a deep question.

"Can you hear?" Parsival wondered, getting a little impatient. His mother had told him: try not to be so impatient, but he was always anxious to get small things out of his way.

The man's finger still traced inside the frayed and greasy leather ring. His eyes showed nothing at all.

"Who sent ya here?" he suddenly asked in an empty, flat, angry voice.

66

"No one. I'm wet and hungry. I'm looking for—"

"They fancy they put one over, do they?" The man snorted. Shook his head, once, violently. "Another wide mouth to fill up, eh? Well, they'll think again, they will . . ."

"No one sent me here." Parsival restrained himself, trying to make sense out of the conversation.

The man looked skeptical.

"Out in the rain, are ya?" he asked.

Parsival waited. He couldn't see what else to do. He wiped the water from his eyes.

"Yer a poor fool," the man told him, "struck by God. I could see that when I looked at ya." He now took to scratching his stubby chin. Suddenly he sketched the sign of the cross in the air before the boy, as if he'd remembered this omission and had to make up for it as quickly as he could.

"Be off," was his next admonition.

He waved his hand in the air as if at a fly and started to close the door except (as he later told his wife) it stopped as though it had hit a tree when the boy put his hand to it. The serf strained to shut it, face reddening, seeing Parsival, expression calm, standing there with one arm effortlessly up. Whatever the man might have thought, the young king was remembering his mother's insistence that he be kind to the weak and poor and keep his temper with the baseborn and old. He smiled through the streaming water that bathed his face, discovering how obvious it was, how simple: if he were angry he would make himself uncomfortable and spend his force for little or nothing when his focus, his intent energy should be saved (he was sure of this, it hung clearly before him as a palpable truth) for winning honor and fighting darkness. He saw that every wasted motion took him from his true path. He smiled, still half-unconsciously blocking the door, feeling proud of his ability to react and profit by new situations. He hardly noticed the man, paler than before, scurrying back into the dim room, tripping over the child who began instantly, reflexively, to wail in exaggerated anguish as, simultaneously, a woman's voice bit into the air from somewhere in the depths of the place, scolding as if picking up without interruption from some previous flow of mechanical rage just as the man reappeared, bowing at the door, holding a coarse black loaf up at Parsival.

"Here's the best we got, young man," he declared.

The young man accepted it, plucking off some mold, then taking a bite.

The unseen woman's voice railed over the violence of the child's breath-timed wails:

". . . an' yer damned friends at the door an' I-don't-know-what a great shitful thing you be lettin' in the damp with one ear cropped as 'tis for choppin' master's wood you'll be hunged and left fer crows—"

Jerking a bow at Parsival, he darted and vanished back into the room, then there was a loud single smack of flesh on flesh, a grunt which could have been anybody's, then silence. Even the crying stopped, stilled as if a sponge had blotted and soaked up all sound and life in there.

The serf reappeared.

"I sees yer no fool," he said, confidentially.

The water softening the bread made it easier to chew and Parsival worked away at the loaf.

"I want to find King Arthur," he said, mouth filled.

The man wiped at his truncated nose several times then blew it into his fingers and shook the mucus off onto the floor, thoughtfully.

"So ya do," he said, "so ya do . . ." Nodded sagely.

"Am I on the right road?"

The man's head bobbed up and down, the flat, empty eyes not looking at anything.

"Straight on," he said, "no doubt of it . . . straight on you go . . ."

"I thank you for the food," Parsival told him, bowing his head slightly.

He turned and walked in his soaked rags back across the muddy yard and mounted Spavint. The little man rubbed inside his collar and stayed at the doorway. No one could have been sure if his eyes actually followed the horse and rider as they moved unevenly off and vanished into the misty sheets of rain . . .

# xxviii

Broaditch was pointing to the south where dark, towering clouds were piling up, bright only thousands of feet above where they broke into sunshine.

"If they move this way we'll have a wet night," he said.

The hills now rose and fell like dunes at a beach and even Broaditch was feeling queasy as they lurched on like foundering boats. Alienor had dismounted and was walking beside Waleis who had nothing to say at the moment, angling himself along, eyes fixed on the ground.

Suddenly the trees began to thin out, then through a break they looked across a field of motionless, rich rows of goldenrod. The earth smoothed out here. There was a rough-shaped, small castle and with the low sun in their faces the structure was a dark, squarish outline without details. Its shadow stretched toward them.

They stopped and looked at it for a few moments.

"Many lords are friendly enough," Alienor said.

Broaditch thought the place was too still. Though it was a small one ...

He urged his mule on and rode past them, bouncing rapidly and heavily on the slightly sagging beast.

"Wait here," he ordered.

They watched him bounce on up to his hams in the bright flowers as if he floated forward on a brisk, choppy current.

He wasn't halfway there before he knew what it was and he slowed the beast's pace to a steady walk as if to postpone the actual fact a little. His breath went out of him slowly and steadily when he saw the first one: a peasant, he realized, thinking: *free of the neckring but that's no real gain it just gets you back to being full naked when your*

69

*clothes are off . . . this fellow now has all the world or*
*nothing depending on how you turn your head . . .*

The man was on his knees, face tilted up, held from
falling by the spear angled into the back of his neck so that
the head seemed (until he came closer) to float peacefully
atop the fuzzy blossoms, mouth gaping, a black hole, a
darkness, a soundless shout of darkness. There was no
odor of decay caught in the stinging perfume of the field:
the flesh was dried and shrunken, the leather clothes
cracked and stiff . . . on bare ground near the walls, clumps
of dried-out bodies outlined the shape of the past battle as
scattered leaves show the passing form of a wind: weapons
held and unheld, shattered and struck home, spears,
swords, spiked clubs, chains and maces, friend and foe
tangled together indistinguishably dressed; hands, arms,
legs, even fingers scattered like the pieces of a puzzle . . .
finally he saw the first dead knight, armor stained with
rust and blood, mail gashed and torn, no face visible in
the dark hollow of his oversized helmet with a great fish
emblem with wide pop eyes poised on top. *There are
never many dead lords,* he remembered. His hand softly,
unconsciously strayed to his side and fingered where the
old, knotted scar ran thick as a rope . . .

Stopped the mule and sat there for a moment, peering up
at the walls he already knew there was no point entering
unless he were hungry for the sight of rats, weeds and
brothers of the dead. The moatless gates were battered in
and gaped like empty mouths. The stone was sootstained
and the smell of fire washed out by past rains lingered . . .

As he headed somberly back he saw the lady's body: the
torn silks had rotted to wisps and whitened ribbons, sinis-
terly suggestive around the bare, withered, violently out-
spread legs between which another spot of dark shadow
gaped at him . . . He sighed deeply. Her head was hidden
in a wash of flowery weeds; just the yellowed legs thrust
startlingly out, knees up. . . . He turned away.

"There was rare sport here," he murmured. Lifted one
square, sunwrinkled hand to his eyes as he rode slowly
back to the other two, across the golden field, noticing,
suddenly, the steady drone of heavy bees stirring and
fumbling everywhere . . .

# xxix

Spavint was limping now and his tendency to drift left had been aggravated. He strayed like a boat in a cross-current. He would wander to the edge of the boggy road only to be constantly reheaded by his rider.

Parsival was sniffling continuously after days of gray rain, of huddling to sleep on chill muddy ground wrapped in saturated travel blankets or crouching under wet boughs.

He had passed no dwelling since the serf's hut and had met only one traveler, a stocky friar who strode barefoot leaning on a staff, barely glancing up at the youth in passing. Parsival decided there must be paths and crannies in this country that he was overlooking. He felt people lived just out of sight around dark bends or over hills nearby. The road, for one thing, was obviously used. From time to time he left the road briefly to reconnoiter but never saw anything except more dim, misty, damp woods and rough hills. He had half decided this must be the country of the dark one, and wondered if they would soon meet.

He was riding, listening to his teeth rattle together as he shivered, watching himself with interest because this had never happened to him before when he glanced up and saw it dancing over the road under a huge chestnut tree with a steady, somewhat jaunty, but very dignified step and he thought: *a new manner of man light enough to tread the air!* And stopped the horse and craned his neck to look, to learn what he could. The rain was recently down to a mere drizzle and each drop could be heard when it percussively went *spatt* on the soaked, blackleaved earth.

The dancer creaked and turned with the sluggish breeze. The thin chain around the neck was corroded black and stretched up invisibly into the treeshadows. Bones creaked

as the hands gestured with (for Parsival) tantalizing significance and the feet did a little kick. The vacant face suddenly turned to look down at him, the eyes black pits.

"Greetings," the young king called up. "Will you speak
with me? How can you tread the air without wings?"

He decided to limit his questions for the moment.

The skeleton suddenly gave him his back as if in rebuttal
or whimsical rejection. Parsival blinked at it.

"Is this your way with a stranger?" he asked, annoyed.
Then thought for a minute. "You must eat only air," he
stated.

There was a rich, deep, somehow ruddy laugh behind
him and he twisted in his saddle taking in another surprise,
delighted at his sudden good fortune.

*A being of flame,* he thought, heart jumping, then saw it
was a mounted knight, the horse covered with red samite
and armor, the man (twisting off his helmet and resting it
in his lap) redhaired, skin thick with freckles, in fire-red
mail trimmed with red, the hilt of his sword red, red lance
and steel tip.

"Boy," he said, pleasantly at ease on his horse, "you are
a precious fool."

The precious fool studied him, happy to see how the
helmet was detached.

"Speak further with your fleshless friend," urged the
red warrior, laughing again at the delicious thought of it.
"It was a rare discourse! Discuss his daily menu with him,
why don't you?" His own wit set him rocking slightly in
the saddle.

Then Parsival worked it out: he remembered the bones
of a bird, related them to these and these to the form of a
man. He smiled with pleasure. The knight accepted this expression as evidence of the last stages of feeblemindedness.

"God shield you, knight," said the boy, "my name is
Parsival."

"This I saw instantly." He grinned, his teeth shockingly
white and even in his ruddybronze face. "You look every
inch the king on your charger there."

"I am looking for Arthur, king of Britons."

The man cocked his head to one side.

"To joust with him, no doubt." The pale blue eyes only
were laughing now.

"They say he will make me the highest knight."

"I'm certain you'll be raised up there, boy. King Parsival,

or is it prince still? No matter. We're both in luck. We ride the same way. I'll make sweet, grudgeless Arthur a present of you. It's only just since I want a gift of him."

The knight went on speaking as people do before a dog or cat.

"Ride with me, king," he went on, "and I'll present you to many more flying air-eaters like this one." He tilted up his red lance and rattled the empty bones on their chain, shook them so that the feet flailed out in a mad, wild jig.

"Is it far from here, knight?"

"Do you know where you are, king?"

Parsival shrugged at this.

"What matter?" he wondered, not understanding why the man suddenly lapsed into several wheezy guffaws.

"One place is very much like another, eh, Parsi*fool?*"

"I have not found it so," the boy said seriously, looking up again at the swinging skeleton who had now turned profile to them, hand sticking briefly in a gesture of disinterest.

"Like him, do you?" the knight inquired.

"I have never seen such a thing before."

This new companion raised both coppery eyebrows.

"Then you must come from fairy realms," he declared, "for there are uncountable many of his bony race in this world."

"Where do they come from?"

The knight grew thoughtful.

"They are born," he said, at length, "of justice mating with kings like Arthur." He laughed. "I mean by *fucking,* boy. Have you to do with fucking?" He grinned at the blank face of Parsival. "Come," he told the boy, "spur your noble charger, gentle King Parsifool, we're off to the delights of court."

He hit his heels into his horse and it barreled forward in a gust, hooves hammering and splashing through the leafy mud, Parsival behind, urging Spavint on to his best rolling limp . . .

"Why are you red?" Parsival wanted to know.

They had halted to water the horses in a ditchlike creek that ran beside the roadway at this point. The still surface reflected puffy clouds and greenblue, intensely clear sky after long rain. The country here was open with scattered rows of trees crossing the valley.

The knight was standing half behind a tree, leaning against the trunk.

"So no one mistakes me for another," he answered the boy who was watching him struggling with something there, strain showing on his face as he muttered: "A hog's backside may your mother kiss! . . ." he gasped for a moment, the pain in the sound startling Parsival. "May serfs rest their whangers on her breasts! . . ."

Parsival was stunned.

"My mother?" he said, unconsciously reaching over and gripping the spear that was secured along Spavint's flank. "What are you saying?" he whispered.

Holding the spear he strode around and saw the man crouching forward slightly, leaning on the tree, his mail cunningly parted at the crotch where he gripped himself with both bare hands, sighing a little in pain as (Parsival noted) a feeble stream trickled and sputtered from him and bubbled on the grass.

"Ahhhhh," said the knight, sighing, "it's like fire . . ."

"What's wrong?"

The man winced, then replied:

"I have some plague . . ."

As he straightened up, Parsival studied how the steel codpiece worked. *So even a knight still has to do that,* he reflected.

The man went over to his horse and patted its armored rump.

"There are more perils to knighthood than you know," he said, ambiguously.

Parsival hoped that didn't mean he would have to suffer such pains too. Was it part of knighthood? He shrugged and supposed he'd have to bear it. He decided not to pursue the subject just then. He went and resecured the spearshaft to his mount.

"That's no fashion to speak of my mother," he ultimately said.

"What?" wondered the other, distractedly, staring across the fields toward the hazy far end of the valley. The sun was lowering toward that point. "We'll be there in the morning," he said. He stepped away from his horse and suddenly drew his sword which, as Parsival expected, was dyed red.

The boy was completely absorbed by the speed and grace of the man's sudden movements. Now he posed, light as a dancer, for all his steel mail and plate, knees just bent, feet firm and still, sword held straight over his head, eyes concentrating with terrible fierceness, watching everything at once, still but fixed nowhere.

"Arthur," he whispered, "I offer you this beauty."

And half-turned, gracefully dropping to one knee as the blade fanned through a perfectly flat arc with a shrill, percussive whistle, seeming to the boy to simply disappear and reappear again in a new position. With delight, astonishment and suddenly checked breath he watched a slender single tall sunflower top that was now behind the again perfectly motionless knight waver and separate itself from the unshaken stem and drop to the grass, so swift and neat was that invisible cut. Parsival's lips parted, the back of his neck prickling, feeling physically giddy, feeling intensely electrically alive, feeling such a strange joy that he was close to weeping and already, in his mind, that sword was in his own hands . . .

He stood silent as the Red Knight slammed the blade back into the red sheath and remounted his nervous charger.

# XXX

The two horses went at a walk. Puffy clouds slid rapidly overhead, their shadows flowing over the green valley. Long, steady breezes kept gathering with great rustlings of leaves and brush and billowing, tugging at the riders with long, steady swells in a vast, breathlike pulsing . . .

The hooves clacked on the smooth neat paving stones, so tightly laid that no grass grew between them. Parsival had been wondering about this wide, white road for several miles. The Red Knight had been silent for some time now.

"There are no ways like this in my land," Parsival offered.

The man said nothing. After a little distance, the boy tried again:

"Arthur must be a great king to have made a way like this."

The knight snorted, not turning his head.

"No man alive has seen them who built this road," he said.

After a while Parsival followed up:

"Who did it, then?"

"What? . . . Oh, the little dark men."

"Where are they?"

"They went back across the sea." He chuckled. "There were none like them for war, they say. Arthur would not long be troubled by ruling anyone if they came again with their machines and magic." He nodded to himself. "But no man knows where they are."

Abruptly he reined up his horse and dismounted. He pointed across the valley.

"There's where you go," he said. At the head of a long, smooth cresting of hills stood a hazy outline of walls and battlements, with one round, thick, tall tower dominating, seeming to tremble slightly again the horizon clouds. "Can your head hold a message, boy?"

The knight saw the distant scene reflected in the wide, calm, greenflecked blue eyes of Parsival. For an instant something unsettled him, the depth and purity of that look —but a moment later he assured himself, it was but the tranquillity of the idiot.

"I can read one," the boy informed him.

This statement was not even dignified with a snort. As he was about to speak the knight winced suddenly.

"Hold," he said in a strained voice and quickly went across the road and into a clump of bushes. Only his bare head, bright red hair curling like stylized flickers of flame, showed as if it rested on the thorny branches. Parsival watched him bite down on his lips, sigh, grunt and mutter curses again. After a few minutes he came out, a little paler under his clusters of freckles.

"Tell Arthur," he said, irritably, "I send you to be granted the honor of knighthood. Tell him he knows what to grant me. Tell me I am coming with my empty hand outstretched." He nodded as with great satisfaction. "Tell the bastard that," he concluded. "Well, repeat it!"

Parsival did.

"Good," said the knight. "You have a holding mind for all its whimsies. Still, I once saw a fool who could reckon great sums . . ."

"I don't think I'm a fool," said Parsival, but the man had turned away and was staring with deep concentration across the valley in the direction of Camelot. He set his spiked helmet on his head carefully.

As he started to ride on, Parsival noticed a chipped stone pillar set in the earth, half concealed by weeds. He poked it clear with his speartip and read the letters carved into the top: SPQR. He started to ask about it, then decided to let it pass.

"Come up," he murmured to Spavint, hitting his heels lightly into the withered flanks.

He passed through the gate with a crowd of peasant women carrying widebrimmed baskets of fruit and grain. Once inside he dismounted and tied his bony horse to a hitching rail near the great gate. Above, on the wall, a man sat looking over whoever came in.

Parsival was amazed by the sheer size of the enclosure. There was a church in the center of the heart-shaped space made by the curving walls. Men were small beside it, he could see, yet it seemed, he thought, low as a serf's kennel against the fortress and massive central keep. To his left, horsemen were maneuvering on a long field; to his right, hundreds of serfs, servants, peasants, merchants he took for nobles and some lords and ladies were trading for food and goods on long tables set up under canvas tents. Children and dogs raced and played. Armored knights moved here and there, erect and aloof. He saw ladies in long, manyhued gowns going into the church; under the near wall by a town of stables a smith worked, naked but for a breechclout, the blows of his hammer tolling across the vast yard, flame and smoke billowing around him, hot sparks spraying, then dribbling down from each stroke . . .

He couldn't take it all in: turned one way, then another, then locked in on a bearded old man, dripping with gold and jewels, glittering clothes trimmed with ermine, shaking a sparkling finger at a common fellow who was holding up a hooded bird. A falcon though Parsival didn't even know that yet.

He stopped, had to duck back into a puddle as an unarmored mounted knight cantered past him, not giving an inch with distant arrogance as mud flew up from the heavy hoofs.

Then his head rocked and he was jarred blank for a moment by a spattering impact. He was wiping the foul mud from his cheek as he whipped around and saw a crew of young peasants and serfs, shaking with high glee.

"How d'ye like it, witless?" one called out as the others shook and danced with laughter at the remark.

Parsival started for them across a muddy space of ruts and dung, fists clenched. A couple of the peasants raised thick, crooked staffs, stepping forward, still chuckling. Then the young king caught himself, turned around again amidst a surge of derision and several clods of muck that broke and scattered in the air, raining down wide, and aimed himself for the bearded man who was haggling for the hunting bird as a slender youth in fine gray linen took his arm in a friendly way, saying:

"You showed wisdom just then, turning from a hopeless fight. You surely cannot be silly to the bone."

Parsival disengaged his arm with an ease which mildly startled the page.

"I have to greet the king," he said.

His new companion seemed disheartened by this as if Parsival had failed to confirm his suspected intelligence.

"No doubt he expects your arrival," said the page.

Parsival pointed.

"Is that the king, Arthur?" he asked.

The young man's eyebrows went up fractionally and he shook his head in mild sorrow. He kept looking into Parsival's face as if it were a great wonder to him.

"Where can he be found?" was the next question.

"Why must you see him?"

"He has to make me a knight. So I may win honor." He reached into the leather bag at his hip, then drew out and opened his hand. A large gold ring gleamed on the palm. The page held it up in the alternately dimming and swelling sunlight, studied the carved jet stone: an eagle's beak. He frowned with recognition.

"I would rather hold a snake," he told him, "than this—" he hesitated, "—favor of yours." And handed it back.

The baseborn youths had moved forward in a cluster and now stood just across a very long, wide puddle as though on the other side of a river. Several small children had joined them, filling out the halfnaked, muddy group.

"Give us the fool, young sir," called one, "we wants a word with'm." His face was browned, brow knotted, eyes wide apart and squinty. The others with him plainly approved of his respectful request but the page directed an infinitely cool look at them and they stood silent, watching, with various degree of intentness. The one who'd spoken out spit into the water and seemed happy to watch the spittle drift. Then everyone turned away as a dogfight suddenly erupted near the market stalls: yapping, squeals, shouts, men rushing around swinging sticks, scattering the animals with terrific skill and suddenness.

Parsival replaced the ring in his pouch.

"I don't believe you're a fool at all," the page remarked. "But you're certainly uncommon enough. Still, I doubt if Arthur will—"

"Where is he?"

Raising a single eyebrow this time, his slender friend pointed straight across the noisy yard at the gigantic pillar

of greenish stone, smooth, broken only by narrow slits and
one tall gate.

"In the great hall," he said, yielding to Parsival's stolid
determination.

The walk took him past the log barracks where men-at-
arms were quartered. He wondered who these men were,
obviously they weren't knights, squatting on the ground,
exercising, sitting in the unshuttered windows, in sketchy
armor or none at all, polishing weapons, testing long
spears, talking, joking, swearing. . . . One evening, a year
before, sunset a greenred stain across the hills, the moon
rising bright and full in the east, he was coming back from
the forest passing quietly through the cool, dreamlike shadows, looking around, then moving up to the castle wall and
slipping the long spear into the deep crevice at the angle
of three roughhewn stones then, nervously spinning around,
sensing, then seeing, a heavy, tall shape detach itself from
the deeper shadows behind him where the trees seemed a
dark, dimensionless single blot, strained to identify the
man, and waited as Broaditch came closer and stood silently in the hinting twilight. "Will you tell them?" Parsival
wondered. "No." He didn't say "my lord." "My mother
forbade me so I keep it here." "I know. You feel a great
power in you when you wield it." "Yes." Broaditch stood
perfectly still and grave, arms folded. "At your age," he
said, mysteriously, "you'll play with one spear or another.
What mother can stop you?" "Did you know I came here?"
"I have a way of stumbling over things." Parsival remembered a question he had and asked it: "Broaditch, they say
my father died in a battle." "So you know about that too."
"That's a fight?" "Yes." "Like when the common men and
serfs quarrel? Like when that man hit the other's head
with a stone and his brains spilled out?" "Did you see
that?" "No. But it was told." Broaditch sighed. "That's
what battles are," he said. "Common men get their brains
spilled." Parsival thought it over. The bluishgray moontints
lay calmly everywhere, blurring the dim outlines. "He died
that way?" he wondered. Broaditch made a slight motion.
"When you boil it down," he affirmed, "that's left in the
bottom of the kettle."

He remembered that conversation, now, looking at these
rough men: there was a group of them crouching down in
a small circle, staring intently at the ground. Suddenly one

or another would throw up his hands and curse or shout while the others paid no attention.

Fascinated, he stepped closer. Meat was broiling close by and the smell set off his appetite. He never understood how his mother could eat only vegetables.

One man in the group, Parsival decided, was displeased with the pebbles he had because he kept snatching them up and casting them back down on the hardpacked clay again with jerky, furious motions, cursing as he did. Each time some one or another would groan or laugh, tossing down and picking up coppers, elbow the man beside him, spit in the dirt, call on God until the young man was convinced they were all madmen. No one else seemed to pay any attention. As he was about to go over and ask them some questions he glanced up and the first thing he saw was the young page running toward him, mouth wide, shouting something, mud splashing up, dovegray tunic fluttering and the next thing was the squinty, bumpy face of the hostile serf and, as though frozen, the expressionless features, eyes invisible (so he seemed, he distantly thought, like something dead) that filled his concentration in a moment that felt endless while his hands moved in a blur of reflex, one catching the thick staff arcing for his skull (he distantly heard the fellow grunt at the shock as though the blow had hit a wall) flinging the other fist like a stone into the thick chest (which was only a blur because the face dominated everything) until it flew out of focus and an instant later was looking up at him from the ground, mud and water still raining down from the terrific impact. The serf's dark, toothless mouth gaped wide, colorless eyes popping as he struggled like (Parsival thought) a fish on the shore as the breathless page arrived.

"Well then," he said, panting, grinning, "what will you want with sword and lance?"

# xxxi

They entered the great circular hall in the immense tower. The round table was in the center. As Parsival came closer he realized the four shapes he'd taken for goblets were actually men sitting there. The scale of the place startled him. *You could ride horses on that table,* he thought.

Glancing around he noticed torches spaced around the distant walls and small groups of men and women in conversation, their voices a faint murmur . . .

The page led him to the table where he faced the four men. In the center the king sat bareheaded, graybearded, nervous-faced, a rather slight man with very long, powerful hands, wearing an unmarked yellow robe. His dark, still eyes held the boy's attention so that, at first, he barely noticed the others: one knight (Galahad) in silverblue; another in brown silks, stocky, near forty; the fourth man a monkish fellow, massive, thickened, bald, with bushy gray beard, somehow ageless-looking, wrapped in a coarse, black woolen mantle, eyes squinting shut so that he gave the fleeting impression he might be blind.

The king's stare held him: deep, absorbing, unmoving eyes that seemed to reflect no light.

"King Arthur, God shield—" he began but was elbowed silent by the page at his side.

"Wait for the master to speak first," he whispered.

"Is this some sport?" Arthur wondered and the huge, bald man (whose veins, Parsival noticed, stood out like snakes on his skull in the uneven torchlight from the iron ring that hung above on chains that vanished up into the gloom) said, in a deep mellow voice with firm, massive certainty:

"No."

"Who is this pretty lout?" Arthur asked, mildly, eyes quiet and impossible (the young king found) to see into.

"King Arthur," Parsival said, "there's a red knight coming here. He said you would make *me* a knight as a gift to him which is what I came here for in the first place. And he also told me that you know what to give him when he comes . . ." He knit then unknitted his brow briefly. ". . . he's coming with his *empty* hand outstretched."

Arthur nodded slightly.

"It's no sport," he agreed.

"If you seek to be a knight," the page said quietly, "you could at least bow when you meet your lord."

"I never bowed at home," Parsival stated, "except to my mother."

"This knight," Arthur went on, "all in red, you say?"

"Yes. Even his sword."

The knight in brown, at the king's left, said:

"That son-of-a-bitch." He leaned his chair back. "Where is this armored red dung, Welsh boy?"

"How can you tell I'm Welsh?"

"By your elegant speech," he was informed. "Answer me!"

Parsival got stubborn for an instant, then decided to save all energy for his purpose, so he said:

"Across the valley. He said he was coming."

"Fuck his sister!" snarled the man.

Parsival blinked at this, unable to relate it to the matter at hand. Dismissed it.

"He said you would give me armor," Parsival added, not wishing to overpress the issue, but wanting some touch of certainty. "When you make me a knight."

Arthur glanced back at the young petitioner as if from far away.

"Make you a knight, boy?" he asked.

Parsival unconsciously scraped the now dried mud from his cheek. He nodded, looking mildly at the king.

"Is this what squires wear in Walesland now?" his majesty wondered.

The bald giant tilted his head back (even more like a blind man, Parsival observed) and said:

"What is your name?"

The boy hesitated, briefly held rapt by the vibrant, soothing tones, the clear calm in them was somehow as if the green richness of the earth itself spoke through him. Parsival hoped he'd speak again but when there was only a waiting silence, he answered the man:

"Parsival."

Arthur looked up, eyes very still.

"HerzeIroyd's son?" he asked.

Parsival nodded. Arthur considered this.

"You surely have rejected your father's tailor," he said.

"His mother is daft," put in the brown knight, "isn't she?"

Parsival let this chatter go past him. He was staring across the vast room at the flicker of the distant torches. Then he looked up toward a thin blade of light that cut in from a high windowslit. He thought about his mother for a moment, thought he had a number of questions for her . . .

"If you're the true son of Gahmuret and Herzelroyd," Arthur was saying, "then I'm bound to give you what you ask for." He seemed amused. "A steel suit. But God knows you are an ignorant prince."

The knight in brown stood up and leaned across the table: his nose was bent out of the true and a ragged scar clipped one corner of his mouth. When he spoke his eyes snapblinked constantly.

"You have to be strong and brave to be a knight here, princeling," he stated bluntly. "If you are a prince."

"He is surely strong," murmured the page.

Arthur half-turned to the huge, bald man who said, in those resonant tones that seemed to still all other sound:

"He will have to prove it eventually."

"Exactly," said the brown knight.

"Well, Kay?" asked Arthur.

"You have to lose a dog or two to get a boar's head," he pointed out, then leaned closer to Parsival, his garlic breath flat and stale. "If you want armor, take the Red Knight's gear."

No one said anything. Parsival noticed that the bald man had opened his eyes just a slit now and he could see the hint of a glinting there. Perhaps he wasn't actually blind.

"That's the king's gift to you," concluded Sir Kay, the seneschal, smiling with a piece of his mouth. "Then tell that shitwit, Sir Roht, when you take it, that we'll give him all he asks." He seemed, the boy perceived, very pleased with himself for some reason. He didn't notice (and would

not have yet understood) that the king seemed vaguely
sheepish, that Galahad wouldn't look up from the table,
because it was all going fast now and he didn't see (or
want to see either) a way of slowing anything down though
he sensed something was strange here and that he'd
reached some crisis, some crossroads and didn't dare hang
back because he was suddenly no longer drifting, things
were sharp, tense and the movement felt irrevocable, and
for the first time in his life he felt a sense of tension and
pressure, so he said:

"I'll go now."

Sir Kay was watching Arthur and Galahad and he said:

"Sire, what should we fear? If this boy is truly the son
of Gahmuret, why he will prove himself. If he be a witless
boy with royal names on his tongue, what is lost?"

Galahad shifted uncomfortably. He seemed about to
speak, but didn't. Stared at the wood where his hands
rested, limp and open. The king held his pointed chin in his
hands, the steely beard spilling around his long fingers. The
motionless eyes watched the young man, followed by the
page, walking rapidly out of the shadowy hall, a diminishing figure against the tall, fuzzy, overbright doorway.

The massive man stood up slowly, steadily, until he
loomed like a dark mountain over them, eyes fully open
now: large, greengold gleaming, sunflecked, forest colors.
He didn't appear to focus them.

"That prince," he said, "will be greater than a king."

Kay raised a goblet to his lips.

"Who," he asked, a deferential yet vaguely contemptuous
expression flickering over his face for an instant, "is greater
than a king, priest Merlinus? Do you foresee he will be
pope of the Italians?" He sipped the wine.

"Kings know," was his answer, "who is greater."

Arthur sighed and slumped in his rude seat. Leaned his
head back and stared into the darkness beyond the ring of
hanging torches.

"I used to believe," he said, reflectively, "it could be
found. . . . Now I don't know. . . . I used to believe in all
that . . ."

"You are but a king, sire," said Merlinus.

# xxxii

The sun was at perfect noon. Nothing stretched a shadow. The field was flat here at the base of Camelot hill. Parsival turned his head and saw the young page following, running to keep up, then stopping abruptly, standing and watching as Parsival turned front and saw the red horseman (who was suddenly very close) slowing from a trot to a choppy walk, his bright lance held straight up, helmet in place, and as Spavint swayed forward, the young man felt a kind of shock at the actual weight and force of the warrior, his heart loud and quick, seeing each motion, each form and color with intense clarity, each detail of the armor (anticipating like a child his gift), each glint, each rippling step of the thudding charger, the flash of the pointed shield, hearing his own voice, dry and much too loud, he thought, saying:

"The king has given me your armor and shield and your horse too. That's my gift. Then they said you'll get what you want."

And the blank steel face, bright blood red against the distant bluegreen of sky and hills, turned toward him, the muffled voice booming, sudden, ringing:

"Go back. Tell them to send out Galahad."

The horses' shoulders almost touched. Parsival reached for the knight's bridle.

"You don't understand," he said. "You're supposed to give me—"

But as his hand closed on the leather strap he saw the lance start to move and then a blank space and he was looking up (not feeling anything yet) at the two horseheads and mounted man against the shimmering sky, the long lance just tilting back upright and then the pain

86

*Parsival battles the Red Knight*

slammed into his head and he winced and wiped a smear of blood from the swelling lump on his forehead; his legs gathered themselves under him, not even angry, moving in emptiness as if the blow had knocked him free of past and future and left him only exploding energy, a knot of concentrated motion, staying just ahead of the bulk of rage as if swept forward on the cresting peak of a massive wave that carried him around Spavint's bony, quivering flanks, snatched his spear as he went by and in the same uncoiling motion threw the shaft point-blank, the head hitting at the joint of faceplate and neckguard, the metal bursting with an explosive shriek (Sir Roht's sword was incredibly drawn and already arcing down in this same instant, the arc failing, going limp) and through a bubbling scream a jet of blood sprayed around and down the shaft, drizzling in a hot light mist over Parsival's face, the dark, blank, slitted eyeholes of the visor seeming to gaze profoundly down at him, neck tilted against the angle of the spear, the left hand that dropped the lance now holding the shaft, loosely, lightly, near the spurting wound, Parsival holding the other end, now as still as the knight, the spear between them seeming to freeze them both in a strange communication, communion, a profound link joining the two, as time and place rushed violently back into motion and Parsival thought: *It's good that it's red because the blood won't show* . . .

The horses had walked off and were grazing together on the sweet, low grasses. Shadows had started to move out from them, from the scattered trees, the hill, the crowd of people hurrying to the field and the page who was walking not too fast or slow, toward Parsival who'd been standing for a long time looking down at the fallen knight before suddenly kneeling beside him.

He felt spent and his body was shaking slightly when he knelt. Sir Roht's hand still loosely held the spearshaft though the blood had stopped pulsing.

*If I'm afraid I can't win honor,* he thought.

So he reached and tried to wrench off the helmet but the spear pinned it firm to the neck. He shut his clear, mild eyes briefly and jerked it out: it came free with a scrape of metal and a liquid gush. Then he freed the man's head and studied the face, the eyes halfopen and filmed over. He touched the pupils. They didn't blink. Then he slipped a finger into the wound to see what that was like, concentrating, biting his full, lower lip. He heard a gasp behind him and the page's outraged voice:

"What are you doing? What unseemly . . ."

He broke off, watching the young man fumble at the rest of the armor, trying to loosen it, then, remembering, gripping the iron codpiece so that the gathering, excited crowd stood shocked and baffled as the now (by right of combat) Sir Parsival with much straining and struggling, working intently, gleaming blond hair stirred by the light breeze, managed to expose the dead man's sexual organs before leaning back from the impossible armor with a frustrated but infinitely determined look on his face.

# xxxiii

Broaditch was first to spot the man ahead where the dusty track bent under a dense overhang of trees. He was standing in the bluish shadows, the dazzling sunlight across the flat, open stretch between them quivering in heat mirages.

Waleis was leaning on the flanks of Broaditch's mule, limping slightly, staring at the ground. Alienor dozed lightly as her mount swayed along behind.

"I don't know what you expect to gain," Waleis suddenly muttered. "He don't need us. An' will he be grateful for what news we bring? Pah! He'll sniff it like a mare noses a gelding's pecker and—"

"Be still!" hissed Broaditch. "Don't look up."

Waleis looked up instantly, shielding his eyes.

"What?" he wondered.

Broaditch sighed.

"What's wrong?" Alienor asked, rubbing her eyes, yawning.

The man stood perfectly still as they came slowly abreast of him. He was leaning against a tree. Broaditch noted he was barefoot, wearing frayed and patched leather that once might have served a man-at-arms in some lord's army. His sunchapped arms were folded, his ax-shaped face bent slightly from the true as if (he thought) knocked into that shape by a blow. *He might just chance to be standing there, why he may dwell nearby,* Broaditch was thinking without conviction, unsurprised when the man spoke in a neutral, high-pitched voice:

"Life is hard, comrades."

Broaditch kept facing straight ahead, letting his nervous-eared mule drop back a little so that Alienor and Waleis passed him. The pace seemed dreamlike, slow, like struggling underwater, and his heart began to thump in his ears. His mind rambled somewhat: ... *we can't risk running these beasts yet* ... then his anxious thoughts were cut short as he saw Waleis start to turn, inarticulately shouting as two more scruffy men emerged (*Is this all?* he wondered, taking in their size and shape with adrenalized concentration: one tall, skinny, in black rags, knotted hair waist long, a few flies arcing and cutting near his head, face like a crow; the other squat, dwarfish, light on his feet, in a single tentlike rag, one eyesocket raw and open, ears cropped), both swinging cudgels as the man under the tree (Broaditch saw peripherally) reached down and lifted a long, rusty, bent broadsword from the grass and minced up on their rear, raising the weapon with a little trouble over his head (*It's too much blade for him*). Broaditch realized there was no alternative and seized the bridle and violently yanked Alienor's mule around to face the single man behind (the others now formed the two base points of a triangle enclosing the travelers) kicking and twisting his own mount through a quick half circle (mind saying: *Ave Maria, Ave Maria* . . .) drawing his long dirk from his belt, shouting:

"Waleis, this way!"

and charged his struggling, puffing mule past Alienor straight at the swordsman who, surprised, gave ground (*a warrior would have stepped parallel and closer*), shaking the too-heavy weapon, screaming with sudden hysterical rage, shrill and high:

"Stop there, you bastards!"

then swayed forward to aim a sweeping side cut at Broaditch's back who saw the weight of the sword pull him slightly off center, then, as the edge cut for his shoulders he twisted to catch it on his knife which shattered, stinging his hand, but stopped the blow and then the mule bounced heavily past, flanking Alienor. *Now just ride,* he thought, *now just ride.* . . . Heard the cries and again there was no choice, cursing, turning the mule (long ears flopping, eyes rolling wildly, foaming around the bit), yelling:

"Don't stop!"

to Alienor, then charging back, seeing Waleis rolling in the dust as the huge sword missed by inches and stuck fast in the earth, the man tugging and swearing, the other two striking down at him as he rolled and bellowed and wept with fear. *All they want is blindfolds,* Broaditch thought,

*and him oinking.* Then the leader freed the blade and
rushed at Broaditch, raving, spittle flying, as the mule
veered into the brush, crashing along shoulder deep in
brambles and long grass, heaving through, braying high
and wildpitched, eyes spinning wide and mad, floundering
in a circle back toward the roadway again, Broaditch
sweating, cursing, pulling the long neck almost straight up
by the humming reins without measurable effect, the robber
with the sword following in his crushed wake, screaming
continuous invective. They crossed the road, breaking out
of the brush a few steps ahead of the pursuer, hearing the
dull hard sound of a club hitting meat and bone (glancing
away from the wild, gape-mouthed mule head that he
swore he was going to bend back into his lap if he had
to), seeing the tall, crowfaced man holding both hands to
his back, face ash pale (he remembered, recounting the
tale later), racing in a tight circle on feet and knees alternately, scrambling, stricken, roaring gargantuan agony as
the stocky one bounced up and down like a distraught
child, shouting:

"Arr, misjudgment! . . . Misjudgment! . . ."
as Waleis crawled, then sprinted (like, Broaditch later remarked, rattling broomsticks) after Alienor's diminishing
dust-cloud; a moment later Broaditch and the foaming
mule careened into the brush and trees on the other side,
branches stinging his face, whipping and tearing at him in
a welter of snorts, brays, howling of the struck man, pro-
tests of the dwarf, and the shortbreathed, then, hysterical
shrieks of the rogue behind him . . .

# xxxiv

There were no stars. The air was damp, almost chilly. The three of them were sitting around the vague embers of a tiny fire. The mules were dark, still blotches, resting on their knees, nearby. Broaditch was smoking his long, small-bowled, skillfully carved pipe about which all he would ever say was that it somehow fell to him after some famous battle. He never said which or when.

Alienor was lying flat on her back against the gentle slope. The pine forest was dark and silent, muffling Broaditch's mellow voice:

". . . he was still hot behind me as that demented beast charged into marshland, all reeds and black stinking mud . . ."

Waleis was crouching forward, bent almost double, bony fingers restlessly plucking at weeds and pebbles.

". . . that filth behind me, why he's sickly mad, never ceased screaming babble. Spent breath like a lord's pimp." He sucked deeply on his pipe. "When last I looked back through the reeds he was in poor plight, glopping to his knees in mud, flailing that outsized warblade." He puffed. "Still," he reflected, "we were lucky enough."

Waleis didn't look up, saying:

"O we're lucky, we are. . . . Where are we? That's my question. . . . Here's Brac-the-Fisher's boy, hunted like a hare. . . . Where are we?"

"Are we far enough away?" Alienor asked.

Broaditch shrugged. Cocked his head to one side.

"Hark," he whispered.

They listened. Waleis moaned, softly, unconsciously. Not too close, muffled, possibly voices . . . possibly . . .

Alienor sat up. The sounds didn't come again. They were

very still for a long time. A drizzling rain began to softly
fall. She groped and found his hand. Squeezed it and held.
A drop hissed faintly on the dark coals . . .

At dawn they were walking through a lukewarm, steady
rainfall, leading the mules over steepening slopes and rocky
ground. The dark, misty woods were intercut with long,
wet, natural walls of mossy rocks so that they were constantly being forced to change direction. Broaditch kept
turning them back against the grain of the country, moving
deeper (though with great difficulty) and away from where
the bandits might be waiting or searching.

"But don't you think," said Alienor, slipping a little on
the soft, steamy earth, "they'll go back and hunt for easier
game?"

Broaditch half-dragged the mule through a tangle of
skinny, dead trees and dried brambles, waving his thick
arms to snap the rotten wood, trampling down the brush.

"I've known others like that chief of cutthroats," he
said. "Born under the scorpion. They seethe and persist in
anger past belief."

"Ah, no doubt of it," said Waleis, leading the second
mule along Broaditch's track. "Just let me get home and
I'll—" He turned and yanked at the briefly balked mule.
"—Damn you! . . . Just let me get home and I'll patch my
old nets and trust the sea for my fortunes again . . ."

"And how will we find our way in any case?" she
wanted to know. "Which of us has the sense of a home-
finding dove?"

"Just let me smell the sea," Waleis said, "and I'll make
for it straight."

"Though it seems against nature to say so," she couldn't
resist remarking, lifting her skirts as she stepped along,
"your nose is too short."

Broaditch guffawed.

Waleis muttered something. Then said:

"Where will you lead us, Broaditch the wise?"

The wise one was looking around at the dense forest and
massive rocks. He marched steadily on.

"Waleis," he said, "I have just enough wit to take my
hand from the fire."

# XXXV

As Parsival kicked his spurs lightly into the warhorse's flanks and felt the knotted strength between his locked, armored legs seem to flow into him, as though he were suddenly rooted within the nerves and fibers of the charger, the field abruptly streaming past, the curious crowd from Camelot turning their heads as one to watch his gallop, lance and shield banging, leather creaking, hooves thumping . . .

The wind rushed through his opened helmet. He felt flushed and light, floating faster and faster, the two one, shouting for joy and sheer life, riding straight and aimlessly down the long, gentle valley . . .

A squire who'd watched him go was standing with the group beside the near-naked body of Sir Roht. He spoke to the page who'd been friendly to Parsival.

"He's mad," he said. "And now he'll run that fine beast to his death."

"He has surprising ways enough," the other allowed, watching the bloodred figure shrink into the distance. "I'll not contest that."

"Where does he ride to?" asked another man.

"It's not clear," said the page.

"Will he return here?" wondered a noblewoman, appetite showing in her veiled eyes.

The page shrugged.

"He said he was off to win honor," he remarked, looking down at the body now: the throat wound was dark and wide; the blood had stopped pulsing out. A fly flickered near it, a speck of sudden iridescence in the sunlight.

A squire snorted.

"Honor," he exclaimed, contemptuously. "With his

shield a-flop, holding that lance like a fisher pole. Let him but meet a true knight like Gawain and his saddle won't pinch him for long!"

The page knelt and closed the dead man's eyes, flat, bright, unseeing blue, void as the sky now. He heard the fly buzz near his ear and flicked his hand at it.

# xxxvi

Parsival had been riding for less than half an hour, passing into deeply shadowed narrow spurs of trees, then out into the brilliant sunshine and rolling fields again. He was just settling into his dreamy, easy, sweet drifting pace when a sudden glittering caught his attention half a mile or so to his left across the valley.

*Knights,* he thought instantly, *adventure . . .*

He turned the horse and followed at a fair clip. He could make out two riders moving across the sloping country. He had no specific ideas about what adventure meant, at this point, but he'd heard enough about it already to speed him in pursuit.

They were heading up Camelot Hill before he was within a hundred yards of them and one twisted back, bareheaded, and spotted him coming on behind. Moments later both knights were yawing their mounts around in a tight half-circle on the fairly steep slope: the first slammed his helmet on his head as both angled their lances down to set and aim.

Parsival had a pretty clear idea what was coming and he wished he'd kept his spear instead of that outsized lance. He wondered if all adventures turned into fights. He hoped not, as the two came barreling at him with terrific downhill momentum, stones and dirt flying from the crashing hooves. He tossed the heavy pole like a javelin and it (not surprisingly) bounced short and tangled under the first horse, the tip catching in padded armor and tripping

the front legs so that the rider was spilled to the side
where the slope was abrupt and the knight rolled, banging
and clanging and raging helplessly down into the gentle
valley as the second struck Parsival a solid blow on the
shield, which he was holding awkwardly out at arm's
length, so that the impact drove it back into his face and
knocked him over to lie, for an instant, on his horse's
rump, feet still locked in the stirrups. Parsival bounced
upright and as the fellow reined close and chopped a
swordstroke at his head the young knight, forgetting his
own weapon in his rage, caught the downstriking arm with
both hands and heaved the shocked man up out of his seat,
across his own horse's neck, and spinning down the hill
after his companion who was still rolling, quite slowly now,
in the lush green field.

Parsival made up his mind to question Arthur or perhaps
the big, bald, blind-looking man about the point of these
adventures and the best way to go about such things hereafter . . .

King Arthur was looking out across the greenblue fields
and hills into the horizon. There seemed to be a dark haze
gathered there, a stain on the pristine shimmer of day.
He'd decided it must be smoke. He was seated on the
windowledge high in the central tower so the view was
vast. Galahad stood just behind him in silken robes, leaning on an undrawn sword as if it were a cane. The sun
was low, reddish beams steeply angled into the deep and
shadowed chamber.

"That's due south, my lord," Galahad said, "as you
feared."

Arthur looked weary. He rested his long head on the
stone windowside and shut his eyes.

"How long before we can attack?" Galahad wanted to
know.

"Soon," the king replied.

"We'll drive the bastards into the sea."

"Will we?"

"You doubt it, my lord?"

Arthur opened his eyes and stared across his kingdom at
the distant black smear.

"That's very likely a raiding party," he observed, "unless

it be a natural mischance. Their main force is still further south." A pause. "We won't meet before the snow flies."

"Why wait so long? How many can they be? Who can stand against us in any case?" Galahad swung the sheathed blade back and forth like a pendulum.

"Did you ever ask yourself why we fight?" Arthur said at length.

"Hmm?"

"I don't mean single combat or jousts, mind you. To spur time or fire the blood at bit. Why do we fight wars, Galahad?"

"Why, because others force our hand," came the thoughtful, frowning reply. "Or to gain something or other. . . . What care I for reasons? There's no choice. It's the way of things. Let those who can't stand up to it turn priest or wear gowns and simper. I care not, my lord."

Arthur wasn't looking at him. He still stared across the lush, late afternoon at the imperceptibly expanding dark blot.

"I tell you this now, Galahad," the king murmured, "because it's my fancy: it is all hollow at heart. This have I learned in my time. When you come to the center of all you did and meant to do there's emptiness."

His vassal stopped swinging the sword and scowled and scratched around his mustache.

"What a bent thing to say," he declared, hotly. "Consider where you have reached in life. You've done as much as any mortal might."

"I did it all," Arthur said, "because I feared to be still." Nodded to himself. "Drenched fields in blood, calculated everything, used even my love—" Galahad raised an eyebrow at this remark and said nothing. "—yes, kept myself busy so I wouldn't have to see it. . . . Each battle won I knew again that nothing had changed. Men went on with love and hope and fear and shat and ate and died. . . . The sun still rose the same and the seasons flowed on, the serfs scraped at the earth . . . nothing changed . . ." Turned and looked up at the other man. "Nothing will. I learned this long ago. I feared to stop because I knew this emptiness. Even now, Galahad. So I will go on with it to the end . . ."

He looked away. Galahad frowned, but kept silent this time.

"The best moments in my life," said the king, "come

when just waking and for a precious few breaths I don't
remember that I'm Arthur or what I must do that day or
what I have done before. In those moments I see the dawn
and hear the waking of the world . . . and in those moments nothing is absent save my foolishness and weary
schemes . . ."

Galahad shook his head. His fingers were nervous on
the swordhilt.

"This is strange to me, my lord," he announced.

"Is it, Galahad?" He stood up and locked his thumbs
under his gold mesh belt. "How often have I wished to let
it go forever . . ."

"But what would a man *do?*"

Before Arthur could attempt to tell him, a deep, mellow,
resonant voice sounded in the shadows behind them and
both turned.

"Good day, my lords," Merlinus said.

"Ah," said the king, "you must have news to toil up so
many stairs."

"The red knight has arrived," Merlinus told them.

Galahad looked uneasy, the king sardonic.

"Well," he said, "he slew the boy. Now someone's got to
slay him." He glanced at Galahad. "You see how it goes on
and on?"

"No," said the priest of the druids, "the armor is the
same but what's inside has changed."

Arthur nodded.

"I see," he murmured. "I begin to believe you," he said
to Merlinus who stood there, massive, motionless in the
dim, fuzzy light that washed in from the window. "What
does he crave?"

"Much," came the answer.

"Shall I see him?" Arthur asked.

"No," said Merlinus, "that boy is my trouble."

"Yours?" Galahad wondered. "I can believe it. He must
have used magic to overcome Red Roht who could, I
swear, stand up to Lancelot himself!"

"Will you train the boy in wizard's ways?" Arthur
asked.

"No. He seeks deeper than tricks. As others once did."

Arthur looked faintly ill at ease. He brushed his hand in
the air as if to wave the shadows away.

"Never mind that, old one," he said. "What's found is

found. Galahad, go down before us . . ." And when the knight had left: "Will you tell me now?"

"Why?"

"I believe in tricks, Merlinus. Only in tricks. Will you tell me?"

"The outcome? Will you live or die? Will the army fail?"

A long silence in the dim room. The rose-red light darkened and faded in thin, vague threads. Outside, far down, someone was clanging a bell in the fields to call in the workers. At length Arthur sighed.

"Alright," he said, quietly. "You have me. I don't want to hear. It doesn't matter." Merlinus waited, motionless as carved stone. "Actually it never did. . . . There's no choice, in the end." He walked back to the dimming window. "This boy, Parsival, is special then? As I was once said to be?"

"Yes," came the even, deep voice that seemed to have a mass of world and time behind it.

A pause. Arthur stared out into the violet glimmering twilight.

"I still believe only in tricks," he finally said.

"Yes," Merlinus agreed. "Still."

"But my cause is better than theirs."

"Perhaps. Do you believe *this?*"

"I have to believe it." He didn't turn around when he asked: "Do you care for me, Merlinus?"

"I must."

"Hah. I'll win. I'll beat them. Always. To the end. . . . Do you truly care for me, old one?"

"Yes," was the reply as it might have been spoken to the woods or the earth itself, "I care."

Twilight was a grayish gleaming in the courtyard when Merlinus found Parsival standing beside his horse near the gate, drinking a dipper of water through his open visor. The first stars were softly out.

"Why did you return here so soon?" Merlinus wanted to know.

The young man replaced the dipper in a pail on the ground. The sky glowed in the water: it seemed to him like a strange hole in the earth . . . He turned to the old man with interest.

"I didn't mean to," he said. "I followed two knights. Then we fought."

"I know. I understand. But you're going to have to be serious soon, Parsival." He reached over and gripped the young man's bare hand below the wrist of the armor.

Parsival found the hand smooth, hard, neither hot nor cold, and much larger than his own. He felt a trembling, steady energy somehow pass between them. For an instant he felt as though his vision sharpened and the twilight brightened. He blinked.

"You have to look even more closely at everything," Merlinus told him, firmly. "You're still missing a great deal. Far too much." His tone was reproving, even faintly mocking. "Do you think you have forever to pull your mouth from the teat?"

"But I'm learning," Parsival stated.

"Others who know much more than you—" Merlinus released his hand and Parsival felt somehow sorry, the grip had been soothing, "—do they seem so content? Is there great joy sparkling in their clever eyes?" Parsival considered this in silence. After a few moments Merlinus went on: "It's more than learning. It's *looking*. And *listening*." The old man's voice suddenly went up in pitch almost as if another person spoke for a moment. "Else you shall hold it in your hands and let it fall again . . ." Merlinus breathed very deeply. "Let your heart be your eyes and ears. Your mother would like that."

"You know my mother?"

"Yes, young man." He motioned down the dark string of road that fell from the gate into the hushed, faintly glimmering valley where a scattering of fireflies winked like reflected stars. "Now go. We'll speak again."

"I should go?"

"Yes. You have learned all you need to here. And the king . . ."

"Yes?"

"You're too special to be easily endured by the great. We'll speak again," he said in dismissal and turned and walked quietly across the nearly deserted yard toward the castle keep.

Parsival meditated on this: Trust old, gray men with beards, the fellow had said. Well, he'd try, and see where that led to. He mounted and rode out past the guards who were just lighting torches and preparing to shut the barred door. One of them watched him go, become merely a blot, a vague shadow as the moonless night sucked all the day away . . .

# xxxvii

Earl Arbil of Rei slouched in a lowbacked, cherrywood chair, staring out across his parklike lawns. Nearby, under a shade tree, his wife and her maids sat sewing silks.

He was sipping wine from a silver goblet and sucking a fat red plum, the bright juice staining his white whiskers. A young priest stood beside him, shifting from one foot to the other, making nervous, choppy gestures when he spoke, leaning away to listen, impatiently. The earl stared straight ahead whether speaking or silent. At the moment he was talking, voice remote and sure:

"And I have heard all the arguments. When have I stinted on saints' days? Has a beggar in the country been turned from my side gate? Unless he were a famous rogue." He sucked the pit into his mouth and worked it around between teeth and cheek. "I have given justice. Wherein have I departed from good usage?"

The young priest sighed.

"Nowhere, my lord," he said. "That is the worst of it. *Quoad capax.*"

"My serfs are content. Should the mule drive the farmer to market?" He sipped from the tall goblet. A page hovered nearby. The priest grimaced and clasped his hands together.

"There is no truth in custom," he declared. "Custom is but habit. A dead thing."

The earl motioned to the page who bent and wiped his lips for him with a linen cloth. It came away blotched with wine and juice. The boy rubbed lightly to clean the beard.

"Good habits," said the earl, serenely. "Isn't that the way of priests as well as laity, John? Holy habits?" He lifted an eyebrow, still pondering the vast green space before the castle, looking where the valley road was traced by a twin row of poplars. "Or are you weary of them too?"

The young man shifted uncomfortably.

"There is much good in the Church," he said, sighing under his breath.

"Ah? I agree. The church knows how to keep the goods they gain." He smiled. "They sell invisible property at a visible price. What merchant fails to envy them?"

"There are fine men there," the priest said. "They try their best. The Italians and Frenchmen have corrupted every . . ." He checked himself. The earl smiled again.

"But you weary of them," he insisted, "as you wearied of childhood sports before. What will you turn to next? Become a juggler? A minstrel, like your uncle?"

"Uncle writes down the old tales," was the impatient reply. "You know that. He's learned, almost unique for a lord in this—"

"This family is ridden with," the earl paused, "unusual men."

The other sighed.

"You pace a narrow track, my lord," he murmured.

The older man narrowed his eyes, still looking straight ahead.

"Do I? Thirty years ago we threw back the barbarians. We waded in blood to do it. It was a wide enough track then. If the wild men came back today the likes of you would fall like wheat to the reaper." Murmured: "What a son you are." Shook his head slightly.

His tall son paced away, then back. The earl's wife looked up, then turned again to her work.

"One blow leads but to the next," the young man said. "And the next to the next after."

"Should we have surrendered?"

"Look at the world you fought to preserve."

His father belched softly and cleared his throat. Jabbed: "You weary of praying. You weary of everything."

The young priest kicked at the earth with his sandal heel.

"I see this world is unjust, dull and ugly," he said. "I don't intend to leave it as I found it. I'll not walk through it with my eyes looking at the ground two feet in front."

"And so manage rarely to stumble," said his father, alert

now, watching the horseman turn from the road and head across the smoothly curving field toward them, coming fast, a startling bright shock of color.

"I am a knight," Parsival announced, looking down from his armored mount, visor up, rust streaks showing on his fair cheeks. The earl, family and several attendants were contemplating him, covering a wide range of incredulity with their various expressions.

"Ah," said the earl, pleasantly, "you might have deceived me with your looks. I would have taken you for a carpenter."

"Have you come far, Sir Knight?" graciously asked his wife.

"Yes, lady," was his reply, "and I'm pretty hungry and tired out."

"What courtesy," murmured a sarcastic squire in the background.

"Well," said the woman, "come down from your steed and put off your gear. You may rest and eat if it please you."

Parsival seemed to weigh this idea. Then he said:

"No. King Arthur of Britain gave me this armor, lady, and I've only just started wearing it. Just let me have some bread and cheese." Then he frowned slightly. "Though I stood by the biggest table in the world, I think, no one gave me any food from it."

"Well," said the earl, "come inside. Your beast will be all the fitter for you if he rests. And you will soon find out no man can live in armor forever, red knight."

The young man considered this for a time.

"Where are you bound for?" asked a knight, bulky, shortish, wearing a kind of robelike shirt.

Parsival knit his eyebrows, concerned.

"Should I be going somewhere?"

# xxxviii

He opened his eyes suddenly: two narrow, glassless windows faced the bed. Bright, goldgreen leaves shook and rustled there, flickering the sunlight and brilliant shards of blue sky. The morning air was mild and sweet. He sat up, the white ermine coverlet slipping from his torso, and he had already swung his graceful legs over the edge of the soft mattress before he saw the three girls, one of whom was just tossing a handful of rose petals into a steaming tub. They smiled and didn't quite look away as he stood up innocently and stepped into the tub saying:

"My mother used to fill my bath."

One of the girls bit her lip and laughed slightly, helplessly, blushing. Another, willowy, darkhaired, sharpnosed, softeyed, said:

"Had she noticed a change in you?"

"What change?" he asked, still standing there as they half didn't look, tilting their heads one way then another. The darkhaired one, the eldest, was poised and sisterly.

"Did your mother teach you," she wanted to know, "to always stand before women, even in the bath?"

There was a gush of laughter, and continued tilting of heads.

"No," he replied.

"Then is it pride that keeps you on your feet? I fear you make too much of yourself, sir."

One girl (a creamyskinned blonde) sank down, leaning against the polished wooden tubside, shaking slightly, helplessly with laughter, as Parsival sat down, unperturbed, the sweet, perfumy water sloshing around him.

"Ahh," he murmured.

He leaned back and looked through the curling steam at

the bright windows, enjoying the firm scrubbing of the
girls as they worked him pink with sandy soap and rough
clusters of leafy twigs ...

At one point, the willowy girl with the dark, confident
eyes, reached into the water a little deeper than the others
and closed her firm, gentle hand, looking straight into his
face. His eyes widened slightly, surprised, then misted over
with a new delight, lips parting.

"How like you this?" she asked him, lightly biting her
lower lip.

"No doubt his mother scrubbed him better," said the
third girl: big boned, puffy faced.

The blond, redcheeked giggler giggled.

Parsival rested his head on the edge of the tub and
smiled as that amazing hand stirred in the soapy depths.
She looked faintly surprised now herself. Her left hand
vaguely pretended to scrub at his neck.

"What do you think of our country here, shameless Sir
Knight?" asked the big girl.

Her willowy friend, mysteriously joined to the young
man, no longer a part of the general situation, had sagged
against the warm tubside, her visible hand now more or
less still, holding his round, smooth shoulder. Her bitten
lips trembled.

He floated, shut his eyes, felt a startling, almost frightening unfolding within himself, a melting and opening, something profound, resistless, and he tensed, a vast tide seemed
to be lifting him and as he was about to let it take him,
the big girl with the sinewy forearms spilled a bucket of
icy water over his head, the shock sitting him violently
upright, gasping, spluttering and a moment later she began
lashing his back with the twigs, expertly (if unknowingly)
stranding him, bringing him down to the dreamless facts
of flesh ...

# xxxix

Stunned by the music he knelt on the marble floor with the rest in the chapel in dim, greenish stainedglass light that (his host had instantly seen) he had no idea was uniquely valuable: few churches in the country could boast even a single cloudy pane. Parsival had barely glanced at the dingy glow; he decided the window had been blocked up somehow. But the two musicians were another thing, sitting bent over their flaremouthed, curvingly hornlike instruments with the third pressing the wide stops of a little box that roared and droned with a full, somber thunder that trembled in the walls, floor, the very insides of the hearer as several choirboys wailed the lilting dirge of a *graduale*. This was something astonishingly new! Before this he had heard only priests' chants and the light tunes of minstrelsy. All the world seemed held in those sounds and as each voice shifted it was still part of one texture and reinforced the whole with its separate wanderings: a sense of all things somehow united filled him. He felt how the air washed over the earth and the light vibrated in the air, how all things moved apart yet in some hushed deep sense overlapped. . . . He felt as if he floated at the center of the sound without a thought, part of a vast expanding, boundless order as if the pure voices of men and instruments created a space that was like a narrow window letting in the immense, intense light of the sun and so he felt that, somehow, these sounds were like light . . .

He fell away from this thrilling center when he noticed the face of the priest on his knees gripping the sides of the altar with large, pale hands, a knot, a lump of scar on the right one. In the dim light his flesh seemed bluish, features clenched in on themselves, trembling, the eyes, he thought as the music went into the background, bright with pain, staring, unblinking, at the rounded ceiling as if he meant to burn a hole through it with his terrific intensity. Parsival wondered if the man were ill . . .

# xl

No one spoke much as they pressed on through the dark forest under gray skies. Enough days had passed now to leave very little to talk about. On a diet of berries, roots and mushrooms, in a land where nothing ever really dried out enough for a fire, Broaditch had already lost at least ten pounds. Though he wouldn't have admitted it, he felt better. Waleis looked unchanged except his eyes bulged slightly more. Alienor was paler against her dark traveling cape.

Waleis hadn't recently mentioned the fact that they were lost without stars, moon or sun for help. *Moss grows here,* he'd repeated often enough, *on all sides of the trees.*

The steep ground was so crossed by sudden ravines and lush undergrowth that any straight course, even if it could have been mapped, was out of the question.

# xli

Layla, the slim, dark girl who'd held him in the bath, stood at the dung-strewn, hoofchewed outskirts of the jousting grounds in the edge of the crowd, watching Parsival mount in full armor and soothe the nervous horse. The earl, in silk and leather, was pointing to a stuffed stick figure set up at the end of the grassless track. She'd been coming to watch him practice for the last two days. She never came close enough to speak and couldn't tell if he'd actually noticed her.

There was a fairsized group gathered to watch because one of the local favorites was armored and on the field today. There was talk of a combat.

Now Parsival closed his helmet and set the long red lance under his arm, aiming at the dummy with the dented shield strapped to its torso. He gripped the reins with his left hand and dipped his head partway behind his pointed shield.

Layla had insisted to herself that she wouldn't come here again. She sighed, thinking, here she was in spite of her wishes. . . . She'd been depressed and distracted all day until she made up an excuse, went outside the gate as if meaning to pick fruit in the orchard, then sighed and accepted reality and half ran around the slope, only slowing up, heart fluttering, at the first flash of the red armor down in the field . . .

"That's good style," said the earl. "Now you're ready, Sir Parsival!"

And the red armored horse burst forward with short, chugging steps, churning and spraying black earth, fast, faster, and then the locked lance hit, split the shield and shattered the figure to broken shreds and a spray of hay like an explosion.

The mounted knight, in black and gold armor, nodded his bare head. A number of people applauded.

"Now I believe," the knight said to the earl, "that he won his gear."

"Care to try him, Schent?" the lord asked, smiling faintly.

"I know how tall I am already," the man replied, chuckling. When the earl looked quizzical, he finished: "I don't need to measure my length in the field."

# xlii

Twilight, gray glimmering, a thin new moon was following the sun down. The woods were humming: steady drones and contrapuntal undulations of crickets blending with katydids. The grass was pale, elusive gray, silvery; the trees vague darkening blots. Parsival was sitting, legs crossed, looking at the evening, smelling the lushness, the faint crispness too, the first hinting of autumn.

He smoothed his hands over the silky, sheeptrimmed lawn and felt the sun-soaked earth giving back the day's rich heat. He wasn't thinking, his mind quiet, deeply alert, watchful, taking in the steady, wordless, pulsing of the living world around him. He took a deep breath and let himself fall back on the sward, linen shirt open, air mildly cool on his bare chest ...

Still mainly empty of preconceptions, he was unsurprised (though it was totally unexpected) when a light, soft but firm hand stroked smoothly across his ribs and stopped.

He turned to look at her: the slim, dark girl. From the bath several mornings ago. He smiled, remembering ...

"You move quietly," he told her.

She was kneeling there, sitting on her bare heels, wearing a ghostly pale chemiselike dress.

"You never came to see me," she said, hurt in her voice.

He was puzzled.

"About what?"

A pause. The twilight was deeper and dimmer. Gradually, almost imperceptibly, they seemed to become less and less substantial in the subtle, sourceless glow.

"They say you're only half among us," she said, as if she hadn't wanted it to be so, and yet it was some consolation.

He made little of it.

114

*Layla finds Parsival near the woods*

"I think," he remarked, "the air itself breathes. At times I can feel the breathing in of everything around me."

A pause.

"My name," she told him, "though you haven't asked, is Layla. I know yours."

She took her hand from his torso. He was aware that his body was reacting to her closeness and it interested him. He took her hand and placed it between his legs. She whipped it free so fast she tilted and fell over on her side, then started scrambling to get away except he sat up and held her by the shoulder. Saw she was crying.

"I don't understand," he said.

"So you make me a whore," she said, voice husky. "You never came to see me after . . ." She bit her lips shut and sat still now so he took away his hand.

"I don't understand," he said at length.

"Because you're a fool. They all say you're a fool."

"Well," he responded, "I'm not. But I have things to learn. I learned a new thing from you."

"Oh," she murmured, looking down. "I have my weaknesses." She thought a moment. "But I'm not as bad as my sister, for instance."

"One of those other girls?"

"No. She's at home. I'm visiting here. . . . Sister says Mother was like us."

"What way?"

She sniffed a chuckle through her nose.

"You're one of a kind," she told him.

"Why did you take your hand away this time?" he asked, suddenly.

He was so serious she giggled a little and shook her head.

"Someone has to teach you," she said, with a mock sigh. "They must have raised you in a cave somewhere or else you come from Ireland, Sir Parsival." She took his hand and kissed it tenderly. They were two close, shadowy blots. The stars were coming out now. "I'm wayward," she murmured. "But I want you to love me." She kissed his hand again, then pressed it to her warm cheek.

He smelt her hair, flesh and breath, and his belly tingled; he felt strange and dizzy; air seemed to catch in his throat. As with fear and in fighting, he noted, what he thought had no effect on anything.

He put his parted mouth to her neck and moaned faintly,

unselfconsciously, felt her soften and flow against him. She gasped. Their mouths came together and he was briefly startled, then it was sweet licking and sucking and in his mind there was an image of a bee working, fumbling, buzzing its way into a deep buttercup . . .

She held hard, arms and hands stroking over and over as if to be certain he was real . . .

He remembered the duchess in the tent where he took the ring and parted her clothes, moving finger and palm all over and along, behind, between, amazed, kneeling over her now, kissing the fragrant body as she turned, twisted, struggled in invisible bonds and probed her hand under his tights; then with turnings, strainings, embracings, they were more or less naked, pressing, separating, gripping, heaving, sighing . . .

Suddenly he pulled his hand away.

"You're wounded!" he said, heart beating with fright.

"What?" she murmured, pushing his hand back where it was. "Don't be silly. . . . Oh, that's nice, my sweet love . . ."

Still frightened, he probed deeper, was beginning to understand.

"Kiss my mouth, my love," she said.

At one point he came to be lying on top pressing rhythmically against her closed thighs.

"No . . ." she protested, head lolling on the soft, dark lawn. "No . . ."

"No?" he asked, kissing her neck.

"Please," she whispered, "don't . . . oh don't . . ."

"Don't what?" he asked, still unconsciously sliding against her, feeling a knotting of pain and ecstasy, feeling infinitely better and worse with each stroke of himself.

"Don't fuck me," she replied, breath a warm gush in his ear that tickled and numbed. "Don't fuck me now, love . . . not now . . ."

He kept sliding, braced on elbows, night air cool on the sweaty length where their torsos parted. He was puzzled and his mind, apart from the main thrust of this stunning experience, began to consider the problem.

"Oh, lover," she was saying, "don't force me now. I don't want to spoil anything . . ."

She shuddered, parted her legs suddenly and locked them around his hips, heels tapping lightly on his thighs.

"Be chivalrous, Parsival," she pleaded. Her fingers floated over his back.

"What is *fuck*?" he wanted to know.

He wasn't aware that a dim moonshadow had suddenly fallen over them where they tangled and strained together . . .

# xliii

Three days later he was standing on the church steps at sunrise watching the priest and others coming across the manor field with the sun shaking immense shadows out before them that reached their dark wavering almost to his feet. Layla's father and mother stood stiffly on either side of him, dressed in glittering silks and velveteen, looking miserable, tired and tense. He felt faintly bemused and expectant.

"I really don't understand," he was saying, "what was wrong with—"

"He doesn't understand," the fleshy sharpnosed lady raised her eyes as if seeking God in the Gothic archway itself. "A priest discovers your shame like . . . like the wickedness of Lot and—"

"Lot wasn't said to be wicked, my love," her husband dourly put in.

"—well, whoever or what, can't he understand the sin he did? You understood well enough what to do with a young girl, hmm?"

"He's her age himself," the man put in mechanically, as if used to correcting her whether it was important to him or not.

"And to have to see you marry my precious girl," the woman cried. "God!" She sighed, rackingly. "This nameless, penniless fool!" She couldn't go on.

Parsival seemed interested in trying to puzzle all this out.

"But Layla said," he reflected, "that you and her sisters do the same thing. She said you take off your clothes and lie down to fuck with young knights, so—"

The woman made a strangled noise. Her face revealed a

certain displeasure. Her black and gray bearded husband
raised an eyebrow. He suddenly seemed faintly interested
in the proceedings for the first time.

"That little tart," her mother whispered. "Well, that certainly sounds just like your daughter," she informed him.

"Parsival," the man said, neither kindly nor unkindly,
"those are dishonorable remarks."

"Are they false?"

The middle-aged, goatish man sighed and looked distantly at the approaching members of the wedding.

"That's not at stake," he told the boy. "You don't say
such things be they real or fancy."

"You don't even deny it?" she wanted to know.

He waved her remark aside. The shadows of the oncoming group shook and crossed over the three of them on the
steps. The bright sun tilted higher, pulled free of the fuzzy
horizon. Inside the open door in the deep, cool dimness,
Layla and her sisters and maids of honor were waiting by
the altar with hushed whispers and giggles. The raging
matron turned her narrow, snapping gaze in their direction.

"Is it actually a sin to fuck?" Parsival insisted on knowing.

With a derisive snort the unintentionally baited lady
aimed herself through the doorway toward her daughter
with ominous determination.

"Like drinking and shitting," her father advised, with a
ghost of a grin, "it has its proper place." He frowned.
"Also," he added, "remember, it were an ill thing to strike
a priest."

Parsival blinked and agreed.

"So I still believe," he said, "for my mother told me men
of God, for all their sins, deserve respect in His name if
not their own."

"Well put," the father grudged.

"Yet that one ought not to have laid on so fiercely with
his stick for my arse is still sore as a boil from that treat-
ment."

His almost father-in-law looked at him with weary resignation.

"In any case," he said, "there's no choice for any of us
now." He took the young man by the arm. "I have some
sound advice for your future days and happiness," he said.

Parsival was still preoccupied with the other issues.
Layla had been doing something wonderful with the burn-

ing sweetness between her legs that promised to melt him down into joyful dying when the first blow hit and a raging voice sounded from far away and, while the first impact across his bare buttocks felt almost good, coming when it did, the next was less satisfactory and after another two he looked up, saw the robed figure and concluded the "dark one" was upon him at last and leaped up with a frustrated warcry to the attack which was met by a storm of futile blows, Latin and Anglo-Saxon curses until Parsival's stone-like fists struck home . . .

"I don't think your wife is pleased to call me son," he observed.

"Ah," breathed the father, "that's apt. That's apt. Now heed what I say and you may win wits and honor yet."

"But you know," the young man murmured, tapping his cheek thoughtfully with his forefinger, "I'm not so sure I even got to the end of fucking. I wish someone would explain in more detail just what—"

"Peace, boy!" commanded the father, frowning just as the priest—who looked warily and triumphantly at Parsival through a sorely bruised, squinting pair of eyes—and entourage arrived. "Now lend ears to my counsel and heed me for the sake of your future good." He smiled thinly. "Good morrow, priest Beera. Now all will see with what joy I wed my sweet child to this noble young knight."

Priest Beera smiled maliciously and nodded.

"Aye, my lord," he said.

After they passed inside the father continued his discourse to Parsival:

"The first thing is," he told him, "not to lie with Layla again until your success is won. This is the most important point. Otherwise you'll lack the strength to succeed where all others have failed." He looked gravely into the boy's clear greenblue eyes. "You must swear your oath to me on this, Parsival."

# xliv

The streambed had become a road at some uncertain point and so the three of them came struggling down from the far side of a dead end, the muddy, rutted track becoming less and less overgrown until they actually passed a serf's kennel in a clearing, a set of ravens perched on the roof, their eyes watching, dark and quick. The collapsed-looking little structure was otherwise deserted, or at least temporarily empty. Broaditch poked around and announced that it had been a mere matter of weeks at best since a fire had burned on the hearth.

They went on and within a mile passed half-a-dozen more deserted shacks, the rank smell of the inhabitants still in the perpetually damp air, before they came to a cluster that suggested a town. The air was so misty it was impossible to tell which way the castle might lie. They struggled through shin-deep ruts that slashed the drenched space between buildings that vaguely resembled a street. A gaunt, knobby pig looked apathetically up at them from rooting in the mud; two naked children crouched in a dark doorway staring at the travelers with bright, voracious, suffering eyes; a thin, wobbly woman toiled with a load of firewood through the sucking ooze to a hut door. She turned a grim, pinched face to them.

"King Hunger rules here," Broaditch murmured.

"God's mercy," greeted Alienor, calling to the woman who had stopped, up to her shins in the muck. She seemed to reflect deeply.

"If you be looking for that," she finally said, "you come wrong."

"We want food, woman," pleaded Waleis, "a bit a' something hot! We been living on bark pie and grass pudding."

122

"Then you been doing well," she said, somberly, plodding onward, lifting her legs high with each weary step. They watched her go on until she went inside, shutting the door.

Broaditch looked around. The two children were gone and that door was shut too now. No other opened.

They continued picking their way along the miserable road. At one point Waleis dropped to his knees and stayed there for a minute or two raging at the squat, grim dwellings all around. He threw clods of mud at one impassive door, loudly questioning the lineage of the presumed inhabitants and casting a verbal pall over their prospects in the hereafter which, he declared, was nearer than they thought. He sat there, pale and exhausted, until Broaditch helped him up again and they plodded on through the cold, steady drizzle.

Broaditch kept one hand under the saddle girth of the mule and let it tug him forward. Waleis and Alienor were riding again.

"No menfolk in sight," he thought out loud, "no food, no standing crops . . . are they all in service?"

"I don't know about menfolk," Alienor put in, "but that woman was several months along her time; thin as she was, the wood didn't hide it."

"How long can a lord keep them to fight?" Broaditch went on musing. "They all cheat but still . . ."

"Maybe they're all dead, then," put in Waleis, despondently. "As one I know and love well soon will be if he don't eat."

At the edge of the settlement, surrounded by the heavy, sluggish, yellowish mist, Broaditch made a decision and led them into the yard of the last shack in the town row.

"We need shelter," he muttered as he went and kicked the door which simply fell open with a soft, rotten crash. A pair of quick eyes blinked at him from the foul and musty depths of the room. A rat's look, he decided. A furtive male hiding from the levy? Maybe a cripple.

"Has there been a plague here lately?" he asked the man as he stood in the doorway letting his eyes adjust: a figure gradually defined itself from the shadows.

"Aye," said the man, "and I alone have lived."

For an instant the sadness, the bitterness in the voice made Broaditch forget that he'd just seen other living people.

Now he could see it was neither peasant nor serf: a minstrel with a stringed instrument strapped to his back, sitting on the floor, seeming to chew something he held in his hand. The eyes bulged slightly, Broaditch saw, and the nose bent up at the tip paralleling a pointed chin. The head was thick, not thin. A raw boldness about the expression irked Broaditch for some reason.

The eyes narrowed now with a kind of slyness.

"What do you want," the singer said, "with a broken old man?"

The voice, despite its control and easy lilt, was too thickened, too hoarse. A drinker's voice, Broaditch realized.

"You're well preserved then," he told the fellow, moving into the dank room out of the drizzle, followed by the others. Waleis instantly sat on the clay floor and began working his way on his buttocks toward the minstrel, eyes fixed by the sight of him biting and chewing behind his hand.

"I come from a far land," he told them, "where men neither age nor hunger." His voice was suddenly vibrant, eyes seemed to look down from vast, unguessable reaches of time and space, a godlike, fathomless look. "Nor suffer pain."

Again the voice held them for a moment, it seemed so compelling and soothing, so calm and true. Waleis ruptured the strange mood, saying, wheedling:

"If you need not eat, sir, pray give me your morsel there."

The eyebrows shot up, eyes danced, face showed the delight of the kindly father who bestows a gift on a beseeching child. He took the hand from his mouth and held out an empty palm. Broaditch perceived a faint, malicious flicker before the voice took charge, saying:

"I ate but air." Looking grave and wise. "But you may share it, my lords. And lady."

"You take us for lords?" Waleis wanted to know.

"He takes all of us for what *you* are," Alienor jabbed. The minstrel chuckled, then grew grave again. It was impossible to tell if any of his expressions were emotionally prompted.

"Why are you crouching in here?" demanded Broaditch as the middle-sized man stood up, long, thick head cocked to one side. When not putting on an expression the face was oddly vacant, only animated, it seemed, by farce.

"If you've come to this little cessflower of a village you must know yourself," he said, seriously enough.

"We came from the hills," Alienor explained.

"Well," said the man, "keep going and you'll become wise enough."

Then suddenly, meaninglessly, he capered, kicked his heels and spun around. A strange, automatic gesture. Waleis alone seemed to enjoy this. He clapped, grinning. The man looked at him with infinite scorn.

"I care nothing for my audience," he announced, airily. "My art speaks to God and to me alone." His face was suddenly gentle, aloof, saintly.

"If that's your art," Alienor allowed, "then what does God reply?"

The man laughed.

"We've no time for fool's tricks," Broaditch said, irritably.

"A fool, big man?" The entertainer seemed angry. "This fool has an estate you couldn't walk the length of in a day!"

Broaditch was peering out into the foggy street, looking for signs of activity.

"So you grovel here eating air," he retorted.

"I wait my time," was the answer. "But you should go on." He went to the doorway and pointed out where the rain was spattering. "A fair journey to you, clod."

*At least his contempt seems real,* Broaditch thought. He noted that the fellow was wearing a small fortune in silks and furs, in fact. *If he's rich why needs he act the fool unless being so deep in the habit he's unable to check it now . . . or many's the dunce gets rich, gold being a poor measure of wit . . .*

Broaditch knelt and prepared a fire in the sagging chimneyspace. Alienor eased herself down on a rancid spilling of hay, sighing over her chilled boneaches. Waleis stretched out where he was, mumbling to himself.

# xlv

The entertainer had been sitting in a far corner, the fire-shadows wavering over him so that his wispy body seemed to shake. He hadn't spoken in hours. Now he was pluck-ing his lutelike instrument and humming softly to himself.

"When you have talent," he suddenly announced, "you can prosper in any condition of life. William of St. Blahe gets a bag of gold for each tune he writes down. The Great Giles gets—"

"Who?" broke in Alienor.

Waleis looked up, morbid interest revealed in his expres-sion: a kind of hunger.

"The actor, Giles," said the minstrel with contempt. "A wonderful fellow. Natural as the morning. Why he has more put away than many a king. When last I spoke with him he—"

"I heard a' him," put in Waleis. "Do you have lots a' gold, sir?"

The man made a sly face, a burlesque of avarice.

"I'm really a Jew," he said, clasping and unclasping his hands. "I have no gold, ah, I have no gold, good sirs. Be-lieve me, I have nothing, nothing . . ."

"Ha ha, very good, very good," affirmed Waleis. Alienor seemed indifferent. Broaditch spat into the fire.

"Your rare skill makes my knees to tremble," he said.

"Ah. A man of wit," said the other.

Broaditch spat again.

"I know what I know," he said. "You're a great figure to be sure, hiding out here telling lies to strangers."

The man's face suddenly expressed infinite hurt and sorrow. How misunderstood, how spurned and degraded. Despite himself Broaditch was almost touched and found

126

himself wondering if he hadn't misjudged this sweet but unfortunate fellow. He looked away in disgust at himself.

"I like to please all men," the humorist replied, as if someone had actually asked a question.

"I thought you didn't care what anybody thought?" Alienor wondered.

The face grew thoughtful.

"That was but air," he said, and after a moment Broaditch realized he was actually serious and, in fact, seemed to be getting angry about something. "Parody. I hate that sort of clod! What use is a truth that no one heeds, a beauty unseen?" His eyes were intense now. Broaditch decided he had the look of a man defending his house or a thief his spoils. "Bah. Men care little for truths. They want to laugh and hate and forget their misery. Give them what pleases them. Don't argue with a lord's ways or off come your ears or at least your purse. Prosper and be damned." He nodded as if that proved his point. "You'll be damned anyway come the end of it."

Alienor digested this, then found words coming from herself that surprised her a little:

"The swine thinks all the earth a sty."

The man cocked his ready, quick face at her, saying:

"A pig knows the reek of another."


The fire was out and they were all crouched alone with their hunger when Waleis sat up and said:

"Would you tell a tale?"

"Can you afford his price?" Broaditch sourly asked, in an undertone. He was engaged in picking the peeling skin of a callus on his heel.

But the man needed no urging and Broaditch was surprised to discover that, in spite of anything he might say about it, the telling of a tale seemed to unfold of itself from the fellow. His personality (which gave Broaditch a griping stomach) seemed to melt away and his face became pure, open, delighting and delighted, and as the story came to vivid life in the dimly firelit room, the rain rattling steadily on the leaky roof, the teller became only the mellow, guiding voice of it and they all quickly became absorbed and shared it, apart, silent, yet together, intimate . . .

# xlvi

Parsival was riding through cool, dry, steep country in
crisp, faded autumn sunlight. There were streaks of redgold
and bare brown among the thinly spread, spiny mountain
trees. His charger, Niva, moved steadily on with a brisk
and chunky gait. His mail links clinked faintly.

That dawn he had been just mounting the horse by the
castle's low outer wall, squinting against the rising sun
across a field of shrubbery and sandy soil. In the distance
he could hear what they had told him was the eastern sea
breaking against rocky coast.

When he'd glanced back at the square, low building she
was standing behind the wall a few feet away, watching
him. She said nothing and made no move to come closer.
Her dark hair hung loose and long. She blinked against the
sunglare.

"Goodby," he said.

After a silence she spoke:

"Did they tell you to go? They can't make you leave
your wife."

"Your father explained to me about the grail. He said
that I will be more famous than any knight after I've won
it. He told me which way to ride."

She bit her lower lip, not looking at him now. She
seemed very intent on something far away. Then she said:

"I hate him. . . . It's just shit. All of it."

"He said it was God's cup. And your mother told—"

"She's a sag-tit bitch." Her lip trembled. "I don't want to
hear this shit spoken." She turned her back and stood
there.

He sat his horse looking at her, puzzled.

"But," he began.

"You're a fool," she said, bitterly. "They were right about you."

He stared, vaguely incredulous. Frowned. She didn't move.

"I'll be back," he insisted.

She didn't move or say anything.

"God shield you," he said, and nudged the horse into a choppy walk.


"Keep the sun ever at your back!" his father-in-law had advised and though it was very difficult to bear true in this rock-chopped country he pressed on fairly well for the better part of a week. He would ride west in the mornings and, true to his instructions, swing around all day and find himself heading east at nightfall. Keeping the sun at your back was easy to accomplish, he decided.

At the end of the sixth day he rode out of a pine forest onto the banks of a long, clear, unruffled lake, tinted rose and green by sunset glow; silver patches showed where breezes stirred then faded away; overhanging trees deeply shadowed the shoreline. The horse stepped along the rocky edge following the curves. Slight splashes sounded, then ripples spread out where fish were hitting insects . . .

Coming around a deep bend he saw a boat anchored well out from land, a single man in it, just dark outlines showing in the glimmering twilight haze. Beyond him, above the craggy hills, a pale sliver of moon was rising.

Parsival reined up Niva and called across the water.

"Fisherman, where can I find lodging for the night?"

Silence. Parsival was about to call out again when the man spoke in a still, quiet voice that carried so well he had a fleeting, confused impression that the speaker was close by, somehow.

"No one lives here," the voice said, strangely direction-less, suggesting sadness too, the young man noted. "There is but one castle in all this land."

Parsival took this in.

"Where is it, fisherman?" he asked.

"Follow the road beyond those trees. Ride straight. There are a great many paths and turnings and it is difficult not to miss one's way."

"How will I know the right road?"

"Not long ago you would not have asked. I wonder if this is an improvement."

"How can you know that? Do you know me?"

"The road you want always rises. If your way levels off or falls you have gone wrong."

# xlvii

The embers popped like a thick cough now and then in the stuffy, warm, dim room. Broaditch stared at the thick ash grayly coating the red glow and listened to the steady, expressive, slightly drink-roughened voice seeming to suspend the images, smells, sounds of the story in the smoky air. Outside the night was still now, the rain no longer streaming over the roof. A cool draft seeped through the crevices.

". . . so when Gawain arrived at this doorway, the fair maid at his back, he regretted having courteously left his sword in the prince's chamber as now those vulgar men with mace and halberd made for him, mouths filled with curses and threats. So he took down an iron bar used to lock shut the door and stood in the center of them as they spilled through the doorway and the lady ran to the far end of the hall and tossed to Gawain, still armored in his nightshirt of green pfelle silk, the marble chessboard and kept the pieces for herself. This lady was about to strike out a gambit of her own devise! So Gawain parried the first spear thrust with the board and shattered the haft with his heavy bar. Then as a mace spun close to his ear he dropped to his knees and whizzed the iron across the shins of the attacker and the bones sounded like snapping brittle twigs in winter and that man was full of regret. . . . Next Gawain struck down another as an ax splintered the chessboard . . ."

"Ah, yes," murmured Waleis from where he lay on the floor near the vague glow of coals.

". . . And then the lady played her knight and castle, for the pieces were of solid silver and large as a hand. She soon followed with queen and pawns and the men she

131

checked held bloody heads and found the game a great
strain to play. . . . And soon, between the two, they were
all mate and taken off the board . . ."

Waleis laughed and even Broaditch found himself grinning at the image. Alienor, knowing nothing of the game,
had her mind on other aspects of the story.

"Did he marry her?" she wanted to know.

"What use," snapped the minstrel, "just to tell you?
That's gossip over washing, not a tale! " His voice went
distant again. "No. . . . A proper tale is in no hurry like
a breathless messenger who shouts the news. . . . We want
to see how it took each person, what the day was like,
what each said and what their feelings were . . ." After a
pause he took up the story again, voice measured and
flowing.

". . . and Gawain, having come all this distance in hopes
of finding the way to the grail climbed the steep stairs
within the vast tower and came at last into the inner, top-
most room where twelve windows looked out on the world
and where he had seen the twelve figures from a distance
that now had vanished . . ."

The fire was out. A soft wind soughed in the roof
thatches. Broaditch lay, hands locked behind his head,
listening with shut eyes. Alienor stared out into the dark
room. Waleis lay close to the minstrel whose voice seemed
disembodied in the blackness.

". . . he went through the great door, that took two
normal men to swing open, and found himself on a polished floor as slick as ice. Ah, he could barely keep his
feet walking there, slipping, sliding, twisting as he made
his way to the Wonder Bed that stood on round ruby feet,
like wheels, in the center of the big, twelve-sided hall. This
bed was of jasper, chrysolite and all rare stuffs and the
covers were rarest fluffs and furs and silks beyond price or
compare . . . yes . . . and as he edged closer the bed, like
an irksome horse, moved away from him, rolling on its
silent, smooth wheels . . ."

"Is this true?" asked Waleis. "It must have been magic."

"He sees right to the heart of a thing, bless him," remarked Alienor.

"Things are true in more ways than one," said the teller.
"Finally Gawain leaped and caught hold of the mattress,
then pulled himself into the bed and at that moment it
spun and sped around the twelve walls of that room with

half again the speed of a racing stallion! Yes, it banged and
spun until the fortress resounded with the crashes and in
his armor with his heavy shield Gawain rode to joust after
joust and if every drummer ever born was to be raised by
the good God in that place and were to drum for a sack of
gold apiece the noise wouldn't have come near to this
sound I tell of! No. . . . And with a prayer our hero covered himself with his shield. That was no place to seek a
good night's rest. . . . Or a good *knight's* rest either . . ."
Waleis laughed. *Like a child,* Broaditch thought, *he seemed
to have forgotten all his terrors—except there was a faint
hysterical note in it.* ". . . Soon the bed stopped its wild
career and stood still in the center of the floor as a volley
of iron pellets came speeding down from high in the roof
where hundreds of deadly slings fired themselves with good
aim so that the hero's shield was punched through in many
spots. . . . When that game was over hundreds of unerring
arrows sped unto him and more than one pierced even his
mail links and cut his sore bruised flesh. . . . If you seek
rest I advise you to pass up this bed . . ."

"That's no place for me!" cried Waleis.

"I know that bed well," Alienor said, quietly, and Broaditch smiled to himself in the shadows.

"Ho, ho," said Waleis, skeptically. Alienor sighed and
the teller went on with the tale.

"When there were no more arrows shot Gawain sat up,
painfully bruised and cut as he was, and looked around the
great room. At that moment a churl appeared wearing
stinking garments sewn together from the foul skins of
fishes. . . . That's not what you want to see after a session
in that bed. He came in carrying a club with a knobbed
end thick as a loaf of bread and had a jaw to chew stones
with. He came toward Gawain, who could have lived to
be very old, content to have him get no closer than he was.
So he stood up and looked sternly at the base fellow who
started back a little and said: 'You need not fear *me.* Your
death is hard by the door!' And with this he withdrew but
left the portal open and shouted for Gawain to prepare
to meet the guardian whose visits, he could assure him,
were often memorable. And then, my friends, the door was
filled with a huge, quivering shadow and a terrible grating
and buzzing sounded as though steel chains were being
pulled across saw teeth . . . indeed . . ." And the steady
voice paused both for breath and to let the mood ripen.

". . . Yes, and next one, two, then three and four, five, six black, spiny, hairy claw-tipped legs scraped and clacked into the doorway there and a fat, stinking body, like black mud, eyes dull, evil green like swamp-light glowing, great, hideous wings buzzing so that a hot wind pushed our hero back where he struggled to keep footing on the slick floor. Have you ever looked at a fly up close? Much like a fly it was, this monstrous thing, bigger than a man, that came scratching and scraping over the floor, my friends . . . yes . . . and it lifted up in that high hall, then settled back, then lifted again, buzz, buzz, buzzing till the ears ached to hear it! . . ."

In the pause Waleis cried out:

"What did he do then? Say what happened!"

Even Broaditch was anxious to know, as he reflected that though there were no giant flies in the world yet they were real. He started slightly as something touched his leg, then identified Alienor's hand. Took it in his own as the voice released the story again, with a little rush as if the pause had built up a palpable pressure:

"Gawain, averse as ever to yielding ground, held his battered shield above his head and raged to find himself in retreat and though he struggled to run forward yet he could not even keep his place where he was. . . . He waved his keen blade and fumed . . . and then the giant creature struck down at him, one evil claw hooking the shield and flinging it off as if it were mere parchment! And still being blown backwards across the immense hall, our hero whipped his blade fiercely enough but only fanned the air but little less than the grim creature itself . . . yes. . . . And then it rose above him and the gusts of wind drove him flat onto his back where he seemed ready for an embrace and kiss he had not invited nor longed for much. . . . And as the fanged face fell toward him the blade stabbed up and was a cold comfort to the terrible beast; though it went in deep where men find pleasure there was no joy here . . . by no means, friends . . . and that monster, cut through and through, flurried and thrashed and tumbled and a hideous black blood spilled all over man and floor. . . . That fly had the face of a raging lion but now it was still and Gawain pulled himself free and sat there a little dazed when a woman as fair as that churl had been foul came in through the door and placed a wreath on his battered helmet, saying: "Thou art now lord of the marvels of the world.' "

"Did he find the grail?" interjected Waleis.

"The grail?" wondered the storyteller. "Gawain—"

"Hark!" broke in Broaditch.

In the silence they heard a faint clinking and the dull steps of horses in mud. The storyteller scrambled on his knees to the door they had propped up and peered out through the widespaced boards. In the dim glow now outside his shape was visible. Broaditch crept over and knelt beside him. Looked through a crack himself and saw patches of stars where the clouds were pulling apart and the half-moon sailing among them; saw the dark shapes of the village huts and then the glint of armor: a line of a dozen or more mounted men filing past, dark shapes on huge horses, muffled, a cough, sucking footsteps in the ooze. . . . Beside him the minstrel whimpered faintly.

"What are you so afraid of?" Broaditch hissed at him. "Have you never seen knights ride past?"

Trembling, the other replied:

"They've come . . . I knew they'd come in time . . ."

"Who's come?" Broaditch wanted to know.

"Why did I wait?" the man asked himself bitterly. "Why did I waste my breath telling tales to dull fools while . . ."

He just sat there huddling by the door, dejected, resigned; Broaditch didn't see to what.

"Damn you," he said, "be clear!"

"Clinschor's men," he said, dully.

"Who?" Broaditch was frowning furiously. A pause. The man didn't repeat it. "Clinschor? In Britain?"

"He didn't land yesterday," the minstrel said. "Last week they were still fighting in the south . . ." He sighed, leaning against the doorframe as if life had drained suddenly from him. "Now here they are . . ."

Waleis pressed close to Broaditch.

"We're going to die!" he suddenly whispered.

"Calm yourself," Broaditch said, squeezing his arm, gently.

"I want to go home," he said, like a child.

"The riders are gone," Broaditch reported, peering through the cracks.

"More will come," muttered the storyteller.

"What will we do?" Alienor wanted to know, kneeling near them.

"We'll see," Broaditch soothed, thinking: *Is it really true, can this be so? The royal gelding in our land* . . .

"He's cruel," said the minstrel.

Alienor remembered the story, how that handsome prince of Sicily was found sleeping with his lord's queen, his father's sister, and how they left him alive but smooth between the legs. They said he became a magician and only lived to hate. Lived on hate, took it for meat and drink. They said he'd built a palace out of the bones and skulls of his enemies. He and his barbarian allies had a death-grip on the kingdoms of Europe and held (they said) a knife to the throat of the Holy Emperor himself . . .

"I was a fool to tarry here," the minstrel sighed.

"Whatever," Broaditch muttered soberly. "We'd do well to leave now."

He stood up and pulled aside the door, then stepped quietly out into the cool night that brightened and dimmed as the moon passed through the clouds. The storyteller sat huddled on the doorsill; Alienor and Waleis moved past him into the yard beside Broaditch who at that moment half-turned, started, then shrugged and shook his head as two tall knights came around the corner of the hut, moonlight glinting on dark, silvertrimmed armor. Their visors were down and the helmets were formed into demon and beast heads, jeweleyes gleaming in frozen ferocity. Not looking he felt Alienor press close and thought he heard Waleis' teeth rattle together as he sank to his knees. Then he bent himself, a trace stiffly, and said:

"We don't live here, sirs. We're but travelers."

The two stood still, swords at their sides, and said nothing. The moon dimmed and they seemed shadows, a darker stain on the night. When it brightened again they seemed to float up from some faint depths, faintly gleaming, like some haunted fish, Broaditch thought.

"We've lost our way," he said, "perhaps my lords can help us?"

# xlviii

An amount of time Parsival was never certain of had passed. Even since meeting the fisherman on the shore of that mountain lake whole sections of life seemed to have blurred by him with color, sound and shape but no measurement: his experiences in this period (he later was to say to friends) were halfway between a fairy tale and shivering awake from a bad dream . . .

In this haunted, shocked state he found himself riding through roadless miles of forest at the cool, brilliant peak of autumn. Though dazed in spirit, he felt very strong and confident otherwise. He felt that soon he would come to something solid, something perfectly lucid . . .

Jeschute, Alienor's former mistress, who'd lived a normally difficult and unsatisfying life as wife of a violent duke before Parsival stumbled into her tent, was riding along the forest trail in the sparkling autumn morning. The white mule rattled his forelegs through the drifts of leaves on the twisted trail. She wasn't thinking about her troubles, about the rags she now had to wear, the unjust penance the duke imposed by driving her on through the countryside in disgrace, because the day was so bright and clear and there were no strangers here to mock her shame. Her husband always followed just out of sight. He was waiting for her lover (as he supposed it) or anyone else, for that matter, to try to help her. Sometimes, in the beginning, she'd wished someone would. It was a nightmare. That was when she first understood none of this was done for love or ordinary jealousy. It was pride and spite. The understanding had sickened her. Now she was dulled and weary and didn't care anymore. . . . And who would stand

137

*Parsival encounters the Lady Jeschute in distress*

up to her husband without good reason, in any case? . . . It was a dull, old nightmare now, months of nightmare and she didn't even hate the mad boy anymore. . . . Pride and spite and a dark anger: he actually enjoyed this, she'd realized, that was the worst, enjoyed parading her, enjoyed the respect and sympathy of other men and even some women. . . . She was dulled and didn't think about it anymore . . .

She heard the leaves whooshing around a bend before the red knight came out of the brilliant fire and gold of the trees. She just watched him as he reined his horse up close to her. She was about to warn him that her husband was somewhere behind when he lifted his visor and she recognized Parsival. He obviously didn't recognize her in her present state. He blinked his clear eyes and smiled. She wasn't angry, there hadn't even been anything to forgive and she knew that, but she had to say:

"You put me on this mule last time we met. Now do you mean to have me killed, too?"

He looked puzzled.

"My lady?" he said.

"And yourself too? I don't know how you got that armor but it won't guard you from—"

"I remember," he suddenly said, beaming with pleasure. "*I* was in the rags then!"

"I don't really care anymore," she said, bowing her head, sighing, suddenly weeping too, feeling hemmed in to her soul by these cold, hard men and unthinking fools. She hugged her ragged, soiled silks over her torso and murmured: "Let me die, it doesn't matter . . ." And surprised herself as she heard the words come out, the sound of another horse coming behind down the trail now, and knew their truth: "I still love him. . . . God, why?"

Parsival was about to say something to her when he saw the knight come around the bend straight toward them. She spoke again but he didn't hear it. He thought: *so this is it, then* . . . setting his faceplate down and bracing his lance between arm and side, Niva seeming to float laterally, feet chop-chopping the turf; swallowing, feeling his heart's pounding, mouth metal-tasting, dry. Glancing around for an instant everything seemed burningly vivid, the sky flashing blue like cut glass, the intense autumn colors, air seeming to vibrate, and he had an impression of having infinite time, that between breaths and heartbeats and

sounds of wind-shifted leaves there was an endless space
in which all things though moving were strangely, totally
still and it seemed incredible that in a moment he would
be riding to joust, to crash against the advancing knight
who seemed to be suspended (though moving rapidly) in
his dark armor against the golden fire of the trees and then
this somehow delicate perception vanished like a pricked
bubble when he peered through the eyeslits at her tortured
face, purple flesh under her eyes, long, trembling hands
twisting the rough rope she had for halter on the mule,
weeping for no reason he could understand and he asked
her about that, voice muffled and harsh inside the steel
helm, and she asked why must they fight and he said
knights were supposed to, everyone knew that and it was
the way to honor and perfection and he wondered vaguely
(he and Niva starting to move up the path) why she shut
her eyes and drooped her head and then in a few steps
they were charging, storming at one another, the road zipping past under him, the near trees blurring and he had
the feeling, as he tucked and aimed, that something like
the wind was blowing them together, faster and faster
until he felt a shock and terrible, mounting pressure on
him that seemed endless while a shrieking tearing of metal
filled the world and went on and on, in the actual space
of a blink, and he strained against it and then it popped
away and he was free and leaning forward, half falling
from the saddle, then tilting himself back upright and
wheeling around in the narrow space between the trees,
turning to see the other down in a mass of fallen leaves,
the horse still galloping straight on past Lady Jeschute;
and walking Niva slowly he looked at Orilus flat on his
back, arms and legs starfished, unmoving; and then felt a
dull pain in his shield-holding forearm and noticed the
metal was buckled and torn and spots of his own blood
showed . . .

She just stared at him as he rode slowly to her, standing
there by the bony mule, up to her ankles in the golden
leaves, hands tightly clasping the rope that loosely knitted
her silken rags together, pale, bare flesh showing everywhere. The bright air stirred and rustled the woods. She
stared and didn't turn to see where her husband's legs
poked out from the leafheaps beside the path. The horse

was around the bend but could still be heard crashing on . . .

Parsival stopped. She just stared up at him. His struck arm was pulsing painfully now. He didn't know what to tell her. He felt only confusion about the whole business.

He started to speak several times. Finally said:

"Is something wrong?"

She started to reply, checked herself, then shut her eyes and bowed her head.

"Is there?" he pressed.

She let out her breath and said nothing. He sat waiting for a few silent minutes; then she whispered:

"God keep you, boy or knight," under her breath and turned away, walking slowly toward where the duke's armored form lay spreadeagled in the bright leaves.

"Wait," he called after her but she kept going on, steadily, head tilted down, wading through the leafswells, each step crackling and scraping.

He turned in the saddle and watched her until she reached the fallen warrior and stood over him. He saw her sit down, wearily, at his feet. Parsival wondered how long she was going to stay there like that. After a few more minutes he gave up the whole puzzling affair and cantered Niva away, looking back once over his shoulder just before the road bent and glimpsed her dark in the distance, like a shadow against the vibrant, crystalline brightness . . .

# xlix

Broaditch on his knees held her half under himself, feeling her tremble silently. His right eye hurt, head still numb from the blow, and he felt the slow blood pulsing and sticking in his matted beard. Smoke stung his eyes: on every side huts were blazing and lashing flamelight showed shadowy, fluttering, dodging figures, old men, women, children and the looming horsemen in black and silver steel flashing into and out of the darkness beyond the lit area, silently riding people down as they sobbed, screamed, fell and crawled in the mud, pleaded crouching over their children as the killers grunted and the swordcuts zipped, horses snorted and Broaditch tried to reject the sounds, the terrible slicing impacts . . .

He saw Waleis lying flat on his face covering his ears and eyes; the minstrel had turned his back and stood silently among the unspeaking captors. And then the violence swirled and shifted further down toward the end of the village and Broaditch watched an old woman crawl, eyes and mouth gaped wide, firebright flesh seeming to form and then dissolve to shadows as the flames gushed and wavered. She struggled forward with infinite and futile labor through sucking mud that squished to her elbows, hopelessly straining, barely moving (*why won't she at least lie still*, he kept thinking) the warriors silently looking until one started over, a mace and chain swinging at his side, then hesitated where the mud deepened, then minced around the puddles and mounted his horse and cantered across the mire, gargoyle visor down like all the rest, his tall, black animal nimbly high-stepping, hooves plopping straight up and down until he loomed over the still struggling half-swimming woman and Broaditch looked away as the spiked ball went up in a long, looping arc, humming and hissing . . .

"Why are you doing these things?" Alienor suddenly cried out at the knights who seemed indifferent as stone. "Why? Why?"

"Save your breath," the minstrel said. "These are Clinschor's mutes."

"What? Are they all deaf men?" Broaditch cried.

The minstrel still faced away.

"Try to plead with them," he suggested. "Try to bribe them."

"Who can order deaf-mutes to battle?" Broaditch demanded, half-hysterically, as if the reality of all this might actually be called into question somehow.

"Their master makes himself understood," the minstrel said.

# I

Dawn was a gray, misty glow. The chewed and rutted road was mud now, dry, cold and hard as iron so Broaditch's feet were swollen sore as he marched with the others, driven on by the blackarmored riders. The collar and chain chafed his neck: the links were strung down the long row of men and women who tottered forward, gasping, numb, miserable past even misery. There were no children or old people in the line. Alienor and Waleis, he knew, were somewhere behind him.

Looking around he saw fogs dissolving from the low wooded hills; autumn seemed already winter here, trees gray, leafless. . . . He twisted to look back for Alienor: there was a thin, shivering teen-age boy staggering directly behind him, holding their mutually joining chain with both hands, his hair matted with dried blood; next back, a woman; then a man; and a long, long row of others. . . . He wondered how far this procession they'd been joined to stretched each way. . . . He had stopped wincing as his feet hit the jagged earth and it wasn't long before he stopped thinking too and there was nothing but the endless walking, clinking steel, gasps, moans, weeping here and there and the dead silence of the dozen captors who never seemed to raise their helmets for air or light that any slave ever saw as the road went on and on through empty, barren heath-country; there was the swaying of the links which gradually bowed his neck, cold winds, gray days and vacant nights and now and then a brief stop when someone fell dead in the line and was loosed and left beside the road until even time was lost to him. . . . Each village they went through was deserted and burnt out. Once they went past a great fortress and there was a flicker of interest in him, weary and sick as he was, to see the astonishing sight of walls shattered almost to dust in places, of stones that looked actually melted. . . . He briefly tried to imagine what engines could have done it; none he'd ever seen . . . and then they were past and his mind dropped everything but the unending pace where it seemed the earth was pressing, grinding against him and that his feet weren't walking so much as desperately trying to push it away . . .

# li

The wind was chill and gusty: the leaves were billowing past, swirling, breaking loose in sudden rushes from the trees, flashing and rustling in the sunlight. Three knights were keeping a fast pace through the forest, armed and armored, lances at rest, horsehooves clunking like drumbeats on the firm ground, spraying the bright leaves like oncoming bows of ships.

"Gawain," said one, "can you still see the track?"

"I know the way," he answered.

"Then you know more than I."

"Which is no new country for me to find myself in," said Gawain.

"Look," said the third, needlessly, as through the bright snow-like fall of leaves a red knight with red-armored charger came toward them at a walk and the three reined up and sat there watching.

"Do we know him?" said one.

"That was Sir Roht's gear," said Gawain, grinning, "so this must be him."

"Who?" asked the first man.

"The boy prince. The bent-brain. Parsival." Gawain nodded, pleased. "His conversation is supposed to shame the greatest jesters."

"Ah," said the first, named Erec, "he's said to be a bear for strength."

"And for wits too," rejoined Gawain, sitting up tall and lean, eyes quick, bright, alert.

"Why don't we knock him flat?" inquired the third, a stout, pox-scarred, unsmiling knight.

Gawain shrugged, said:

146

"Do what you please, Rammes."

Then raised his eyebrows, satyr-like, as Parsival halted his horse and without a word turned aside to give them a wide berth.

"Hoy!" called Gawain and spurred after him and a moment later the other two followed as the red knight kept edging across the windy little glade where the leaves were swelling and breaking like surf over rocks and horselegs.

"Wait," called Gawain.

Parsival opened his helmet.

"I'm not sure this is the right thing to do," he said.

"What?" Gawain wondered.

"This knight business," was the lucid reply.

The horses were standing now, ears restlessly cocking, tails nervous. The other two came up beside Gawain and stopped.

"You're Parsival?" asked Gawain.

"Yes."

"If you want to go your way," snarled Rammes, "yield yourself and maybe I won't crack your head for you, you red dick-licker."

"I just fought again," said Parsival, "and I'm not sure I like it."

"There's a hole in that shield," observed the first knight, a medium-sized, soft-spoken man.

"There'll soon be one where his fucking nose used to be," stated Rammes. He rode closer, pointing his lance at Parsival's face. "You hear me, boy? Do you?"

"Why are you angry?" Parsival wanted to know.

"What? Boy, I'm angry at every man on earth I haven't knocked on his ass!"

"Who did you just fight?" Gawain asked.

"Orilus. He fell dead. . . . There's something I don't like . . . I don't understand . . ."

Gawain cocked his head to one side, thoughtfully.

"Listen," he said, pleasantly, "when a fledgling has hopped from the high branch it's too late to ponder the mysteries of flight, Sir Parsival. He'd damned well better flap his wings!"

"You killed Duke Orilus?" asked the first knight.

Parsival nodded.

Sir Rammes snorted and jabbed his spear viciously at the youth's bare face.

"Slay me, you squished shit!" he said.

Rammes held aside his shield and lance, offering his breast-plate.

Parsival started to speak, then didn't. He sat his horse, frowning in thought.

"You'll have to fight," Gawain pointed out, not displeased by the prospect.

Parsival decided that since he didn't really understand yet he would have to trust the advice he'd been getting right along. Not that he didn't enjoy the speed and impact, the struggle and clash, the moments of skill . . .

"It's the only path I know about," he mused aloud, "that leads to the perfect blessing. But I think there ought to be another . . ."

"Leads to *where?*" Gawain wanted to know, face unsure whether to grin or frown.

Parsival closed his helmet and wheeled Niva in a long semi-circle to the far end of the glade as Rammes made himself ready. Gawain sat sidewise on his steed, leaning on one elbow to watch. He felt a shiver of appreciation as Parsival lowered his lance and began his terrific, compact charge . . .

No one helped Rammes to his feet. His horse had gone down with him and lay stunned and quivering. Gawain nodded approval of the match.

Rammes managed to rise to his knees and swayed there, battered, blood beaded on his chest mail, as the three of them rode on together.

"We'll meet you at Arthur's camp," Erec called back to the fallen knight.

"Parsival," Gawain said, grinning, "welcome to our company."

The three of them went on across a twilight sea of leaves where the forest at last opened out into a rolling plain spotted here and there with tall clumps of trees, vague silhouettes, blots . . .

Parsival listened intently to their conversation. They rode on either side and spoke across him.

"Arthur has called up every vassal and begged and bought those he could not command," Erec was saying.

"He's afraid," Gawain commented.

"He seemed unhappy when I met him," Parsival recalled. "I meant to ask him several questions but things happened so fast . . ." He stared, thoughtfully, into the gathering evening. Gawain glanced at him.

"I never thought to see him show fear," he said to Erec, who twisted uncomfortably in his saddle.

"This gear pinks my ass," he complained, "grease it as I will." He shook his head. "I was riding south a three-month past," he said, grimly, "and I saw their work. I can understand showing fear. I had gone to visit Enid whom I had not seen since—"

"Whose work?" Parsival broke in.

Erec and Gawain looked at him.

"You'll soon discover that, youngblood," Gawain told him, "and we'll find out if you need a winecork in your bunghole when you see the enemy." He grinned in the dimness.

Erec laughed but without much energy.

"I found myself on a road there," he went on, "lined on both sides with spearshafts, thick as a fence. I had just crossed the stone bridge over river Thames." He paused a moment. There was a great rush and twitter overhead as a mass of swallows blew like a dark cloud and settled in a massive, shadowy tree that loomed above them dim, mountainous. "I lie not," he continued, "thick as a fence along both sides of the way and on each spear was the head of a woman, child or beast . . . I was sickened at heart . . ."

They were silent for a time. Then Gawain finally asked: "Did you see the invaders?"

"No," Erec replied. "It was dusk, even as now, and in the fields before me I swore I saw . . ." He broke off.

"Saw?" Gawain pressed.

"I know not what," Erec said, thoughtfully. "Shadows in the distance. . . . Shadows. . . . I changed my direction. The spears and heads went on into the woods beside the river." A long pause. "They say those are not natural men."

Another long pause. Just the sound now of horselegs swooshing the leaves.

"Well," declared Gawain at length, "soon we'll see if they can bleed."

It was virtually night when they passed through a screen of hedge and stopped before a long, low peasant's hut in a grove of trees. When Gawain thumped the door a servile head popped out, nodding bows as if the man had actually been waiting for them. *Unless,* Parsival reflected, *he knows to greet everyone the same.*

Inside, their host and his woman, both sturdy and active, nervously offered water, cheese, bread, dried fruit. . . . The firelit room seemed overwhelmed by the shadow and glint and mass of the three armored men. Parsival noted that Gawain and Erec showed little courtesy to the people. He wondered what his mother would have said to that . . .

"Will my lords honor our house?" the man asked, bowing as his wife lit extra candles on the table, nervously.

Gawain sniffed the air.

"Where are the rest of the pigs?" he asked.

"All in the barn, sir," she said. "An' we have cows as well, and even with the levies it were a middling good year for grain. We have divers substance left us, four solid deal stools for the table, my lords, pewter and good knives if—"

"We'll eat in here then," Gawain announced. "It seems tolerably clean."

"I've had dealing with noblefolk before, my good lords," the man said, jerkily bowing. "I've—"

"Whence came all your wealth?" Erec wondered as the three knights sat down at the table. He smirked, slightly.

"Ah," said the woman, bustling, setting out knives and wooden bowls on the rough, solid wood, "I wouldn't say we were rich, by any means, sirs, but we have fresh meat more than salt! Our lord is a kindly master, and my husband has rights of trade in skins for all of Drahcir and—"

"Who is lord here?" Gawain wanted to know.

"Ah," she said (her husband had gone out). "My lord baron."

"His name, woman."

"Baron Leffacs," she said, setting a pot on the fire now and stirring it.

Erec frowned.

"I thought you killed him?" he asked Gawain.

"His brother," was the reply. He took the two knives from in front of them and set them in the bare center of the table facing his own. "I met Leffacs and some other bastard on the high road from Camelot last year . . ." He deftly slid the single blade between the other two, aiming straight ahead. "They gestured and made a great show of challenge but I kept my head bent forward and my lance in my stirrup looking weary from wounds or grief . . ."

Erec nodded; Parsival looked curious.

"So you didn't fight?" he asked.

"Woman," called Erec, "any beer?"

"No, my lord," she said, whirling around, "but we have wine."

She said it as if to apologize, but no one but perhaps Parsival could have missed her sly gloat.

Erec blinked.

"Wine?" he said. "Bring it then, though it must be swill."

She curtsied and went into the next room.

"When I was right between them," Gawain was saying, "you see? Right here . . ." The single knife lay straight between the other two, "they were gaping, asking, 'What ails you, knight?' trying to decide whether I was worth striking a blow at, I let my lance fall limply from my hand, you see, and fell forward against my beast's neck . . ." Erec was grinning and shaking his head.

"Ah, Gawain," he murmured with admiration.

"So," Gawain continued, "they came close, no doubt moments from cutting my purse, and quick as you please, I drew . . ." He spun the blade between his fingers and the other two tinkled and skidded off the table, ". . . and hit them both fair in the face with one long turn." He grinned. "And now his brother is the baron here."

"You were surely born under the ram," Erec said, nodding slightly. "These are a master's words, young Parsival," he concluded, almost piously. "Right over the horse's head, he had to strike! A difficult technique."

The young man looked unsatisfied but said nothing. The woman came in with a skin of wine which she poured proudly into mismatched wooden cups.

"You handled yourself pretty well today," Gawain offered to Parsival, who still looked thoughtful.

Erec guzzled some wine, winced, wiped his mouth. Belched.

"It's fit for a salad," he remarked, "but it swallows at least."

"It was a gift from my lord," the woman put in. "My husband, Yerm, brought him fifty—"

Yerm came in, head perpetually tilted forward, eyes quick, ever-moving.

"Is everything alright, my lords?" he asked, "Woman, is supper on? Do your lordships want for anything?"

Gawain looked wistfully at him.

"Were you Jesus Christ," he said, "you might not have the power to supply my needs."

The man nodded, screwing his face up into a semi-parody of wisdom.

"I see, Sir Knight," he murmured smoothly. "Ah, the needs of love, sir, I see."

"Is your bed a bug-nest?" Gawain demanded.

"What, sir? Oh no, sir, no. By no means is it such. A fine large bed, why all three of you can comfortably—"

"That's good," Gawain told him, draining his wine cup.

Parsival sipped and made a slight face.

"You freemen," Gawain said, "are an independent lot, are you?"

The man's face became grave as he pursed his lips and shook his head.

"No, no, not at all, my lord. Not at all. Don't pay attention to *her*."

"Your lowborn dog," Erec declared, meditatively twisting his winecup on the table-surface, "though he steals enough to be rich or wins a sort of honor in the field, why he never can have the true grace, for that must be born in a man. . . . There we see God's will made plain."

The peasant nodded readily.

"If I had such things," he affirmed, "what would I do with them?"

"Riches or honor?" wondered Gawain.

The woman was setting steaming bowls around the table.

"Either, my lord," said the man.

"Don't have much gold?" Gawain asked, all innocence.

"Gold?" He shook his head as at a great wonder. "Gold?"

His wife looked uneasy. Her husband's eyes were looking at nothing.

"Why," pondered Parsival, "do men set such store by gold? My mother said it is like filth and that a man who rubs himself with offal stinks of it all day long."

Gawain grinned, tearing a chunk from his crisped chop and chewing with vigor, the food on his tongue muffling his words somewhat:

"Your famous dam," he said, "ever wise. Ever wise."

Erec frowned over his food.

"And foreign fashions are the worst corrupter of men," he announced.

"I know one," Gawain let on, between chews, "that won't soon be adopted here . . ." Belched suddenly. "In the far north islands there live people who count their wealth in beads and common stones . . . that's right. . . . They hoard these like many a miser here keeps quiet gold . . ." He glanced at the peasant who wasn't looking at anything with increased concentration now. ". . . It's truth, by God's wounds, and if one thinks another man has many such hidden away, even if he *have* not, he treats that man like a lord just for thinking he has the stones. . . . Ah, and they steal and kill for such trifles of substance . . ."

He twisted and cracked the bone and fiercely sucked out the marrow, lips squeaking air. He looked innocently at the woman who hovered nearby ready to serve them.

"How are your children?" he asked.

"Children?" she repeated.

Gawain squinted one eye and studied the bone with infinite care.

The two squires leaned into the king, supporting him as he laboriously limped across the shadowy hall; watching him come Parsival felt chilled and inexplicably weak. He tried to move but his limbs seemed locked and then the sad, gaunt, holloweyed king was there looking through infinite pain and despair at him, removing one hand from where it had been pressed down the front of his breeches, which Parsival hadn't noticed until the man actually moved, and extended it: the fingers were stained with what seemed thick, dark blood and then the king's voice seemed to sound though his lips remained tightpressed: *With all your strength why can't you move? Why can't you say something?*

He opened his eyes in the dark room and the figures were gone. His body tingled: rapid tickling vibrations seethed up and down his limbs though he didn't move at all. His bare back rested on the cold earthen floor. He'd kicked the covers away. Then a voice whispered close to his ear and there was a pause before he realized it was Gawain:

"Make no noise, pious Parsival," he said. "An adventure waits for us."

Barefoot, wrapped in a flannel mantle, following Gawain carefully and quietly across the pitchblack room that trembled with each of their host's long snores, he slipped out into the cool night, crossing the hard, cold ground under shocking-clear stars, moving in the narrow space between the dense trees, keeping the other vaguely in sight a few steps on, breathing deeply to clear his head, and then striking a knee-high wattle fence, swaying, hopping and twisting desperately to keep his balance, then, silently, going over and down on his back in soft, reeking mud: something stirred massively beside him and in a brief near panic he struck at it, hitting dense, slimy flesh (he had a fleeting thought about the demonic invaders Erec had talked about on the road), evoking a gurgling grunt, looking around a little wildly, trees overhanging here, the night almost as dark as indoors, seeing the huge shape raise itself and (a blot, a blur) heave, move, then rolling away from it in the muck as it seemed to try to get on top of him, rolling into two more, on his knees now punching, kicking out, scrambling, falling over another body that heaved up and moved with sudden violence and he gripped it and rolled over and over, trying to get a deadly hold on the fat, smooth, slimy creature that grunted and fatly wiggled in his embrace until he finally realized these were the hogs he'd often seen in peasant yards and in a spasm of rage and disgust threw himself free and staggered back over the fence, the beasts falling silent almost immediately and settling back down in the sour, silent darkness . . .

He took off his ruined mantle and tried to wipe himself clean, looking around for Gawain. Nothing. He picked his way along the low fence for what seemed a long time and then headed, naked now and reeking, through the trees thinking to cut back into the cleared area. The stony cold earth was hard going and he limped around trees and bypassed dried thickets. Suddenly a dark shape loomed up, eyes flashed and he tensed, knotted his fist, then practiced whispering some of Gawain's curses when he recognized a cow . . . *Is this an adventure?* he asked himself.

He stepped out from between two trees dead into a wall of rough stone. In the darkness there was no telling how far it ran and it was much too high for climbing. He felt his way along it, slipped, quickstepped and suddenly the earth opened and he walked space, then a terrific shock that he didn't realize was cold for almost as long as it took him to perceive it was water. He pulled himself out, not even shivering yet, groped and found the wall again except the angle had changed and then there was an opening. He realized it was a building and pulled himself through the narrow window and crawled through a mass of warm hay and was nearly dry by the time he got to his feet and stood in the rich tang of dung and sweetish, cloying, ripe musk of cows and acrid note of hens that stirred and clucked briefly. He blinked at bright flame near the floor and moving nearer got another raw smell that he almost recognized, thinking as he saw the movement there, and made out Gawain sitting at his ease, that he had been brought to see a strange, deformed creature, a demon-stunted human with, in the guttering light, disturbingly twisted limbs and convulsive, gasping motions and that penetrating smell as Gawain said:

"So you got here . . . I always check the barn. It pays." And Erec knelt himself up from between the short, full legs and let himself roll aside and sprawl into a litter of hay. In the dim quiverings of flamelight Parsival saw bare, sweat-gleaming skin, a young, round face, lips making a silent O, wriggling her back into a more comfortable space, the smell, as he stood over her, triggering a kind of sagging within him and with a strange weak, fierce desperation, blood feeling thick and rich in his face and throat, he half-fell on the wet, pungent softness, hearing her husky, somehow remote voice saying:

"Have you a whole army out there, knights?"

Parsival sat Niva at the edge of a rolling field where an army was camped. The tall grass was browned, air raw, clouds steely, churning in the bitter gusts.

He looked absently at the thousands of tents and fires. He kept drifting off from Gawain's intent discussion a few feet away in a group of armored knights. He felt nervous, restless . . .

He barely reacted when Gawain turned to him, saying: "You're in luck, Part-of-val. There's work to do."

Parsival nodded, vaguely.

"Is he *ready* for men's work?" asked another knight in

the group. There was a scarred lump instead of a left eye in his head.

"Push him and see," grinned Gawain, slyly.

"This is going to be one misery of a war," Erec complained, shifting uncomfortably in his saddle again. "The invader already holds half the southern lands."

"It will be long," Gawain said, obviously pleased, relishing the statement.

Parsival kept staring off. He kept thinking about the peasant girl. He wondered if they could ride back past there again. There had been a faint glimmering gray wash of dawn at the stone barn door and still he had gone back to her for one more time though she kept struggling vaguely and falling asleep by then, barely stirring under him, soft, loose, breath sourish as he gripped her shoulders and thrashed himself into her, stabbed and wrung, as if he had to use it all up at once, weary but unceasing. Dreams and thoughts kept flashing through his mind but his body went on and on and the girl sighed and stirred faintly. Erec snored in the haypile nearby. Parsival dug his toes in the packed cool clay, knees scraping and banging, jaw a little slack, eyes hurting. . . . At some point he glanced across the dim room where the cows were moaning faintly with milk-strain and starting to stand up, big, shadowy, in the vague glowing. He saw Gawain stooped over, digging a stubby spade into the earth floor, breath coming short. He'd already ripped up half the area. He suddenly gripped his hands into the loosened clay and clawed out a small sack, shaking the dirt off, tearing it open, clinking a handful of metal that Parsival didn't realize must be coins, saying, with delight:

"Ah. . . . The barn, always look for the soft spot, that's where to dig!"

As Parsival knotted up, cried out a little, locked still for a moment with biting pain and needle stabs of pleasure . . .

# lii

As elsewhere Broaditch staggered to his knees with the others in the long, chained line when the leader leaned his demon-faced mask down at them and pointed to the river: he lowered his face toward the stream, chain tugging as others tumbled in with grateful gasps and cries, seeing the bushy, gaunt reflection that for a frightening instant seemed a stranger, then cupping palmfuls over his face. He noticed the bitter taste and brownish, sluggish flow of the stream. . . . As they were being driven back into line on the trail he felt refreshed enough to wonder what kind of a barren country this was with fouled water and knobby, scrubby, burnt-out trees on the low, dark hills. . . . *A fit place to enter as a slave,* he decided and then it hit him, because he'd been holding it away through all his pain, shock and misery, keeping it somehow temporary and now, for an instant, he faced it testingly, and felt like a falling man about to grip air . . . and then the chain jerked the iron collar and he groaned and accepted the now familiar dull chafe of pain and stumbled on in the line, heart still pounding from almost facing what was happening to him, his chapped and bitten lips trembling a little . . .

How many days they were driven on into that harsh and bitter country, he never knew. At the end most of them were staggering and falling. At the end of it he'd accepted death with that free part of his mind, the part that wasn't hurt and numbed into stiffness. . . . And then they'd arrived and were fed, after a fashion, and rested though he still believed he was dead, in the free part. . . . He squatted in grimy torchlight on a sooty field, now chained to a small working party of about a dozen other men. The

torches were set on high poles jabbed into the earth about
every ten yards, stretching on, curving up a hill and out of
sight in both directions. The long, fluttering bands of flame
gleamed on the spears and axes of squat, bushbearded barbarian warriors who stood impassive, menacing watch. The
lights outlined a palisade that ran such a vast curve it
seemed at any point a straight line.

He chewed the hard bread and got it down well enough
except one tooth seemed a little loose. He poked and tried
to wobble it with a forefinger. Inconclusive . . .

The man beside him, actually a shocked-looking boy,
face caked with mud, hair plastered flat, sat holding an
uneaten crust in his palm, slouched forward, sighing with
each shallow breath. Broaditch took note and said:

"Better eat."

Nothing.

"You're going to need what spunk you've got, lad," he
tried.

"Aye," said the man to his left, a thick, shapeless-faced,
middle-aged fellow whose form expressed the kind of
doughy resilience that seems to endure life with neither
sickness nor health. "You'll work here till you pays the
dead fee. I been here workin' some months a' days . . ."

Broaditch painfully twisted around to squint at him:
gray, squat, filthy, shapeless.

"What work?" he asked.

The man laughed, cackled, spat, then worked his lumpy
jaws around.

"You're for it here," he pronounced. "These outlander
scum are the worst goin' . . ." Spat again. Jerked his head
out at the blackened branches and charred stumps that
made an artificial desert as far as was visible in the unsteady light. "Takin' out all the woods."

"Burning it out?" Broaditch asked.

"Hah. That's it. Choppin' and burnin'."

"Why?"

Another man spoke from the shadows, just his bare
knobby legs stretched out into the glow.

"Go ask them then," he commented.

"They don't want no woods close by," said the doughy
one. "The pus-suckers."

Broaditch turned away and peered at the guard: short,
dense, grim-looking in pointed helmet gripping a thick-

hafted spear, fireshadows hollowing out his face, blacking out the eyes as in a skull . . .

He wondered where Alienor and Waleis were now since they'd been separated inside the palisade. . . . At least he knew they were still living. . . . Everywhere he'd seen armed men, serfs and slaves; roads jammed, hills thick with new hovels, tents, people sleeping out in the open, ceaseless work and drill . . . he wondered how long they'd been there . . . wondered if the islands would unite because it was said they had once before in such a time as this. . . . Or was that just hopeless legend too?

He sighed. *And does it matter who holds the whip handle?* he asked himself. *They all love war and we bleed.*

# liii

Gawain and Parsival were riding with the army through the damp countryside. The trees were ragged, wet leaves gone to dull gray and brown, sky solid gray like tin, mists a rising tide among ghostly groups of knights and fighting men, spears upright and clumped, the billows swirling higher and thicker as they moved on and progressively submerged and faded . . .

"So it was no bucket of cold water that time?" Gawain said, cheerfully.

"It was a priest's stick," Parsival said, smiling faintly. He held his helmet in his lap as Niva moved easily along beside Gawain's dark mount. Gawain guffawed, shifting himself around, twisting his body strangely. Parsival looked curious.

"I always get an itch when I'm armored," Gawain explained. Parsival nodded. "So," he said, relishing the tale, "they made you marry her? You fell for that?"

Parsival shrugged.

"She's very nice, I think," he said.

Gawain was shaking his head with a concentration of worldly understanding impossible to describe.

"No doubt," he allowed. "No doubt. . . . God's bones, but you're a rare fellow."

"I thought I'd fucked with the best of them that night," Parsival said, thoughtfully.

"And now you know better," Gawain approved. "You're blessed you met me, lad. They won't be fooling you so well in future."

Parsival looked with perhaps a trace of sadness across the misty field where trees, horses and men floated and faded.

"Yes," he murmured, "but . . . I don't know. . . . It was different then. . . . It seems so long ago . . ." He sighed. "Everything *meant* so much," he tried to explain, "it was so simple and—"

Gawain was grinning, intent on the picture before his mind's eye.

"So," he said, "you never even guessed what your dangler was for?"

"Past a point," Parsival replied, "no."

"You were a wonder of the world," Gawain concluded.

They went on in silence for a time. Every so often Gawain would smile or chuckle as he recalled some fine point of the story . . .

"No doubt," he finally said, "they hoped to bring down a richer dove with that fair hawk. And they got *you*, pretty withal, but off-center to the point of sinking the boat." He shook his head. "How that goat father of hers must have cursed that priest for finding you. He was stuck." He laughed. "By a saint's fart!" he exclaimed, "what a crick in his schemes!"

Parsival smiled but he was looking away where the mists folded and unfolded over the army like Hades' gray surf . . .

"And so he chased you off to get lost or butchered," Gawain reflected, "and will call her a widow in due course."

They could no longer see the rest of the army in the swirling, thickening fog. Only a small, wet circle around them was open. They could hear the muffled noises of men and horses not far away and every few minutes a long, low, wavering blast was sounded on a horn . . .

"Men talk and tell tales," Gawain was saying. "You have to accept it." He unfolded a cloth from a saddlebag and wiped his armor where the fog condensed like cold sweat. "Why, I was drinking in a stew with the whores and some fellow was telling a tale of great feats and astounding achievements so that I was amazed to hear it. Later I learned it was Sir Gawain himself who had done these things." He chuckled. "I was glad to learn of them."

"Yes," Parsival said, looking around at the yellowish, impenetrable mist, "but you'd just kissed the girl in the castle keep." Parsival looked wry. "I suppose the next you knew *you* were married."

"What?" Gawain skinned his teeth, tucking the cloth back in the pouch. "*I* wasn't raised by a mother who saw visions. You don't catch Gawain so easily, even in tales."

Looking somewhat sly, Parsival said:

"This world of yours is just too much for me."

Gawain raised an eyebrow.

"That's a hard case to try," he declared. "Well, I went inside with her and we sat down together, side by side. I shifted my chair closer . . ." He shut his eyes, smiled faintly. "She kept saying no, I kept asking what harm it would do. For the better part of an hour. It was a nice, quiet room there . . ." He guffawed. "She said she thought I'd gone far enough already. I said that was like telling a man who's just mounted his horse that the journey must have tired him out!" They both laughed. He shut his eyes again as if to set his memory. "She didn't even know who I was or where I came from, she said. Complained. That's right. And I thought that in a dark spot with eyes closed in the heat of love did she plan to repeat the names of my parents? A dismal idea . . . I told her I was my aunt's brother's son. Did she need more details than that? I asked her not to let my relatives or their geography keep her from giving a sweet favor to her ardent knight, and so forth . . ." He rode on silent and self-satisfied, for a bit. ". . . Her body, you could see from her breasts, it was so ripe . . . so ripe. . . . We drank some wine, the ladies and the servants left us and in mid-protest I slipped my hand under her mantle, God, so sleek she was! I can't describe it! You'll have to imagine for yourself . . ."

"What's the good of imagining?" said Parsival, deadpan.

Gawain wasn't really listening. He sighed. The gloomy horn sounded and this time it seemed to be more behind them. Parsival frowned, then redirected his horse, Gawain's automatically following.

"I tell you," that knight insisted, "we were a few short breaths away from it! That's all. . . . Did she pull away? Did she leap up?"

"You ask me?"

"But then that fat, pox-riddled, scurvy whore's son whose oily liver I'd like to roast and feed to rats, that portly turd popped his numb head into the chamber and heaved a great, stupid cry of outrage. 'My sister!' he bellowed. . . . Picture this. No stray priest who I would have dropped on his neck, if I'd been you, but the well armed,

inept brother himself barking for the rest of the motley
dogs. . . ."

"There you were," remarked Parsival, cocking his ear
for the next blast of the horn. They seemed to have lost
the sounds of the army somewhere.

"That's truth. There I was. 'You murdered her uncle,' he
yapped, 'and now you ravish the niece!' " He sighed. "I
was set upon by half-a-hundred rabble and second-rate
knights. What a damned mess that was . . . I took an iron
bar, whacked a few loose from their brains, then fled like
a thief . . . lost a good sword . . . I wish I'd slain the lot,
uncles, aunts on to the sixtieth cousin!"

A few voices rose out of the general sound of the army.

"So I says to her, 'Grip it fair or I'll dump yer off the
cart!' "

Laughter and jeers.

"He's a lover, he is," another voice said.

Then a third, "He ought to a' been a priest, then."

Another, "Priest? Arr, a damned bishop, no less!"

He was staring into the limits of the mist, at the shapes
his imagination created in the roils and swellings there: a
winged dragon coiled over the ground, shifted into a magical fortress whose cloudy battlements rose up and up . . .
mysterious beings moved within the changing walls . . .
from a slowly manifesting gate a dark, massive troll or
demon figure half emerged . . . Parsival blinked as a black
armored giant on a huge horse suddenly appeared, blurred,
ominous, shadowy, but not imagined—he was instantly
sure and his skin prickled and his heart raced.

"Gawain," he said. "Look there!"

And then the fog shifted and became totally blank again.

"Where?" Gawain wanted to know.

Parsival was already riding at what he thought was the
spot, lance leveled. Gawain partly followed.

"Something was watching us," Parsival called back,
thinking: *Was that him, at last, was that the Dark One?*

Nothing now. Not even tracks.

"Well?" Gawain shouted. Parsival shook his head.

"It's gone," he replied.

They were still following the horn later. The fog was
just as dense. They heard the muffled rumble of hooves,
feet, voices, whinnies, grunts, clinkings of steel. . . . Twisted

trees would loom slowly up like enchanted shapes and slide past . . .

Parsival was trying to understand what had actually happened to him from the time he met the fisherman on the lake. He was telling Gawain the story of his search for the grail castle. After his wife's father had advised him to seek it and in those days, he said to Gawain, he accepted all advice without concern for motives. So he'd searched and come to the shore of that lake and the man had said to follow the road that always climbed.

"So I thanked him and went on," he said to Gawain. "That was a very strange time for me. I have trouble remembering everything. It seemed very clear then but . . ."

"Did you find anything there?" Gawain prodded, shifting in his saddle.

"Yes. There must have been a hundred crossroads and forkings on the way . . . I can't recall . . . I wasn't worried, I just climbed on and on, watched the sun and the clouds pass over and the moon at night. . . . There were no *ends* of things then, for me, no edges." He shut his eyes briefly, remembering. "I found the castle."

"Did you try your arms there?"

"No. That was an immense place. The moat was more of a river. But they received me well enough, I think."

"I would have challenged first," Gawain interjected. "There's more respect if you lay a few stout boys to rest among the grasses." He smiled. "What did they call the place?"

"The castle of the grail," he replied, quietly.

Gawain blinked, tilted his head to one side. "Ah," he said after a moment, "and fairies flew you up over the walls."

"No," said the young knight, "though that might not have surprised me."

"Castle Mundsalvache? Do you still think so?"

Parsival nodded.

"What they call the grail," he said, "they brought it out to show me."

Gawain frowned, his crinkly-eyed, humorous face reflecting a succession of uncertainties.

"Nonsense," he finally said. He studied his companion's serious profile, bobbing slightly as the horses made their muffled way across the misty, soaked downs. He felt a prickling of gooseflesh on his nape. As he didn't know what to think he repeated himself.

"It's nonsense. They tricked you. They saw you were, well, a little simple." When the other failed to respond Gawain pressed: "What did you think you saw there?"

"The men wore white," the red knight said, voice distant with remembering, unconcerned or unconscious of his friend's skepticism. "The women were lovely. Like my mother. Very pale, very fragile . . . like a breath. . . . The king—"

"Anfortas?"

"—Yes, he was there. They told me he was sick. He looked ill enough. His hair was white and his face seemed to have no blood in it."

Gawain couldn't get over all this.

"You were really there, you met the wounded king?"

"Would I lie?" Parsival mildly wondered.

Gawain leaned out from his mount closer to his companion.

"But tell me, damn it," he insisted, "is the grail *real?* What did you see there?"

"When I came into the hall they gave me the queen's cloak to put on. It was very beautiful. Deep blue silk. With a white cross." He smiled and rubbed his chin with his bare hand—his gauntlets were tucked under his belt. "When I mentioned that the fisherman had sent me they seemed a little disturbed. I never found out why . . . but you must know, many things that night made little sense."

"Am I to wonder at that?" Gawain wanted to know. "But go on, Parsival, for Jesus' sake." He knew he still didn't believe it. Not that he disbelieved; he simply didn't believe it.

"They were all sad folk, Gawain. But they were kind to me. And I nearly struck a man there. They were leading me into the great hall which was lit by more candles than you could picture, they were thick as the stars on a clear night . . . I swear it was bright as day. . . . So this man snarled at me: 'Go in there, doltish colt!' he said and I'd learned enough of life by then to clench my fist before the others explained that he was so happy I'd come he couldn't control himself, which made about equal sense then as now."

"So . . . so," murmured Gawain, "but?"

"But I have to tell you, there were four fireplaces heaped

with logs and spices and that room was like a sweet forge. Yes. And the king lay wrapped in fur and blankets, shivering, not sweating a drop. . . . They said it was his cold sickness but I said nothing, not wishing to put my big foot in it again as I seemed always to be doing . . . I'd made up my mind not to go blurting out things anymore. I was tired of 'you fool' this and that. . . . And then a page came into the hall holding up a rusty old spear smeared with fresh blood. And you must hear that blood dripped down as from a living wound. I know because I'd seen a few by that time . . ."

"The spear!" murmured Gawain, crossing himself.

"You know about it?"

Gawain seemed very, very thoughtful, suddenly. He nodded.

"The spear of Longinus," he said, looking at the ground past his horse's neck as if his eyes actually were focused on something. *How can I believe this?* he asked himself except that he did now and knew it. "You saw this," statement, not question.

Parsival shrugged.

"Yes," he said.

"Well, I've seen a little magic in my time."

"The page went around the room holding it up. I saw the blood stain his sleeve. Everyone there began to weep and then they brought out food." Parsival was still disturbed by that. Gawain smiled, wryly.

"Hardly the right sauce for the meat," he agreed.

"It was passing strange, Gawain," said the red knight.

Twenty years later there was a big, sturdy, steelgray-haired man slouched in a wickerwoven chair, his legs stretched out, telling the story to three children (two boys and a girl) who sat in the dusty yard beside the stone house in mellow evening summer sunlight. His big, rough, wrinkled hands held a long, carved, unlit pipe. He was looking at one of the boys. They both had dark, shaggy hair. Their sister's was coppertinted.

"Well, father," he asked, "but what was the grail like?"

The weathered face tilted back in reverie.

"Who can say, lad? Only one who's seen it, I ween. It was the perfect wonder of light and truth, they say, beyond human speech, and in its glory sat Sir Parsival . . ."

"And he didn't understand," the girl put in.

"He was still simple," the other boy said.

"No," said the father, "but unripe . . ." He stared up at the seamless, greenishblue sky. "They say the grail is the spot where heaven forces its way into earth, where God breathes life into all the world. . . . It is too beautiful to be false, children. . . . If he hoped for food he found it on his plate, if he wished a wine it filled his cup." He smiled, looking at them, their serious eyes. "You'd like that, wouldn't you?"

The air was warm and still, sweet with the scent of universal ripeness.

"And yet, they say, Sir Parsival understood little of this and so he ate and drank and grew sleepy . . ."

"And he never asked the king the question," the little girl anticipated, innocently self-righteous.

"True, my Tikla," her father acknowledged. "He sat in silence through it all . . ."

The fog had thinned somewhat for the moment.

"But did you *see* the grail?" Gawain wanted to know. "With your own eyes?"

Parsival was watching the marching men, moving in slow coils into and out of the drifting mists: one moment seeming vague, shadowy phantoms, then suddenly, as the fog would thin, becoming solid, crunching along with grunts and mutters, shifting the weight of their weapons.

"I don't know," he finally replied.

Gawain was aghast, furious. He stared at Parsival as if his eyes could pierce his skull and let the secret out into view.

"You *what?*" he more or less shouted.

"There was never such wine as I tasted there and I was too worried to pay close attention . . . I think I fell asleep . . ." He sighed and nodded. "Many times, I think. . . . It seemed my goblet was always brimming. . . . Ah, but it was hard to tell which was the dreaming and which the waking there!"

The crackling, spurting fires all around; the rich hangings; musk-scented air; myriad candles blazing; a young page kneeling, holding out a blue velvet cushion on which richly gleamed two silver knives, keen blades without handles and he thought: *how can these be held?* And there was music, tinkling and reedy, in the background and then

music in his mind and it was now hard to distinguish
them; the sweet musks caught in his nostrils and chest,
the room getting so close and warm like (he vaguely
thought) being wrapped in a huge, stifling fur . . . the
bright candles blurred and seemed to shift, dance and at
one point he felt a strange chill shame looking across the
room at the Grail King who half-reclined on a soft mound
of blankets and pelts, shadowed eyes shut, pale, feeble head
lolling on a blue silk pillow . . . and then the air, walls,
people, everything seemed to waver, shake like wind in a
dream and there was a deep, rushing, roaring sound like
(he dimly thought) thousands of rivers flowing and the
crowded room seemed far away and he had the impression
that the king was suddenly standing before him, face tender
but in deep, unending pain, hopeful too and beseeching
. . . then despairing, agonized, silent, eyes bleeding tears
. . . then the golden brightness flickered and again there
were only candles and the crowded, noisy, stuffy room . . .
he must have been asleep . . . as the party went on he
thought he noticed (but was in no shape to be certain)
hostile looks aimed his way and about when he'd decided
to ask about this he heard himself snoring which seemed
to wake him up and then he lost waking and was being
carried (he felt he floated) down endless vaulted corridors
and then (he believed) he was set adrift on a vast, white,
billowy bed where dream after dream washed over him
and he felt serene, cozy, safe in a soft ecstasy of comfort
and peace not even aware of the maids and pages undress-
ing him, covering him though he did recall (and told
Gawain) giggling, feeling a deep, gentle, sweet stirring and
heard his own voice cheerfully announcing:

"Alright, bring out the tub . . . scrub me, for God's sake
. . . I'll marry whichever one first touches my dangler . . ."

As best his gear permitted Gawain was bent forward in
the saddle resting weakly against the horse's neck, shaking
with deep, rapid convulsions. When he could speak, he
said:

"Jesus of the bloody feet, what courtly grace!" He went
on laughing for a time. Then said: "Parsival, you are past
price and reckoning!"

The red knight sat there, rocking with the charger, staring at where the tide of mist now rose over the marching
men again.

"And past redeeming," he murmured.

Gawain peered at him, a trifle suspicious.

"So you really never *saw* the grail then?"

Parsival sighed, staring.

"I don't know what I saw," he said.

He parted his eyes and the light stabbed his brain so he clenched them shut again and just lay there on the lumpy bed, breath coming short and shallow as a dying man's. The covers were knotted and sweaty. It took him a few minutes to understand that the moist, sour smell rose from his own open mouth; once he did, he shut it stickily.

He groaned softly, shifted his limbs and tried his sight again, squinted against the hard, white daylight that slashed in the windows. His stomach rocked uncertainly when he forced himself to sit up and look around the large, bare stone chamber. He heard no sounds in any direction.

He wobbled getting out of bed and went and looked out the window. As he leaned forward his head cracked on almost invisible, fine glass and he put his palms over his eyes and groaned thinking he'd been struck by an enchanted mace. After a while he looked out again, discovered the glass, touched it, marveled briefly, then studied the autumn-streaked forest, leaves cresting over the rough slopes under a pale, clear sky. He watched a hawk sail slowly past, veering with an almost sinister ease, then riding a roll of wind around and out of sight . . .

Dressed, he wandered through the dim, long halls calling out every so often and getting no answer but an echo. He finally found his way to the main chamber, now empty, tables clean and bare, all the candles melted down to gushes and dribbles of wax.

He found his armor there and two swords: a new one, a gift. He drew it and was impressed by its sheer mirror gleam. Then he dressed himself and went outside where he discovered his saddled horse waiting, spear leaning against the flanks. The turf in the castle yard was chewed up and the thick trail of hooves led straight out through the open gate. There was still no one in sight. He shouted several times. Mounted Niva and rode out onto the drawbridge and shouted again and again. . . . Nothing . . .

Just as he reached the far side the gate slammed shut behind him and he jerked around.

"Who's there?" he cried. "Show yourself! Who's there?"

Silence. He heard a long drawnout bird call deep in the crisp, redbrown forest. No human sound. Then the bird again . . .

"And so," their father was saying to the children in the little arbor, as the sunbeams slanted lower and shadows grew away from everything, "Sir Parsival followed the plain trail of the riders before him. As he went on through the twisting paths in that deep, still wood, the tracks he followed became fainter and fainter as horsemen broke off to follow different ways . . ." The three children sat still and grave, bigeyed. ". . . And finally there was but one set and then that faded out too . . ."

"And he was all alone there," the younger, a slim, dark-eyed boy, said.

"Aye, Erik," responded his father, nodding. "Alone in a great forest he'd never seen before."

"He didn't understand the grail," the girl said softly. The boy nodded.

"True," said his father, "and it passed him by. He was beginning to know, he who wore armor as though it were fluffy cloth, he was learning how heavy is the gear all men have to wear. The weight of growing up. The kinks and the pain and the sweat, my doves. . . . Aye. . . . By the time he thought to close his hand, there was naught but air in it . . ."

The fog had closed down again. They had aimed themselves at the last hornblast, having discovered they'd drifted away out on the flanks of the again invisible army. But when the next deep-throated toot sounded it came from the totally opposite direction and was suddenly growing faint. Parsival was startled.

"Something's wrong," he said.

Both peered into the blank mists. Gawain was alert.

"We can't lose a whole host," he remarked, frowning.

With less than twenty feet visible in any direction, they rode as quickly as they dared for the last sound. When it came again it was even fainter and far to the left and they knew this was going to be serious. Neither spoke as they changed direction and went dangerously close to a gallop, twisting past trees and deep ruts that would suddenly appear as if lunging at them with personal vindictiveness. As it was they both nearly rode over the edge of a ravine full of fog. The sound of rushing water came up from far below. They stopped and just looked at one another. The horn was heard again, this time moving away across the gap under their feet.

"Sorcery," muttered Gawain, looking pale. Parsival seemed nonplussed.

"This is fairly strange," he said, at length, his old, expectantly curious self coming to the fore.

They rode with extreme caution now. The wall of fog was so close if they thrust their arms out in any direction the hands all but disappeared.

"What can you hear?" Gawain wondered, twisting around in the saddle.

"Nothing."

Gawain stopped his horse. Parsival drifted on a little further and by the time he looked back it was too late.

"Gawain!" he called.

Nothing. Then a muffled sound that might have been a shout.

"Gawain?" he called again, aiming Niva at where the voice apparently came from. His own cries echoed strangely, he thought. No answer. He wiped the condensed wet from his eyes and stared fruitlessly into the wall of mist. Then he heard the sound again, straight ahead, as if leading him on. Straight from where, however, was a mystery: no idea of direction existed for him at this point. For all he knew his mount's next step might be into the abyss which he believed was behind them. At least, he thought, he couldn't hear the sound of the rushing waters . . . He followed what seemed a lightening of the fog: there were shadowy forms, dark, damp, twisted hemlocks streaming wet smoke, a limbless trunk seemed to move and he almost cried out and moved to attack the expected shadowy giant before realizing a cowled man had stepped into his path, shaking his head as if in deep disgust. Then threw back his hood. Parsival recognized him: the gray-bearded bald man who'd been seated beside King Arthur the day he'd arrived to demand knighthood. Who'd sent him down the twisting road from Camelot. The idea of the time that had passed, for some reason, shocked him, though it was not even a year.

"What do you want with me?" he asked and realized it came out a little harsh, impatient.

The man tilted his head as if to study him better. His rich resonant voice seemed to echo in the very earth itself:

"You are just about a complete warrior now, Sir Parsival."

The young man frowned.

"Is this a wrong thing, old man?"

Merlinus sighed.

"Wrong for you," he said, "for it fails to content you."

Parsival considered.

"That's partly true," he allowed.

"What are you going to do, Parsival?"

"Do? What do you mean?" A pause. "Find Gawain and the army." He looked around. "When this damn fog lifts."

He heard the gray man sigh.

"I wonder if the fog will ever lift, Parsival, king."

"King?"

"Your mother died, infant. You almost have to grow up now, don't you?"

"My mother?" He frowned and thought. "But is this really so?" He touched his sword hilt. "Don't taunt me, old fucker!"

The graysteel eyebrows went up. The thin lips smiled faintly.

"You've mastered new conversation, boy," said the man. "She died not long after you left." The astoundingly deep voice was rounded off with tenderness suddenly. There was a considerable pause. The moor was still, the fog billowed, unfolded . . .

Parsival was staring not at Merlinus or the soft, turbulent blankness. His hand unconsciously relented on the hilt.

"Where is the grail these days?" Merlinus asked, after a time, smiling faintly.

The young man didn't respond. He slumped a little in the saddle. Stared. Then shut his eyes.

"You found me here," the rich voice was saying as if the earth formed words, "I didn't lead you. And now you're wasting the moment. Do you imagine you have a thousand years to learn in?"

Parsival kept his eyes shut. He idly wondered why even when it was dark out, there were always spots and streaks of light behind the lids. He decided the light was somehow *in* the eyes itself and then wondered where it came from . . .

"You are blessed," said the voice into his distracting private darkness, "that I have no patience at all for had I any it would long since have worn out with you."

*Mother's dead,* he thought. And when he opened his eyes a few moments later with a question to ask the bearded old man he was alone and for some reason this frightened him, the nerves in his belly pounded once or twice and he felt dizzy for a moment, shook his head as if to wake himself.

"Where are you?" he cried, craning around.

"Here," said a voice behind him and he turned in the saddle just as Gawain emerged from the mist which was thinning, curling closer to the ground.

Parsival kept looking around. He realized that a year ago he would have just taken this in stride too, unsurprised because a year ago nothing was ever strange . . .

At dawn the air was cool and clear. They worked their way around the ravine and crossed the unmistakable wake and litter of the army up ahead.

"Well," Gawain said, pleased and relieved, "we'll catch up soon enough. You'll taste life and death then and stop worrying about old men in the fog."

Parsival was depressed and confused. Was his mother really dead? Why was he going to this battle? He was tired of questions. He hated questions, all of a sudden.

"Look," he said, pointing up the stony slope that tilted before them.

They sat their horses and watched ten mounted knights approach at a fast canter. The pale sun was just rising behind the netted gray branches on the hillside. The grasses were yellowing on the fields, Parsival noticed, as he asked:

"Should we prepare to fight?"

"We ride straight at the center of their line," the expert veteran advised, "then break on my signal for the opposite ends and take out the last man on each side. That way they can't concentrate against us and have their numbers tell." He banged his steel fist against the younger man's helmet. "Take that from your lap and clap it over your head where it belongs. It's time. After we take out the first two we circle back and repeat until they learn to come singly to their doom and disgrace." He grinned through open visor, eyes quick and excited.

"Wait," Parsival said.

The line had stopped short and a stocky knight in white and red mail opened his helm and shouted:

"Are you friends to King Arthur of the Britons?"

"And if we were not, oaf," Gawain muttered, "we might say 'yes' and cut your throat some other day." He shook his head with a feeling of letdown. "That's Lancelot himself," he told Parsival. "What he has for brains makes the flowers grow. But it's as well to pass him in peace if you can."

"What? Water?"

"Hmm?"

"Makes the flowers grow?"

"He's in reverse. He squats down to think and wipes his head when he's done." He called out: "Greetings, Lancelot!"

"Who's that?" came back the question. Gawain and Parsival were riding steadily closer and the others held their lances ready.

"The Angel Michael and his son," Gawain claimed.

"What's that?" Lancelot demanded. Parsival could see his furious red face and golden mustaches. "Angels never marry."

"He's a bastard then," Gawain retorted. There were guffaws among the other knights.

"You seem mortal to my eye," Lancelot insisted, not entirely certain, however. He was squinting and frowning. "I know you," he said, ponderously. "Gawain."

"You're quick as ever," that lord returned. "Where are you bound?"

"A raid. There's a petty baron near here who's gone over to the devils. We'll see that they get him to keep."

"Why would he?" Gawain wondered.

Lancelot shrugged.

"None can say," he declared. "What matters that? Join us if you will."

"Gladly. How was his treachery revealed?"

Lancelot shrugged again.

"Someone said so," he answered.

"That's solid proof enough," Gawain said, with sarcasm totally lost on the other. "Where's the main force now?"

"Camped ahead," another knight put in.

"We'll catch up by morning," Lancelot said, spurring his bulky horse forward.

"Come, Parse," Gawain said. "What is it you always say? Ah, you'll learn a new thing today, I promise you!"

# liv

Parsival didn't steer his mount, drifting across the withered fields, narrow strips and sections marked off by poles flagged with rags. Visor up he watched Gawain and the others drive a shattering charge through the little knot of armed peasants, breaking spears, splitting skulls: one sturdy man ran a dozen or so steps headless, blood fountaining; two others screamed as the massive armored chargers danced on their bodies . . . then the group broke and fled, the knights wheeling around to make following charges and to turn their flanks in and close them in a loose bag. A few broke through and sprinted in panic for the nearest woods.

A teen-age boy, tall, lighthaired, holding a scythe, came toward Parsival, who'd drifted between him and a spur of trees he had some hope of reaching before the horsemen behind ran over him. Parsival watched him as if from far away, seeing his bright blue eyes, strongboned, not-coarse face, saw steel flash as he desperately hooked the tool at Niva's eyehole in the gleaming red chain mail hood, and as the horsehead jerked slightly and the dented blade chinked dully on mesh steel Parsival felt all confusion dissolve in him. A moment before he'd wanted to hide, to blot out the horror he was watching and at the same time telling himself mechanically that it was part of knighthood and what he had to do. He'd been in conflict with the thread of his quest depressingly lost, become a smoothness with no edge to grip and, wanting to run, a void had opened before him now because he'd never had to plan anything, had followed, flowed with what he encountered and to turn away offered a vast and terrifying blankness. *That old man*, he thought, *had done this, somehow. . . .*

176

Then the boy's blow released him, concentrated him in a focus of fury that swept conflicting thoughts aside as if that blond hair and blue-eyed face were the Gordian knot of the questions and confusions that had been twisting tighter day by day. He didn't want to think so that even as his sword flicked up—and he knew there was no stopping it as if its power passed through not from him—even then his mind cried *No!* and he struck in a kind of frenzy, desperately plunging over his head into irrevocability, wanting to be past all this, wanting peace and freedom, breath, not hearing his own booming shout:

"Leave me alone!!"

As the blade zipped through its arc and was motionless at the horse's flank before a brightred, threadlike line opened diagonally across the surprised face, seeming to crease the parted lips. The boy raised one hand vaguely toward his face, then, still holding the bent scythe, face split at the bloody seam as if two expressions were badly fused, he took an absent step and fell flat, legs kicking up a little from the impact ...

Teeth clenched, eyes slitted, raging but strangely, darkly elated as if he'd somehow proved something and freed himself, Parsival sent Niva crashing after a knot of men and women who were scrambling over a log bridge that crossed a deep, narrow stream with three other knights in close pursuit. He galloped beyond his doubts now, thinking over and over how the sword made things simple, how one stroke freed him from intolerable pressure, how all the intrusion and perverseness of another creature was simply swept away and left neatly. . . . Other people were always pushing, always wanting something, always poking into his life, aiming him this way and that, weeping and plotting and upsetting the flow . . . why wouldn't they leave him alone? . . . now they'd see, now they'd regret!

And he united with the gleaming, massive armored shock of the others, pounding down on the frail, fleeing prey as if to wipe out their confusion of screams and curses.

He reined up just in advance of the others as the log was still falling, splashing down, the last peasant, in a frenzy of terror, scrambling on hands and knees into the screen of brush on the other side. He snarled, furious, thwarted. The other horsemen were already wheeling back across the dark, bare fields. Stinging black smoke from the burning huts drifted low and dense, covering the scene. . . . He galloped now, in and out of the smokedrifts, eyes tearing, looking for someone left alive to kill. Nothing but bodies: men, women, youths, children. . . . Then, slowing, wiping his hand in the air as if to clear it, he spotted moving forms, bare flesh.

The smoke thickened as he aimed for where he'd just seen the figures. When he broke into clearer air he violently checked Niva and stared, blank for a long moment before he could assimilate what he was seeing: an armored man held each ankle wide, a third knight, naked except he wore his closed helmet, sat above her head, gripping the wrists, squarish, hairy feet digging hard into the woman's shoulders while the fourth man, nude below the waist, mail shirt flopping loose, pressed himself between the long, sinewy legs. *Why are they holding her?* he wondered. He stared for a moment at a strawberry mark on the sole of one of her feet. There was a bleeding slash across one shin.

The horse ambled closer and, still trying to take it in, he saw the breasts flattened against the steel chest, her bruised, straining ribcage. He froze. There was a rush of heat to his face and groin, heartbeat stuttered with excitement suddenly and he dismounted, feeling giddy, sword forgotten at his side, moving closer, entranced, barely noticing one of the men on the legs grinning up at him.

*Will they let me next I don't want to wait,* his mind said.

The woman's bruised, scratched face turned to him: she wasn't young and somehow that stunned him. He blinked. Her eyes didn't beseech, showed no pain that he could read, were not even dull and, worse, weren't even seeing him. Her face was strong, chapped, crinkled at the eyes. His mind registered everything with strange clarity, and her look made him feel she was enduring all this the way someone puts up with a sickness, even to death, accepting a fact neither outrageous nor desirable. He grasped somehow that she was living her life, even at this moment, that life was not just when you were comfortable or following hope or fleeing despair, both of which wedged you away from the reality of the living moment . . .

He suddenly noticed that his energy had drained away. He felt boneless. And sick to his stomach.

"You can have her next," the naked man above her said in the hollow of his helmet.

He wanted to do something. Didn't know what. Stood there, blinking, uncertain. . . . A billow of smoke broke over them and flowed away. . . . Didn't know what. He was sure he should do something about it but there was such a limpness in him that he only sighed and turned away, leaned against his horse.

He was shaky. One of the men said something and laughed but he didn't hear or care. The raw air came in through his open visor. He took off one gauntlet and touched his eyes. He didn't quite understand why, but he was weeping. He sighed and gripped Niva's mane.

# lv

Alienor strained to keep her footing in the slick mud, the
swaying weight of the massive kettle, hung from the
wooden bar that rested on their shoulders, wobbled her
continually as she and the other woman struggled across
the tumult and confusion of the fortress yard in the chilly,
misty morning: soldiers everywhere, knights galloping in
and out of the gates scattering servants, slaves, men-at-
arms; archers drilling, a sudden gust of arrows audible
every so often; spearmen working out; a constant clank
and shout and bray and neigh . . .

"Easy, dear," said the woman, stout and strong, face reddened and leathery, eyes crinkled to knots, old, hard grime
permanently creased into her flesh, hands splayed and
stone-smooth where they gripped the pole. "You'll pick up
the way of it."

The steamy smell of a fresh cooked meal did nothing
for Alienor. She decided she was beyond appetite at this
point.

"Oh, there's great doin's here," the woman confided,
managing to express both awe and a kind of unsophis-
ticated cynicism. "All manner a' doin's day and night . . .
grandlookin' knights . . ."

They stopped short as a pair of riders splattered past.

"Curse you," the woman muttered at the horses' hinds.

Long tables stood in rows in the barracks area where
female teams were ladling out porridge from other kettles
as the men were slamming onto the benches, cursing,
jostling, fighting over hunks of bread, swilling down morning ale . . .

In the middle of all this several armored knights came

riding through the area clashing swords on shields with a
sound like a forge, shouting:

"The lord comes, the lord comes!"

And Alienor murmured to the woman:

"Do you mean God himself?"

"Mind!" hissed the woman just over the din as the men
unhesitatingly leaped from their places, halfeaten food hot
before them and Alienor reflected that it must be the good
God indeed to rouse them from breaking fast with such a
will and when she was about to speak again the woman
gripped her arm and shook her quiet. The yard was suddenly silent and a thousand or so people were standing
still and watching the great gate.

The rows of black and silver knights with demonfaced
visors came barreling through into the courtyard.

The press of the crowd behind urged them forward so
that Alienor had to struggle to keep clear of the stream of
mighty black horses and massive riders and through the
confusion she caught glimpses of a swarm of personages,
enclosed by the troops, in furs and jewels and glittering,
studded armor and they in turn enclosed a single rider
aloof on a gray horse wearing an unmarked gray cloak,
hood down, head bent, hair and long mustache coalblack
against a startlingly pale, bony brooding face and she
thought *He must be a prisoner poor sad man* . . . and she
worked her way back through the crowd to where the
woman and the kettle were and by that time at the far
end of the large enclosure the glittering leaders were arranging themselves on the high steps that led into the massive castle keep. They all stood under the great door that
gaped like a mouth. She stood on her toes to see: the man
in the dull gray tunic with the deadwhite face was in the
center and she was wondering what they meant to do to
him when she heard the voice. She squinted, trying to see
where it was coming from; the sun was rising just to the
left of the building so it was very hard to be sure, even
with shielded eyes, so she actually listened for an appre-
ciable time to those tones that seemed to effortlessly, con-
versationally fill the vast open space before realizing that
the gray man was speaking and it was longer before she
even bothered with the words themselves, just the sound
thrilling her as if, she later thought, the earth itself
trembled in support of the strangely accented speech. . . .
She blinked when the man suddenly, in a terrific knotting

of violence, raised his fist and shouted so that the crowd sighed and swayed and Alienor stepped back, unconsciously, as if to free herself from a kind of soft, sucking ooze:

". . . and now, as one . . . as one . . . as one single mace, as one single blade we rise and fall upon their skulls!"

And then the swaying roar of the crowd blasted the air: swords clashed, spears were shaken, and Alienor stepped back from what seemed the bestial howl of a single monstrous animal and her flesh crawled as she resisted the merging force, a thing that drew and drew at her as if physically and then the speaker was gone (*almost like magic,* she thought) as if he refused to witness the effects (or didn't have to) of his invocation and now, she thought, the warriors seemed like daftmen, howling and cheering in mad groups, knocking one another aside, some fighting, mock-dueling, some rolling on the earth in a frenzy, kicking it, punching it . . .

She looked at the woman who was calmly arranging the empty kettle. Alienor took her end and they worked their way back to the kitchens, moving wide around the hysteria. Even the knights themselves were cavorting on their horses, cutting in and out, riding short, half-jousts. She fought not to run when the barbarians in their furs and ironsewn leathers formed a great circle and began to dance and chant in an ecstatic, guttural awe and anger . . .

It was quieter in the kitchen area. The cooks were bustling as if nothing surprising were going on. As they set down the kettle the woman confided in Alienor:

"It's always like this here." She turned to the nearest cook who was slitting the belly of a suckling pig, unknotting and freeing the guts, tossing them into a yellowish purple heap beside his board that was half a man high. "Ain't it, Turken?"

"Aye," he replied, nodding emphatically. "It's that true. She's all nasty little men here."

Alienor leaned on a rude stool to steady herself. She wiped her matted, greasy hair from her eyes and thought how good a bath would be as she asked:

"Who was the one, the voice?"

"Him?" asked Turken the cook in his turn. "Ah, that's himself."

The woman nodded with grim sagacity and knelt to begin to grease the huge pot.

"That's him," she pronounced.

Turken the cook chuckled.

"Why, we've heard him said of even on the bitter islands at home," he reflected.

"An' who hasn't else?" interjected the woman. "Him a wizard. . . . But no great arts can grow back all that was uprooted . . ." She chortled with wise satisfaction. "No. . . . When some jewels is stolen, my dear, it's no good chasin' the robber, eh?"

Turken was delighted, grinning as he flopped another pig down and slipped the blade effortlessly along the underbelly with a sucking squish and tearing.

"Takes but one proper· cut," he gibed, brandishing his bloody knife at Alienor, who wasn't following all this.

"Maybe," offered the woman, "his magic's what's kept his voice from running high."

The merriment this provoked spread the whole length of the kitchen, which was wooden, wall-less, just a low roof supported by thick posts. But, Alienor noticed, every remark was prefaced by a careful glance over one's shoulder.

"So that was Clinschor?" she asked.

"Who?" squeaked Turken in a falsetto that caused snorts and convulsions in the whole area.

The woman squinted up at Alienor.

"Lend a hand here," she said, "Lady-too-good, if you please."

Alienor sank wearily down beside her.

"Would they let me look for someone here?" she wanted to know.

"What? An' who then?"

"A man."

"Husband?"

Alienor hesitated, then nodded.

"Took you both," observed the woman, "did they?"

Alienor nodded.

"They'll have him on the works," said Turken, sympathetically.

"I had two husbands," reminisced the woman, pausing in her work for a moment.

"Did you now?" remarked the cook.

"You know it well, Turken, both good rogues. . . . But you do best to marry an older chappie," she proposed to

Alienor. "When you're outta his sight why he don't think about you which myself says is bad for lovers but good for them wed." She nodded agreement with herself.

"Will they let me look for him?" Alienor insisted, suddenly discovering she was a little hysterical, that she hadn't even wanted to face (or dared) until this moment the actual absence of Broaditch. It had just been a numbness until now.

The woman and the cook looked silently at her for a moment. The woman sighed and then said, not quite harshly:

"Put off your foolishness, dearie, and lend a good hand here."

# lvi

Broaditch leaned against the hut's outside wall, legs lolling straight out before him in the black, half-dry mud. His eyes were red and bleary. He felt bonechilled. Raw wind drew steadily across the sagging collection of low, dark, shacklike buildings where dozens of other morose-looking men sat in their chains, some, like himself, staring at the endless file of troops moving past on a road already churned to a dark, rolling smear so that he thought the men waded along rather than walked . . .

He was in the same hungry, tired state that he woke and fell asleep in day after day after day, dulled and cold, when a few of the older and lightly disabled guards who were being left behind to handle the serfs got them all into line and marched them off to resume the day's digging down into what Broaditch called the pit to hell: a hole, just a vast hole, hundreds of feet deep already, that narrowed to a forty-five-degree tilted tunnel, going down with a purposeless straightness. Thousands of men were driven in to dig it every day. Nothing was ever brought out but dirt and rock.

They were moving dully along an ashy track through the leveled, burned-out forest. The wind blew gritty powder over them, stung their eyes and every face was black as if they mined coal.

He hardly glanced up at the line of gibbeted men and women except the last one wore such fine garments that for a moment he wondered if they'd actually hanged a lord . . . and then, as the wind twisted the corpse, the stiffened limbs pirouetting, the bent head of the minstrel went profile to him as if nuzzling the noose and his heart caught for a moment with recognition and he thought:

185

*why is it always more when you know some fellow, however slightly?* . . . and then he saw Waleis chained with a work party and under guard, standing near the gibbet-poles, eyes bulging and hopeless, seeing nothing and Broaditch called out:

"Waleis! Here!"

And the other looked up, blinking, turning his head to follow as Broaditch marched past as slowly as possible. His eyes were wild, outraged, in pain and he cried out harshly, a little madly:

"They make me hang them up!"

"Have you seen Alienor?" Broaditch demanded as Waleis just stared at him. "Have you, damn it!"

"They make me," he said, petulant, almost.

The line was backing up against him and he was forced to take a few more steps, now craning to look back at Waleis who was standing, lower lip pouting just about under the minstrel who was now rocking with the breeze, mouth open, teeth showing, tongue thrust out violently as if in infantile mockery and disgust. For a flash Broaditch remembered the Gawain story, thinking *it wasn't true anyway*, realizing he'd never hear the end of it, at least not that particular way in that particular voice and manner and wondered why he thought this as he called back, the sound surprising him with its vehemence and fear:

"Tell her you saw me living! Tell her that!"

# lvii

Alienor set down the tray with the earthen wine jug on the single white marble table and stared around at the vaulted, long narrow chamber designed to mimic a chapel. The table was where the altar would be. She'd been told to come straight back to the kitchens but couldn't resist looking around.

It was very still in there; indirect, gray light glowed in narrow windows. She walked around to study what was collected in the workspace: parchments of what she knew was Latin because it looked like what priests read. While staring at a map of what she assumed was Britain, there was a clinking of scabbards and mail in the hallway and she jerked back and in an unnecessary and unreasoning panic ducked behind some floor-length tapestries depicting what seemed a knight in horned helm riding what looked like a winged snake.

She crouched on her knees, pressing close to the cool stones. A thin ripple of light traced down where the hanging touched the wall. The dusty fabric smell caught in her nose, her eyes watered and she nearly sneezed.

Then two men were talking. She heard a chair creak as one sat, close to where she knelt.

"The genie of the lamp," one was saying, "wants to check his prophecy."

"Hush," cautioned the other voice. "The Devil tells him tales."

"Tells tales to himself, you mean," said the first.

"Have a care, Cydner."

After silence, the first voice, Cydner, spoke again:

"I'd like to know what he does with her."

The other grunted. Said:

"Ah. The master has pondered well all the arts of the East."

"Watery shit," the first declared. "There's no magic will grow *them* again."

His comrade sniggered, hesitant, nervous.

"Hush, hush," he murmured.

"What, will the mutes tell him?"

"Anyone can don black armor and all men might be mutes till they speak. And some were better mute that have their tongues."

"He comes," said Cydner, without particular emphasis and the chair instantly creaked and she pictured the second man springing upright as a pair of feet padded quietly over the paving blocks from the direction of the doorarch.

"Master," greeted the second voice.

"My lord," said Cydner.

Silence from the new party. The footsteps had stopped somewhere near the massive table in front. The silence dragged on and she was sure her presence was sensed. She had an urge to crawl out and beg mercy. *Why was she hiding there? It was mad, how did it happen? What possessed her? . . .* So her mind paused before actually registering Cydner's voice:

". . . and it may be a near thing, my lord. Your significator is most powerful and yet, the same Mars jointly rules the growing power of your enemies."

Then that voice she'd heard thundering in the courtyard rumbled in the narrow, resonant room and she found herself slightly stunned again by the muted, seemingly limitless force of it:

"Are the signs against me?"

She thought she knew where he'd stopped but the sound didn't seem to come from any particular place. She rubbed her fingers nervously, unconsciously, together. They were slick with sweat. Her knees were starting to hurt but she feared to move at all. She had a sudden thought that the voice was going to somehow single her out, command her irresistibly to do some frightening thing . . .

"No, my lord," Cydner, sounding all at once like a sheepish schoolboy, "by no means against, and yet, not for. There's a . . . a mixing of effect and portent so that—"

The threatening thunder broke closer now:

"Even if ill I'll force the stars against their proper course if need be! Do you see a better time than now, astrologer?"

"No, my lord. As is said, *inclinate non—*"

"Quiet."

Silence in the room. She heard someone's deep, unsteady breathing.

"The purpose of astrology," said Clinschor's voice, now seeming at a vast distance, reflective, the throbbing, unwavering power upholding the universe, "of all human art, is to agree with the concentrated will of one who is the center, the heart and brain of the time. . . . This concentration is the truth itself and all else is mere interpretation. The stars but measure contradiction and confusion but the true master sweeps all that aside. Is there a mind in your hands and feet? There is one mind and that mind directs the whole body. Do you see? When the decision is directed by the master will then the stars must agree before they're asked . . ."

Alienor hardly followed the remarks. The voice seemed calmly persuasive. She blinked, found a tune tinkling in her head; knees were getting numb; she was cramped and beginning to wonder how long she'd have to sit there as Clinschor warmed to his subject:

". . . therefore the function of new information is discovered by seeing how it fits in with the vision of the master . . . that which fails to fit is false and must be ruthlessly discarded or else confusion develops. Here we see the test of truth: does the so-called *fact* fit the true vision?" He chuckled, the voice mellow and delighted. "This is too often misunderstood. The master's power lies in his perfect focus, so when ordinary beings slip and slide, he remains unshakable. . . . A serf, could he but master his inner force, could rule the rulers!"

In the pause following she thought she heard the nearest man to her sigh faintly.

# lviii

The warriors posted around the lip of the vast pit looked, Broaditch wanly reflected, like sprouts of weed against the tingray sky. He moved with the line over the stepped terraces that circled the excavation. He was down to the lower levels now where the diameter shrank to less than one hundred yards. It went down, and down, like a tilted funnel.

*It's mad,* he thought, *they bring nothing out but dirt.*

Another string of filthy, sagging, rot-reeking men staggered up toward the light from the deepest circle that resembled a drainhole. They struggled past, swaying under wicker baskets of dirt and stones, wormwhite streaks of flesh striping them where the muck had been partly sweated clean.

He was always tired, he always ached but his energy stayed high. In some respects he felt physically good: the meaningless work and routine, despite the scraps of food, endless hours, misery, had hardened him while others had broken and dropped. He'd reflected that no one who'd seen him set out (an eternity ago) would easily recognize this craggy, angular, callused shape even after a scraping, bath and trim . . .

The steep shaft narrowed as it slanted into the earth, became hot and dark. Torches guttered, dank oily smoke gusted in the drafts, men toiled like phantoms in the uncertain shadows . . . human stinks, gases, damp, grunts, scraping, clinking tools, air fouler and fouler. . . . His head began to throb as he labored to breathe.

At the very bottom of the pit he took up a rough picklike tool and in the blotted light where flames barely flared, he joined in chopping away at the dull rockface, pressed close with dozens of other straining, sweating men. When one collapsed he'd lie until he recovered or was dragged away. If he died, he went up on one of the carts at the end of a shift . . .

# lix

She was afraid her bones were going to lock permanently if she didn't move soon. The stale air behind the tapestry tickled her throat and she had to keep dryly swallowing. The little crease of light where the fabric loosely draped along the wall was much dimmer now. She realized it must be twilight already.

There had been a long silence (seemed endless) since one of the men (Cydner, she thought) had gone out. Just as she was contemplating a peek around the edge to see if they all hadn't somehow slipped away, Clinschor's voice rumbled again:

"Is it necessary to set up counter-forces before my main battle is joined?"

A pause, then the other voice:

"Master, can you be sure . . ."

"I have every reason to believe," came the slightly impatient answer, "that such forces exist. I've performed similar rites on a smaller scale, of course, but I have every reason to believe in our ultimate success . . ." He seemed anxious to pass over the details though Alienor was in no condition to mark subtlety.

"But such as these?" murmured the other.

"Well, well? What of that? A small torch or a great fire, it's all the same flame. . . . It's necessary to achieve my purpose and how many men could comprehend what that purpose is? They think me merely a great conqueror. Let them think so. How many, Linkmer? How many of these barbarous swine I lead?" He chuckled, a throaty rumble of disgust. "Not many," he replied to himself. "By shattering all the old ways, rooting up the world, stamping out the Church and its stinking politicians, making each petty lord bow and add his small voice harmoniously to the great descant, wielding in my person the supreme power . . . and it *is* here, my friend, don't doubt that, I didn't speak with more than one forbidden priest for naught . . . it's here, and there's one man living at least who knows where and I'll speak with him soon . . . with that I won't even need the earthdemons, I won't have to bow to their king . . . this will be a world fit for gods to walk in again, as it once was. . . . A world for true men, not pigs and cattle. . . . Yes, the necessary blood will flow and stir the energies in my favor, as it was in the golden kingdom and, anyway, it will leave us less pigs to kill later. . . . Have you inspected the digging?"

His voice seemed oddly childlike with pleasure, she couldn't help but note. For some reason that quality, joined with the throbbing, organlike tones, repelled her.

"Yes, master," said Linkmer.

"Well?"

"It goes down."

"Are there enough workers?"

"Yes. They don't die as fast as they did. More food did the trick."

Clinschor sighed.

"Think," he said, "if they break through."

"I confess, master, I'm somewhat—"

"We have enough army to ensure our hides, even against inner demons."

Alienor's heart caught a beat. Gooseflesh tickled along her arms and nape.

After a long pause, Linkmer said:

"Those priests are at it tonight."

"Don't trouble me with details," Clinschor muttered.

There was very little light now. Just a grayish thread that seemed almost a trick of her eyes.

"I don't like those old priests," Linkmer said. "*Barbarians.*"

"This is no petty cause!" Clinschor suddenly thundered and Alienor nearly screamed. "This is necessity! I use

whatever tools come to hand!" A pause, then more quietly: "When there are no more enemies the sword can be—"
the slightest hold, "—dispensed with. Until then, Linkmer,
let it be swung."

# lx

Sweating, hands sore, chest laboring, each breath fire,
Broaditch struck the crude pick at the blank shale wall,
struggling in the foul, shadowy din, packed in the reek of
himself and the naked, swarming, grunting and gasping
others, pressed by weight of numbers into the tip of the
immense pit . . . then his ears filled with a vast roaring
and his sight was eaten by sprinkling dots, then spreading
rips of void and he knew he was falling, dimly registering
everything from far away as one gaped until all the world
was empty and he tipped and dropped into the vast emptiness of himself . . .

There was time and no time and he had an impression
that the surface had swallowed him . . . he was resting on
a darkly invisible floor; when he made any effort to focus
his eyes the dark deepened but at other times he half saw
or sensed figures at the rim of his sight. When one or more
of them seemed to speak he somehow understood . . .

# lxi

Naked men, women, girls, boys, chained together, neck to neck, were being herded in a long silent line across the moonlit and torchlit fields by the blackarmored knights in silver inwrought face masks. The queue ran past huge standing stones, roughly squared pillars tabled by flat blocks on the scale of a giant's furniture, immense, portentous in the misty darkness. When torches flared in chill gusts of damp wind the great shadows wavered.

Waleis could see where the line topped a rise and passed under an arch that seemed to be tilting forward down the slope as mist streamed and twisted past it. He stood shivering with about fifty other slaves looking across the field, trying to see what was going on within the torchring that enclosed the whole silent hill. At this distance the people seemed vague, pale, insubstantial congealings of the fog itself . . .

He sighed and hunkered down. He wondered how anybody could bear being naked in the nightchill. *It was cold enough for snow,* he decided.

"Cantly," he whispered to the tattered, bowed and sprung figure squatting beside him on the smooth, hard earth. "Cantly, what's all this, that's what I want to know."

Cantly worked his jaws from side to side, then spat. His face was jowly, pale, streaked with lank beard and strings of hair.

"Arrr," he commented.

"What hard things I've had to see," murmured Waleis. "Why am I not bent in wit? I ask meself . . ." Shook his head, eyes wide, restless. "I once had a life with small pleasures . . . now here I am . . ."

"Here you are," Cantly affirmed, sagely. "Alive too.

That's a spare crop these times, the livin' is all flowers in Janery."

Waleis hugged his knees, rocking nervously, feeling the cold seep through his burlap wrappings. He kept glancing up at the long ghostly line undulating slightly over the crest of the vast barrow. A horse snorted in the shadows. Someone coughed nearby, racking gasps, cursed . . .

"I could sleep in the sun if I'd a mind," Waleis remembered, "eat good fish from the north waters . . . What devil got me to leave that land? . . ."

In the distance there was a sudden percussive sob or moan.

"Did you hear that?" he nervously asked Cantly.

"Un? Me bones are too cold for the chatter. . . . Takin' us off our proper work." Spat.

"Proper work?" Waleis exclaimed. "Hanging up dead ones? You call that—"

"I've done worse and seen worse yet."

Waleis shifted his eyes to the hillmound again: the thickening fog swelled like the sea around the standing stones.

"What devil," he whispered to himself.

# lxii

Parsival and Gawain were back on the track of the army. Their fellow raiders had scattered for one reason or another: a few had gone looking for another settlement somebody swore was nearby; Lancelot was last seen sleeping in a barnstall, naked in the damp hay, sword beside him, one arm gripping a cask of ale, the other circling an immensely fat woman whose snores, Gawain remarked to his youthful companion, were enough to raise the local dead for judgment!

The two of them were following the chewed turf where the mass of men had passed. Parsival was still depressed and uncomfortable about his most recent experiences . . .

"It was just sport," Gawain insisted. "Your blood quickens in the field. You know this yourself, now. You're not momma's blond dearling anymore, lad."

"But . . ." He frowned, "I don't know . . ." He was staring at the withering countryside, feeling very distant.

"Just high spirits," Gawain repeated, nodding to himself, chewing a piece of dried fruit meditatively. "A fighting man has to let out his spleen at times . . ." He shook his head. Chuckled. "Did you see Lancelot and that sow?" Shook his head, chewing. "The great Lancelot," he muttered, making a face.

They went on in silence. The horsehooves punged on the earth steadily. The sky was gray and heavy.

"I didn't like it," Parsival said at length, staring . . .

198

# lxiii

The wriggle of grayish light had melted into total blackness before Alienor would poke her head around the edge of the tapestry: the room was dark, empty.

She crawled out on her knees. Then, stiff with cramp, she gradually braced her feet and stood up. Sighed, eyes smarting.

Near the archway she stopped, starting with fear when a man coughed out in the hall, just around the corner. She thought, *Holy Mary what would they do to me for spying?* She felt ill. There was no getting out of it now. She was certain of that . . . She thought about the kitchen and it seemed warm, secure, remote . . .

She backed along the smooth, cold wall, staring at the dimly outlined doorway, heart jumping each time a blot of night seemed to move, continually expecting a black figure with fixed, grimacing silver mask to loom up. . . . All the shadowy terrors and mysteries of this place seemed to be beating dark wings in the still, ghostly chamber. . . . She wanted to run somewhere, anywhere . . . then her arm touched wood and she huddled into a low doorway she hadn't noticed that afternoon, straining her sight, certain something was moving across the open space toward her and as she struggled against the door it soundlessly swung inward.

She was in a hall (she decided), moving, touching one wall lightly, the other hand stretched out before her. She groped into an utter blackness along a slightly curving passageway. After a couple of dozen steps all sense of time and orientation was lost . . .

# lxiv

There seemed to be three persons or beings: he caught
glimpses of them whirling at the edges of his vision and
he knew his eyes weren't seeing this. And there were no
words in his mind: he seemed to touch the experience as
if mind and substance were one fabric. The figures appeared as though a wind rippled them, vibrating, always
moving though at the same time nothing moved at all and
he knew this too . . .

*why waste your strength?* one seemed to ask.

*I am a slave,* he somehow answered, wordlessly. In the
background he feltheard a steady rushing, deep and immense, within and without him as if he was the sound too
as well as the hearer . . .

*we know that,* one pointed out, *and in more ways than
you realize . . . we will never be found by scraping the
earth.*

*we are forced to dig,* he told them.

*but you are not forced to be a fool,* another, or was it
the same, or were they all one voice? *you do not even
know why you searched for Parsival yet, did you expect to
profit by it?*

*I don't understand.*

*why do you waste your strength? you have come nearer
us than all those thousands and yet you imagine you are a
slave.*

He had a sense that he was twisting, falling in some unknown direction. There was no frame of reference he
could grasp. He assumed he was dead now and lying on
the stone floor; he *knew* this with one corner of his perception but felt distant from that, indifferent. He felt the

figures were moving with him, keeping pace as the rippling, windlike effect flowed by.

*is this a dream or death?* he asked.

*why do you want everything to be what you think it is? free yourself, Broaditch, use your great strength.*

Suddenly cold, he began to shudder and shiver and the world vibrated in a bewildering complexity of color and shape and as if a fabric were rent and flapping he found himself both in the mine shaft and still in that other inexplicable place too and then he thought he cried out and fell, rocking and swaying into darkness . . .

# lxv

Dawn. Wet, gray sky. A light drizzle misted down.

Shivering, Waleis was being herded with the others across the wet fields up the slope to the standing stones. He was in the second work party and could see men laboring on the flat, circular barrowtop and his body jumped before his mind actually interpreted what was happening: the workers in their grimy, tattered rags were gathering naked corpses into twisted stacks, heads, limbs lolling . . . coming closer under the spearprods of the black knights he saw a man dragging a dead female child by one stiffened arm, saw the face, the dark gaping mouth much too large, disturbing, and as he was wondering how a mouth could be so far down he realized it was a slashed throat that flapped at him and then he looked at all the others, hundreds, all sliced the same way and everywhere the grayish earth was crusted over by what he'd taken for frosted pools and now the light was intense enough to register color and he saw they crunched across a field of frozen blood, the thin, dried grasses pushing through exactly as in an icy pond . . . Waleis pressed his chilled, bony hands to his face and deeply, softly, rendingly moaned . . .

# lvi

At the end of the long, utterly black corridor Alienor came
to a door, slightly ajar. After a long hesitation she eased it
open, nearly cried out when a long sighing moan broke the
muffled silence. She prayed silently as her eyes adjusted to
the vague light of a single taper that fluttered near a vel-
vet-hung wall. A woman's or girl's voice:

"You promised," it said, with an unidentifiable (at least
to Alienor) accent, in a wearily petulant tone.

Then there was another loud sigh. Straining her vision
she thought she saw figures standing; then it seemed like
a bed across the chamber; thought someone got up and
sat down but couldn't begin to be certain of anything but
sounds. That, and the rich smell of perfume like wet fields
of violets after rain.

"I'm sick of this cold place," the girl said, and there
was a silken rustle of what might have been bedclothes
as if she moved. "I want to go back to Rome. . . . What do
you care about me?"

Then there were kissing sounds, wet, sucking smacks
and more deep sighs that bordered on being shudders.

Alienor was still too curious to move until the rumbling,
hoarse voice stunned her and after the moments of shock
she turned and ran.

"I love you!" it thundered in a desperate whisper, with
pain, longing, hope and insistence; then kissing sounds,
and again: "How can you doubt me? . . ." Kissing, breaths
seeming to be torn from him. "How? . . . Ah, I love you, I
love you . . ."

And as Alienor was already heading back along the
corridor she heard the female voice, indifferent and a little
impatient, saying:

"What you call love."

And the wet, sucking, kissing sounds and the terrific sighs . . . and then she was actually running afraid of the dark like a child and she never understood or remembered how she went back that whole twisting way without once ramming into a wall . . . and then she was pounding through the vaulted chamber, the doorarch, down halls and stairs into the courtyard, voices calling at her as she fled (and once someone seemed to reach for her) feeling nothing, not even the bursting in her lungs until she fell on her face in the warm kitchen straw, in the dark, and lay there feeling alone and miserable, thinking about Broaditch, her lost mistress Jeschute . . . her childhood home . . . until her breathing gradually eased and at some point she was crossing into sleep and the last thing she heard was someone kindly telling her:

"Rest for a while before you come home, child."

# lxvii

As they rode on Parsival was feeling better. When the subject of the grail came up it seemed very distant now . . . he talked about it but it was as though he were telling another's tale . . . It was the same when he thought about his wife or mother . . . he kept wondering what he was going to do after the coming battle: it was as though, he suddenly realized, a void had opened before and behind . . .

# lxviii

Broaditch opened his eyes, blinked, saw gray, shadowy, blurring, strange, distorted shapes, semihuman, he decided, dissolving into the blank background; they moved with a slow, strange rhythm and he thought he was in the land of the dead and those were the endlessly bound shades. . . . He shivered, wondered vaguely why his own shadowbody should be so chilled and seem so heavy. He decided it was an effect and tried to move, blinked and the water in his eyes spattered and he lifted his head in the icy rain which was mixed now and then with gusts of light snow. He was somehow disappointed to see that the mysterious forms were just the slogging laborers slaving in the concentric pit; he lay heaped with the dead at the vast lip of it. After he grasped that he was alive it took him another moment to decide that he alone should know this fact: he made up his mind to wait for dark. His body felt nothing and he hoped he'd be able to move it when the time came. He wasn't really rational and knew that too. His decision seemed to implement him rather than the reverse. He sensed there was some immense, external importance to all that he now would do with the rest of his life. Somehow, he felt serene. . . . The rain plucked steadily at him, swooshing down everywhere in the slimy, black muck. . . . To avoid notice he kept perfectly still as they were loaded on an uneven cart later and pushed and pulled through the sucking paste, the stiffening dead stacked like firewood . . .

# lxix

Waleis backed off, choking when a windshift puffed a cloud of greasy smoke from the blazing pyre into his face. He gagged at the stench under the unmoving scrutiny of the black guards. He wiped tears from his stung eyes. At one end heads were being gathered in bloody sacks. The huge stacks crackled, logs and bodies swelling and bursting with heat, the whole charnel hill dense with blackened fog, a pitch cloud filling out above; through everything he heard the fat bubble and hiss and he gagged again . . .

Later they were marched back across the bitter fields in staggering, grimy, bloody dozens and it was as if a voice spoke (though he heard no words) telling him he was about out of time, that he'd better get away, hide himself. . . . He looked around: just the shuffling, beaten slaves and the black riders as they passed into the outskirts of the stunted, burnt-out pine forest, feet and hooves raising a fine ash dust that caught in throat and nose and he knew somehow, without even thinking of a voice this time, that he had to act and it was as if an invisible hand gripped and flung him flat on his face in the ashes and he heard (without immediately making sense of it) whirring rushings in the air and a ripple of thuds, cries, gasps, chokes, then desperate shouts, flurry, stampede, men dropping all around and over him so he just shut his eyes, bitter dust thick in mouth and nostrils and never even peered up to see the archers as the arrows whizzed, it seemed, interminably and then he heard the splashing impact of blades. . . . A light rain mixed with snow started to fall . . .

# lxx

Night. Sky cold and clear. No moon. Broaditch's ragclothes crackled with frost as he crawled, then hobbled on half-frozen feet across the ironcrusted earth. He believed he would die shortly unless he found shelter and a fire. Though he had no notion of how he might manage this there was no question of turning back to the ring of fortifications behind him. He'd been dumped with the dead outside the gates and that was that. He wasn't even shivering now, as if his tight, resilient body had compacted, tensed with his will and hardened beyond the power of mere earthly cold to breach.

He still wasn't thinking in his accustomed way: his mind was remote, sharp, heatless, abstract and he walked on among the broken, burnt-out trees aware that a totally new action was waiting for him, that his past was with the heaped dead or somehow sunk in the bottom of the senseless pit . . .

# lxxi

Waleis was tramping steadily over the light, crusty snow, beating his arms and hands across his chest, breath steaming out, gusting in the dim, gray dawn.

He hesitated, sniffing the air through a mildly red and runny nose. Smoke and meat cooking. Frightened every step of the way, he followed the smell over a rocky hill, working his way painfully up to the top of a short, icy cliff face and then peering down into a dell where a few evergreens still stood unhacked or unburned. A lean spearman in leather armor sat with his wide back to Waleis, leaning over a low fire, chewing, biting from a bone he held in his hand. A naked man lay in the shallow snow, indented, face split, blood bright red on the trampled white; a second warrior seemed crouched asleep under a tree near the flames and pale smoke.

Waleis was already easing himself backward when the spearman suddenly twisted around and stared up at him and Waleis started to throw himself down the slope at all risks as the fellow stood up, grinning, calling out:

"Waleis, you look like a starved weasel. There was a time when you only looked like a weasel."

So he climbed down into the hollow, realizing it must be Broaditch. Face-to-face he was stunned by the lean, dark, carved hard-looking features, the black, glinting eyes that gave him a queer transparent feeling, somehow. But it was Broaditch all the same.

Who smiled, almost as if reading his feelings, his voice warm and he realized for the first time he felt really close to him, really taken seriously.

"Easy, my friend," Broaditch said.

Waleis looked at the dead man, then the other whom he'd thought to be sleeping. He wasn't.

"Put on his gear," Broaditch told him. "We have work to do." He nodded. "That's right," he confirmed, "and I'm glad you found me."

"Work? What work?"

"We have to find her."

"Go back there?"

Broaditch nodded.

"Back there," he confirmed.

Waleis crouched by the meagre fire, seeming to suck at the warmth, hugging himself.

"First eat something," Broaditch suggested. "Tell me how *you* got away."

Waleis shook his head.

"I don't want to tell," he said.

A pause. Broaditch nodded.

"Alright," he said. "But eat something."

Waleis peered up at him, eyes dulled, desperate.

"Can we go home?" he wanted to know. "After whatever you have to do, can we go home?"

# lxxii

They heard the sound undulating like the sea long before the dense woods ended, their horses laboring chest deep in powdery snowdrifts at times, cutting along, spraying and splashing like ship's bows as they mounted a long, easy slope, where the pines thinned to a trickle, toward the continuous roaring and clash. Now individual sounds separated out: shrill neighs, cries of rage and pain, clashing of arms, the earth vibrating profoundly as thousands of men and riders shifted and collided . . .

A recent snowfall had almost totally effaced the vast army's track: there were only vague ruts and stretches of rounded roughness.

Parsival was flushed, excited, anxious: finally the battle! Everything else, Gawain had insisted, was boy's play and now they'd have man's work!

The spray from Gawain's stallion needled back into his face and clittered on his mail and shield. He kicked Niva on hard as they topped the crest finally and looked down an easy hill into a long level valley where the armies milled in an immense, writhing mass that stunned Parsival's attempts to take it all in, to sort and pattern the sweeping action spread out before them. He first thought of bees swarming: countless dark dots against the blinding white, sunshimmering snowfield, clusters shifting, wheeling, scattering, coalescing, the two sides merged into a single, ponderously heaving mass and he realized he had no idea which was which and he called ahead to Gawain who half turned and shouted back to him voice wild, exultant:

"Speed, speed! It's magnificent! . . . Magnificent!"

Driving his horse on in a fever of haste like a parched man runs to water.

211

"But I don't know . . ." Parsival tried to shout.

He spurred after him, fascinated by the vast conflict that seemed one colossal creature struggling with itself . . . closer now he could see, when a tidal heave shifted the outlines, men lying still, writhing, crawling, hobbling in the snow, and all the shout, cry, clatter, crash merged as if one single throat cried out in pain and terror . . . the hair prickled up on the back of his neck . . . closer, closer, Gawain holding his lead in full charge over trampled, shallow, hardbeaten footing, passing the staggering wounded, bright blood specking and spattering the snow, now on level ground, careening into the shifting mass of men, passing some who were just standing, talking, resting on a knee, a spear cast from the melee and then in a sudden wheeling hundreds of swordsmen and spearmen locked in close combat cut him off from Gawain and a moment later a line of pike wielders charged him and he wrenched Niva to a violent kicking halt and before the line could reach him a wedge of black armored knights—he'd never seen so many alike before—slashed through the men who were actually (he realized) fleeing . . . he tried now to circle back because there was still no way to tell friend from foe. Without Gawain he knew there was no chance unless he found Arthur or Lancelot and what hope was there of that?

Then a madly struggling gush of foot soldiers and horsemen engulfed him, bright armor, blades, shields flashing, sounding, zipping arrows, horses toppling, screamneighing, he saw a knight pulled down as his mount stumbled, a brief space was cleared by three riders fanning mace and blade the way (he thought) a swirling hand shallows out a pool and then the water rushes back, dribbles and spews around the futile fingers . . . then a pike was rammed from the ground at him: he turned it almost lazily with his shield, another glanced off his mailed side so he slammed his visor shut and drove the nearest men back shouting his question:

"Who stands for Arthur?"

into a din that swallowed all individual sounds.

As the battle whirlpooled around him he, distracted, struck a few men down . . . soldiers were staggering and dropping everywhere, legless, armless, headless, split, skewered, battered and sliced to shreds . . . the snow was slushy in places with blood . . . he was stunned watching a knot of goresoaked men-at-arms, with mace, spear and ax, slipping and crawling across a patch of bloodreeking, steaming earth, howling with mad, wild, infinitely concentrated rage, hurling themselves in frenzy back into the struggling mass as if a fragment of the great beast had been flung free and was drawn to a macabre rejoining . . . through the tumult ahead (he was now solely concerned with getting away from the storm of incomprehensible fury, of men who all looked the same) he saw a line defending what he first took for a low hill: fifty or more knights were charging partway up the slopes only to be thrown back like (he thought) breaking waves on a rock and as he came closer he saw it was a hill of dead men half-standing upright, leaning like bundled wheat against one another in a welter of spears, lances, swords, arms, legs and at this his mind seemed to suddenly clear to a point and it seemed, through all the immense violence, there was an uncanny silence, an even vaster movement of silence and for a moment he felt shrunk to nothing, a pinpoint, a shock of fear . . . a sudden calm and he followed that calm, concentrated focus of tranquillity as if it were a path through the massive warring, feeling released from deciding anything, from any thinking at all . . . no one touched him as if his release had rendered him invisible and Niva trotted easily right through to the outskirts of the fighting and only then he looked back at where the howling, striking, raging undulations went on and on . . . he tried to think about it: he didn't know who to fight so none of it made sense and since he had no place in it just watching was too horrible so he understood that and each time he did the calm returned . . . it was suddenly very funny, he grinned, then laughed. One of the straggling wounded looked up at him as if he were mad . . .

Niva slowed to a walk up the easy grade toward the fir woods that edged the field, their blue shadows intense in the snow, bright coppery suntints on the lush iced limbs that crackled in the icy light . . .

# lxxiii

At nightfall they edged along the road that crossed the bridge; beyond it stood the gate in the outer wooden palisade—which in later times would be called the barbican and made of stone. The road itself was pure mire: stones that had been dropped in were half-lost in the ooze. Beyond the track of mud greenish-rose twilight glimmered on the snowfields.

Every few minutes a collection of riders came splashing out through the gate booming over the timber bridge and ploughing away along the mucky track. Broaditch assumed that the great battle he'd kept hearing about must now be raging in the east. He glanced at Waleis toiling along beside him, spear swaying awkwardly in his uncertain grip. *Well,* he reflected, *they'd seem wearied soldiers, splashed to the thighs with mud* . . . He'd decided to pass the gate by claiming to bring a message from one of the vassals.

As they neared the gate, guards were visible against the afterglow, leaning and pacing on the walkways behind the spiked top. Waleis glanced at him but didn't speak, in a situation, he noted, that in the past would have coaxed a virtuosity of complaints. He smiled faintly, grimly, for a few moments regretting even those uncomfortable lost days.

Then there came a steady, massive beating of drums, broomboom bababoom broomboom bababoom, and a shrill, raw, braying flourish of barbarian horns as the gates swung wide and a wedge of foot soldiers came pounding out at the double. Waleis and Broaditch fell back on the shoulder. Waleis was trembling slightly.

"This has nothing to do with us," Broaditch assured him.

As the straining troops came sloshing abreast, a sergeant at arms paused to look them over.

"You two bastards," he raged quietly, "the war's the other way." He set his massive hands on his leather-girded hips. Gave them a hard, lingering stare from his flat, bearded face under the twinhorned helmet.

"We were ordered back," Broaditch improvised.

"Deserted back, you mean," the man snapped as his troops trotted heavily behind him, spattering the raw mud. It sounded like a butterchurn, Broaditch noted. "The fucked woods is full of desertin' bastards."

"If we deserted," Broaditch reasoned, "we'd of headed for our lands and not back here, by Christ."

"If you was my men," the sergeant declared in his tempered, raging voice, "you'd sweat blood and shit!"

Now a mass of the silver and black elite horsemen with their terrible face masks was coming through the gateway. Before them slogged the brass and drums.

"Himself is comin' to the fight," said the sergeant, suddenly conversational, glancing at the oncoming masses. "They say it ain't goin' as it should. Well, by God, we'll slice a few fuckers for bacon!"

With a formal snarl he fell in beside his men and trotted off, cursing inflectionlessly, mechanically, with heatless fury.

The knights with their grimacing masks drew abreast and smartly passed. Waleis shuddered and averted his eyes. Then followed a line of richly dressed lords in light mail and plumed helms; then, one alone on a glistening jet black stallion wearing silver armor polished like a mirror so that all the faint evening glow seemed concentrated there in a dreamlike gleaming and Broaditch stared at the frail, bony, pale face, the upcurled mustache (*like a Turk's,* he thought) that seemed almost comical for an instant until he caught the eyes which he thought for a moment feverishly touched his: they appeared expanded, pupilless as a cat's at night and for a moment his stomach pulled with terror: *hollow!* he thought then *no it's the light Christ I'm cold sweating . . .* then something crashed against his back and he stumbled to his knees in the mucky road gasping as a fierce voice barked behind him:

"Down dogs before the king of the world!"

And he was pulling himself and Waleis back from the path of the following mass of knights and all he saw for a moment (as he later recounted) was a welter of hinds and hind legs and tails and steamy droppings "that fell like poison stars." And then he'd made it back to the snow-bank under a confused impression that the push and voice he'd heard were supernatural until the face of a thick-bodied warrior leaned down into his, saying with energy:

"Fall in at the end of this line and march or I'll lose a spur in your stinking bungholes!"

Parsival had nearly reached the line of glistening pines that stood like a wall before him. Only a scattered collection of wounded had dragged themselves this far. He noticed that a wedge of blackarmored riders had broken loose from the general mass and were galloping through the icy slush on an angle that would take them between himself and the woods. He kept Niva at an easy canter. The snow was less tracked and getting deeper here.

When he next glanced up the black horsemen were riding as hard as possible, much closer now, and he wondered if they'd all decided to desert the battle as he did . . . had the confusion been too much for them too? If you can't tell friend from foe, whose deaths to cheer and whose to deplore, whom do you strike down, whom help? The knights were crashing through, scattering the stragglers, massed flank to flank, a single missile, and Parsival estimated a dozen or more in the group. While he was thinking and watching a childhood memory flashed into consciousness: he'd been playing alone in the snow in his leather and woolen leggings and wraps, running in wide circles on the hillside behind the little castle, jumping through the brown, spare hedges, plunging through in an explosive dry crackling, spilling on the packed snow, laughing, rolling, up and running again, breathless, flushed, then at a steep crest overlooking the village he let himself fall and roll down and down, blue sky, white earth, sky, earth, sky, earth . . . then suddenly the tilt was too steep and he starfished to slow himself then skidded into empty air, tumbling, catching revolving flashes of huts and houses, animals, a moment of sinking thrill and terror, a dark rush and bump and he was on his back staring up through several feet of snowbank that he'd sliced neatly into and just lay there for a time, winded, comfortable, looking at the crystal bright blue . . . when he finally knelt his feet under him and peered out of the drift across the common yard, squinting against the sunglare he saw a rough pen crammed with men and hogs, the mass seeming to seethe, desperate beasts thrashing and snorting and the astonished boy watched axes rise and fall, spurts and sprays of hot blood, the raw metallic stink of it, slicing impacts, bubbling shrieksqueals, blows, blows, blows and then he was climbing and clawing, running through the deep snow and up the slippery hillside, terrorized, shaken . . .

The black knights suddenly wheeled and scattered like an explosion, enclosing him with marvelous ease in a loose circle. *What terrible faces,* he thought an instant before realizing they were silverwrought masks. As they all stopped he reined Niva in and looked around at them: the one in front and nearest had a long pointed chin, slit, tilted eyes, stubby, gleaming curved horns hooking out from the silver temples, flashing the sunlight when he moved. Parsival was curious about the workmanship. Dark, rich armor and mirrorbright masks against snow and gleamingly iced trees were impressive. He wondered how he'd look in gear like that. *They're made up to seem devils,* he thought. *What would I have done if I'd seen them back home? Would I have wanted to become a knight?* He wondered if they were with Arthur or the enemy.

"Who are you?" he asked, cocking his head.

No response. They were working their horses closer, he noticed, by inches.

"Name yourself!" he demanded.

Nothing back. He drew his sword, the bluebright blade from grail castle. Several of the riders were unlimbering hookended chains, not so much to kill as to tangle and hold. The rest moved in with mace rather than sword. He had an impression that they didn't mean to slay him.

As one released his chain in a looping arc Parsival spurred Niva and the links rattled around his back so he bent forward and the whiplash spun the hook away and then he was driving into a slowmotion charge straight at the horned rider too close to gather real momentum but still closing as a second chain hummed and lashed

*Clinschor's black knights attack Parsival*

around Niva's forelegs, the hook failing to take hold, and then he was close enough: the rider snapped his massive mace at the horse's head and, stunned, it stumbled to its knees and Parsival, raging, stood in the stirrups and cracked a sidecut that split the waiting blacksilver shield neat as cheese and the silent man drew back the stump of an armored hand (blood jetting from the slanted slice) and gurgled wordlessly, horribly, air hissing, trying to scream inside the fixed grimace of the mask. A hook caught across Parsival's chest, metal singing as the rider hauled at him and under his demon visor may well have looked surprised when the red knight, unmoved, simply gripped the tensed links with his sword hand and casually yanked the opponent loose from his saddle maskfirst into the snow, tugged the hook free and got Niva back (if unsteadily) to his feet as two more mace-wielding horsemen moved in on both sides (the maimed one now was bent over his mount's neck trying to stanch the bleeding, the second trying to get to his feet in the deep snow) and like precisely geared machines struck simultaneously for his head (he had an impression this trick had worked often for them) except he leaned forward, both blows missed, then he twisted in the saddle and before they could recover their momentum he backswung, his blade disappeared then reappeared a foot behind one's neck (just above the line of his shield where the helmet was tied at the joint of throat and tilted chin) with barely a flash of sparks so incredibly neat was the stroke: the head wobbled, the knotted features of a raging bull gazing blank and unchanged, then like a stone rolled and dropped and vanished in the pure snow as the steaming blood geysered and in the same motion Parsival hissed a downsweep at the surviving man which sheared away part of the shield as the rider desperately backturned his charger to get clear of the following cut which creased the silver snakeface chipping loose one blank crystal eye.

The red knight twisted around. The rest were coming on and in the raging background another group had broken free of the fight and were coming across the white field. A flank seemed to have been turned down there but there was no telling (for him) whose.

"Why won't you speak?" he shouted, opening his helmet. "Whose men are you?"

They just came silently on and in disgust he reined Niva away, circling around the one he'd pitched into the snow.

"War," he reflected as he rode, "is stupid."

# lxxiv

It was just dawn when they reached the battlefield, Broaditch and Waleis marching at the rear of the van with the supply wagons. They'd moved into a country of small fires, tents, wounded, weary, chilled men. There was no sound of combat, only a gusty, whistling wind inflecting the sighs and groans and muttery conversation. Long, twisting bands of smoke from the fires threaded up and stained the clear sky. Broaditch was astonished by the unending numbers stretching away across the vast, unsheltered plain. On the low slopes beyond he could make out Arthur's battered forces and he realized, from conditions around him, that they were witnessing a terrible stalemate.

"I knew it was my time to die," Waleis sighed.

Broaditch was staring at where the wagons were being unloaded.

"There's still breath in you," he remarked.

Waleis dropped his spear with disgust.

"What will I do with this?" he wanted to know.

Soldiers moved here and there with burning brands and kindled fires. Jugs of a raw, brandylike drink were being passed around. Meat was broiling.

"The army doesn't stink so much in winter," Broaditch observed, more or less to himself.

"I'm not brave," Waleis said, decidedly. "I know it. I don't pretend to be."

"We'll come out of it," Broaditch replied.

"I don't pretend . . ." He squatted down in the snow and stared at nothing. "I never had any fortune with women," he said. "That's why I went with you . . . it's true . . ."

Broaditch glanced at him. Frowned slightly.

221

"Give yourself time, Waleis," he told him.

". . . I thought I'd get a position, a grant of land . . . what dreaming . . ." He stared on and on. After a few minutes, during which Broaditch went back to studying the wagons, he muttered bitterly: "I'm not even hungry! . . ."

"You can smell the uncertainty in the air here," Broaditch mused.

He had watched the women setting up to cook for quite a while before he actually realized it was Alienor carrying two plucked geese and flopping them down on a long, rude table. A stout soldier paused between them to relieve himself and Broaditch moved obliquely to keep her in view. He couldn't believe finding her.

Cooks and scullions were busy now, fires blazed up. He drifted closer.

*I must have a fair aspect, this day,* he thought.

He stood near the head of the table and looked at her: she was bent to her work, chopping vegetables with a square knife: potatoes and yellowish greens. She seemed stronger than he remembered and her cheeks had a good color but he detected threads of gray in her hairline and her expression seemed so utterly set as if for life: neither happy nor sad, just steady, sharp and steady. It was as if he were first seeing her, he thought. He realized he hadn't really paid attention the last night they were together, it hadn't seemed urgent then and now it was clear: you couldn't imagine you had all the time in the world to love, to feel, because only when you understood that the loved might vanish forever in a moment, any moment, was there enough intensity to appreciate the vast tenderness of it . . . he watched the lean, strong, worn fingers gather stalks for chopping, the light on her reddened face, her very breath like magic frosting before her, made visible by the clear cold as other clearness revealed unseen things to him. . . . Then she looked up as an Irish-speaking warrior snapped at him:

"None of your filchin' ways here, buck."

The widefaced, lopsided fellow tossed underhand a hunk of stonehard black bread to Broaditch.

"Gnaw for a bit," he invited, "there'll be hot soup for all soon enough. Forgive the lords eatin' first, will ya?" He grinned. Broaditch liked him. Grinned back. Saw Alienor looking up at him now.

The Irishman glanced quickly around, then said:

"The great master don't use magic spells on his belly, buck." Tipped a wink and moved away, munching and crackling crust.

Broaditch held the bread as Alienor came around the table and gaped wide-eyed up at him. She pushed a hair-strand back behind an ear. She seemed beyond hope or amazement and he wondered if she might be reacting as he just had . . .

The moon was full or past it, and bright on the pine-and tent-dotted snowfields. Spotted among the shadowy forms low fires winked. Under a mile away on the high ground the lights of the opposing army showed.

He'd left Waleis sleeping and was making his way carefully, feet poking through the glassy crust. As a boy he'd loved that sensation: the hold, then sudden crunch. . . . He passed near a campfire; two men swathed in furs were talking:

". . . an' if you laid them dead ones end to end you could walk home an' no mistake."

"Aaah," deprecated the other, "this Lord Clinschor, he always knocks the shit loose from them, don't he?"

"I don't like it."

"You never like it."

As he went carefully on their talk was absorbed into the wind's chill rushing whine. When he checked around at the cooking tents he noticed a few black and silver clouds were passing the rising moon.

"Alienor," he whispered loudly and she opened the flap and gripped his hand. Her touch was burningly warm. He entered, embracing her, standing in the dark, stuffy, spice-smelling interior.

"No one's in this tent," she murmured pressing her cheek to his chill face.

His hands moved over her back, went under her loose, rough shirt and scraped and pressed with wonder over the hot, smooth, tender flesh . . .

She made a little sound, half whimper . . .

Wrapped in blankets with her, drowsy, utterly comfortable, relishing the sweet moment, the faintly sharp smell of sweat and hair, he sighed to his bone foundations and wished for a pipe.

"Pleasure," he murmured philosophically, "never sates itself, it just reminds you there is more waiting."

"You want something else?" she asked with a partial yawn.

He sighed and was serious again. Not that the seriousness had ever been altogether gone, just coated over for a brief, sweet time.

"Did you pack food?" he asked her.

"It's in a sack by the door." She readjusted herself so she could gently nibble at his nipple.

"You kept in practice," he said, cupping a breast, marveling at the liquidy texture, thinking how she seemed deceptively lean and hard when dressed.

"I've had no men since you, Broad One." She nipped him and he winced. "You made a weakness in me, I think."

He smiled in the dark.

"We have to leave before dawn," he said. He was, he knew, half-convincing himself.

"And cross to Arthur's side? But won't you have to fight there as well?"

He squeezed his eyes open and shut.

"I half wish it," he said. "I never thought I'd come to that, but I've got to do *something* . . ."

"You still hope to find the boy-king?"

"Who? . . . Oh, Parsival. God's wounds, I'd actually forgotten. . . . All that seems a strange dream now . . ."

"Look where you woke."

He sat up with a brief effort and sighed again.

"Don't move so sudden," she complained. "You let the cold air under."

"There's more cold coming, woman," he informed her. Squeezed her firm, lean rump.

"Great pinching fingers," she whisper-cried and twisted away, burrowing deeper into the bedclothes. In a moment of silence she asked, seriously: "What's that *something*, then?"

"What's what?"

"That you mean to do?"

He was out of the pallet now, shivering, snapping on his stiff clothes.

"I don't know yet," he replied, "but I'm not leaving things as I found them. That's something enough, by Christ."

"How?"

"How what?"

"How will you leave them?"

"I don't know yet . . ." He thoughtfully tugged on his boots. "I'm going to help."

"Help who, then?"

He bent and snatched the covers away and she gasped.

"Help you get that arse and muffin up and going," he informed her. Then took her by the shoulders and kissed her warm lips. She held on. Her skin prickled in the cold air.

"How can you be so merry?" she wanted to know, a little breathlessly.

"Because I came back from death," he replied, seriously. "Like a stinking Lazarus, and I've got a life to live."

# lxxv

Now it was snowing. The sack of provisions tied to his back swayed heavily as he picked his steps, leaning on his spear like a staff; Alienor close behind, Waleis last, leaning into the stiffening wind, feet crunching the crust in knee-deep drifts. They all blinked and tilted their heads against the stinging flakes. Not a hint of light in sky or earth was visible. A solid blank black, steady tinkling hiss of snow on snow . . .

He knew they must have passed the sentryline by now and prayed they hadn't strayed too far north or south. He calculated that within the hour the sun should rise in their faces behind Arthur's hosts. There would at least be a glow there to guide them.

Shielding his eyes with one hand, he muttered:

"We must be in the battlefield somewhere . . ."

The wind kept picking up force, sweeping straight into them and he thought: *just so it's from the east* . . .

She called out and he turned: she'd fallen on her side and was struggling to rise. The two of them swung her back upright.

"I'm alright," she gasped, the rising wind washing away the words so that he had to huddle close to hear and speak.

"It can't be far," he called at her from inches away.

She nodded, gathering her willpower. Broaditch squeezed her arms and chafed her hands and cheeks.

"We're lost," Waleis cried out suddenly.

"It can't be far!" shouted Broaditch. His words seemed faint in his own ears. The storm moaned, shrill and hollow, snow needling into their flesh.

Gripping her hand he went back into it, braced on the

spear and ploughed on into the wild, swirling, crackling,
shuddering darkness ...

On and on and then something caught at his calf and
he struggled to free himself. *A branch,* he thought, stoop-
ing and taking hold of (he realized a moment later) a brittle hand, iced, that reached up as from the frozen earth
itself to pluck at him. He pulled loose and struggled on;
tripped and caught himself, stepping over buried obstacles
that he knew weren't logs or stones and then they were
in a thicket of tilted spears and arrows that swayed and
vibrated in the storm, stepping over and around bodies;
next climbing a sudden, slippery, steep hillock strewn with
dead and it wasn't until, on the top, his foot skidded on
icy armor and sunk down past the knee, finding no earth,
that he grasped this was a mound of heaped corpses ...

As a grayish, vague glow began to seep into the billowing blizzard the puffs and waves of snow became gradually visible. In a few minutes it was letting up, little by
little, as if the weather were timed for sunrise. After a
while they could see several hundred feet of brittle field:
here and there a lance or broken spear poked up through
the surface which otherwise rolled smooth and unmarked
as the sea.

They couldn't see back to the army they'd escaped but
before them were rows of snowladen tents; tethered and
blanketed horses and suddenly several yapping dogs appeared and then a knight in bearskin and another in fox-
fur stood up beside a low fire and studied them.

Broaditch wiped ice and snow from his beard, holding
Alienor close to his side, nervous as the two men mounted
warhorses and began ploughing through the drifts at a
ponderous gallop as the snow died to a light powder and
the air became bright gray.

He waved his arm with the spear and called out:

"My lords!"

He was feeling weary and sick already at the sight of
them drawing their swords and leaning over their horses'
flanks looking like the mechanical toys of later times.

"My lords!" Broaditch tried again. He could clearly hear
the grunting of the laboring animals now, rattle of metal,
hiss of snow spray from forelegs and chests. "We're friends
to King Arthur!"

And then, silently, Waleis threw down his spear and

was running back the way they'd come, arms, legs and loose clothes flapping as he highstepped through the drifts. The horsemen veered toward him as Broaditch shouted:

"No! Waleis! Waleis!"

And then, falling and getting up again and again he struggled in a wide circle until one rider passed close to him, Broaditch continually shouting, though he never remembered what:

"Don't fly from them! Run at an angle! Waleis, don't fly! Run at an angle, they can't turn horse so fast as—"

And then stopping as the rider flicked a casual cut as though swatting a fly . . .

# lxxvi

The snow dusted down featherlight into the dim pine woods. Dark gray sky was ripped with whitish strips. There was no sound above the horse's breath and steps. Parsival was glad for that. *It was as though,* he reflected, *I had actually to reach the battle before I could realize I'd outgrown yet another thing. I'd made a wrong turn,* he told himself, *and am going straight back to the grail castle without a single detour to pick up the lost track . . .*

He came out of the woods on a smooth knob of hill overlooking a long valley where a frozen river flashed the sun that was breaking out as the clouds were shredded in the winds.

He chafed his reddened hands together to warm them and looked around at the snowscape: the sun went in and out and the ice seemed to brighten and dim from within. The light effects fascinated him: the bright, clear air like cut crystal, pure white and blue, rainbowed ice . . . he felt giddy, overwhelmed as if he'd never seen anything before, as if his eyes were just created and somehow he felt he could embrace and hold the shimmering, penetrating, magical clarity . . . Niva's eye regarded him as the horse cocked his silky head: deep, lustrous, rich gleaming, the intelligence and reality there, the warm palpability of living flesh dazzled him like the day . . . He touched the warm neck and mane and smiled with pure delight . . .

Down the valley he saw dark low clouds, long tangles of smoke unwinding. Shielding his eyes, squinting, he made out a collection of burning huts and houses.

"War," he informed Niva, sadly.

He wondered if it were going to greet him everywhere; how far he'd need to ride to be free of it . . .

229

Passing through a pine lane he caught a woman's face at the corner of his sight. She seemed to be standing in the brush at the edge of the trail. He twisted in the saddle to speak and was startled to discover there was no body. He reined up and stared: a woman's head on a thin pole, her eyes rolled up as if in prayer, mouth parted, dark. . . . He sighed. . . . He was getting almost used to such sights and wondered what that meant. . . . Nudged the animal on and then there was another, an old lady, the stake hidden among the sharp, brilliant green needle sprays so that the face appeared to float or hang like fruit. The lady was looking down toward the crusted earth. . . . He refused to look at any more until the last. He stopped again: a battered knight's helm with shut visor gleamed, reflecting the green and bright snow. He drew and reached with his swordtip and wedged open the helmet and knew the face. Knew this truly meant something. Erec. Erec, pale, blood streaked as if he'd wept it. . . . Parsival thought: *God, this is a strange world I left my mother to find.* . . . He let the visor bang shut over the still face, then slashed the pole away. The helmet dropped out of sight in the snow and shadow . . . He glanced back at the mute gallery along the trail.

"I wish I could say something to you . . ." he suddenly cried out and then was silent. He sighed and urged Niva on . . .

At dusk he came to a deserted, partially burnt-out barn and sheltered himself and Niva there. He realized there was no hope of recovering the way he'd followed with Gawain because the storm would have covered everything over long since. Still, he wasn't too concerned since he knew the general direction: ride at the setting sun . . .

He struck steel over tinder, as Gawain had taught him, and got a fire going just where the roof had fallen away. He boiled snow water in his helmet, added dried herbs from a pouch and had a thin meal of soup and hard biscuit.

After a while he wrapped himself close and lay back on a scattered, whitened bundle of straw and let himself fade toward sleep . . .

Almost there a picture formed as if a dream were beginning: his mother, sitting on the highbacked throne. He watched her and didn't feel really sad though the image had a profound effect on him, deeper than sadness . . . much deeper and he knew that this image was somehow all she was now and all she ever was, a purity without substance, a glowing effect deep within him, and his mind said: *that's all she ever was* and he started full awake, afraid as if a pit had suddenly opened below him. Eyes open hard he felt his heart pound, looked at the dim embers, the icicles glinting faintly around the gutted walls; outside the rising moon spread its light across white fields. . . . He held all thoughts blocked for a few moments and when he reshut his eyes he fell into an instant, utter black sleep . . .

# lxxvii

As elsewhere Clinschor was sweating in the stale, cold air inside his tent. The dark hangings muffled everything. A few tapers thinly flamed around the table where he sat, moving his fingertips restlessly over his sweaty palms. The low coal fire smoked faintly up a crude tin chimney lashed to the center pole.

He sat wrapped in his furs, alone, staring at the gold and silver inlaid plaques lying on the tabletop arranged in the shape of a cross plus a vertical row. He chewed his lower lip and worked his hands.

"Damn you," he said, throwing himself back in the carven chair, vaguely luminous eyes distant, brooding. The empty tent was quiet: a golden suit of armor hung up; a rack of swords; silken pillows. Outside just a few muffled voices singing in the camp; the impatient whinny of a horse . . .

He whispered to himself in quietly raging frustration:

"Damn . . . Damn . . . If you had flesh I'd kill you!"

He leaned forward and stared at the layout, the inlaid figures on the plaques (which in later times would be pasteboard cards) holding wands or stars or strange devices. . . . He stared at the one at the head of the spread: two crossed swords supported by a blindfolded woman. He tapped his fingers now. Then hissed:

"That's no answer!" and swept the clacking pieces from the table just as the tentflaps parted and a dark, rounded-off, middle-aged woman stepped through and took the situation in: the gleaming divination tiles scattered on the rug.

"Is that all you do?" she wanted to know.

He glanced at her, silent, brooding in rage.

232

"And feel sorry for yourself," she said. "You know you do. You get yourself sick this way."

"All I ask," he declared rhetorically, "is one damned clear answer. That's all I ask." He rubbed his eyes. "What do I do? I go on and on . . . I'm tired of these fights in strange lands . . . I've given everything for the work of the gods and still the answers are obscure . . ."

"I can't stand it when you get yourself sick like this." She held her ermine wrap close around her short, rounded body. Her hair was coiled in dark braids. "I want to go home."

He rubbed his clammy brow. She went and knelt by the brazier coals.

"You always want to go home," he said. "I'm the one who's tired, *I'm* the one who should go home."

"Good," she told him. "Let's leave then." She turned her hands over the heat. "This miserable, freezing country. I don't know what you want with it. You never stay with anything you win."

"You close your mind to everything," he said, looking away from her.

"I know," she said, dryly, "you want the secret power. You tell everyone about it sooner or later. It's a wonder they believe you in anything."

"You have no imagination."

"Thank God. And don't make speeches at me. Nobody likes them anyway."

"I'd like to kill you," he muttered, without real heart. The dispute was mechanical since he could feel the depression, the emptiness sucking at him steadily, relentlessly . . .

"Good," she said. "I'd prefer it to an unnatural life in these barbarian sinkholes." She sat down on a silken cushion in an Eastern fashion and opened her cloak slightly.

He wasn't really listening.

"My life is given to this," he was saying, "and I must finish my work. . . . Minds like yours can't grasp this. I hold them together with my will, they're all so stupid and fearful . . . so petty . . . petty little lordlings with minds on plunder and fucking, they have no sense of the large scale, the shaping of the world which—"

"They're blessed then," she cut in. "Plunder and fucking doesn't sound so bad if—"

He stood up and jabbed his finger at her, the pointed nail glinting in the taperlight. Shrieked:

"You're just like your father!" He sputtered. "No vision! No vision!"

She watched him, her large, deep, liquid eyes quite still and unreadable. She could see he was weeping.

"Bitch," he whispered. The depression drained and drained at him and there was a strange pleasure in letting it now, in sinking down with it into lightless despair. She could see he was weeping. "Foul bitch," he whispered. He put his hands to his face and sighed in misery. She just watched him.

"What do you want from people?" she wondered.

"Taunt me," he said into his hands, "but you'll see what I do! . . ." He rocked back and forth. "Ahh," he whispered, "gods or no gods, you'll see what I do . . ."

"I don't know what you want," she told him.

He wiped his face and swallowed hard. He was feeling slightly better. He sat back down at the table. *Win this battle*, he thought, *find that boy*. . . . The work, the intricacy of planning was beginning to absorb him again. He hardly noticed her sitting there. *No cause to despair. There was much to do.* He nodded to himself. The depression was definitely lifting. The goal was a warmth and light: he felt it. He leaned back in the chair and let the goal take one of its forms, began filling in armies, crowds of grateful peoples, tall temples went up in lucid, Mediterranean sunlight and graceful, beautiful men and women moved joyfully at work and play as glittering armies marched on and he tried to imagine the lands beyond the edges of the maps where they would go; he wasn't in it, he simply looked from an increasing height on a singing world distilled from every springtime. . . . He smiled. She was crosslegged on the pillow, looking at her favorite ruby, turning it, catching him at his table, everything, in its lucent depths.

# lxxviii

The captains were gathered on a hillock backed by a bright wall of pines. The roar of the conflict broke around them like the sea. Their mounts were restless, wildeyed, overwrought. Messengers struggled across the snow, mounted and on foot. All before them in the smooth field the armies heaved and spilled together.

Arthur stood up in his stirrups, pointing toward a low ridge at the right flank of his host. He was shouting at the battered, bloody Galahad whose helmet was part sheared away and a broken arrow caught in his armpit.

"Go back," Arthur was saying, "overwhelm them at that spot!" He swept his fist in a tight, fierce semicircle. "Crush in from the side and we roll up their flank."

"But, I tell you, I have not thirty-five sound men and six knights," Galahad insisted. "The horses sink in the snow when we try a charge. . . . Men can do no more than we have done. I've lost three companies entire since noon and we stand in the same frozen blood we started in!"

"Are you all cowards?" Arthur cried, looking around. "Attack! Attack! Attack! Do you hear?"

Galahad raged, breath steaming out in gusts:

"Aye. I hear madness!"

"Madness is it?"

"Aye, my lord. When we're all dead will you change your opinion?"

"Courage will carry the day," put in Sir Kay, who was beside the king.

"Then come forth and lead us, you son-of-a-bitch!" Galahad invited. He swept his notched, bloody sword back and forth. "This battle can't be won today and well you know it."

"Then fly, coward!" screamed Arthur, face red and tense.

"You call me coward?" Galahad was white with fury.

"I do! It takes no courage to die. Any weakling can do that as well as you. To *win* takes a man!"

"There's no winning here, Arthur Pendragon," Galahad cried as he spurred his foaming charger back toward the battle.

To the captains before him Arthur commanded:

"Attack everywhere to the last man! Slay and slay and slay!" He brandished his sword above his head. His teeth gritted together in his frenzy. "If there be one man left living after this fray let him be a Briton!!"

With a cheer, almost involuntary, the knights wheeled around and galloped back for the fight, horses leaping and scrambling over the freezing mounds of dead and wounded.

Panting, Arthur partly turned to Kay who was watching them rejoin the titanic battle that now spread over a mile across the countryside, resembling, from this vantage point, a great, darkly glittering, barely writhing snake . . .

"Where is Merlinus?" Arthur demanded.

"I have not seen him this day."

"Have him found, do you hear? I want him now. I have need to know certain things. . . . Have him found!"

Kay rode off with a few remnants of the king's guard. The rest stayed in a loose circle around Arthur who hissed into the stinging cold wind that blew into his bared face:

"To the end it must be . . . To the end . . ."

On the other side of the battle, out of view of the fighting, in a sheltered dell, Clinschor crouched on his knees on the fur floor of his tent, incense sticks and candles smoking all around him, a map spread there, sketched on pale, tanned hide. He was rocking and chanting, holding a skull-shaped silver bowl full of blood on his lap and, with his fingertips, sprinkling little red droplets on the sheet as if he were marking the undulant shape of the battle . . . After a time he raised the bowl to his lips and deeply drank, a crimson dribble staining his chin and pale, bared chest.

His stout, exotic-eyed woman came into the tent with a gust of chill air. She looked at him without expression.

"I came to say farewell," she told him. "I'm going now."

He twisted around, working his blood-smeared lips, mustache and teeth under those glaring, hollow eyes.

"Look at you," she said. "What do you call it? I've never seen this little routine before." Shook her head. "Farewell. I'll see you at home if you ever get out of this miserable country."

"I called *them*," he said, and she couldn't tell if his eyes actually saw her. "I never dared before. . . . They'll come soon . . . soon . . . I called them and they'll come . . ."

"You've lost it," she said.

He set down the bowl, carefully, still staring.

"They'll come and the fire of hell will sprout and bloom in this forsaken land," he whispered.

He could see it: the monkeylike, nameless shapes rising from sudden pits of utter shadow, fierce fish with legs and teeth creeping through the fields, hounds dripping fire bounding everywhere baying like steel scraping stone, a host of skeletons under a banner of flame, charnel winds of darkness, men with hawk faces and iron eyes, black and red shambling things bubbling from the wracked earth, blazing winged ones hovering over villages and castles, all the land sinking into black, bubbling pitch, the earth opening like fanged jaws. . . . His stained hands clenched before his pale, feverish, convulsive face.

"Hear me!" he whisper-shrieked. "I loose you! Come to me, I free you! Break forth!" The roiling clouds of vision swirled about him. His voice gathered and seemed to shake the cold earth itself and stunned her for a moment. She backed outside and shut the flap. In the distance she could hear the battlesounds. Close by the wind soughed over the bright snowdrifts and stirred the stiff trees. The tent banner fluttered percussively. . . . Her men were waiting. His blackarmored guard sat horses close at hand. The sun was sinking and long shadows crossed the fields. She halfexpected the earth to open up. . . . But it did not . . . *Perhaps,* she reflected, *it didn't have to . . .*

# lxxix

Parsival was riding at the dawn. He kept his face away from the coruscating glare where the sun seemed to melt loose from the horizon as it rose. Because he was facing down the ridge into the flat valley where the frozen river curved he saw the three people on foot, struggling along, two of them seeming to be arm in arm and he thought it might be a man and a woman. The smoke from the burning village drifted around them, blotting, then blowing free as the wind coiled and uncoiled ...

That strange feeling of peace and kinship had stayed with him through his sleep and he smiled and waved his hand at them, it didn't matter if they noticed him or not, and wished them well.

They were leaving the war too, he decided. Then he looked away and lightly spurred Niva on across the rising slope ...

# lxxx

Broaditch, breathing heavily, thigh aching with each stiff step, blood caked and frozen on his leggings from the slash, kept Waleis leaning against him, staggering him along, hearing him gasp, feeling him sag limper and limper step by step. Alienor, huddled into herself, waded on in front.

He noticed Waleis was sobbing now and, thinking the pain must be too much, he called to Alienor to halt and they stopped in the center of the open space near the river with streamers of black, bitter smoke swelling and thinning around them. He sunk with Waleis to his knees, holding the bony head on his chest with an almost maternal desperation and intensity as the mortally hurt man moaned:

"I feel nothing . . . I feel nothing . . . help me . . . I can't feel myself at all . . ."

Broaditch embraced the frail form in bloodstiffened clothes and felt a bitter anger seething quietly deep, deep within himself. Alienor crouched down near them as Broaditch, in wordless pain, glanced up in time to see a flash of bright red on the sheer white hillside: the knight was just going over the crest. He craned around nervously, afraid more might be coming this way but the blinding bright, shimmering landscape was clear.

He looked hard at Waleis: eyes nearly shut, focusless, watery, lips cracked and bleeding, each heave of breath shaking the yellowish foam that bubbled at his mouth corners.

Broaditch sighed and silently stroked the cold, lumpy forehead with his own stiff fingers. Sighed again. He was feeling pity too as well as that steady, subliminal rage. After a few moments Alienor spoke:

"My love," she said, "can't we go on?"

He nodded. The picture flashed in his mind: the knight swatting Waleis across the chest then coming straight on at him, massive charger rocking in the snow like a ship running before a choppy sea. Keeping himself between Alienor and the rider, a goodlooking, blondhaired youngster, helmetless, whose bright, still, impenetrable blue eyes were fixed forever in the periphery of his memory, the eyes and then the missing ear that set the charming face in disturbing asymmetry. He backed to the side as the blade went up. In the background he saw the other horseman strike at and miss crumpled Waleis. And Broaditch cried, feeling hopeless: "We're friends to Arthur's side, damn you!" then rocking back from the swordswipe as the knight sidestepped his mount to renew the attack crying gleefully: "Better hope you're friends of the devil, you son-of-a-bitch!" And Broaditch turned as if to spin away, slipped, went down, holding the spear out free of the snow as the next stroke hissed near his head, heard the grunting animal, the hooves pounding down, glimpsed, as he rolled desperately, the sleek black hide towering above him, and then the animal was over him and past and he, from a sitting position, wildly swung the spear like a sword and just clipped the back of the rider's bare head. He felt the impact vibrate and sting his swollen hands and as he struggled to his feet he saw the second one wheel away as the first toppled headfirst like a sack and then he noticed his leg was slashed open and he pressed a hand to the pulsing wound. *Now we've got no choice,* he found himself thinking, *now we've got to run from everyone* . . .

"We have to go on," Alienor repeated.

"Yes," he said, thickly.

He held Waleis' face close to his own as if they were lovers and closed his own eyes. In his mind he said:

*Dear God let me do something to help, sweet mother, something in this world to help* . . .

Many years later, grizzled, going stout, Broaditch was kneeling in his rye field on a shatteringly sunny and pale green spring morning, studying the new shoots. His eldest son stood near him. Across the long sweep of pasture and field a faint quiver of hot smoke rose from the chimney of the stone farmhouse.

"You never told me all of it, father," the boy said.

Broaditch eased himself back on his ample hams and stroked his uncombed beard. His fingers were stained dark with rich earth. His look was far away.

"Well," he finally said, "we left him in the snow. I had never really thought much about poor Waleis before that . . . I'd been thrown in with him, you see, by circumstances. I don't think we would have taken one another for friends . . ." He scratched the soil-engrimed wrinkles of his eyes with a stubby yellow nail. Went on: "We left him and I, I felt it so much more than I would have expected, son . . ."

"He was funny, father. Always scared."

"He wasn't the only one, I can tell you."

"But he was funny. I liked hearing about him."

"Yes," his father responded absently. "He was funny. . . . He thought too little of himself, I think . . . he was a person . . . he had his hopes . . ." He stared across the newgreen fields, the fragile shoots quivering in the mild breeze. "We went on," he continued. "That was a trek. No easy pilgrimage and your mother bore it better than a man. . . . The plague was loose by then. Ah, he walks behind war like a sower behind the plough and a terrible crop he seeds!"

"Did you get sick too?"

Broaditch, father, smiled.

"If I had, I would have died, Torky. It's not the small fever I speak of . . ." He grunted and stood up, shifting his weight with care.

"Then what happened, father?"

"What indeed?" He shook his head and rubbed a kink in his neck. "Well, I came upon the maddest of men who was nearly the greatest and a woman. . . . But I'll speak it all out one day."

"Later? Please?"

His father was still gazing over the fields, abstracted.

"Please?"

"Perhaps."

"No, promise!"

His father smiled and turned to him.

"Alright," he agreed, "after dinner. Get mother to help stir my memory."

"A promise?"

"Yes. A promise."

# lxxxi

Parsival recognized the country even under the snow:
brief, narrow, smooth places endlessly intercut with walls
of ridgerock where no horse could pass. He constantly had
to ride parallel to find breaks as though picking his way
through a maze. The woods seemed a woven barrier, a
nearly spaceless netting.

His idea was that once he located one of the roads that
always climbed (he recalled the fisherman's advice) there
would be no difficulty in reaching the castle again.

He was relaxed for the moment: *first reach your goal,*
he told himself, *and everything else will fall into place.*
Except he didn't want to ask yet: *what is everything else?*
He wasn't asking: *what if I fail?* either. . . . He was oddly
conscious that he was somehow imitating his previous
genuine innocence and though he wasn't thinking about
past or future its urgency was always there.

Dinner was cleared away. Broaditch sat at ease at the
head of the table, puffing smoke at the low, solid ceiling.
Candles and the fireplace embers shook light and shadow
over the rough, smokedarkened walls and stone floor. The
narrow, glassless windows were covered with hide. He
sucked the long pipestem, reflectively.

Alienor sat at the other head, the boys and the girl
on either side.

"Your father and I wandered like stray dogs from village
to village," she was telling them, "but only the dead were
staying there. Surely it was a time from Scripture and
many thought the last days of men in the earth had come
upon us . . ." She sighed, remembering. "Weeping and

243

groaning was the common speech. And everywhere it was the same until we finally reached the southern seacoast."

"Now that's a fine telling of a tale," her husband complained.

"What's wrong with it?" she defended. "Those are facts enough, and none can dispute that was the true way of it!"

He shook his head.

"Woman," he said, with mock patience, "you might as well give it out: Ah, we had hard times, children, but we married, grew older, raised a family here and we'll grow older still, perhaps, before we die and then you all will either die or grow a little older before death . . . bah! . . ."

"There's uncommon truth in that," she declared.

"No," he said, "it's common. That's but the spine of the tale. God's feet, that's no more than what's carved on a tombboard! My life comes to more than that bit of raveling, I hope."

"Your life isn't in the telling," she said.

"I don't know where it is. But there's flesh and blood to it."

"But what happened?" impatiently asked the eldest boy. "You never get the story told, you always argue."

"I'll say no more," Alienor said, obviously hurt. Broaditch sighed.

"Ali," he said, "we all love you."

"Never mind," she replied. "I'll be still."

"What happened before you came here, mama?" the girl wanted to know.

"That's what I was getting to," Broaditch put in. "But I think your mother—"

"Say what you will," she declared. "But I for one would rather forget those days."

"But there are things to teach and learn," he insisted.

"Aye," she said, sarcastic, "about fools, murderers, and harlots."

He smiled and nodded, finally getting the point. Finally.

"Harlots," he said, "you mean harlot, don't you, my love?"

"I mean what I mean."

"After all these years and you—"

"Tell your tale or be still, Master Broaditch!"

He rolled his eyes heavenward.

"Alright," he said, wearily. After a pause he went on:

"We fell in with a company of men and women . . ." He paused so as to hear Alienor mutter:

"Women."

". . . men and women running from the war, like ourselves, or so we thought, although, as it fell out, they weren't exactly running . . ."

"Were there children, daddy?" the little girl wanted to know.

"Yes, Tikla. A number."

"Were they scared by the war?"

"*You'd* be scared," put in the youngest boy.

"*You* wouldn't, I guess," said Torky to his brother, with fine sarcasm.

"Everyone was afraid," said Broaditch, "unless they were mad."

His eyes were sore and swollen from snowglare so he rode on with shut visor, peering from darkness out into the blinding blue and white world. He'd been following a road which he kept telling himself was at least level but now finally he had to admit he was sinking slightly. For miles there'd been no crossroad; no break in the walls of rock and woods until he came out at a broad, long, perfectly flat, treeless plain that a moment later he realized was a frozen lake.

As he rode out across it he wondered if it were the same one where he'd met the fisherman. If so, he'd be closer to his goal. He scanned the wooded, snowy hills but could see no trace of the castle. It wasn't far from the lake, he was certain of that, and he didn't think they'd be likely to have moved the place. The trouble was, even if this were the right lake, he had no precise idea of the direction he'd taken originally.

Niva slogged on. Even bundled in heavy furs he was chilled by his armor. Hunger had been steadily with him for a long time now. His insides felt hollow and pinched and whenever he lay down to rest he was amazed by the remarkable sounds in his belly.

Out in the utterly flat, unmarked snow in the middle of the lake, while peering around he thought he saw dark figures moving back across near where he'd left the road. He couldn't be certain, strained to see; but they might have been spots in his vision. *Or animals,* he thought. Whatever they were, nothing emerged from the shadows of the woods.

When it was too dark to go on he'd stop, strike a fire and wrap himself up for the night. But it was increasingly hard to sleep. He'd shut his eyes but nothing would happen for hours. He wanted to dream just to relieve the monotony . . .

One night, the fire guttering, the moonless sky a shock of stars, as he lay staring, thinking restlessly, vaguely, the idea of giving up entirely came to him. *Where will I go?* he asked himself and wondered: *Go back to my wife? Home?* That seemed very far away. Everything seemed very far away . . . At some point he had an impression that his eyes closed and suddenly he could see everything around him and he thought *it must be dawn* except the light was strange: everything was silvery-gray and shadowless and he seemed to see all around at once without having to move his head. He watched some chickadees sleeping in a nearby bush, little balls of fluff, and he felt a tenderness as if feeling, somehow, their faint heartbeats and puffs of breath . . . at some point he noticed that the whole landscape seemed to breathe, to brighten and fade slightly and he sensed a strange life even in the cold air itself and the earth under him seemed to pulse with vast power . . . then he became aware of dark forms deep in the vaguely translucent woods, they were moving, and he felt a sudden chill and a fear . . . suddenly something seemed to pull at him and his body (he believed) vibrated like a feather in a gale and pulsing waves passed through him like prickling needles and as if at the edge of his puzzling field of vision he perceived a man in armor, head bare but fuzzy in outline, a curl of mustache, glint of eyes like stones under dark water. He felt pulled by the figure in some mysterious way as if an invisible cord joined them and Parsival felt himself suddenly, violently resisting: there was a moment of terrific tension and fear and then he was free and seemed to fall back into himself; opened his eyes and it was totally dark. He sat up. The world was still. His heart raced. He looked around and saw nothing. Sat back feeling weak and vague. For the first time he was afraid that something might be too much for him, that he might not have the strength to keep going on . . .

". . . all these folk had died, homes lost, and even in the best of times your serf and peasant suffers what we all know." Broaditch paused. His pipe had gone out on his chest. He slouched in his seat staring up at the shadowed ceiling where lingering threads of smoke slowly unwound. The family was rapt, even Alienor sat leaning forward, staring inwardly at the past. " 'Now is our hour!' that man cried. 'Now is the time to cast down the mighty from their seats!' because, you must know, the armies were breaking up, the country was stricken grievous to the heart and, that man said, it was the perfect moment to strike down the gentlefolk."

"The gentlefolk?" wondered the eldest boy, Torky.

"He was daft," said Alienor. "Well I knew it."

"Well," said her husband, "be it as may, there was truth in him too. More in the wit than the heart, I grant you." He sucked the cold pipestem before going on. "So this John of Bligh, son of a great baron in the west, I think it was, this raging priest who'd torn off his holy robes and made new vows to men, not God, in the name of God."

"Name only," Alienor said and he went on:

"Yes, children, a tall, spare man who walked as if he meant to take two directions at once, or more. . . . He was so poor on horseback I never wondered that they'd made him a priest to start. He sat as you'd sit on a hot stone with a bare ass, children . . ." They were hugely amused by their father's imagery. "When we came into that walled town a few days' walking from the great battle we saw that the men at the gate and in the street were armed and armored but all were common folk. No gentlemen or ladies were met in that place. And it was in the market square we first saw this John standing on a turned-over cart talking to the crowd."

"Roguish trash," Alienor said.

"Your mother served with such exalted folk she's a hard judge of plain men. Were we trash then too, my love?"

"Say for yourself," she told him.

He grinned and proceeded:

"So this long, lean man with his long fingers, in a monk's cowl, pale as death in the gray, snowy air, was shouting in a shrill voice that at first you took for a boy's: 'When Adam and Eve lived in the earth under God's sweet eye, where was your lord and lady then? Were there serfs in Eden too that the prophets overlooked for all their long sight?' And what cheers went up from the people there . . ."

"Cheers?" murmured Alienor. "If the yapping of hungry dogs are cheers of dogs."

"Oh, mother," Broaditch sighed, "there were rough characters, and no deny, but no more than in another place. Some believed in their cause. It was the few who made the many groan. . . . Ah, we had all seen so much misery . . . so much . . ."

His wife looked at him with a sigh.

"When I asked who that man was," he continued, "a woman in the crowd told me he was God's flail, that he was a nobleman who'd lately turned against the unjust ways of his kind. How her fair eyes flashed when she cried: 'We are not beasts to be driven to labor and slaughter! We are none of us beasts but folk!' Well, before your mother can put it in I'll own that some were lawless, some were indeed . . ."

# lxxxii

John of Bligh sat crosslegged on the shattered altar of the ruined, burned-out church. Streamers of moonlight leaked through the broken roof and touched scattered fragments of statues: a ghostly, holloweyed head, staring, tilted; a pair of praying hands suspended alone in the empty darkness; dim, motionless forms and wavering in the still air the hesitant, reedy, somehow pubescent voice of the man, aiming his words out over the solitary figure of Broaditch (whom the light touched too) sitting on a cracked stone pew as if one of the carven people had taken flesh.

". . . the measures may seem hard at times, friend, our tools may be rough, but when the barber cuts a boil blood must flow to cleanse the pus. Man cannot always wait for God's just judgment—which rarely comes in season—man must listen for God's voice and strive himself to realize the holy, perfect plan in his imperfect works. We aren't tasked to tell the plants and flowers how and when to spring and flourish, friend, or to set the sun by our time, but men have free will to err and with that will, which God cannot order unasked, we must work and carve and shape . . ." He shut his unfocused eyes for a second, intensely, as if to pray.

"How do you know it's his you hear?" asked Alienor's voice from somewhere in the shadows in the rear of the ruined chapel.

The priest's eyes opened but scanned nothing.

"Who tells us to do good?" he asked her.

"How do you know what's good?" she insisted.

Broaditch, vaguely irritated, turned his head, wanting to hear more of John's sermonic monologue.

"If ye know this not," John said, "then ye are not one of his."

Broaditch could feel Alienor not replying. How trivial her questions seemed, how picky. . . . He turned his attention back to the vague, bony figure on the tilted altar. *And this is why I lived to this day,* he was thinking, *I had to meet this man* . . . because for the first time he could remember, he thought he saw light far ahead but within reach and he had a sense that the immutable, grinding, daily misery and injustice, always there like a background noise even when things were going relatively well, was actually subject to reworking . . . the sleeping people could be roused, it was so true, so clear, so simple: the world was a mass of habits, stinking habits, and habits could be changed, wake people and they'd see it, they'd have to! And then for a moment his thoughts seemed but words and he quickly spoke:

"John," he said into the dim silence.

"Yes, friend?"

"Are their armies so weakened now? Are you certain of it?"

The penetrating, wavering voice replied:

"They are broken. And even were they whole, I tell you, the truth alone would take a sword and cut them down!"

"How fine that sounds," Alienor's voice said back in the dark and Broaditch snapped at her:

"You find out a crooked seam, woman, in every garment!"

"Peace, friends," said John of Bligh. "For this is the hour and you are now one of my captains to lead in it. Soon we'll be an army so great and strong that none will trouble us. This realm we hold will be called the 'Free Lands,' from this night forward. And we shall spread out until all men are free alike! This," he murmured fiercely, as if just discovering it, "this is the heart of a capital!" He spread out his arms. "And from this spot the golden light of God's hope will shine out on all the sweet children of the earth and all will possess their own lands and pray and work in peace . . . I see this," he concluded in a reedy whisper.

"Well," Broaditch was telling them, soberly, eyes not on anyone in particular, absently twisting the long, cold pipe in his thick fingers, "there was a hope there . . . a great hope . . ."

Alienor looked at him.

"Hope," she said.

He sighed. Tapped the bowl on the rough tabletop and loosened the plug of ash.

"In time," he murmured, "in time the people might have understood . . ."

"Hope," she repeated.

# lxxxiii

He caught up with the raiding party just before dawn. A small collection of village huts were ablaze and he followed the light across the wooded fields. He couldn't tell what was burning until, working himself and clumsy spearshaft through a last spiny tangle of undergrowth, he broke out of the trees and had an unobstructed view of several ramshackle houses in flames. *See that they contain their just wrath against the oppressors,* John had instructed him when he left. But it looked like the oppressors had come here first in any case. The troops from the local castle were supposed to be off at the war. Depressed, he dragged his feet across the bare field through patches of snow, hoping he wasn't going to find the dead and mutilated rebels he was certain were there. . . . His mind went back to the night before, in the soft bed beside her, staring at the slitted window where the stars burned sharp, intense, feeling her cool feet on his calf.

*It will take shaping,* he told her.

*Shaping,* she murmured.

*Aye.*

Silence. She shifted restlessly on the large mattress. He had never lain so softly anywhere, except, he thought, in the sea . . .

*Why must you always cast glooms?* he wanted to know.

The cool feet broke contact.

*Has John taken your balls?* she asked.

*What?*

She shifted and sighed.

*You're a foolish man,* she murmured.

He folded his arms behind his neck and yawned. He felt like a lord in that bed. Sank deeper in the down.

He knew he felt vaguely wrong lying there and suddenly realized all of them were like spiteful children, in a way, always looking guiltily over their peasant shoulders . . . *well, they'd have to grow up and get over that,* he reflected . . .

Alienor twisted beside him.

*It's not even for another woman,* she said.

*What?*

*Why don't you go crush the hay with John, the priest?*

*What? You think me unnatural, woman? Where do you find these words?*

*In my mouth. But you put them there.*

*God's shattered feet,* he sighed, *what are you working to bring forth?*

A pause. Then she said, quietly:

*I want to go away from here.*

*Everything,* he sighed, *is ever a struggle . . . small surprise men wither and die in a few breaths.. . .*

*He has you spun into his damned dreams with him. Like a moonstruck lover and lass.*

*Woman, woman . . .*

*It's true.*

*Woman . . .*

*It's all a daft dreaming.*

He reached over and touched her back lightly with his rough fingers. She shrugged irritably, but he kept contact.

*I'd prefer it were a woman between us,* she told him.

*Than a dream?* he asked, touching her.

*Yes,* she said, shifting herself, backing into his body. *Yes.*

The heat stung his face as he moved between two burning heavytimbered huts. A great log burst with a crackroar and spurted meteoric sparks across the grayish dawnlight. The last of January's thin snow had run to mud and puddles from the heat. He thought how he always seemed to be following death.

He stopped when he saw the two naked girls and the handless and headless boy, emerging from the dawn which was already too bright for the fires to be more than lightless color, their bodies spread out as if in a frieze of fleeing, posed in a kicking struggle behind the turned and twisted forms of what might have been the rest of the family, as if dancing to death strung along an invisible string, emerging from the morning mists, displayed. . . .

He wondered if the rebel band had ever come this far, if perhaps he hadn't missed them along the way somehow.

He crossed the village fields into the sun that, burning off the last wisps of fog, angled its fire straight at him and his immense shadow amplified his movements and he walked as if that shadow were a slow and sticky weight, dragging himself step by step closer to the intact barn, the wattled door ajar, loath to finally reach there, pull it open and lean his head into the musty dimness . . . and when he did, blinking, frowning, the reek of blood and stinking, unwashed male sweat was expected, the unique, gaggingly intense fecal rot that men develop in the field because they really can't scrub their loins even if they have an irresistible urge for hygiene . . . not wanting to see it he felt his eyes adjust and studied the tangle of bodies that seemed to take shape and substance in the sun-threaded gloom . . . at first he didn't register the rasping buzz and by the time he consciously wondered what the noise was he already knew, already understood and his hand clenched around the spear haft as if it were a hard unyielding throat and he sneered with a rage so deep, so sickening, so burning, so acid hot that it was beyond actual expression and he felt faint and ground his teeth together, raised the weapon and jammed it into the hard, chill earth and snapped the wood, turned and strode away, leaving the broken stick quivering there, its narrow shadow stretched along beside him as he headed back, face set like iron, still picking out that raspy sound above the sputtering of the fires, he seemed tuned to it, walking past the pale bodies in the rude, harsh daylight that exposed them dirty, gashed, broken . . . a dark dog crouched nearby, silently eyeing him and on a tilted, charred post a lone crow sat and cocked its head and when it fluttered its wings once or twice an immense, swelling shadow wavered over the barren fields . . .

He leaned forward over the table watching his children's faces. Alienor had turned profile to him, staring toward the hearth. The fire guttered. The youngest boy was fixedly picking at a scab on the back of his hand. Torky and the girl looked seriously at their father.

"What did you see in the barn?" Torky wanted to know.

Broaditch shook his heavy head.

"I didn't have to see," he said. "I heard enough."

"The funny noise?" questioned the girl.

"Yes. They were snoring. Drunk and snoring." He tilted his head back and stared at the smokestained ceiling. Clenched his folded hands and pressed them to his chin. "Drunk and snoring," he said, "all the dung-sweating bastards . . . I didn't even have to see the innocent blood smeared all over them . . ."

# lxxxiv

Parsival reined Niva up and stared along the muddy trail
where sunrotted snow lay in stained and diminishing
clumps and patches under the netted shadows of leafless
trees. The horse was spattered to the flanks with the
syrupy, black muck.

Each sucking hoof plod had been pinching his nerves.
His mother would not have known him, and, but for the
scarlet armor (stained, dented and ripped) Gawain himself might have taken him for a stranger: he was pale and
gaunt, the ridged bones, the long edge of his nose stood
sharply out. He was past being hungry now and too tense
for the full weight of his tiredness to fall on him. His
eyesight had been troubling him for weeks: elusive shapes,
half substantial figures would flicker across his field of
vision. And his eyes hurt, constantly, irritatingly.

He squinted around at the bleak landscape. He was certain they were close behind him. Several times in the
beginning he rode back hoping to meet his pursuers; now
he only looked behind him.

At first he hadn't understood what was affecting him:
he'd ridden on and on across the snow and then over increasingly muddy tracks and the first thing that began to
spread over more and more of his thoughts was the idea
that there might be no food in the forest ahead, that even
the roots and berries he'd started to depend on might not
grow there. It had been a new idea, at first interesting,
then, more and more, disturbing. How long, he'd wondered, could he eat just those, in any case? He'd seen no
game, no living thing beyond an occasional distant bird,
crows soaring high or eagles, a few chickadees in the
brush. . . . Suppose he never found the castle? . . . Re-

cently he'd begun worrying about his body because he kept finding it wasn't reliable anymore . . . he noticed pains and strange stiffnesses . . . his hands often slipped . . . he'd never thought at all about his body before, he realized, and it seemed a sinister, immense oversight somehow . . . and now, staring around nervously, eyelids jerky, it occurred to him that he might never find his way back from here and then knew that the only reason he hadn't turned around before was because he sensed the riders were still on his trail. He was stunned by the unique idea that he couldn't even be sure he'd always win a fight. He couldn't completely trust his body or anything else.

*I'll be alright,* he thought, *if I go home and rest . . . I have to eat and rest I just can't go on like this . . . I'm here alone and what if I do find it what then?* because he remembered last time, that nothing had really come of it. He'd found the grail that everybody talked about, whatever it really was, and then nothing. No, no nothing: he was locked out!

"I'm lonely," he said, lips jerking slightly.

Impulsively he turned Niva around on the muddy trail and started back the way he'd come.

"What if I even find it again?" he asked the still day.

He felt a deep relief now that the decision was taken. He would locate Gawain who seemed, more and more, a very sensible person. Yes, Gawain would be the best one to talk to . . .

"About the dreams," he murmured.

Because, though he'd slept little these last weeks, he'd found it hard to tell dreams from waking at times: the wall between them had partially dissolved so when he lay down to rest or sleep he often couldn't be sure which world he was actually in . . . at times he would see the gleaming women, like water-sheen flowing, walking near him, with a scent of warm greens and syrupy flowers, on the dark, snow-shot fields . . . and in the last few nights he was sure the dark men had found their way to the shimmering, waterlit lands. The idea that they might find him there terrified him . . . with a deeper knowing than he'd ever experienced he realized he had to be whole in both worlds or be whole in neither and if he were trapped in the dream then the waking would be lost and if he kept only in the waking the dream would die . . . he had to be complete in both, awake in both and how he knew this he couldn't have explained even to himself . . .

Night. He sat nervously, back to a knotted tree, starved, aching, weary, staring at the pale embers at his feet. He was afraid to sleep again. He was sure something was going to happen if he did. He felt as if his consciousness was holding a flimsy veil up to the gap in the wall between worlds, against the vast deep, dark stirrings of the unknown . . . there was sometimes no sun above though everything glowed and gleamed with prismatic light, sky sparkling gold, flowers on the crystal grass sprouting like crusted jewels . . . the very air breathed light, and everywhere a ceaseless music sounded and girls who seemed condensations of light and sweet scent, as if those flowers had become flesh, gently begged him to stay and renounce the chill, harsh, grinding lands, *stay with us,* they seemed to say, *where innocence is sufficient for all things, where everything is apparent, where you need learn nothing more* and he kept protesting in their wordless, intimate language that he somehow had to soften the hard world and join the dream to it.

Deep into the night he started suddenly: either he'd actually been sleeping or something had moved out there in the dark, not in a dream. He couldn't tell. Something dim; uncertain shape. He strained to focus his stinging sight and fought an impulse to get up and run blindly off into the moonless obscurity. By looking to the side he could distinguish the vague starlit coil of the narrow path . . .

His fingers, sweaty despite the nightchill, reflexively gripped and ungripped the sword pommel. He wanted to get up and run and didn't find that at all remarkable. . . . Strained to see . . . among foldings of shadow a shadow may have shifted. . . . His heartbeat seemed to echo in the woods . . . still nothing . . . the same after a long, agonizing time . . .

"God keep me," he whispered behind his teeth.

He let his head relent and rest on the wood. The tree felt warm and secure at his back.

"Keep me," he repeated. Then thought: *was it* THAT *I used to feel in everything before, was* THAT *always close was* THAT *why everything was so friendly?* . . . He found himself listening as if for a voiced reply from the stillness all around. *Was it* THAT *or me never fearing or doubting?*

*I wonder if she knew?*, thinking about her suddenly, seeing her bent over her swollen clouds of flowers in the walled garden, the reflected sunlight from them flickering richness over her translucent skin so that she seemed to him not flesh but a thickening of the incredible colors ...

"Mother," he heard himself say out loud.

The fire on the hearth had burned low. The youngest child was falling asleep in his chair. Torky and his sister were still alert. Alienor was nursing a mug of herb tea with a sweet, woodsy odor.

"Your mother and I slipped away from there unheeded," Broaditch was saying. "There was nothing to say to him after that."

"But you saw him once more," Alienor remembered.

He nodded.

"That's true. I saw him again."

# lxxxv

He hadn't quite reached the village yet, after nearly a week's hard walking back, when he realized he wasn't going to leave without seeing John of Bligh (or Blight, as Alienor liked to call him) once more. He had no idea what to say, he wasn't even angry anymore or empty either. He felt strangely calm now. He felt that, somehow, the extremes in his life were over, that either he'd missed something gigantic or been spared . . . anyway, there was no going back and that was good . . .

He was walking tired; the road was dusty, the sun surprisingly hot for early spring; a moment in the shade brought back late winter. The world was the world he knew, the smells, the sights. . . . He felt, oddly, as if he'd dozed off and suddenly started full awake again.

He kept off the muddy center of the road, walking relaxed and steady. He noticed a smattering of tiny green shoots dotting a roll of dark, stony earth. He could almost feel the warm sunlight drawing them up as it streamed life into the stirring soil. Smiled slightly, took a full breath, tasted the vernality in the air, rich and warm in his lungs. Smiled, looked with a releasing, relieving tenderness at the delicate buddings as if the hard winter iron of himself was softening too. Thought of past days in the fields: the growing plants, discovering potatoes under the loosened loam (always a surprise and wonder), remembered girls tangled with him in buzzing glades above the village of his youth . . . thought of Waleis . . . Alienor . . .

In the valley just before the castle town he started passing groups of peasants straggling in all directions across the fields. He stopped as a dour, stocky man, his rawboned wife and mudcaked children clustered around a laden, spindly cart, came abreast of him. The woman gave an expressionless glance and said:

"They all run off. They's an army comin'."

Broaditch paused to talk but the family kept plodding steadily on past, the bent man pushing the cart—Broaditch glimpsed an infant packed in among the sacks and bundles —as if it bore the weight of the world and turned as slowly.

"Who's run off?" Broaditch asked.

"Anybody with sense," raged the man in a flat, uninflected voice and Broaditch realized he wasn't raging at him or anything in particular.

"Where is John?" Broaditch inquired.

The man kept his sour look on the pile of possessions he was pushing. Broaditch turned his head slowly to follow them as they moved past.

"Ar," grunted the man, "the priest."

"Yes."

"Poor soul," said the woman.

"What happened to him?" Broaditch wanted to know.

The woman shrugged.

"Who knows?" she said.

"A daft business," growled the husband, "from the first. Throw down the lords and then who's going to rule?" He never shifted his eyes from the swaying load that he leaned into relentlessly. "What large, daft notions . . . Does the cow milk the farmer? Eh?"

Broaditch, by this time, was looking at their backs.

"Where are you bound?" he called after them.

Without turning the man said:

"To get a damned crop in the earth someplace."

Broaditch started to say more, then shut his mouth. Followed them thoughtfully with his eyes. They went on against the slant of the sunlight, their shadows swelling, the rickety cart teetering as the man plodded his weight into it with a sense of infinite and endless toiling . . .

There was a trail of litter that seemed to twist out of the village street as if a whirlwind had sucked open all the doors and windows and scattered the meagre rags and fragments (things even the impoverished found useless: furnishings and weaponry, rusted, broken, stained) along the yellow dust of the street. As he actually entered the village he unconsciously avoided splashes of excrement and other noxious refuse, picking his way through the litter.

He saw no one until, turning a corner, there was a massive, rotund man, swaying slightly, standing beside a house. He seemed to be painstakingly drawing something in the roaddust with a bent stick. Or writing, Broaditch thought—because for some reason he had an idea the man might be a clerk. He stopped to watch the stick, with infinite laboriousness, trace what might have been some profound design or complex strategy.

As he was about to question the fellow he ponderously turned, rocking, and then the gaping, blasted face was looking at him: the bluish stain of eyeballs that had melted into the yellowish whites, the wordless mouth slobbering a raucous moan. The stick went on working in the dust, in slow, independent convulsions tracing an intricate weave and Broaditch shuddered, crossed himself, and went on.

Closer to the hilltop castle there were a few men and women sleeping under shade trees near the bright blue lakelet. From the slope he could see other groups still struggling across the plains and knobby hills. . . . He stood a moment looking. . . . Sighed . . . Shook his head, then turned and went on toiling up the slope in the raking sunlight.

# lxxxvi

Niva was a little wobbly, foamy lather gathered at the corners of the opened mouth around the bit as horse and rider yawed together down the narrow, twisting paths, screened by leafless trees where, here and there, bright green buddings flashed by.

Parsival kept himself partly twisted in the saddle straining to see behind, face grimy, pale, ferociously, intently gaunt. At the next forking he tugged the horse to a shaky halt and began nervously peering right and left, right and left . . . worked his rough, dry lips together, kept blinking rapidly, twisting to look back almost in a twitch . . .

"Which way?" he muttered. "How can I be sure?"

He suddenly kicked Niva up to the right, then turned and headed back to the left and stopped again. Shut his eyes.

"Which, which?" he asked the air.

# lxxxvii

Broaditch found him on the hilltop in the shadow of the castle walls, pacing in front of an assortment of men and camp followers: an old woman with a wen the size of an egg on her cheek, hair so greasy it stood out in strands, was squatting down beside a tree, dress hiked up, relieving herself with considerable grunting and straining while a runty dog watched her with interest; another, younger sister, was looking with obvious disdain or at least disinterest at everything and everyone; a plump gnome of a man sat on his heels and gnawed a bone of something and peered up at the pacing leader; a knobby man (who reminded Broaditch fleetingly of Waleis and caused his heart to seize for a moment) kept looking covertly at the disinterested woman as a burly spearwielder assiduously probed for lice in his armpits; a gawky, redcheeked boy listened to John of Bligh's discourse with unfeigned interest; behind him two young men pulled sly faces at one another and nodded sagely—Broaditch wondered at what —and then he could hear the actual words as the loose, jerky limbs flailed the erratic body into and out of the shadow of the battlements: John would reach the end of his invisible tether just over in the sunlight and the sandy-red hair would suddenly shine and then, turning on his heel, he'd jerk, splayfooted, on the precise return track (that Broaditch thought he must already be wearing into the earth) and it was as if a light in him went out instantly.

He barely glanced at Broaditch who was now standing on the sunside of the shadow's edge.

". . . no question of giving up the struggle, no such question," he was saying, preaching, now down under the dark, chinked walls, his back to everyone. "We merely continue in smaller groups, we raid the enemy, we nip his flanks until he finally, bleeding, falls . . ." He was striding back, uneven, sudden. ". . . How many wolves to bring down a wounded stag?" he asked and without pause, stepping into the brilliant sun, answered: "Just a hungry few. One keen sword or pair of fangs is worth a hundred dulled blades or toothless gums!" Turned on his heel and metronomically, in his gangling violence, winked back out of the light, voice continuous, uninterruptible: "Let them go, let them all go, they're no use to us or themselves. We'll free them without their worthless help, if it must be, but we'll free them! This I vow. . . . With nothing but the truth of our cause all will fall before us!"

And before he made his next turn deep in the shadow Broaditch was already turning himself and heading back down the grassy, steep slope, the reedy voice still breathlessly wavering in the mild, still air behind: ". . . who won't convert we slay so when all the remaining heads have rolled in the dirt the body will have to learn to live for itself—" And then, somebody up there breaking in, exasperated, raging: "Damn, damn, we have not even one damned knight or a damned army, who are we going to kill?" And the wispy voice went smoothly, flowing on: ". . . Their power is at an end, their pomp fallen, you'll live to see all men peaceful and free because . . ." But the rest was lost as Broaditch, backtilting, went faster and faster on a suddenly steepening angle of hill, digging his wide heels into the loam, squinting at the warm sun, looking out over the woodlands: a flight of distant birds coiling with the winds; clumps of houses and huts, thatch goldenbright; the intense blue glitter of the pond . . . he felt, for a moment, a sense, a partial memory of childhood, sailing down the hill as if he could at anytime jump and sail free of the tilting earth, float off into the freshening, gathering spring . . . let himself go faster and faster until he was running beyond what he would have believed, trees, rocks, scattered figures zipping past and he felt like shouting and he finally laughed . . . down, down, floating, light, laughing . . .

"Your father found me on the road," Alienor told them. He looked at her but her eyes were aimed toward the dim hearth embers. He'd never asked her why she was already going or where. It was in her eyes but not as an answer. It was just there, always.

The tallow flame in the center of the table sputtered, shadows playing wildly over their faces: the youngest was tilted back in his chair, mouth open, sound asleep; the other two bleary but holding on, Torky just setting his jaw against a yawn.

Broaditch heaved his shoulders slightly, sitting there immobile, remote behind his fathomless gaze.

"Clinschor's devils came there," she said. "I think they said it was the next day."

Torky look troubled.

"Oh, *no*," he said.

Alienor set her face against everything and anything so that even her gray eyes were perfectly still and untouchable.

"The fools," she said, "what did they think?"

Broaditch said nothing more. He stared, unreadably, into the shadows. The little flame that touched them all with dim shreds of light flipped and danced to extinction.

"We was well out of it," she said. "Things only grow where they grow. You can't sow wheat on stones."

Silence. The faint sput sput sput of the dying candle was just audible . . .

# lxxxviii

Parsival reeled and reined up desperately, nearly spilling himself as the horse scrambled to its knees and jerked upright again, halfway around a sudden, violent kink in that tree- and rock-locked trail.

He held Niva still and waited, listened. . . . His ears rang and he twitched his head slightly, involuntarily. . . . He'd sensed something nearby, again. He wanted to try another doubling back but didn't have the strength left for it. He was pale and shaky. The country was too dense for him to cross from the stony trail. He felt feverish. Half drew, then replaced his sword, surprised how heavy it had become.

Sweating, he eased forward slowly in the muggy, hazy spring sunlight that was thinned to a vague glow by the netted branches.

Just around the bend he jerked his head back as if pulled from behind and something whooshed just past his bare face and crashed into the woods. He glanced to the side and saw a great war-ax smashed deep into a tree. He'd felt its wake suck at his cheek, it had been that close.

A huge knight and enormous charger suddenly slammed around the narrow trail straight at him. The man bellowed a great cry in his helmet, raising a two-handed mace above his head.

Weak and sick as he was, Parsival struggled to turn Niva on the narrow lane and saved himself by chance as the other horse glanced off Niva's rump, sideslipped, the rider's deadly downswing missing, and slid forward off the steep shoulder of the trail and wedged its armored bulk between two thick treetrunks. There they both were jam-

267

med, their rears to Parsival who wobbled in the saddle, blinking at the sight, painfully.

"Why do you attack me?" he cried, righting Niva while his unexpected enemy and mount struggled to free themselves from the vise their great weight locked them in. Parsival noticed the man was actually chained to the saddle, or so it appeared.

"You soon will discover that!" was the bellowed reply. "Damn you!"

The horse was slowly unwedging itself, scraping backward from the trees' grip.

"I need no more of this," Parsival declared, blinking.

"I warrant!" shouted the other. "But have it you must!"

"I'm sick of all this . . . I think this is a dream . . ." He was very giddy now. "Why are you chained like that?"

The animal worked itself another halfstep out. In a sudden frenzy the knight pounded one tree with his huge mace, shaking it, shattering bark, dead branches raining down.

"My back was broken," he shouted in his helmet, "yet still I live, you bastard!" He now braced and pushed the mace against the trunk to help his mount. "You broke my back, aye, but hate holds me upright!"

Parsival decided to accept that this *was* a dream.

"Who are you, sir?" he decided to ask, to placate the illusion.

"Who? Hah! Who indeed, you blue-eyed scum."

"Who?"

"The man you wronged."

"Wronged?" Parsival swayed. Dark spots danced and spun in his sight. He wished he'd wake up soon.

"Duke Orilus, you pretty bastard."

The horse popped free with a rasp of steel and heaved sidewise and backward onto the trail again. Several lengths of chain did bind him to the saddle. Parsival wondered, vaguely, how he could dismount, then recalled it was just a dream. A sickening dream: his eyes ached, his body trembled, burning bile kept heaving up from stomach to throat and trickling down again. He watched the fever phantom advance on him step by step.

"I've followed you," Orilus said, "and I'd follow you to hell." He wore a grilled helmet and his dense beard bushed out through the latticework. "I'll follow you past death," the duke concluded, "and chew your flesh in the Devil's lap."

Parsival felt a cold sweat draining him. The figure danced and trembled insubstantially.

"I have to go now," he murmured. "I'm sorry if I broke your back . . ." He started riding slowly away, leaning on Niva's neck in a half faint, vomiting a thin trickle that dribbled down his chestplate.

In an immense, roaring rage Orilus struck his steed with a mailed fist, furious that his paralyzed legs could not spur him point-blank after his victim. A blood vessel popped and burst in his eye as he screamed:

"You and that whore! You and that whore!"

The startled animal reared at the terrible cry, and shrieking in his madness Orilus crunched the mace on its skull and with a shattered sound it fell instantly dead on belly and knees and left him sitting, chained there in the sudden stillness, rage having gone past any sound or motion now. Just sitting there as if he and the beast were praying to God . . .

# lxxxix

Elsewhere his wife, Jeschute, was sitting at a narrow window in the tower of her father's castle. The pale daylight barely illuminated the tall chamber. Her older sister stood facing her, soft features showing hard etched lines around eyes and mouth.

"I don't understand you at all," her sister was saying, voice ringing faintly from the bare stone all around.

"I mean to do it." Jeschute's speech was almost a sigh.

"Marry again. Father will see that—"

"No."

"I don't understand you."

"There's no peace out here."

"Forget what happened. You have your life before you still."

"Not out here." She kept her profile to the light. She was thinner, paler, and her eyes saw nothing close at hand.

"You really mean to take vows when you might wed a future king?" her sister asked.

Jeschute shut her eyes.

"Yes," she replied. "I won't marry decay again and lie in bed where fleshless hands can touch me." She hugged herself and tilted forward, shuddering.

"Compose yourself, sister." A pause. Jeschute didn't respond. "You'll feel differently in time."

"Never," her sister whispered. "Never."

# XC

The blackhaired middle-aged man turned his sharply hooked face to the sunset. No light reflected in his dead-black eyes. He leaned in the askew, open doorway and watched the riders cross the level horizon across the flat grasslands. Their dark armor in silhouette flashed points of fire from the fat, haze-shrouded sun. The mild breeze was sweetscented. The earth was rich and renewed. The riders seemed to float, soundless as their drawnout shadows, over the world. They'd passed earlier, he remembered. He had a feeling they were searching for something or someone . . .

"Papa," said a girl's voice from inside.

He answered her, voice burred, lightly mocking, testing: "He's back with us, is he?"

"Yes, papa."

"Alright. If he asks for his gear, you tell him: 'Sir Knight, you lie as we found you.' " He pursed his lips, starting back off across the now empty, gravely glimmering plain where the sun had just sunk entirely from sight. "Say we swore he was just born—naked as he is. . . . His good luck was nobody slit his throat. His good luck we came along."

"Yes, papa," she murmured, automatically.

In the dim room Parsival opened his eyes and looked up from the soft bed, where he lay at full length, across the twilit room at the wiry figure silhouetted in the doorway against a wash of whitishgray.

The last thing he remembered was the stench and his sinking, reeling weakness, swaying on Niva's bony back, sunlight darkening around him, staring at a nightmare of stacked, stiffened bodies where green flies flickered and

271

flashed like nether flame in a buzzing putridity and tangled
horror of limbs stunning his already tentative senses so
that he didn't consciously notice the stooped, hooded
figures standing by a cartload of fresher dead, watching
him as he gagged, clung to the matted, filthy horseneck,
gazed once more around at the flat countryside, the road
he'd halfconsciously followed, the rotting mounds and the
sun and earth tipped, dipped, spun up and over him with
a dull, flat, smothering clasp . . .

"I might have let the lads do him," her father reflected,
turning from the door and crossing toward where Parsival
lay sunk in deep downy softness. He stood over him and
squinted through the semidark. "So you are back, Sir
Knight."

Parsival shut his eyes and flashed the last image again:
bright sun, heaps of twisted and swollen dead. Opened
them: the dim room, dim figures. . . . He watched the girl
go away and come back from the next room with an elabo-
rate golden candlelabra with five clear flames wavering a
warm light that glinted on bright polished silver and gold,
specks of jewelfire, hanging soft, heavy all around the
room.

"Whose castle is this?" he asked and the man chuckled.

"Lord Pick and Choose," he replied and chortled. "At
your service, knight."

He made a vaguely mocking sort of bow and the fragile
light caught his eyes and Parsival thought they looked like
polished jet stones.

"You a lord?" he wondered. "You seem a churl."

"Do you trust appearances, knight?"

Parsival gathered himself and, with a surprise effort,
managed to sit up. He felt vague, weak and giddy, but
sensed his strength trickling steadily back. He looked
around at the strange contrast of thatched roof, loose-
timbered walls partly draped with bejeweled brocades and
rich artifacts.

"This is no castle," he announced and the dark man
cocked his head and Parsival thought there was but one
word for him: *sharp* in every sense he knew.

"Give the guest some gruel, Gainora," he said, grinning
his perpetual, asymmetrical grin.

"Yes, papa."

Papa tilted his head from side to side, reminding Parsival of a perching crow.

"And you're no lord," his guest decided, indifferently.

The man cocked his head. There was no way to tell if he were actually amused, Parsival thought.

"I have done better than that," the fellow confided. "My kingdom can't be thrown down nor my subjects turn against me." Grinned.

# xci

Next morning, the sun well up toward noon, the convalescent knight was gingerly walking under the cool speckles of shade where the trees clustered behind the house. The budded leaves had opened into spears of delicate light green; a few cows straggled and lay at ease on the grassy field.

Gainora came out of the darkwood barn and set down a clay pot, then crossed to where he was resting now with his back to a cool tree. She knelt on her bare heels beside him. They were silent for a time. The day was developing an almost summery quality.

"Where is my horse?" he asked, at length. He looked at her reddishbrown, faintly poxscarred face; deep serious eyes, dark, gleaming hair.

She folded her hands on her knees.

"Nobody wanted it," she told him. "It's somewhere, I guess."

"Nobody wanted it?"

"The other men. When they found you at the dump."

"Is your father a freeman farmer?"

She shrugged.

"He was, but now he's rich. So are some of the other men. But I think he's the most rich."

Parsival wasn't terribly interested.

"Where is my armor and sword?" he demanded, looking away at the sunbright land where clumps of busy trees stirred in clear bluish shadows.

"They wanted those," she said. "But papa has lots."

And she obviously wasn't impressed by such things. She was vaguely patronizing.

"So you are thieves," he said, frowning.

"No. Nobody else will take anything from the dead. They thought you were one of them. Later, when you moved, papa put you in the cart but the rest were gone then . . ." She cocked her head to one side, hands still and neat on her knees. "Isn't it nice here?"

Parsival was thoughtful and that depressed him.

"So the war is still going on," he murmured.

She shrugged.

"I don't know," she stated. "But the sickness is what men fear."

"Sickness?"

She shrugged again.

"God's scourge," she pronounced. "A priest said that to papa. I heard him. I'm not sure what that is. . . . Papa told the priest that the Lord seemed to have scourged every man in a different fashion."

"I wonder if the fighting goes on yet."

"Papa says the war is our best friend . . ." She tilted her head back and stretched, feline, arms over her head. "No one will touch the bodies of them struck down except papa and some others. They run off and leave everything behind."

Parsival was curious.

"Why isn't he afraid?" he asked her.

She stretched again, deliciously.

"He says if your time comes, it comes," she told him. "He says you ought to get all you can before it comes. He says it don't matter if they run or stay because all their times have just come at once. That's what papa says."

She was now looking very intently into his face. Her eyes were deep, with faint golden light in them. There was something deeply, profoundly there (that he sensed without even being able to think it as an actual thought) that belied her life, her words, everything obvious and present . . .

"I never saw a knight this close," she said. Then amended. "Except dead ones."

# xcii

The thin, winterbleached, silky grasses lay in flattened waves across the pasturelands where the pair waded to their shins among the newly green berry briars. The sun was tilting down the afternoon side now and sparkled on daffodils like bright coins scattered everywhere.

He was restless, anxious, preoccupied: whether he thought of going on (wherever that would lead) or staying here he became uneasy . . .

He suddenly realized she'd been talking and turned to her.

" . . . so he won't be back before sunset."

She was standing very close to him again and his body felt it as though she'd invisibly touched something in him and he suddenly wanted to kneel or lie down, felt giddy and flushed and then he never knew who actually moved first except that her hands were pressing his upper back and their teeth clicked as they kissed too hard and she felt feverish and he noticed, dimly, the garlic smell then lost all his senses pouring himself into the long, deep, wet kiss, holding her suddenly as if she were the only firm comfort in all the universe . . .

"Ah, but don't, my love," she whispered, pressing herself closer, bare legs parting over his thighs and he felt, with a mild shock, a searing, sticky warmth (*like hot stones in there* a thought reeled). "Ah, but don't . . ." As her teeth closed on his ear and a rush of her breath stunned him with heat . . .

Now she was flipped open wide on her back, all lovereek and softness, struggling as if with an unseen, painful form, bare heels pushing again and again through the pale, silky grass, full breasts and belly rippling sealike as he

276

lowered himself and she, eyes brownish and full of unsayable need and a distant, mute secret beyond reaching, sucked herself against him like a wave panting in sweet, acrid desperation:

"I am a virgin, my lord, oh, have care with me . . ."

And he sank down into her with a falling cry . . .

Moving steadily now, caught up in their sweet undulance, in mounting convulsions of breath on and on and suddenly his mind went aloof and thought: *it is full large as a cave!* . . . and something happened and she seemed harsh and he felt chilled with warm sun on his back, burning flesh beneath and his own rich blood pounding: chilled and far away . . . alone . . . lost . . . pressing desperately at her and making no contact, felt himself rubbery, slipping away against her now inelastic resistances . . .

She sighed as if distracted and brushed nervously at her hair, eyes shut, head jerking from side to side and he now was utterly remote and his back had a crick in it and his right arm trembled with holding his weight and he was staring at nothing across the sundappled field where an early white moth corkscrewed and sailed the light breezes among the lenghtening shadows. . . . Then she was still again and those eyes with the deep, lost secret were finding him:

"What troubles my sweet lord?" she asked, tenderly gripping, kneading his softness with hers which served only to pop it out into the cool air like squeezing, he thought, a fish.

He rolled on his back. At the rim of his sight he saw a treetop where new leaves rippled and shook. He blinked. Gnawed at his lower lip.

"That's alright," she was telling him. "It was tasty."

She shifted closer to his side, resting her hands on his chest. Her other hand slipped down and loosely held his looseness. He felt like heavy, cold stone, to himself.

"Will you stay here?" she asked.

He stared at the skyrim. Sighed. Felt empty and utterly lifeless. He had never felt so static and he realized that a steady fear was faint at the moment but always there, underlying everything, and had been for a long time now so that when he was still he became uneasy . . . something subtle, unresolved. . . . Nothing was the way it was, he was thinking, and now he couldn't even fuck . . . *I have to do something,* he thought. *I've gone wrong somewhere . . . or else what's the point if this is all there is of grails and jousts and wars and fucks what's the point? . . .* It was so lifeless and silly.

"I'm glad we found you," she murmured at his ear.

He was thinking about Niva, wondering if he could find him again.

"I think I'm falling in love," she said, softly, a little flatly, somehow defiantly.

He blinked at the paling sky. *What am I supposed to do?* he asked himself.

"Please," she said, snuggling closer, "please let me . . ."

# xciii

"You'd be a fool, my lord knight," said Gainora's father, Dennen, with light scorn.

"They always used to say I was," Parsival replied.

"You'd be a fool to go back to a lost trade."

They were seated together on the seat of the wide, mule-drawn wagon that seemed to float imperceptibly forward in the balmy, shimmery day, a light dust breaking around hoof and wheel, bright green trees slowly drifting past in the long, hazy, perfectly flat valley. A murmur of insects; clipped calls of birds . . .

He was dressed in white linen brocade from his host's spoils chest. His long, fine hair was bound by a thin, coppery circlet. He wore a simple sword.

"For it's all done with for the time," the man went on with a lingering smirk in his voice, quick, intelligent, depthless eyes moving rapidly. "The great ones ate themselves alive." The jetblack, pupilless balls stared at Parsival for long, blinkless stretches. "They broke all the land to pieces and only—" he smiled with strange self-mocking and yet insolent mirth, "—only the carrion feeders can fatten today. . . . You have to learn how to chew and swallow death now if you've a mind to live. Without wealth, with vassals dead and dying off like fleas on a drowning dog, ah, you can use your fine lances to ream out your assholes."

Parsival took it all in. They were moving around a gentle, shadowdappled bend through a dense copse of beeches and then the thick stench suddenly puffed into their faces and he gagged and felt clammy. The man slapped a winesoaked rag across his nose and mouth.

"Here," he announced. "You'll get used to it gradual."

Parsival held the sour cloth to his nose as they halted at the lip of the huge charnel pit: dark, slow smoke stained the purity of the greenblue afternoon with its sagging, curdling unwinding. Various hooded figures, faces wrapped to the eyes, stirring the heap with long, charred poles.

"Now here's a trade in fashion," Dennen remarked as he went around to the rear of the wagon and started tugging a sheeted, dead woman by her stiff, bare legs from the wagon-bed and dragged her toward the oily flames.

Parsival twisted around to watch. The wrapping tangled loose as Dennen swung her by the ankles so there was a flash of pale, naked body before she sailed in a spiraling, easy arc into the gaping hole. The flesh flashed an image into his mind: Gainora crouched nude between his legs mouthing his penis (which seemed absently hard to him), watching her strain, suckle, press herself to it, sighing, rocking back and forth . . .

"Just change your clothes and join me," Dennen was saying. "Join me and Nora and your fortune's secure, knight." The unblinking, glittering eyes watched. He paused and rested, hands on hips, back to the stinking smoulder, catching his breath. "I won't deny I stand to profit in many ways by joining myself with such a one as you. As you well can't deny the advantages of such an offer in these days, Sir Knight." The slightest hold. "And my sweet lass." The slightest grin.

Gainora kneeling, looking up at him with a need, devotion and illusion he wanted desperately to meet and match. He wanted to respond, to somehow lose himself and everything, doubt and purpose in her, working every afternoon (and sometimes night) at lovemaking like a chore, trying, trying, holding on, though everything remained muted and very little of moment happened except that he came to understand or at least feel guilt which, he decided, resulted from weeks of watching her from a numb distance . . . there had to be more and he knew he had to feel it, what she seemed to lushly press on him, what those untouchable eyes seemed to silently beg and he tried, wanting to lose himself with nothing coming from behind or waiting ahead of him, he wanted this . . . remembered her crouching on the grass, naked, among threads of honeypale sunlight, holding herself with folded arms, silent eyes showing it to him and then slow, silent, hot tears as she bit her bruised, full lower lip and he asked her *what? what?* and she said nothing not even with her eyes now . . .

"What do you say?" Dennen called over to him.

And he blinked at the pits, holding the acrid rag to his nostrils. Then got down from the seat and stood looking through the bitter smudge at the twisted bodies, charred, half-charred, the hooded men staring at the creeping flames that guttered and spurted.

"It's the best chance you'll get," Dennen was saying behind him.

And her expression again: mute eyes, tearshiny, lost, hopeless. . . . An inarticulate cry welled up within him in the face of his memory . . .

He shut and opened his eyes. Then started walking with absolute determination, straight away along the sunny road that aimed roughly northwest across the valley in the general direction (though he didn't know that yet) of where he once lived, feeling keen anxiety again, a sense that the very hardpacked earth under his feet was profoundly loose and cloudy, a sense that dream and waking were still a problem and that he'd have to somehow comprehend the whole before he could hope to settle with any of the parts. . . . Walking on through the wisps and curds of sickening smoke until the breeze turned into his face and he could toss the rag away and the sweet richness of the land drew or drugged him into a tender mood so that for a moment the lurking fears drifted away and he felt the timeless pulse as though nothing had changed since the morning he turned from his mother in the flowergarden and set out across the billowing summer grasses mounted on the bowed and sprung old horse that, unattended, pulled always in a vast circle. . . . *Like much else,* he reflected.

"I have to find out," he said to himself, drinking in the gold and red flowers, the sharp shadows on the wooded hills, the great hush of cloud shadows, the steady pressure of the sun . . .

# xciv

The cart-incised, narrow road was whitish and faint in the full moonlight. The trees overhung the way. Parsival ascended the mild slope in the warm air. Off in the wood's depths he could hear running water. And then something else, closer. Gooseflesh prickled arms and neck as he froze, hand on swordhilt. He was conscious of his white garment's visibility.

He was sure they'd finally caught up with him. For an instant his body started to run but didn't. He smoothly drew out the blade. It gleamed in the fanning light like a ghostly flame.

"Come on then," he called out, trying to still his heart.

# XCV

A light snow was falling, the clouds were gray smoke and the day was as bright as it was likely to get.

Wrapped in her furs she walked with her mother along the lip of the moat where a scummy ice was forming on the stagnant surface. Across the field there was a low stone wall and beyond it the road where every day now straggling groups of huddled, homeless people with their carts and goats and mules and silent misery were heading north. Once one had died right there and none would touch the body and she went down to see: it was a small girl in rags, face swollen, arms awkwardly stiffened, skin horribly mottled and she'd shuddered and ordered some of their serfs to bury the child but no threat would avail. For a few mornings the body stayed there, preserved by the cold, and then one morning it was gone . . .

"You've never pleased your poor father," the short, stocky lady told her.

"Christ, mother," Layla said.

"It's true. God judge it!"

Their breaths puffed out and wisped away among the snowflakes.

"You bring him no comfort," her mother informed her. "Is our life so easy? The crops are poor, the serfs run off . . . or die . . . the death is everywhere . . . Even the nobles are not always spared by God." Her voice went to a whisper. "We've had to barter with gold we'd kept!"

Layla seemed unimpressed. She was looking across the temporarily deserted road at the gentle slopes beyond where the leafless trees struck her as black fingers clutching at the drifting snowfall. She was thinking with regret how no minstrels came by these days. She kept recalling past songs and gambols. . . . She hummed faintly to herself. . . . Life was a dungeon, and no mistake . . .

"And the quality of food," her mother was saying.

*Am I getting my wish?* she asked herself, seeing what she now was sure was a man coming through the trees not dressed as any peasant, even through the blurring white air she could be certain of that.

"Look, mother," she said, pointing.

"What? What's that? One of these villains looking to cut gentry throats?"

And then she was stunned as he reached the wall, obviously weary and cold and just as obviously indomitable, by the beginning of recognition and she thought: *but it can't really.* . . . She caught the glint of blond hair around the leather cap he wore and somehow she knew and then tried to decide how she actually was going to feel about it . . . and thought: *but if it is.* . . . He was now leaning on the wall, looking up at the castle looming through the snowmist. And then he vaulted over and started across the field toward them and her mother hurried toward the drawbridge calling Layla to come on, holding her full skirts and halfrunning.

"Mother," Layla called after her, "it's my husband."

And the woman stopped, her hand flying to her throat in a gesture that would not have warmed any son-in-law's heart.

"On foot? On foot!" the mother cried. "Come back as poor as that?"

Layla decided she was pleased altogether, not merely her body. She bit her smiling lower lip.

*It is it is and we'll get away from this miserable place!*

And then her body was running toward him as her mother shouted something, lost in the muffling snow, that was certainly not formed in the sweet rhetoric of delight . . .

# xcvi

Her parents just watched him in silence. They sat on either
side of the great fireplace while he ate at the nearly empty
board with a single, ancient, scrawny servant to attend
him. Layla sat at the far end of the long table drinking
mead from a goblet and smiling every once in a while . . .
the only sound in the hall, besides the crackling blaze, was
Parsival chewing and working his knife on his plate . . .

They watched him, whenever there was no choice, all
winter. It almost amused him after a time. Eventually he
got used to it altogether. . . . He ate, hunted in the snow,
and spent the long, long nights wrapped in furs and silks
in bed with his young wife and the pleasure of that filled
enough of his days so that by spring he was fairly content
and had put on a few pounds. Once in a while he was
troubled by dreams or when sitting alone, idle, but as the
season warmed he spent more and more time running the
dogs and just riding, learning to hawk from a visiting
cousin who'd escaped the calamities further south; kept
busy and refused to think about anything in the past
year . . .

On a cool, gray April morning he was riding along a
wheatfield idly watching the serfs chopping at the still hard
ground with matlock and wooden plough. He sat his horse
to watch as an old man with a stiff beard came toiling up
the path beside the rail fence. He seemed to be holding a
ball except when he got close Parsival saw it was the
bloody head of a calf, the tongue poking straight out as if
in human mockery. The old man stood still looking up at
him on the horse.

"What's this?" Parsival asked.

The old serf was distraught and angry. His eyes were lost in crinkles of wear and weather.

"It's no apple," he said. "D'ye see this, master?"

"I do. Is it for a feast?"

"Have I substance enough to kill me only calf for carnival?"

"I know not."

"I don't, good master. I don't. . . . Some filth did this to me and stole the body off, I know not where." He held the head up with bloodied hands as if to offer it to the young lord. The soft calf eyes were empty above the gaped, dark mouth. "I know not where."

"That's a hard thing, old one."

"And left this here head a-standing on a pole out in a field! What else but to mock me? I ask you, what else? Hah? What manner a man lives in these times? I ask you?" He cocked his head.

Parsival drew in his breath and stared into the calf's face.

"On a pole, you say?" he questioned.

"So it was," the old man raged, starting to walk on. "And left but this for my old woman to stew in the pot. God curse the devil who'ere he were!"

Parsival watched him go. Bit his lip. Felt uneasy. The day was too gray, he decided. It depressed him. . . . He suddenly remembered all those months in the woods and the shadows he felt at his back. . . . He looked around the dreary landscape. Felt nervous; shrugged it off. . . . It was just a prank, he said to himself, unsatisfactorily. *I'd better go home soon,* he thought. *I'd better go back to my home . . .*

# xcvii

The fields were virtually dripping with rich flowers. Shadows of the leafladen trees crisscrossed the stone road where a dozen attendants and men-at-arms shuffled in loose file.

The morning was already hot, even for a rider. Parsival was sweating around the hairline. He turned for a careful look behind: saw the wide road running in a shallow curve out of sight into the lushly bluegreen hills.

He was wearing white silks with a blue coat of light mail. His wife, Layla, beside him, in yellow, rode her palfrey side-saddle.

"You never finished that tale, my love," she lightly prodded.

He smiled and looked at her: the dark, smooth cheekflesh, deep violet eyes, the thin, nervous, startlingly full-breasted body. Blinked himself back into the telling:

"Ah. . . . Where was I?"

"In the forest. The mute knights were upon you."

Neither smiled now.

"Or so I believed." He glanced backwards again. *A habit,* he reflected, *fast becoming permanent.* "Half a dozen rogues in ill-fitting tatters of gear. One so poxriddled his craters gaped even by moonlight. Another had but one eye, but what an eye! . . . I said no word. 'Deliver your purse an' pay for your life,' said One Eye. I decided to just wait."

"You didn't smite them dead, my love?" She seemed faintly disappointed.

"No. I just waited, holding my blade ready. Death had become very uninteresting to me, I'd seen so much by then . . ." He smiled vaguely. "When they saw I wasn't waiting to have courtly conversation they went off to seek more gracious company. There are times when silence is a keen sword."

He checked his rear again, not quite consciously.

"I went on and I think they followed, gathering their courage after a time, but something happened back there because there was a sudden howling and cursing and clash of combat and I went running along that little road because I wasn't so sure but that silence may have dulled its edge by then."

She laughed, delighted.

"Was it the mute ones?" she wanted to know, looking behind herself though danger seemed unthinkable in this mellow summer morning.

"I was too swift to ever know," he said. "Either I left the path or it ended and I sped through sparse trees and thick brush and the next event was an immense blow that battered me reeling and down on my back and I was certain I was departing my mortal frame . . ."

"An ambush!" she cried, caught up in the story.

"A wall," he corrected.

She frowned, then laughed.

"The great fighter," she said, "smitten by a wall. What wall, or didn't you ask the victor's name?"

"The champion was called Sir Stone," he said, leaning across to kiss her cheek, a kiss she accepted without demur. "It turned out to be a monastery. A grim enough place . . . I followed the wall—on wobbly legs—to the gate . . ." He automatically checked behind again. The men were starting to straggle as the sun tilted higher. Up ahead, her maid, on a pony, was beside the column, chatting with an ax-wielding soldier. "It was a place where many had fled the plague and it had pursued them even to that holy spot."

She bit her lip and shuddered slightly. The day was suddenly touched with something darkening.

"There I learned some news," he continued, "none of it fair to the ear. The abbot had just died and the monks were falling fast. One of them told me there were no armies left to speak of anymore, that the sickness had eaten both sides to the bone and the black magician, as they called Clinschor, had fled south with the remnants of his host and had taken shelter in the underworld with devils. So they said. But a traveler told me that the mute riders and others who spoke for them were still roving through all the country seeking Sir Parsival and any who knew him."

They rode on in silence for a while.

"Well," he said, at length, "we're far from them now."

She looked at him anxiously and said nothing.

They all went on, feet tramping, hooves clicking, the men sweating along with their packs and arms. Her maid was now singing faintly in a high, light voice. A slow and poignant keening tune . . .

They had stopped to rest and refresh under a cluster of thick oaks in a shade so cool and sweet that someone remarked it was like a draught of spring water. Men were stretched out; the maid was still talking with the soldier; Parsival and his lady sipped wine over the remnants of a cold fowl.

"I never thought to see you again," she was saying. "My father and mother swore you'd never return."

"They convinced me to set out in the first place."

She shrugged.

"I've seen them happier," she said, "than when you turned up."

He leaned back on his elbows and looked through the winking leaves, the little shifting blots and blurs of light.

"Did I tell you I met the old man again?"

"Yes," she said.

"It was in the forest close to Arthur's lands. I had about decided to look for you and was avoiding the roads, of course, because I was a long way from the famous ass I used to be . . ." He reflected for a moment. "Even in trackless woods I found men dead and dying from the black poison . . . beyond belief . . ." shook his head.

"You actually saw Merlinus again?" She rested her head on one elbow. He nodded.

"I chased him," he said. "I saw him crossing a field lower down on a slope and I called out to him and, strange to tell, I ran but as fast as I ran the distance kept the same. Though he never glanced back or seemed to speed up, that I could tell . . ."

Seeing him just beyond a screen of trees, racing around it in the wet, misty bushes where gray drizzlelight hushed everything but his breath and swishing steps and the faint ticking of raindrops on new leaves; running faster over the slick earth, catching flashes of the hooded, cloaked figure through breaks in the foliage, feeling dreamcaught, and for a timeless gap he had a sense that all the living breathing, circulating world was vague, thin, fragile and feeble and that there was something else, something his mind could not actually grasp, something too vast and deep and utterly, utterly still underlying everything else, all the superficial pulse and stirring of life and time and he suddenly felt he was about to run out of the world into that something else where briefly his senses flailed and failed finding no purchase and it was as if he'd been turned inside out, in some inexplicable way, and then with a gigantic, soundless rush the opening sealed itself before him and the world was firmly back and Merlinus was standing watching him from under a widespread, darkleaved yew tree, now-white beard damp and flattened over his gray mantle.

"He scared the shits from me," Parsival told her, draining his cup of perfumy wine, enjoying the coolness. "And he wasn't a great help, either."

"Well, she pointed out, "no good comes of meddling with witchmen."

He lifted an arch eyebrow.

"A witchwoman ought to know," he remarked.

She made a devilish face, leaned over and fastened her teeth in his shoulder.

"Grrr," she said.

One of her hands dipped between his crossed legs and began to mock scrabble at the mail codpiece fastened there.

"God's wounds," she said, "an unnatural man!" Laughed richly, intimately.

He chuckled and freed himself and in the laughing struggle pressed her flat on the warm, scented, resilient earth. Kissed her cheeks, forehead and lips.

"What did the old farter tell you?" she wanted to know, suddenly.

"Who?"

"Merlinus."

"Oh . . ." he eased himself onto his side, propping head on hand. "Not much, I fear."

Merlinus didn't speak for a time as the rain misted down; and then he inquired:

"Why don't you go home and get another suit of fool's skins?"

Parsival frowned and wiped the beading water from his eyes, peering in at the old man in the damp cool dimness under the tree. It was unnecessary to point out that he didn't understand the reference. Merlinus sighed as if relenting from some contemplated harshness.

"Why were you chasing this man?" he asked and it took Parsival a moment to realize he meant himself.

"I . . ." he began, by way of explanation, "I wanted to ask you . . ." and broke off discovering he really had no idea. He simply had a sense that he should talk to him.

The old man seemed to understand well enough to render answers superfluous.

"How can this man help you?" he asked. "If he held it in his hand he would give it to you. Look," he went on decisively, "do you see that tree . . . over *there* . . . against the sky all alone?"

Parsival turned and looked: a giant oak swaying against a pale, dull sky.

"Now we both see it," Merlinus pointed out. "That's the best I can do. I can keep showing you roads but you have to walk them. This man can't possess that tree, he can only look as you can. It's all in the seeing and I can't see for you."

Although Parsival kept telling himself this was all senseless, in a larger way he was aware that he deeply understood, knew that what his mind would remember afterwards would be meaningless. He stared at the massive branches as if, somehow, something profound was about to happen there.

"I couldn't find the grail," he suddenly said, complaining. "I looked everywhere."

"Maybe it's up in the tree," said the old man's voice behind him, mused and wry.

For a second the young knight was about to race over there and look. And again, in the briefest of flashes he felt the world and himself silently explode and for that immeasurably tiny flash there was something he couldn't grasp with anything, mind or sense . . . and when he twisted around again there was no one behind him.

He was staring off past Layla's head, remembering, and she touched his cheek.

"Come back to me," she said, in a serious whisper. "I don't like it when you go away."

He smiled vaguely and focused on her face.

"I'm here," he said, gently, and cupped his hand against the slight, full curve of her belly. The idea that she was going to bear his child had come to seem natural, deeply sweet. And so did going back to where he'd set out from with a queen beside him to rule that remote and armyless kingdom which nothing ever touched but the ordinary tide of time.

"At least," he murmured, "I've found out what I don't like." He sighed, went off into memory again. "I once killed a deer and wept for that . . . and soon after killed a man and got almost used to that too . . . but, Layla, my wife, I always felt some *magical* adventure lay before me, was waiting . . ."

She traced the thin scar that creased his cheek. Her fingers kneaded it gently.

"I saw that right away," she told him. "Your eyes told me that, Parsival."

"I went barefoot through a field of cowshit," he said, grinning, and she laughed heartily. "And I said to myself: 'Under one of these griddlecakes—'" She broke up completely, head lolling back. " '—under one of these mushy treats there's a magic pearl, so I'm going to have to keep squishing on—'" She gave a little shriek and rolled helplessly on the shady turf among the spears and flecks of sunlight. " '—and keep squishing until I catch it between my toes like the farmer in the story looking for his wife's ring.'"

They laughed together for a while. Then he went on, derisive, but deeply serious and still (and he knew it) innocent too.

"I was supposed to learn everything so fast," he said. "And that's true, I did: everything useless like killing things, like walking on shit."

"Stop it," she said, gasped, holding her side. "I'll laugh the baby out."

She lay back for a bit, watching him tenderly.

"I saw it in your eyes," she said, and then the joy gusted from her again.

"My lord, my lord," cried a barefoot servant in brown livery, standing just outside the overhanging treeshadow, pointing back along the curved road.

Parsival sat up and followed the finger and saw a rider sitting a heavy, armored steed about a quarter of a mile back just where the road curved into the wooded hillside. His dull mail glinted. His visor was down.

Parsival stood up and took a few steps forward out of the shade. His bright blond hair flashed in the sun.

The knight just sat there watching as Parsival debated whether to go closer or call out. After a few indecisive moments the rider backed and turned his mount and went down the treelined curve of road and out of sight, leaving the others staring at rich, empty greenness.

Layla was standing just within the treeshadow on the whitish stone road.

"He was afraid to try combat," she said, hopefully.

Her young husband wasn't so sure.

"I wasn't armored," he pointed out. "Why should he fear anything?"

Layla shrugged.

"I think he was afraid," she said.

Twenty years later Broaditch went into the tilted, tiny room by the shaky light of a candle, bearing his sleeping daughter in his massive arms. He laid her down gently on a lumpy straw mattress. The cool air smelt of sweet, damp wood.

He stood there a long moment, studying her face, the stray coppery coils of hair along her cheeks. Adjusted the coverlet around her. Suddenly she opened her eyes.

"Sleep, little one," he murmured.

"Father," she said.

"Sleep," he soothed.

"Did he die, father?"

"Who?"

"Parsival. Did he die?"

"Parsival?" he wondered. Her big eyes looked at him from the borders of her dreams and the shifting light that fanned her face with quick shadows. "I don't know, child . . . I really don't . . ." And although he instantly sealed his mind off from the notion he knew it was too late, that the seed had dropped and would inevitably sprout; suddenly the twenty years were no longer a barrier or protection; suddenly the wall of time was crumbling and he felt utterly naked as if he were already on a long dark road alone out there somewhere; not the farm or family or any of it was going to be defense enough against the last incomplete question which had been his thought (no, not thought but rather certainty) that her voice had betrayed into words, precipitated into the actual world. . . . He knew all this as she slipped toward sleep again, murmuring something that he stilled with his square hand on her forehead.

"Peace, little bird."

His eyes were already gone and going, distancelooking. . . . He sighed with tremulous, infinite weariness . . . and with patience . . . sighed . . .

# xcviii

The young woman in a tattered novice's habit paused as they came out of the thin, scraggly, charred woods and reached the cracked and bilious wavelike mounds of red and black clay as if the earth's inner spew had been exploded in a deep vomit there. Her two dwarfish, slanteyed captors (that she didn't know were called Mongols in some lands) in their strange leather armor and boots, prodded her along with casual, unparticular roughness.

"You go," one said. "Pretty soon see king."

She'd made up her mind they were demidemons: the ill result of mismatching men and un-men. It was told that such matings still took place in foreign lands. These two had (she thought) been in the ambush: she was half dozing on mule-back, hardly noticing the armed men walking before and behind the little group of pilgrims, women and servants they escorted and then, instantly, a seething clatter, a ringing, screaming, raging, neighing, pleading mass on a suddenly bloody stretch of mountain road and before she had time to more than twist in the saddle and gape around (at a monk's head rocking off his shoulders, a dozen arrows transfixing a blacksilk-clad dowager so that she spat bloody foam, a few desperately battling knights in their guard being battered by mace and chain like iron in a forge), she was gripped from behind, smelt a strange, spicy breathreek, felt rough, hard hands and then was dragged into the underbrush and pressed down flat on her face, lips soundlessly and continuously praying, seeing only a scant few feet of sunsprayed brown and green, the weight of one man (she knew there were two) on her back and after a while (surprised when nothing more happened) in order to distract her mind from her probable fate and from the

295

terrible sounds a few yards away she concentrated on an anthill a foot from her face, watching the glinting black creatures seethe into and out of the stray strands of light that leaked and speared down through the thicket, watched with a kind of distant, stunned wonder as dozens fastened on what looked like the twisted claws and bright plumage of a small bird's leg (vast as a hill on their scale) and dragged it with frantic intensity toward the hole that they rioted in and out of with mad precision, which by no stretch of anything, instinct or human imagination, could possibly receive the offering of rotten flesh and bone and she wondered if they had to find it out each time in every case by tugging whatever it was by painful fractions right to the door and then in a maze of confusion and thrashing legs and feelers discover it didn't fit . . . she was briefly irritated with disappointment when dragged to her feet (the sounds, except for a low, whimpering moan which she took at first for some animal, had died down to muffled conversations) before she could see what the ants finally did . . .

Now, footsore, hands lashed behind her back, she was shoved over a soursmelling ridge of clay and nearly fell (heart raced wildly) over the edge, glimpsing a ledge of earth a dozen feet below, then another and another, like stairs, all curving concentrically, and her senses were stunned by a sheer immensity: circles cut into the earth spiraling down to a dense gape of darkness . . . then she was sliding and stumbling, arms held by the hard, scraping hands, over the lip and down to the flat packed level . . . they began walking around the vast and (she soon discovered) almost imperceptibly diminishing circles . . .

# xcix

The sun had set. Parsival, wife, and company were pressing along into a hazy shimmering dusk that glowed like silvered water. Midsummer insects chittered in an undulant, rushing roar. The servants moved on, huddled, worried, hushed; he rode in the rear, looking around restlessly, Layla a little before him. The hooves were muffled by the evening sounds. The air was heavy and fragrant. He kept turning behind. The memory of being lost in the grail woods stirred almost subliminally.

*That was the land of dung,* he thought, with his developing crude whimsy.

Layla was looking back at him, face a pale whisper of light. She seemed more a soft glow than a substantial being.

"Hello, my love," she said softly.

*There must be time for us,* he thought. It was urgent in him. This was new, too. Time for sweet evenings in the calm eye of the world . . .

"Don't fear," he told her.

He reached across the dim space between their mounts as if to assure himself she was solid. She closed his hand in her firm, warm grip. He smiled invisibly in the gathering night.

And he knew even then, though he wasn't going to say it even in his own head, it was still lost, whether called grail or something else, it was missing, a hole in life, love, everything, an empty spot, whether they chased him, found him or lost him, whether he reached home and raised a dozen sons, lived a hundred years, yes, whatever he could say or would be said, in men's and women's eyes, in summer, spring or winter light, going out or coming in, it was lost and even in the lush, sunrich forests of paradise with all the sleek ripe fruit it would draw any Adam to stare through the last hedges with his naked back turned on perfection . . .

Held her hand harder and for an instant he could have wept: touched and briefly treasured the sleek, fine firmness of her living flesh and knew it was only a question of time and so, like an arm held up against a swelling tide, he said:

"I love you, Layla," into the glimmering evening, into the strange, rushing silken stillness of the night.

# c

She had no idea how long they'd been driving her along this endless march around the vast periphery except that it had become totally dark: moonless, starless dark. Her mouth was dry, feet numb; cramped and flaccid she went on and on . . . after a measureless period she had a vague impression that there was more curve to the walls which gave her hope they might be nearing the bottom because however horrible her ultimate fate she now only prayed for rest. Her thoughts reeled on:

Perhaps this was the fabled gate to hell . . . could these truly be demons? . . . she was lost though living . . . ah, but was she living? . . . some said the fey folk had their lands in hollows beneath the earth, the underworld, the foundations of the earth in holy writ . . . some were supposed to have actually visited the inner countries and escaped, there was a miller she'd heard of who told of being taken within the hollow world and released again. . . . And she went on and on in a grinding stupor and then, a stirring of fear sharpening her senses briefly, they were going at a steep angle straight down into the feebly torchlit tunnel itself into a sour reek of close, wet air . . . at some point she noticed the guards: filthy, shabby barbarians armed with clubs and warped spears, squatting and slouching along the greasylooking tunnel walls, staring without interest as the three of them went past, bearded men with horned helmets, sweating and depressed-looking. Several humid, dank levels down the walls opened into a fairly large, recently buttressed, stone-walled and stone-floored chamber: the work had been clumsy enough, viscous black mud oozed between the blocks in countless places. There was a sharp, cloying stink of urine and bad meat and unwashed bodies. Such dainty whiffs were not unknown to her but here they were so concentrated she gagged. She'd decided by now that this was the hall of a troll king. In the shadows between the wide-spaced, guttering torches she saw dim figures in dark armor. They finally stopped well out in the chamber and she stood for a while, swaying slightly on her numb feet . . .

# ci

Parsival eased his horse up past the retainers who'd all
stopped, drawn together along the road in common anxiety
and silence watching a mounted, plumed figure approach in
silvery armor as if floating along the moongleaming stones.
A stout spearman crossed himself and muttered under his
breath as Parsival halted and watched the misty form come
on as if rising, Layla thought, from the murmurous depths
of the sea of night like some supernatural being in a tale.
She loved tales: after hearing a minstrel she'd sometimes
spend hours composing her own poetic adventures, walking alone, shining a soft iridescence of astral realms over
her everyday afternoon, dreaming things so intensely that
they seemed at times to move of themselves . . .

She watched her husband and the ghostly knight sit their
steels facing one another out on the road and part of her
mind spun a story: the dark enchanter had come to take
Parsival in thrall back to the country of lost souls where
all good men were slaves and forced to labor without rest
for rewards (silks, sweetmeats, jewels, rare wines . . .) that
melted to smoke when you tried to grasp them . . .

The ghost raised his visor and the moonlight angled into
his face and Parsival's stomach seized up as if his body
understood before his mind could take in the recognition
and horror: half the face (or very nearly—one ear, eye and
part of the mouth and chin) had been sheared away so
that the teeth there gleamed gritted through the open
cheek. The other half was unmarked. And then he noticed
the left arm's armor had no wrist or hand. He looked up
at the right side of the face: smooth and handsome as
ever though pinched and drawn—and the eye was wild.

"Gawain," Parsival said.

*Or half him anyway,* he thought.

The grotesquely torn warrior twisted his head to bring his

single eye to better focus. Even in the elusive, enhancing moonlight when his mouth moved the effect was indescribable.

"My friend the fool," it said with a flash and gape, without particular emotion.

"I hope I'm your friend," Parsival replied.

Having cocked his head Gawain had only his intact side in the soft light, the horror and ruin lost in visorshadow. After a few moments he said:

"You're changed."

Parsival nodded.

"Yes, Gawain," he said.

"Thinking I'm changed as well?"

Parsival waited, alertly. Gawain chuckled, gestured with his right hand.

"This is nothing," he announced, "none still dare come at me from this side." Clenched his mailed fist.

Parsival waited.

"So you think you know something now?" Gawain said, mockingly.

"I heard the fighting is done." Parsival held a question in his voice.

Gawain grunted.

"No," he said.

Parsival just noticed (perhaps with a shift of breeze) the powerful sour wine smell on the other's breath. Gawain swayed slightly in the saddle.

"You never stood up to me, you bastard," he said, dropping hand to hilt. "I've lost count of all I've sent on their fucking way . . . or the bitches I've pried open . . ." His face turned back again as the eye looked elsewhere and the terrible slice showed in the moonlight.

*How did he live with such a hurt?* Parsival asked himself.

"I'm still a man," Gawain said; it seemed, to the fragrant, glowing night. "Think you are old enough?" His eye came back to Parsival suddenly. "Eh? Want to try me?"

Parsival said nothing and the eye went elsewhere.

"God curse it!" Gawain suddenly cried out with a raw pain in his voice that tore at Parsival. The crippled knight was breathing as hard as if he'd been warring. "God of filth and swine, curse it!" And drew his sword: the blade rippled like watersheen in the moonlight and tore the air like ripping silk as it slashed at nothing for a moment or two . . . and then Gawain just sat there, rocking in the saddle, shaking very slightly, a rough almost sobbing in his breath.

Parsival said nothing. Could think of nothing.

"Get off, you bastard," the older man muttered. "Do y'hear?" And slammed his visor down presenting a smooth, silvery blankness.

Parsival wanted to speak. For an instant he almost knew what it was, what to say . . . and then it was gone and he sat stranded . . .

"Do you hear?" Gawain shouted inside his helmet.

"Oh, Gawain," Parsival whispered and turned away.

And then the crippled knight gathered and stormed his jingling mount past the young man and clattered straight down the road, crashing past the crouching attendants and Layla perched sidesaddle and tentative on her palfrey.

Parsival didn't turn around. Listened to the sparking, clattering hooves until the waves of summer night closed over the fading sounds . . .

# cii

Just about that time one of the dwarfish, yellowish barbarians still standing a little behind her in the chill, stinking, torchlit hall gripped her arms and slammed her to her
knees so that they cracked on the stone. She was jarred
fully awake. And then she saw the three men standing over
her: on the left an immensely fat knight with pale, bloated
face, sweat clinging, streaming steadily over his bulging
cheeks and staining his silken collar; on the right a spare,
bloodless man in black, priestlike garb, eyes faint, washed-
out gray like colorless, still water; both flanked the one in
the center, whom she noticed last, with his square face and
bony forehead and absurd (she thought) waxed mustaches
gleaming and grayed, coiling up around his nose, setting
off the puffy, curdled skin, seeming lost in an oversized
gray robe, strangely large, white hands toying restlessly and
continuously with the loosely knotted tassels.

The fat one dabbed a saturated cloth at his endlessly
sweating flesh; the priestlike fellow bent his slit mouth to
speak:

"You are Jeschute?"

She blinked, then nodded slowly. She was fascinated by
the grotesque hands of the mustachioed man: now they
moved like soft, spidery seacreatures entwining the feeler-
fingers with the black cords.

"Where is Parsival, the red knight?" the slit mouth
wanted to know.

"Who?" she wondered, dully. The hands were now
clasping and unclasping rapidly as if the spiders fought or
mated madly. The face above seemed disconnected from
their motions with its dour, pouchy, emotionless expression.
*He's ill,* she thought.

303

*Jeschute is tortured in Clinschor's dungeon*

A harsh grip closed on her hair and suddenly her head was flipping back and forth, shocking her with needles of pain. Then the grip relented and she gasped.

"Parsival, the red knight," the slit repeated coolly.

She blinked her painful eyes.

"Oh," she said, "the madling boy. . . . But how would I know this? Why do you trouble me with this? I don't—"

"When did you see him last?"

"Oh . . ." She thought. "A year . . . at least a year. . . . Why have you brought me—"

"A year?"

The hands were presently in a frenzy of twisting and twining and interlocking as if nothing else lived on that motionless, slouchy body. The eyes suddenly glowed with feral, fitful life, the mustache moved, the agonized, resonant bass rumbled like distant thunder:

"Did you see the grail?" he asked her.

*They're all mad,* she thought.

"Grail?"

"Did he have it?" The mustache quivered like the hands as the jaw shook. A fleck of spittle struck her cheek and for some reason it made her want to retch.

*His flesh seems bread-dough,* she thought. *What fate brought that boy to me what fate . . .*

"But the grail," she protested, "who still believes that such things—"

The dark, fitful eyes weren't really looking at her and for some reason she was suddenly aware of being terribly afraid. Not like the fear of capture, rape, or even the death she'd expected from the beginning. Something else, something which sickened her with a nameless fear. . . . In the background she heard others' voices, common warriors, one reedy and complaining:

". . . sweat and sweat and for what? . . . it's disgustin' livin' like fuckin' moles what with the blocks slidin' loose all the time and water seepin' in and rotten scraps of food for what? . . ."

And her head was being violently shaken again and this time she found herself screaming.

"Tell me," the thundervoice boomed into her expanding nightmare of sick pain and terror, "where is it? Tell me this! Where is it?"

And she heard herself screaming and screaming as her body began to crumple as jarring blows seemed to come from everywhere out of a devouring darkness and still to the end the whiny common voice was strangely clear:

". . . . eatin' on rats, an' they're all gone mad or I'll be fucked . . . for what? . . . we all look like mushrooms, by God . . ."

And then the darkness shut down solid and she went out with an image of the beautiful boyface in her mind, blond and chiseled, set off by his red armor, sweetly saying to her:

"An' for what, then? I ain't come to die like some fucked mole in the fucked earth with Saint Devil and his unnatural strange gang all with soft turds between their ears. They couldn't even *scare* a mole anymore . . ."

# ciii

"We're come fairly far north," Parsival stated as the party was crossing a heather-rich country of low, rounded hills and massive, glacial rocks. The day was still and perfectly clear.

"What sweet weather," Layla said, breathing it in.

For the diversion of her maid, mounted on the palfrey, one brawny soldier was clapping his hands with vigor and wordlessly singing a dance tune as two unarmed servants cut a quick caper on the white pebbles of the dry streambed that served as road here beyond where even the most energetic Romans had sweated to lay their neat road bricks.

Layla laughed and started clapping in time herself. Then another joined in, humming. It was infectious except that Parsival was now twisted alertly in the saddle staring intently back the way they'd come. He'd heard a crunch and clatter that at first had seemed part of the entertainment. It wasn't.

Back through the purplish shimmer of the sea of flowers there was a flash of steel light and what seemed a mass of moving shadows. He could now hear the stones of the streambed grinding under heavy hooves.

*Oh, God,* he thought.

He drew his sword.

"All of you," he commanded, stilling the gaiety, and then the grinding and clanking and horsesnorts were clear, "all of you run ahead, except for those armed. We'll hold them here for a time."

There was shock and silence. The oncoming noises were unmistakable and terrifying. A woman began to keen in fear; a youthful peasant bolted suddenly, silently into the brush.

"Follow the stream for as long as you can!" Parsival shouted. "Go! Go, in the name of God!" They went, led by Layla's woman on her mount. He pointed after them for Layla's benefit. "No nonsense," he said, "follow them!"

"My love," she said, distraught.

The black horsemen were visible now crashing along, four abreast, stones flying up around them, grinding a powdery dust from the way.

"Go on!" he yelled, "I'll follow!"

And she went leaving him now with the six spearmen.

"How many do you make them, my lord?" asked one, the man who'd started the impromptu dance. Parsival noted he was bronzed, bearded, sturdy looking.

"More than is wise to count," he replied. "They can't flank us here so we'll hold and give our ground slowly."

The soldier nodded and set his men up shoulder to shoulder blocking the thirty or so feet of open space and watched the massive column of heavy cavalry come on, lance tips sparkling, blackarmored, barrelchested horses rocking irresistibly forward.

"I doubt we can do it, my lord," the bronzed man said.

One of the others, skin grayed with fear, looked up.

"They'll crush us certain," he said.

"I'll break the charge," Parsival announced. "They've had a long trail, remember. They must be weary. And they can't re-form if I stop the first four."

*Praise God,* he thought. *And please him.*

When they were twenty yards away he charged them, veering to the extreme left at the last moment so that he only had to actually meet one opponent and with an almost effortless twist unseated the silent knight, his own lance shattering on impact. The tumbled horse and man held up those coming up behind but the other three burst past and rammed the thin line of warriors: one fled, tossing away his spear, four went down (two impaled and flopping at lance end, one with his bowels torn out and spilling around his legs, struggling and shrieking madly in the coils) and only the bronzed man still stood, braced spear deep in a horse's chest, burst through the chainlinks by the force of the charge, blood fountaining over him in pulsing jets, the fallen animal lying on the rider screaming outrageously. Parsival took all this in as he turned his mount and spurred at the two remaining of the first row (he didn't want to look back at what was continuing to come crashing and churning up the stony way) whose backs were to him, one struggling to free his lance from the tangled bowels of his victim and only succeeding in unstringing them in incredible pinkish lengths and loops so that Parsival, gagging in his fury, stunned by the unbelieving, living eyes of the gutted warrior witnessing the unwinding of himself from where he lay on his back, careened into the horseman smiting and smiting in sickened frenzy and horror, sparks flashing as his blade tore, rent, bent and twisted the black and silver armor, pounding, pounding until the man fell silently in a spray of blood just as his companion whipped his sword and scored a blow across Parsival's helm that rang like a bell and dazed, then infuriated him so that his blade seemed to crack like a whip as he buckled the mute's shield into his body and toppled him.

"My lord," shouted the bronzed man, thrusting his bloody spear at the pinned knight beneath the dying, gurgling, foam-mouthed horse, "my lord, they're upon you!"

And Parsival turned to face the next wave of unshouting warriors bearing down on him in a clash of hoof and steel. Head still ringing he turned the first lance with his shield but the next following tore through his armor and side though he managed to stay locked in his saddle for the terrible instant of pressure before the cutting head pulled loose and whitehot pain rushed in: the foe's momentum brought him within stroking range and Parsival folded his shield with a sidecut and then was in a struggling swirl with more coming on with sword and mace now and for a few moments Parsival slashed and spun and parried with such windmilling speed and force that the mass of enemies had to give some ground, though now each breath seared his chest . . . he was cut off from the lone soldier and heard his dying outcry from behind the crowded welter of riders and knew there was no reason not to break off so he turned and galloped up the rising slope away from the nightmarishly silent men, gaining steadily on their heavy mounts. He spurred on until he spotted Layla ahead just catching up with those fleeing on foot, then, starting to recover his wind, he reined up and waited just around a bend where the glowing heather grew so densely among the white rocks as to seem one solid, violet substance . . .

He ached and his side felt numb now. Sluggish blood trickled down the leg of his armor. He felt it squishing and thickening around his foot. He spat a dry cottonball through his lifted visor and blinked his eyes to clear them of sweat and then the grinding charge (at least a dozen strong) swept around the curve of flowers and he snapped helmet shut and raised blue shield to his shoulder and braced for them. There was no choice: if he outrode them not only would they (apparently) eventually follow, but even Layla could not hope to keep up for long. It was not to be risked.

"Still I don't know what you want of me," he snarled as they shocked into him, twisted, gargoylish facemasks shining bright silver.

And then it was all a blurring and flash of arms too fast for thought as blows battered and rocked him in the saddle and he tasted blood dribbling from his mouth then got in one good blow and saw an arm shear off in a blaze of sparks and heard a terrific, muffled blowing of screamless breath in the crabfaced helmet and then he had to fall back again and there were only eleven driving their barrely steeds after him up the streambed which twisted, narrowed and deepened as they climbed the ancient mountainside . . .

Higher, only two could come abreast when he next turned into them, sucking burning air, having accepted his death at the borders of awareness where incidentals were still being dealt with . . . now his senses only worked in fits and flashes: he kept briefly blacking out under the blows that dented, ripped, twisted mail and plate so that in flashes he saw the masks and then (as if in an invisible wind) a lionfaced foeman seemed to blow away and as he struggled on, fleeing, reeling (dark light dark light as blade and mace hit shredded shield and body and his mind found it amusing that they were *black*-smiths pounding his metal), he saw his blade stab through the eyeslits of a serpentface where blood burst from the seams and mouth slit . . . and then he was clinging to the mane, fainting and waking as the animal struggled up the steepening slope . . . and now his mind had an idea that his home (his ultimate goal, the hope and meaning of his life was on this mountaintop: there was an image of a castle of rainbow jewels carved and shaped, prismatically afire and in the bright heart of the wonder and glory in letters of jewel-flame that sounded with a voice as if precious stones spoke: *Parsival you are king.* . . . His lungs seemed permanently flattened, his mouth gaped and struggled like a beached fish's and yet he turned again, finally where they had to come singly at him and he dimly saw, as if from underwater, a goatface, and a bearded, leering manmask, and then, as if sinking in a dream and swinging his sword under the sea in dimming slow motion he checked and blocked and cut and battered each form that rose up before him over and over, hacked and hacked and hacked . . . and then silence and night like a final blow . . .

# civ

The afternoon was throbbingly hot and still. Among the flowered grasses there were faint stirrings of bees. The sun was white fire. A faint smell of baking bread floated from the hillside village up the slope to the small castle. Midsummer was swollen to bursting with green.

Parsival leaned in the narrow window, staring out over the bright fields. He was naked. There was a vague, purplish smear under each eye drawn by his kidneys, a doctor had told him recently. There were wrinkled lines of weathering there too. And everywhere on his body knots and lumps and traces of scarring; several long, wide smooth ones on his sides and back. The years had blended them as much as they ever would. The servants who'd come back with Layla to pick him up said that the narrow streambed was running blood as if a red rain had fallen. They could not believe he lived. His sword was broken off in the helmet of a fishmasked knight. His horse was dead. They'd fled with what they thought was his lifeless body . . .

Parsival scratched his pubic hairs with a forefinger. Behind him, naked on the rumpled bed in the humid stone room, Layla lay, beads of motionless sweat gathering on her forehead and cheeks.

"I'm thirsty," she said.

"Well," he responded, not turning from his reverie, "send for some water."

"Your servants, when are they ever awake?"

"Mine?"

"They're not mine, these clods. You don't know how to handle servants. You never did . . . I don't want any water anyway . . ." She looked at his wide, white back, creased with muscle. "You're always staring into space."

He sighed.

"I was thinking," he said, absently.

"Oh ho," she retorted.

"I was thinking that I missed my chances . . . I was just remembering when I said goodby to my mother, right down in the garden there. . . . At least it used to be a garden."

He was studying the square close to the wall below where rosebeds were being washed over by a tide of spiny weeds.

"To you that's worth a saga." She saw no reaction so she said: "King Parsival takes his leave of his mother with tears and drumbeats . . . I don't care a stain of shit for her gardens either. . . . You're weary of me, with all your talk, that's what the sifter leaves in the bowl."

He sighed again, still staring down the hills where he grew up. In the distance, through the dense trees in their rich bluish haze, he thought he could make out a flash of water where the stream curved, the place where he stalked the deer: the memory flashed vivid and he saw it all, the supple shadow-stippled motions, the arcing spear, the raw blood, the beauty, terror, shock . . .

"You and your chances," she was saying, "for what?"

"I don't want to leave you," he said for some reason, and was faintly surprised by what came out. Still, he knew he meant it. He scratched his navel.

"You don't really care for me," she went on, fanning herself now with a parchment sheet.

A pause. Outside the rich day buzzed and drowsed.

"Things happened to me," he said. "I don't quite grasp it, but I feel something went by too fast . . ."

She rolled impatiently onto her side facing the moist stone blocks.

"It all went by so fast," he was saying. He watched cloudshadows silently speed over the fields and set off the day's burning radiance. "Maybe I should see the old man again . . ."

She tsked, once.

"He's a daft old man," she said. "Magic and mumbling. You're two of a kind."

She was making a picture on the gray wall: a composite image in emerald green armor she called Gawain (based in part on descriptions, in part on other men, unconsciously,

on her husband too) and now she fled with him up narrow
twisting stairs, holding hands, pursued by dozens of fuzzy
outlined, undetailed armed men (though there were features here and there: her father, a cousin, several servants . . .), and high in the tower they bolted themselves
in a bedroom whose door was so massive even the sounds
of pounding and struggle without became muffled echoes
. . . they rested on a deep, glistening green, ornate bed and
after a timeless time while he sang sweet lilting tunes to her
she reached over and discovered he'd parted the mail codpiece and it was sticking straight up and she shut her eyes
holding him with firm fingers and melting soul, then rolled
on her side, scissored her legs and dropped her aching,
devouring mouth over him . . .

"I could have done much better," Parsival brooded.

She rolled over on her back again.

"God's blood," she sighed, "but you act as though your
beard were white."

He turned from the window and sat on the ledge, hands
on knees. He looked idly at her stretched out on the bed,
staring at the vaulted ceiling.

"It's hot," he said.

"Why don't you go have an adventure," she said. "Go
. . . go knock somebody from his horse."

"Oh, be still," he snapped, finally getting irritated.

She didn't look at him.

"You could be jester at my father's court," she informed
him. "God," she implored, "send me a *man!*"

He stood up.

"Layla," he said, "I don't understand you. I thought I'd
learned about this world. . . . Give us peace, pray."

She stared up at the shadowed vaulting, trying to recover
the threads of her fantasy; said:

"Why won't you go and *do* something?"

His heart wasn't completely in it but he went and sat
on the edge of the bed next to her.

"Layla," he murmured. "Please."

He touched her cheek, then shoulder. At first she was
stiff, resistant, then gradually loosened. She put her hand
over his. Took it and kissed it.

He found himself staring past her face. He couldn't stay
with her, with this, with anything, kept drifting off into
vacancies . . .

"I don't know," he murmured.

She held his palm over her warm, dry lips.

"Nothing's what I expected it would be," she said, muffled by his flesh.

He absently stroked her body.

"I touch life with a curse, I think," he said.

She shook her head.

"No, love," she said, muffled.

"I think I do," he said.

She tugged him down to her: the light moved in her eyes like deep reflections of green earth and sky in still water . . .

# CV

Later they lay apart, dozing in their musk and sweat. At a certain point, as if he'd blinked he was somewhere in a forest, following a stream: the light was scintillant, sun hyperbright with a vibrating silvery tone so that the pine needles in this dense wood glistened almost metallically and everything seemed oddly shadowless . . . when he suddenly realized he didn't know how he was moving over the earth he got stuck, strained but couldn't free himself . . . felt a chill . . . then another blink and he was moving through a dark tunnel, somehow floating, and then the tube opened out into a vast dome higher than he could actually see and everywhere soft light, myriad colors sparkling gemlike from trees and flowers that seemed living jewels; beautiful men and women in pastel and white robes, sitting and standing and he had an impression of invisible forces vibrating . . . several glanced up as he floated above them and higher than himself drifted what he took for a shining silver chariot—he realized he could see in all directions without moving his head—then he felt (not heard) a voice sweet and light telling him that it wasn't here, that he couldn't come back here yet because it wasn't here . . . and then he was in a darker place, a cavern or hall; perceived a strangely familiar woman lying dead as if tossed casually aside in a muddy corner and even as he watched a rough-shaped block oozed in a sludge of mud from a wall and sunk heavily to the floor . . . he was moving again and passed two men prostrate before a carving indistinguishable through a dense pall of incense fumes . . . then he passed along a few ropy turns of tunnel and saw with shock and curiosity two naked men embracing on a heap of sacking . . . down another level to where filthy men and women

316

squatted in a circle tearing chunks from some unidentifiable animal and stuffing the bloody pieces into their mouths; the men wore horned helmets, he noticed, and the women knotted rags . . . then he floated through a massive iron door into a chamber filled with gold and jewels . . . drawn deeper still he found himself peering up a narrow shaft, flamelight showing at the opening and then it was blocked out and he willed himself up and into a narrow room where a stooped, miserable figure in obvious pain had just seated himself on a diamondcrusted, ivory ring, set over the shaft, his gray robe hiked above his bony, hairy shanks, large white hands desperately gripping his knees, doubled forward so that his chin nearly touched his fingers there, his upcurled mustaches quivering as he bit his lips and cried out (soundlessly to Parsival) and beat his knees together and rocked his pale, bare buttocks on the priceless seat . . . and then, shuddering, icy cold, he woke up in the warm room in bed beside Layla; the late sunslant barring the air with delicate rose tints above the dim, purplish twilight of shadows . . .

# cvi

It was raining. The downpour beat steadily over the soggy, steamy forest, spattering, echoing, dripping down the gray stone castle walls. Whitish gray clouds spilled endlessly overhead. Beyond the swollen moat the fields ran mud.

Arthur shifted on the windowseat but couldn't get comfortable. The dank chill had, he was certain, penetrated permanently into the bones of his back. The old injury there was stiff and painful. The crease of a pained frown was worked into the flesh between his eyes, which stared out into the misty dark, rocky hills. Even bundled in robes and furs he shivered slightly.

His mind still refused to let the images go completely, even now. The last days of the unended war, the scattered remnants of armies struggling across the snowbound country, men freezing on roads or in burnt-out, shelterless towns, starving, passing through the vast zone of desolation . . . and then the secret death began to stalk them with fever, agony and corruption . . . he and Sir Kay had turned from Camelot road (too long and hopeless) and fled for Morgan LaFay's land . . . Kay had sickened in the saddle, bloated as they rode, burned, choked, raved and died lying forward on the charger's neck . . . Arthur had fled on and on, numb now, unable to grasp the magnitude of the past events . . . he kept seeing dead Kay galloping across a frozen river and vanishing into the falling snowmists . . .

His sister had been watching him from across the chamber. She was standing, eating an apple with delicate bites. She looked young though she was not.

"I'll help you, brother," she was telling him again, "you know that. However I may." He didn't respond. "Your name will still conjure men to arms. The time has come to take back the kingdom." She munched steadily, precisely.

He shook his head, vaguely.

"No more," he finally said, "I want no more of it . . ."

"Someone is going to pluck the fruit," she pointed out. "It might as well be us."

He halfturned to her. His beard was largely white now, she noticed.

"I never set out in life to 'pluck' anything," he said, remembering. "They used to say my sword was magical . . ." Smiled. "That was a trick too . . . Morgana," he said, looking directly at her, "I believed it too . . . I believed . . ." He looked away again. "My bones hurt," he murmured.

"You want the crown," she said, firmly, "you always wanted it. You swore *you* wouldn't fail like father had."

"I swore many things . . ." He pressed his palm flat on the cold stone windowarch. "Father tried too . . ." Shook his head. "I wish he were alive today. I would have much to say to him I never said while he lived . . ." Dropped his hand and shut his eyes briefly.

"Are you so old and weak now, brother?"

"I don't know what I am." Sighed and stared at the stone across from him. "I don't know what I am . . . I wish I could go back to the beginning . . . I wish I could be a boy in the castle woods, in long summer evenings. . . . Ah, God . . . I wish I could go back to the beginning . . ."

"But you can't," she said quietly, "so you'll try again. Don't indulge yourself. It always disgusted me when you indulged yourself like this."

"What do you know of it?" he frowned.

"Heed me," she said, tossing the core to the floor for the dogs, "you will try again. You can't live otherwise. I know you well, brother."

He sat, silent, his back to her now, facing the rain and fog below.

"God help me if that be true," he finally said.

# cvii

Parsival sat uncomfortably in the tilted chair in the dense shade of a yew tree. The day was hot and close. Flies buzzed around a partly eaten haunch of beef. He flicked his hand languidly at them when they circled his head. At the far end of the banquet table Layla was in intense conversation with a graying, darkbearded knight in neat, rich garments. Parsival thought he had a sly eye. Didn't like him much. But didn't care much either.

His stomach was sour, gas pockets stirred vaguely in his bowels and he swore he could feel the twists in there. The heavy woman on his right fingered the wen beside her nose and then wiped her greasestained lips with the back of her hand. She was working, he could see, on starting another conversation with him. He imagined no salvation from the old man on his left: frail, whitehaired, crisply wrinkled, glazeyeyed, with the perceptive faculties of a weathered stone. They were, at least some supposed them to be, relations of Layla's. That was all he knew. They were in company with the handsome mature knight who apparently was not a relative—at least not too close a one. Watching them use their eyes on one another Parsival tried to decide which was the snake and which the bird—and ultimately gave up. He stifled a yawn and considered the circling flies, the little greengold flecks and flashes over the changing meat. He gently pressed his stomach. There were some years of softness there now. He'd heard someone remark that you could often tell a man's age like a tree's age by the rings on him.

"To this day," the woman grimly pronounced, "fear of the plague keeps even bandits and trolls off the roads." She sucked her forefinger clean. "Arthur himself, they say, has shut himself in and begged preserving spells of his wicked sister. Ah, but we were turned away from many a castle gate on the long way here. My sweet father spurned like . . . like," she hunted for an appropriate word to express the infamy of it; meanwhile she sucked another finger. ". . . like a stray dog from a table. . . . Ah, if my husband were living—" Crossed herself, denting her shapeless bosom and burping moistly. "—God preserve his gentle soul. If he lived still they'd have had to answer for such insults. He'd have ridden back the whole way to each gate to seek satisfaction. But then, there are no such men today . . ." Another finger went in up to the second joint.

His bleak reveries and the tale were interrupted by a stone striking the halfdevoured centerpiece with a dull thuck, scattering the flies in a glittering frenzy. Then came a piercing childscream.

A bony little redfaced girl about six had pressed her hands to her head as if in a paroxysm of agony, breath sucked so deep that the anticipated sound was suspended and then torn from her as if, he thought, the darkest damned in hell had found an outlet through her larynx. In the background, looking uncomfortable, was a boy about four, dustcovered, windblown, wiry black hair streaked with trails of bright, fine blond. Behind them both a stout, depressed-looking peasant matron hovered anxiously. Layla was up out of her seat like, he thought, a drawn blade.

"Damn you," she was crying out, "what have you done now?"

Parsival turned away to look for the flies.

"Lohengrin," cried the girl, "he won't give it to me!" And then wailed again her disproportionate howl.

Parsival looked back.

"You wicked boy," Layla said, "what have you done?"

"He won't give it," the girl reaffirmed.

Now Parsival was watching a serving girl flirt with a young man over by the cooking fire. From her short, shapeless sack of a dress, beautiful, lean, barefooted legs flashed the sun as the couple mock-wrestled, hands locked, pushing and laughing. His narrowed eyes went up and down her legs, the arched insteps, sleek calves, faint twinkling of living thigh muscle . . . His hunger toyed with her and he barely noticed the yowling and sharp words on his left.

"You just flatten your ass on that bench!" a voice, he

correctly identified, of penetrating scorn was saying, he realized, to him. "And stare at wenches."

He looked up, irritated and faintly embarrassed. The little girl's mother (a fullbodied lady just reaching the far side of her prime) was on one knee comforting her child; his son's bare back was just winking out of sight around a loop in the castle wall; Layla was standing, hands on hips, frowning down at him.

He mumbled something about her talking nonsense.

"He'll grow into a woodsbeast," she averred, "or simple as his father."

"I love the boy," he replied, not quite relevantly, he knew, and wondered why he had to say that. He felt halfhearted about it though he certainly *did* love him . . .

"You can *say* anything with ease," she told him. Then she headed down the long table, smiling at the knight who was petting and patting a large, bristling dog who'd just planted oversized paws in his lap.

"Ah, good Boarfang," he was saying, "good my lad . . . This is a true hunter," he called up to Parsival and the others. "The apple of my eye. . . . Wait until you see him in the field." He nuzzled the dark neck, joining his own beard to the dark fur and very nearly provoking an unpleasant comparison from his host. His eyes laughed up at Layla as she seated herself again.

The roundish mother released the child who promptly went off in the direction taken by Lohengrin.

"He better let me have it," was her last word.

The lady shook her head, smiled at Parsival, and came to the table.

"Children," she said.

The old, wizened fellow stirred himself.

"Is there a pasty course to come?" he wanted to know.

"True courtesy," the relative with the outsized wen pronounced, "is taught among the gentlest nobles from the *cradle*. Respect of women being the first law of refinement." Now her thumb went into the mouth for a solid sucking. Then she spoke on: "But if you speak of good pasty, well, at the table of Prince Talric of Elausus, in Cornwall, let me tell you all, that . . ."

Parsival was elsewhere. The old man was scratching himself under his tunic, lips moving soundlessly; Layla was up strolling with the dog's dark master; the peasant lass and lad were on the grass eating leftovers with the

cooks; the flies were settling down in restless clumps on
the meat while a few flicked up and down around a fish
head that gave back (Parsival felt) the same stare glazed
and melancholy as his own; a new dog was bellyinching
toward the table; the sunlight imperceptibly shifted its
slant; a pocket of gas burbled deep within him. . . . He
vaguely noticed that the plumpish mother was watching
him very closely . . .

# cviii

The night was humid, warm, full moon flashing in and out of silverhemmed clouds. The breeze was fragrant. Taper light trembled in a few castle windows. Down by the pond frogs and insects united in an astoundingly loud chorus.

The wine he'd taken in was a steady pressure as he teetered down the stone steps and stopped and stood on the sloping field of grass. Looking up he noticed two moons sliding out from a cloudbank. He shut one eye and chortled to himself. Decided human senses were silly. Not to be trusted.

He strolled out along the hillside, peered down at where the peasant huts clumped together. No lights at all there. He started down in that direction, placing his feet with care and thinking about those long, lean legs from the afternoon.

The silver light blinked out.

He stopped, fumbled and opened his codpiece. Held himself with both hands and squirted out a high, stinging arc that drummed softly on lush ground. Hummed a snatch of tune. Then, for some reason, remembered something: the Red Knight urinating in pain . . . the memory of those days came rushing back and for a moment, though he didn't know why, he felt like weeping. . . . Then giggled:

"Why, he had the pox," he said, "and I wondered what caused his pain . . . I was simple, it's true . . ."

Then he remembered killing the Red Knight on the field at Camelot. Frowned.

"That was a stupid business," he muttered as if angry at something. "Stupid . . ."

Went on a few steps. Remembered the bright blood

spraying down the spearshaft that he'd held locked to the knight's throat.

"Stupid . . . knighthood . . . dunghood . . ." Brightened and chuckled, pleased.

"Fuckhood," he said, grinning, weaving down the slope, the air cool through his opened pants.

He remembered the girl in the barn with Gawain and the other man, Sir-what's-his-name? Erec . . . His head looking gravely from the pole. . . . Her eyes like sea colors, a helpless lost look in them, untouchable, a strange innocent boy there too, but nothing which particularly included him. That bothered him and his mood went down again as the moon popped out. Something there in her he could never reach or touch. Like the fish in the boyhood stream he used to try to catch with his hands and even threw stones at because they were so vibrant and mysterious and then finally spearing one it became just a dead fish . . .

"It's all like that," he announced to the night. "No way to get a grip on anything. . . . Trust me, it's true. . . . Just like grails or what you will . . . easier to catch fish or fucking than grails though . . ." He laughed at that. ". . . All fucking grails though . . . all of it . . ."

"Indeed?" remarked a woman's soft voice at his shoulder. He turned, slightly sobered, to see the roundish woman. She was wrapped in a mantle. Feet bare. Surprisingly small and pretty, he noticed. Well, she wasn't really *fat*.

"Indeed, my great ass," he told her, for some reason.

"Is it, my lord?"

He paid no attention.

"You're Lila," he said, as if it were a momentous disclosure.

She smiled and lightly touched his forearm, traced the chiseled muscle lines, the fine hairs.

"You've had much drink," she murmured.

The peasant legs seemed too far away all at once. He nodded agreement with this idea.

"So you don't deny it," she remarked.

"Lila," he said.

"Yes?"

She was near but as he reached for her she stepped back.

"Pray," she said, "spare me a minute's courtship."

"Courtship?"

"Am I a wench in a stew?"

"What?"

"I'm a woman," she said.

He swayed and took thought.

"Why don't we fuck, then?"

She laughed.

"When I was a girl," she told him, "knights spoke in wondrous poetry when they courted."

He was dimly interested.

"They did?"

The moon went in and quickly out again. She turned her face up to it.

"In tales," she whispered.

He was debating whether or what to do. He had a fuzzy suspicion there was going to be a price to pay if he stayed here. He wasn't sure what.

"Age," she was saying, "is a narrower cage for a woman."

"Don't you want to fuck?" he asked, baffled.

She took a few steps away from him and looked down at the looming, deep, elusive shadows of the old trees, the gleaming fields . . .

"Ah," she said, pointing, downslope, "lovers come out in the night like white moths."

He couldn't entirely follow this notion.

"Is that poetry?" he wondered.

He suddenly was annoyed at his numbed head. Wished he were much drunker or totally sober.

"Of a sort," she said, pointing. "Look there where some clods are doubtless off to country sport." She was whimsical. "Even in the sty tonight," she sang, "the pigs feel the passion of the moon."

"What pigs?" he asked, squinting down the knoll where she pointed and then she leaned in against him, soft, warm, a gush of womanly perfume. Her robe parted and he felt the moist heat of her. *Something is moving down there,* he thought.

"My husband says I'm a pig too," she whispered at his ear. "Says I'm a common pig."

# cix

He had turned her on her knees, facing away from him on the grass. The moon was down now and her soft, bubble-round body was a dim outline. *It was easy to smell where she was,* he thought, grinning within the numb reaches of his winestung mind. A sweet and reeking mix of him and her: sweat, semen in spicy sauce. She wriggled and tilted her rump higher, impatient. He rested his hands on those wide, white buttocks. She sighed and pressed herself backward, snorting her breath so that he suddenly understood her husband's nickname because it was very close to oinking and he smiled and gripping himself with a sort of satisfied indifference lifted forward to join with her, balancing on knees and toes: soft, lubricious, hot, slick and easy contact and he pressed more oinks out of her past even noticing now, feeling himself all run into his groin, concentrated there in a dense burning, punching himself volitionlessly at her, into her, anonymous organs drawn by their innermost suctions and then he burst, locked himself to it, bursting as with a shuddering sob of a sigh the bubble of ecstasy swelled and then popped far too soon and there was a sinking in his stomach and cold sweat on his bare flesh as he looked around at the dim shapes and he realized that was what she'd seen and with his fear he felt absurdity as she kept squishing herself backwards in search of what was already a memory and he settled back on his heels aware that the figures were all around them and that in his present condition there wasn't much to do but sit on his heels and wait—and then a mealy voice said:

"Who's got hot water?"

And Parsival thought: *so they're not all deaf and dumb.*

"Hot water?" a shrill voice asked and mealy replied:

"What you throws on two dogs, lout."

General laughter.

Parsival just waited and listened absently to his pounding heart. The woman understood now and crouched silently on her knees, covering herself with her hands—*like a picture of Eve,* he thought.

Then a crunching, steelshod kick took him in the ribs and pitched him on his side where he could while away some time struggling for breath.

"Rutting bastard," the shrill voice declared.

Another voice, reedy, authoritative, demanded:

"Is your king home tonight?"

"You have poor courtesy," mocked still another; one that even in his pain seemed familiar to Parsival. "There is royalty at your feet. With his cod a-dangle as ever. He was never altogether the fool he was taken for."

Then a sharp, then dulling pain behind his ear, bright light, dark . . . blank . . .

# CX

It couldn't have been too long: the dawn was cloudy, landscape, graylit, brightening gradually. His eyelids quivered, stuck, then popped open. He was still naked; his hands were bound behind his back. Men sat and stood on the slope. He twisted to look around: the woman wasn't in sight. A few of his men-at-arms were looking down from the battlements at this body of men before the gates. *All they have to do,* he realized, *is keep the bars up and this crew will never enter. Pity I'm out here.*

The blunt morning dissolved the shadowy terrors and revealed lumpy and lank rogues in mismatched gear where he'd expected silent, black demons. Only two were fully caparisoned, obvious leaders, and stood apart. One wore his visor down; the other, standing over Parsival, had a long, narrow, restless face, sandyred hair and eyes that didn't seem to actually pause on anything; and, though Parsival didn't know it, was called John of Bligh.

"Where is it?" he asked in what amounted to a whispery shriek.

Parsival forced himself to sit up and promptly vomited. He recognized winereek mixed with the sour bile. Several of the gentlemen were tickled into considerable delight. Now that he was up he wished he were down again. His head was very bad. The repeated demands by the bony man didn't help.

"Where are you keeping it?"

"Be damned," Parsival muttered. He was staring at a seated varlet whose lumps of flesh swelled through his ropebound snatches of mail like, he thought, a bound roast beef.

The large knight in the background stepped forward and squatted facing him.

"Best give it up," he said in his muffled but familiar voice.

"I know you," Parsival said.

"There's no help for you in that," the voice said.

"Why waste breath?" inquired John of Bligh, pointing his blade at the prisoner's crotch. "For our sacred cause we must have it. . . . Speak or you'll do without what you abuse anyway!"

"Just take off one and clept him the Great Wizard," the fat man with the mealy voice called out.

"He means it," said the still visored knight.

"Gawain," Parsival said.

The visor blankly regarded him, eyeslits dark.

"Gawain had two arms," it said, "and a whole head entire. This is something less than Gawain."

John pressed the point just over the root of Parsival's mischief. Bright blood welled there.

Parsival stared at Gawain's left hand: the right reached over and stripped off the gauntlet revealing wooden fingers.

"What do you want with me, Gawain?"

"Nothing with you," whispershrieked John. "We want the Holy Grail."

Parsival shut his eyes briefly.

"You think it's in my pocket?" he wanted to know.

"I care nothing if it's up your arse," Gawain said, muffled but conversational.

"Don't try to deceive us," said John. "God has led me to you and he will unmask any treachery."

Considering the sword point nicking above his organs Parsival restrained his boiling remarks.

"I don't know anything about it," he finally said. "I never did. I don't even know what in hell it is."

"You'd been to the castle," Gawain said.

"That's true. But I never saw it. . . . Whatever it is."

"He lies," offered John. "All know its power. The devil Clinschor sought it with his might. Sought you. With these few men and the power of the grail a new life, a new world will spring from these grim ashes like the double bird of legend." Warming to his topic John withdrew the blade and turned his face and moving eyes more toward the sky than anywhere else. "A new force, a new truth, a world where—"

"Peace," said Gawain. "We need this power," he told Parsival. "Give it to us or show us where it lies."

Parsival shut his eyes and shook his lowered head.

"I'd be happy to," he insisted, wearily, "if I knew. I could never find the castle again. I tried."

A pause to consider. Parsival kept looking in wonder at Gawain's wooden hand: the surface was gleaming and polished. It wore rings.

"It's rare workmanship," Gawain informed him, noticing his looks. "Wrought in the East."

"It's handsome, indeed," Parsival allowed.

John of Bligh strode around nervously.

"So you must die then," he announced.

"What for?" Parsival wondered.

He wondered if his wife were up yet or still lying abed with that, he thought, aging rooster. He felt disgusted with her and himself, with everything. The idea that he was going to be murdered seemed ridiculous. Stupid. He wanted to go to bed, mainly. He squinted his blurry sight at a group of these men heading down the slope toward the village.

"Where's the lady I was with?" he asked.

"One last chance," John said, desperately, raising his sword above his head. "Speak!"

"He's not lying," Gawain asserted, calmly. Then, to Parsival: "What lady?"

Parsival sighed and looked away. He'd never felt so sick in his life. The other men in the raiding party were getting restless. The fat man with the mealy voice was standing up now.

"Let's go down to the village," he said.

Another stood up.

"What are you doing with them?" Parsival asked Gawain. Who shrugged.

"I think there is a grail," he said. Paused. "I might as well. It's as good to believe as anything."

Parsival looked up at his castle. The men above were watching. There were more of them now, against the dull gray sky. It felt like rain.

"Don't kill me," he suddenly said.

Gawain's mask was pointed at him. John of Bligh

seemed lost in anxious thought. His lips moved slightly as he paced around.

He finally knew he had it: it came to him like his breath. It was everywhere, like the breath of everything. Layla was in it, his child, all of them, Gawain, the motley band, Merlinus too. . . . His sight seemed very clear now, though he still felt sick that didn't matter, and he looked at the rancid gang of them, scarred, patched, filthy, cruel, foolish and he felt an inexplicable tender pity, a general pity that named nothing in particular, that included himself too . . .

He felt as though he was starting out again for the first time and he realized that nothing he'd done had really marked him deeply and saw it was true for them too, that all the ugliness was on the surface, that they could all stop where they were (as he realized he was doing and would keep doing because it was so right it was an ecstasy) and start from the beginning, the root, the center, the heart beginning of themselves . . . and he smiled and nearly laughed with shock and delight . . . everything was within reach, everything, alive like the day itself: Layla, Lohengrin . . . he wanted to weep too . . . alive like earth, air, sky . . . everything breathing and that was it: just to grasp that it was all living in a magnificent, rich, endless surprise, every moment the first moment and he wanted to tell them too, that one with his hand digging downdeep scratching the crease in his backside; another, flatfaced, chewing a dried hunk of meat; another rewrapping the grip on his sword; the nervous leader (John) pacing around full of obvious silliness and dreams; Gawain nursing his hurts behind a silly blank front . . .

He stood up, the air cool on his naked body; the irrepressible smile crinkling lips and the corners of his blue eyes as well. He wanted to see Layla and Lohengrin and hold them tenderly.

*Where shall I begin?* he asked himself. *How can I best tell them?*

He felt as though he'd awakened from a nightmare. How precious everything was. He was savoring each breath. He felt giddy.

The leaden clouds were moving rapidly overhead, showing whitish where the winds stretched them thin.

Gawain stood up now and Parsival could see his own

reflection in the smooth, blank visor. His hair curling in the breeze, his smile distorted by the curve to seem exaggerated, foolish, which made him smile the more.

*I have to tell them . . .*

He saw other reflections behind his, moving in the mirror-clear steel where the sky and earth too were bent.

"What do you have to amuse you, Parsival?" Gawain asked, hollowly in the metal helmet.

It took him back to seeing the knights first coming across the still glade, flashing the sun with a shocking intensity so that he imagined a profound and miraculous experience had come to him, there, by the stream, years ago. . . . *They didn't think they were gods,* he said to himself, remembering how they'd chuckled at his questions.

So simple, so easy and effortless, perfect and pure . . . so silly to fight it . . .

For a moment he almost embraced Gawain, armor and all. . . . Felt free and calm . . . remembered riding Spavint across the golden, sundrenched fields, drifting timelessly on and on in what now seemed one endless, unstained morning . . . undiluted breathing light here too and everything in it infinitely real and fascinating and he wished he had a thousand hands to touch with and eyes to drink life in with, to embrace everyone and everything, to cry out that it was simple as love and wind . . . and he shut his eyes and everything stayed so vivid he gasped and felt the inexplicable heart of earth and air' and the speech and stirring of all life and thought: *How could I not have known you? All of you?* Wanted to kiss something . . . ah, something . . . he knew, now he knew . . . he wanted to laugh . . . he knew where the grail was now . . . everything you touched spoke and everything touched you and revealed all secrets . . .

Opened his eyes again and looked at the bright, false reflection of himself and the dim shadows of the others in the metal. He smiled, peaceful and wistful.

"Don't kill me, Gawain," he said, gently, almost (the startled knight thought) sweetly.

*There's not even anything to pity,* Parsival discovered, turning to watch a bluejay rush up above the trees and sway and soar, a clear, stainless spot beating with the winds . . . on and on . . . tossed his hair back from his eyes . . .

# cxi

On a clear summer morning under a clearing sky with rain-pools glistening like jewels in the fields, wet, drooping trees, heady air, Broaditch stood looking down the road to where it hooked under a wave of willows, where pond-mists drifted and the eaves of a neighbor's house were faintly visible. Beyond that, high on the darkgreen mountainside the lord's castle caught the rising sun. He leaned on a bowed staff. A sack was roped to his back. He meditatively scratched the stubble line of his chin where the graywhite beard sprouted.

Alienor came out of the house, barefoot, noiseless, in a shapeless faded workdress. She handed him a package of cheese and bread wrapped in cloth. The morning light on her scrubbed face showed the intricate netting of fine wrinkles, the darkening reddish hair tints, the direct, quick eyes. She looked at him without a word for a while. He kept studying the road. A squirrel bounced from the brush: bright, nervous, rapid. It sat up in the first fingers of sunlight, then flicked into the shadows. A cock crowed in the distance.

"So," he said, finally.

She just stood there.

"Keep them well, my love," he said.

"Keep yourself," she retorted. Then, remembering: "Beware of lost women you meet by shallow waters."

He didn't remember:

"Women?" he wondered. "It's not women I'm looking for."

"Nor was it before. How many years now?" She thought back on it. Seeing them coming (Waleis on the mad mule, Broaditch weighing down the other) splashing across the

334

stream and recalled thinking: *between the two I swear I favor the beasts.* And then: *but he has a gentle look about him.*

After a few moments Broaditch said:

"Well, I'm off."

And he felt how easy it would be to stay, to go back in the house, get out his pipe and slip into the day's routine. He sighed and felt a tingling in his belly. Wanderfear, it was called. Sighed.

"It's just a sort of pilgrimage," he said, still not looking directly at her. "It'll do me good."

She still studied his stolid face, the tiny red veins whorled on his cheeks, the round nose. She absently straightened his collar.

"Who can say but that I'll find him," he said.

"Who can say," she murmured softly.

"It's just a sort of pilgrimage," he repeated, distantly.

The sun tilted higher. The wet grass glittered. The road was drying fast. The mists were dissolving and shadows barred the landscape with bluishblack bands.

"Go on then," she said, gruffly, "before old age takes you where you stand."

Then she kissed him dryly on the cheek and stepped back before he could turn and hold her.

"Go on," she told him.

She watched him for a time from the splitrail gate, hands holding her shoulders, arms crossing her chest. Watched him moving toward the hook in the road, a sturdy, slightly bowed figure crossing the strips of tree-shadow, winking into and out of the steady, hot, rich, mellow sunlight. His feet raised a faint dust now as the day's heat began to set. Then she looked up over the mountains at the immensely towering clouds vastly coiling into the west. Folk were said to live in such clouds and for a moment she tried to imagine their airy forms, their lightness. . . . The idea amused her and she smiled, faintly, distantly, before she turned away.

# notes

Like most Arthurian cycle stories *Parsival* is not set in "real" historical time. Facets of medieval life covering centuries are compressed into one semi-imaginary period. History is not the issue because Parsival's has always been (on one level) an initiatory tale, an adventure in spiritual alchemy. Parsival (aka Percival, Parsifal, etc.) is the holy fool in the tarot deck moving in perfect innocence into the world of pain, edges, limitation, desire, pleasure. If he finds the grail he keeps his innocence and puts on ultimate wisdom and power as well. The *spiritual* grail, then, is a benediction; a self-transforming enlightenment; a recognition of the total field in which the individual is an inseparable waveform and like a wave cannot be removed from the medium, the whole, and so *is* the whole. So no human being can seek and find the grail because there's no place to go and look. Rather, the nature of the self has to be revealed.

Before and during World War Two the S.S. went hunting in the Ariège for the "occult" grail. Like Clinschor, they wanted the jewel, chalice or tablet of psychic power. Some said it was a set of magical writings passed on to King Solomon by the last Atlanteans.

The Clinschor in Wolfram's version of the story may have been based in part on a real person, Landalf da Padua. About the time I was finishing the manuscript I read that Adolf Hitler may have believed himself to be a reincarnation of Landalf! Hitler was deeply interested in grail lore, partly as a result of youthful immersion in Wagner's *Parsifal* and the teaching of the (now) infamous Thule Society to which he belonged. It was an occult organization promoting distortions of very ancient spiritual ideas.

Merlin becomes Clinschor's opposite number in the "black" versus "white" magic system. Black magic suggests using the psychic forces of self and nature to manifest and fulfill the ego's appetites, grasping power to enhance the self or its projections. The white magician or alchemist uses basically the same powers to improve the self's environment. Power, of any kind, does not lead to enlightenment and applied without insight into the harmonious nature of self and universe is essentially destructive. This is one of Parsival's major discoveries.

My first contact with the tale was in college. I had to read Wolfram's epic version for a class. I skipped a lot but the gist of the story made a deep impression. Somehow, everything I knew seemed to be there, in the inexplicable metaphor of it: the search, discovery, loss; the painful process of becoming hardened to life, the reawakening of innocence and love when it seemed forever buried, what had grown stiff and flat opening into deep and fluid vistas of discovery; the endless, rich joy of it, which is always possible whenever you look at life as if for the first time without past or future, as the lover who never tires of the play and unfolding of his love.

No work of mine ever flowed so easily or taught me so much. The vision has already effortlessly persisted into the first chapters of the sequel. Writing *Parsival* brought home a humbling truth about creation and the ego: the self as a semi-continuous, conditioned collection of memories and techniques can create nothing. There is no artist, no creator, only creation, a response to a state of awareness. I've been asked in writing workshops: "That all sounds profound as hell but how come one person can create a piece of art and another can't?" Because one person has practiced and developed an expressive technique to respond with—and knows when and how to shut up and just listen and look. Approaching a character, for instance, is the same as approaching living beings. If you come at a person, image, or any question with love and total interest, if understanding is life and death to you, then you forget your self, your theories, fears, ideas, obsessions and give absolute attention and you learn. There's room for something new in you and it comes in. You can't force it, it simply comes. If you look at anything through a clutter of prejudice, dreams or certainties (however sophisticated, entertaining or clever), there's no movement into discovery because there's no space within you for it. So an artist has to make room in himself and the humbling fact is that anyone (and probably dolphins, too) can have creative insight. There's no special "gift" involved, just a passion for the unknown, for the delight and wonder of what's beyond yesterday's inner horizon. In one sense, *Parsival* is about this and helped me see that my opinions and intentions, my dead yesterdays, have no magic in them.

In the beginning chapters of the novel, certain specific elements of the older versions were used. Medieval authors almost always worked from sources (as did Shakespeare) and this seemed an excellent way to plant the seed of the piece. Broaditch, Waleis and Alienor appeared virtually out of nowhere and took charge of the story. They were a delight to work with. There was always more to them than I could ever quite catch up with. I missed them when the piece was finally finished until I realized that Broaditch had guaranteed a sequel.

## About the Author

RICHARD MONACO, a successful screen-
writer, playwright, and poet, teaches at the
New School for Social Research and Mercy
College. He co-hosts the "Logic of Poetry"
show weekly on WNYC. He is the author of
*The Grail War,* coming soon from Pocket
Books.

# Non-Fiction Bestsellers from POCKET BOOKS